Fantasy R
From New Voices

by C. C. Brower, J. R. Kruze, S. H. Marpel,
R. L. Saunders

FANTASY ROMANCE ANTHOLOGY

First edition. October 13, 2019.

Copyright © 2019 J. R. Kruze et al..

ISBN: 978-1393649441

Written by J. R. Kruze et al..

To all our many devoted and loyal fans -

We write and publish these stories <u>only</u> for you.

(Be sure to get your bonuses at the end of the story...)

Introduction

OF COURSE, WHEN YOU talk to your readers, you find out that they have many questions.

My typical response is to send out some of the earlier stories my authors have written in order to answer them.

Often, these stories were standalones and have fallen "into the stacks" and never made it as part of a series anywhere.

That was the case with several of these romances.

All our authors write romance into the books, in one way or another. Because most people like (or will tolerate) a little romantic interest.

For those who like a lot of it, this anthology is assembled.

What you don't see here is the "Universe Notes" which tie the stories into longer story arcs where the universes these books take place in have evolved.

So – sorry, these books may raise more questions.

Of course, in that case, just check in the back to find other stories by these authors which will (hopefully) answer those questions and resolve certain story arcs.

But this anthology was collated to help the Romance fan to see how love truly does make the world go 'round – and is the universal solvent for many things.

It also tends to who that two heads are better than one – and couples rule when solving mysteries and dealing with adventure.

Here is then a big tome of Romance that you can curl up to over a long weekend and binge-read.

Of course, all these short stories can also just be fit into your commutes and odd moments where you need to escape for awhile.

Please enjoy. Because that's what they were written for.

ROBERT C. WORSTELL
  Chief Editor, Living Sensical Press

On Love's Edge

BY J. R. KRUZE

I OFTEN COME OUT TO the end of the dock on nights like tonight. Where the sky and the water seemed to meet at the edge of nothing. Both reflected each other so well that it never seemed like one ended or the other began.

This was when sky and water formed a perfect union, a marriage of two souls so deep that they didn't exist without the other.

All I felt was the passion of the last time we were together. And the aches of those times we had since spent apart.

But the wild thing was that we had never met.

THE STARS AND THE SKY opened up that evening and we simply talked from our souls over an endless distance, it seemed.

But for all I knew, he could be just on the shore of the pond opposite, just beyond the myst, standing there among the trees, just watching. A slight smile on his lips. As if the whole thing was a joke or a pun, or some sort of clean and harmless limerick.

"I never saw a purple cow, I never hope to see one..."

Life didn't have to be difficult, it didn't have to be hard. Love seemed to make things just meet and match and fit. One of those wooden puzzles that are hard as hell to figure out if you never saw them put together, but you never want to take them apart if you did see them that way. The wonder was how they were built at all.

I would send my love out to him from the end of that pier, that long dock, and I'd feel the response instantaneously. Like there was no time or space, just love.

I WROTE HER SHORT STORIES with no plot. Just some character doing something or saying something that didn't have to go anywhere. I could see her face in my mind's eye – twinkling eyes of her own, all hazel-blue and full of laughter. She gets the point immediately. She sees that the story could only be short like that, because it didn't have to be long at all.

A pooh-bear story. No adults present. No judgment of what was wrong or right. It just was. And fun, always.

That was the joke that came up when we'd talk in my mind, when she would seem to come and sit beside me as I wrote - tip-tapping out the story on the worn keys that had seen so much adventure through my fingertips.

And now were simply writing a love story out of the motes of stars and water and cloud. A story that simply flew across the sky, the endless distance and resounded in a massive orchestral chord.

Love is like that. It doesn't depend on money or being somewhere, or having fine things around you. It means that you care for each other so deeply you just become the other. Finishing sentences, walking hand in hand without bothering to sweat from discomfort, because it is the most natural thing you can do.

Even though you've never met in body, you know she's out there and she is always sending her love to you. Even when you are upset and quarreling with yourself or some character you are writing out of whole cloth.

I WROTE TO HIM AND of him as I crafted my stories. And often could simply just look out into space as my fingers typed away. We would be of one mind. A proofreading soul looking over my shoulder or through my eyes at the scenes as they shone through the page.

I was his female voice, he was my masculine influence. Together, as yin and yang, we wrote perfect stories in any genre - in every genre.

Any action had a romantic interest, had a mystery, had thrills and horrors and pure distraction from the world and all its difficulties.

A woman knows when a woman is writing, as a guy knows that somebody out there is probably sitting in a corner of a bar with a laptop - or a coffee shop - and is cranking out another adventure he would always like to take.

When it's time to hear from the guy, it's all brusque and cheeky and direct. While when the girl is talking, there is care and support and softness, the subtle hints of things unsaid.

Of course, it's also true when the characters are together in a scene. He writes the descriptions of the guy and then I'll come into write all about the gal.

He drags his fingers through his thick mane to force it rudely out of his eyes. Should have gotten that hair cut a month ago when I first thought of it. But it was one story after another and then four weeks were suddenly gone. How was a guy supposed to keep track of such things.

When I read through these words, I could almost see the plaid flannel he wears in winter as he types away, knowing that he didn't want to bother with getting his hair cut or running trimmers over his chin more than once a week – because he was "supposed to be writing, dammit."

And when I wrote the descriptions of the girl, she was always tenderly brushing an errant lock off her forehead and behind an ear. When lost for inspiration, she would twist the end of a strand around her finger and look off into the sky beyond the walls of her own room to a mystical place of lavender clouds and light brown tree trunks just starting to turn gold for the fall yet to come.

There was a difference about actions, descriptions, conclusions.

Male and female, yin and yang on the same page.

Both of us typing away from the same two pair of hands.

He was writing in his remote farm cabin, I was in a high room on a small and sturdy table set into a corner and by a window.

Yet we were as close together as if born twins.

WHEN WE WRITE THE LOVE scenes, it can get really bad. No, there's no on-page sex, but the teasing and touching leaves us both moist with expectations. Often I would take a long walk to clear my mind, especially if I had to get the character out of some dire situation – and this cuddling was just a short break in the action before he jumps back into solving things.

Or maybe he has an angel who shifts in from another universe wearing little, just to tease him. And might wind up in his bed when he wakes in the middle of the night, kissing and caressing him, but then gone by morning – a complete dream, except it was so very real.

There are few ways for release at that point, even in rolling over.

Often it's the only decent thing to do is to get up, turn the lights on and type out the story that's been racketing around my brain, or mind, or whatever you want to call it.

Romances are best when they are brief. But that's not love talking, that's coming from the hard-tack life of building things, of organizing things to run better, it's from herding your animals through pastures and fixing the fence when some storm drops another dead branch heavy onto it, crushing and twisting the fence so any calf will take that opportunity to show the other calves and their moms the fastest way out to new grass.

And the herd will act as a single beast does - they turn and twist and go the other way. Herd as you like, you cannot make them come back out of a new pasture to go into an old one. Once you go back to get the others, then the first bunch start back through.

So you just change your temporary polywire fence to at least keep them in that new small spot with a nice, potent shock on it to remind them why they are where they are. And when they all go out for water, you shut them back again and roll up that temporary fence once more. Or maybe you then let them into a larger space out there, now that you've been able to adjust the size of temporary pasture to their use.

But that's a guy thing. Hot sweaty days where you have to get them back in anyway, and after all that walking, to get some rolled wire and a tin bucket with a sturdy wire handle that holds all the fasteners you could need. Along with that set of fencing pliers that can cut and twist and hammer all in one tool, so you don't have to take three with you.

The sweat doesn't go away, but some days need two bandannas – one around your forehead to keep it from stinging your eyes, the other around your neck to keep the biting cow-flies and mosquitoes away, to cool your neck on the back of it, regardless that the heat outside is not too much difference from inside. And the worst days where it's much hotter outside than in.

Either way, you have to keep going and doing and fixing until it's done. The cursing that no one hears out deep in the woods – where the fencing is the weakest to hold and the toughest to get tight again. Where the stagnant water in the creek and the ditches just keeps the air humid and dank. Where's that damned wind when you need it?

That's a guy's job to do. I've heard women discuss it, but always talk as if they have help with them. A guy will go off and do it by himself and rarely say anything when he gets back except that, sure – it was hot.

IN THOSE TIMES, I WISH I was there to help him. Not that I'm strong like him, or could help much. But just to be there and help him. Somehow.

Actually, even if he won't admit it, I am. I'm the reason he takes those breaks and looks around to see if someone is in earshot of his cussing. Or when he gives his cows a scratch just where they want it, and leans up against their bellies full of this year's grass and their next Spring calf. Those brief moments when he feels something that is nurturing and that quiet warmth that flows through his fingers.

Like the love you feel when a dog wants your petting. When they interrupt your typing to tell you that it's time for another break. Because you've been at it way too long and are working way too hard for something so simple. That your word count is way down, and getting another cool drink from the fridge (maybe with a snack) would bring your speed back and give your muses a chance to re-charge.

LOVE IS ALL AROUND, you just have to ask for it.

But sometimes it comes even without asking.

That's when you simply have to let Love find you and flow over its edge back to you.

All you've invested in everything, in your writing, in your fencing, in your job – it can come back, compounded with interest.

Because you deserve it.

All this I see from my own quiet little desk, where the room is painted in a rose-pink, with ruffled curtains pulled back from tiny windows that rattle when the wind moves them, propped open to let slight breezes come and go.

I think at those times that you are here and moving those curtains as you climb in the window, shifting through the glass and screen like it wasn't there. Come behind me and wrap your strong arms around me just to cuddle. Your stubbly face scratches my own, and I can smell where you've been out there today. Even though you've changed your shirt and run water through your hair and combed it roughly away. I can smell the rust, and dog, and cow on your hands. I see where the brambles have scratched you again, and feel the iron in your muscles where they are sore, the bruises from having the hammer slip in your sweaty hands.

And yet I can also feel the smile on your face as you hold me.

You've come to tell me to take a break with you. We can sit on the veranda in the shade and feel the breeze while we chat about nothing and tease each other with senseless jokes or just enjoy the quiet of that time of day.

Finally, I rise and you rise and we go back at it. You phase out to that world of yours with your cluttered desk filled with stacks of books, and a second screen, plus other computers just to research in. How you put your feet up on a makeshift stool just to anchor yourself into a typing mode to crank out your stories.

Mine, I like to persuade my stories to uncoil themselves onto my pages, to breathe life into them. I can feel them steaming from my bust in a quiet heat as they come to life on the page. I can hear their voices, their discussions. For I'm only here, just outside of that conversation, listening in and making quiet notes.

WHILE MY STORIES RAM through my head-mind like a moving picture in front of me. I can almost hear the projector flickery-flick as the celluloid strip is pulled and wound through, over the hot light to project the moving pictures against a bare wall where they can't escape before I see them.

The action moves. The hero's only reaction is how he stands and does nothing, but should be. Because something has happened to the woman he loves and he can do nothing. Raise an eyebrow, perhaps. But the long shot – where you see him just standing there, his face in shadow – speaks more than if you had a closeup on his craggy features.

That's how he shows his love. By moving when he's supposed to, by defending against uncounted dangers, by standing still when he has nothing better to do. Or simply slamming the door on his way back out the the fields so he won't say something he would regret later.

Even the slamming door is a statement he regrets. But he loses himself in his work and lets the emotions flow out of his hands through the fencing, through his trudging boots into the hard-packed ground. Stomping isn't worth the effort. Stalking off miles, maybe.

Or, if the snow is heavy on the ground, the wind too bitter cold, then he gets a fire into the old cast-iron stove in the machine shed and clears off the work bench to fix something. Or several somethings. And when he's fixed or rebuilt, or torn apart to save what he can out of them. And his mind is clear again, then he can come back into the house.

Quiet, respectful.

She's made you another pot of coffee and some cookies.

But doesn't expect you to talk. And she looks for some signals from you that you wouldn't mind her sitting close to you.

And she doesn't say anything, because whatever ticked you off is gone now.

She smiles and kisses you lightly. Then goes upstairs to her little room with the short ceiling you bump your head on.

You go to your own cluttered, crowded space with the tall shelves stacked and cross-stacked with books by long-dead authors. The ones you pull down every now and then to read for a bit when inspiration doesn't come. Styles you hate, styles you love. Plots with holes in them. English from earlier ages that inspire you not to duplicate their twisting and convoluted torture of English, but the phrase turns and the descriptions, or the scene shifts that keep you in the story regardless.

I LIKE TO COME DOWN when he's worked all that angst out of his system and put a few thousand words down on the page.

I can see his shoulders are relaxed and he wants just to keep going because he wants to make a word count – or more probably that he's gotten the characters into a real mess and wants to get them out of it before he leaves them for the night.

I know he won't be long, though. So I walk with enough noise not to startle him and lightly brush my hand across his broad shoulders without saying anything.

My clothes have already changed to nothing but a long flannel gown. And he can smell the scent of my hair as I've let it down.

No words are needed.

In the bed, I'll push my pillows up behind me and pick up that novel I've been slowly getting through each night, a bit and piece of it at a time. Often several stories stacked up on the nightstand. So I can be in Arabia, or Punxsutawney, or Abilene. And lose myself in the hers and shes of times long past or never-were.

He's got his own night stand, but will as often read from a phablet, having a spare with the same set of books on it, or different ones.

But he'll change into his sweatpants and t-shirt before he slips in from his side.

If we feel like it, we'll make love. If not, we just enjoy each other's company for awhile before sleep.

And waking in the middle of the night may have inspiration, may not. But the night will be filled with love.

Even though we've never met in person. And we don't know where each other's home is.

We meet at love's edge. Where our stories intertwine, and nestle like spoons.

Root

BY C. C. BROWER & J. R. Kruze

WHEN A.I. GOES WRONG, it goes horribly wrong.

Chip-in-a-brain is no different.

In order to make massive changes to any computer program, you have to have administrator access: "root".

Integrating chips into humans had become almost a social media requirement. Fear of Missing Out had the latest enhancements available to anyone who could afford them. Soon, legislatures legalized a simple audio "bio-hack" now available through over-the-counter pharmacies and installed as simply as a ear piercing. The chips had "momentary" root access to your brain. (It said so in the tiny type of the TOS.)

Soon, advertising-paid versions made the cost of implants virtually free, as the massed populations of major metropolitan and coastal megalopoli were all connected. Software upgrades were free and frequent.

And then the "fad" of the timed dopamine "rushes" started - where everyone stopped mid-action and enjoyed the smooth burst of calming hormones while a Macarena-style tune played. Like an elevator-music-sponsored pomodoro break where everybody simply went on "pause".

After that, "accidental" deaths became more commonplace. Some regained their motion faster than others, an advantage for petty thieves - and others.

A single teen-ager saw a pattern to the deaths - as murders-for-hire. But who ever listened to an underachieving high-school student with a conspiracy theory, no matter how detailed. Except this one girl with some serious connections...

But the hacks also worked in reverse. Soon they were pursued - by those people who "returned" a split-second faster than others.

And wanted to keep it their little secret...

I

IT WAS ONLY POLITE to stop and stare.

Also, it meant that the cops wouldn't bust you or ship you off to some "facility" where they kept "people like you".

Because in this city, everyone here - except for us extreme few - were all wired in. This is where social media led us. For a few moments every hour, like some sort of enforced pomodoro break, people would zone out wherever they were and whatever they were doing. They'd all later wake up on cue, smile and carry on.

The rest of us had to play along. Or else.

Because when 99.99 percent of humans around you all did the same thing - you'd better, too. People had not-so-funny ways to dealing with people that didn't. Especially as they were vulnerable - everyone was vulnerable - during those moments. So it was a matter of "public safety" that you pretended to zone out along with everyone else.

Just another reason for the walls around the city, and keeping people out as much as keeping them in. To keep us safe from everything else "out there". Where they weren't necessarily all plugged in. The rumors were that those were all the Luddites and 'deplorables' who were so 'backward' they couldn't see the obvious advantages to plugging in. "Just above their station in life", they explained.

Like that was a bad thing.

ME, I COULDN'T BE BOTHERED. I had my studies to do. I had things to figure out. And going without their mandated TV and their "socially-required" plug-in's just gave me more time to work things out. Working things out gave me peace, helped me understand the world, let me live with less mandatory conformity.

For now, I could almost count down the days, hours, and seconds before I was no longer required to attend their truly dreary "schooling" to get my mandated so-many-hours of "education" so I'd be one of their "well-adjusted" and "productive members of society".

More double-speak. "1984" was one of my favorites, along with "Animal Farm". And some classic humor like "Gulliver's Travels". I always chuckled when he got in trouble for helping put out fires in Lilliput. That was also my attitude toward the too-numerous regulations and regulators: piss on 'em.

THE "MUZIK PLUG" HAD been available for some time, but was regulated as a health device. Then some politicians soon "got interested" in deregulating it, making it available as an over-the-counter device that wouldn't require a shrink's script to pick one up. Right after that, they made a "ad-sponsored" version for free - and started the fad. Especially, since installation was almost as simple as getting an ear-piercing. And could be done at home, no adult supervision required. If you had a steady hand, you could even DIY your install. Even multiple versions if you wanted.

If your mind could take it.

The idea was simple - feed a sequential play-list of your favorite tunes in the background of your consciousness, so you always had some beat or other going on. If you ran out of your own tunes, you could have the device select and play the most popular ones for you.

Ads played in between each song for 15 seconds or so.

A lot of people reported it helped them improve their working conditions. Because their jobs were already mind-numbing. The muzik just helped them get along with each other. That was the name for this noise. They borrowed it from old Depression Era company that urban legend said wired background music into mind-numbing elevator trips. To make everything more enjoyable. But it was updated for people who had no clue where the original came from and were used to everpresent ear buds anyway.

All its programming was also generated under some sort of "open source initiative". (Meaning it couldn't be traced easily and liabilities for misuse would be impossible to prove in a court of law.)

Hacks and upgrades were plentiful after awhile. The mental-music called "muzik" could be attained from a number of sources, which were all themselves trademarked and syndicated.

A little research led them back to some shell-companies who were owned by other shell-companies. But it all meant the same thing - one or a handful of companies were profiting off these ads. And paying people to look the other way since it was "harmless".

Of course, those same companies owned the tabloids and media. So they soon made it a fad, a "fashion statement" and the "next big thing". For all practical purposes, "everyone" was wearing one, conspicuously or not. Customized or not. As long as they left it alone, in its basic functions, they were safe in using it.

And when some lawsuit did make it to court, that was the usual excuse that threw the case out. Their "customizations" violated the "root" clause.

Root access meant control. And it was supposed to keep the device safe for everyday use. And gave it control over some of your "autonomous" functions.

Generally, it seemed safe enough. You took their little boring device that played music and ads into your brain incessantly. Even "helped" you go to sleep and keep your dreams "pleasant". So all the media said.

At some point, the idea of taking breaks to improve productivity came in. And the idea was to stimulate the dopamine levels in the brain so your next 20 minutes of production would be at the same or better level.

Everyone got on board with that one. And of course, it was backed up with all sorts of scientific studies published in the top "peer-reviewed" journals. (Which were owned by those same media conglomerates - big surprise.)

HOW DID I KNOW ALL this? Because I loved research. And you'd just as soon find me in a library vault somewhere looking up material, or at my terminal in the half-way foster house I was assigned to.

My whole research was under their radar. Because my grades were barely above passing, and my attitude was about the same. Just enough for everyone to give up on me ever amounting to anything.

Well, until I bumped into her - literally.

II

"HEY BUD, WHY DON'T you watch where you're going?" I was incensed. This dull, unaware nobody had blocked my path so suddenly, I couldn't do anything but grab onto his dark jacket to keep from falling down.

Of course, all my books and laptop and everything went flying. At least he helped me pick them up.

All the time he didn't say anything. So I decided to help him come up to speed, once I knew I had all of my things back in my arms again. Whatever he was carrying didn't matter.

"Thanks, clumsy. Nice you could stop and fix the mess you made." I added in some extra sarcasm to salt the wound.

He just nodded. But looked into my eyes with his puppy-dog sad ones, and then looked away to get his own books back before they got stomped by the crowd.

Something in those eyes. Certainly not in the way he dressed, which was some throwback to a pre-industrial age – or hand-me-downs from Salvation Army refuse bins.

"Muzik too loud or something?" I tried to get his attention, but he was looking down again.

My right hand went to his chin to pull it up. And that got his attention.

His own right hand flashed up to my wrist and held it in a grip that was commanding, but gentle. Then his eyes met mine again.

This time they weren't sad, but a light of defiance burned briefly.

"Sorry. My fault. You're right." Then the dull look showed again. He let go of my wrist and dropped his hand.

But I wasn't going to let it go.

I pushed my arm in and put my hand by his ear below that dark gray stocking cap. Yup, he had a muzic chip there. Older model.

Then his hand flashed up again to grip my wrist. This time the defiant look stayed.

"Look miss. You've got every right to be pissed. I said I was sorry. Now let it go and get on with your privileged life."

I was shocked, my face showed it, and he saw it. But he didn't let go.

"Whassamatter? Nobody ever talked like that to you before?"

And the shoe was now on the other foot.

He was taller than me, lean, and his loose clothing hid the power behind that grip.

Meanwhile, we were both almost invisible in this crowd of people - who were only nodding to their own tunes and not really looking to us other than how to avoid our unmoving block to their progress. All muziked-out.

I jerked my arm free so I could reach up and dial my own muzik down. "What's your name?"

"What's yours?"

"I asked first."

"So? That's your privilege talking again. Tell me yours and I'll think about answering."

"Always so obnoxious?"

"Always so privileged?"

Now he was deliberately getting under my skin. "Look you—you – throwback! Let go of me before I start screaming and the authorities come to handle you."

He gave me a wry smile. "Oh, you must have missed the memo. No "hall monitors" anymore. Or school rent-a-cops. We only have time to get to our next class, and everyone is on their own "best behavior.""

He cocked his head to the side, and peered into my eyes. His were a decided green. "Looks like I'm not the only one with the muzik jacked up beyond safe levels all the time."

No one had ever talked to me like this. Since forever. It was obvious that he wasn't tense about this situation. Sure, he had a grip that could cut off circulation if he wanted. But he wasn't threatening me.

I saw the muscles in his face relax. "You're Jean. I'm Tom. And I'm sorry to interrupt your day. But then, maybe not. Of course, you already know you're cute, so..."

"How do you know my name?"

"Your spilled books."

"Tom, I..." And couldn't think of something else to say. It was his eyes. And his touch. Like he cared. And I hadn't felt being cared for since my Mom passed. It had been an endless chain of servants since. Dad was always busy with his business, and I was in the way more than not. Too young to attend his booze-soaked parties, and my calendar was filled with extra-curricular activities. And disinterested tutors who knew their job was to simply to make sure my homework got done. We'd both crank up our muzik and ignore each other until their assigned time was up. I was their job. To me, they were just another supervising nanny in my life.

"Look, Jean, I am sorry. But you've got something about you - no, it wouldn't work. Forget it."

Tom carefully shifted his books into one arm and turned to move around me.

"No, wait. Tom - please."

That stopped him in his tracks. So I caught up with him and turned him around.

"I just wanted to say 'thank you.'"

His face was really shocked now.

"Tom, I'm the one that's sorry. I was rude. Please forgive me."

Now he was the one that had no words.

So I smiled. And that brought his quiet grin back. Then the warning bell sounded. We had seconds to be in our last class for the day – and out of the hallways. The swarms of students were already thinning.

"Hey, Tom, let's ditch this last one."

"Whoa - you with the platinum hair, and a no-account like me?"

"Not an option. You're in. Hold onto your books." I grabbed his arm and started pulling him behind me. His strength seemed to melt as I did.

The echoes of the hall were louder now without the muzik beats buzzing in my ear.

Then I remembered that he'd never turned his own muzik down. But heard everything I said.

III

ONCE JEAN GOT ME INTO the stairs by the second floor, I held back to get her attention. And she dropped her soft hand on my own wrist. I put my finger to my mouth and then pointed to an access panel in the wall.

She looked around on the ceiling and saw that the camera's were all pointing away or missing.

It didn't take much to get that panel open, even though there weren't obvious handles, just recessed screws. A couple of taps and it sprung open enough for my fingers to pry it open. Then I climbed in, set my books down and turned around with both hands to take hers out of her arms.

All that was left was for her to climb through.

When I reached out for a jury-rigged wire handle inside that panel door, she got out of his way and I secured the panel with a couple of clicks.

Reaching nearby for a switch brought the red lights on. She could see that the panel had little spring-loaded latches in place.

I noticed what she was looking at and smiled. But put my finger to my lips again, then motioned her to follow. I picked up the short stack of our books and gear, then led off.

Soon we wove our way through a series of maintenance tunnels within the walls, to a wide space where an older monitor sat with its keyboard and nothing else on a small metal desk. Here there was a regular yellow light in place overhead. The display was the various hall cameras. And those halls were empty.

"I can get into your class if you want, and even get the audio for you."

Her face lit up. "This is so cool! How did you find out about this?"

"Blueprints and schematics. All online. Just had to hack the janitor's password. As long as I don't leave a trace of being there, nobody cares."

"Wow. But why do you do this?"

"Too much juice running between my ears. Hereditary genius. Don't ask me if it runs in the family, I don't have one. But I know you can't teach that stuff in school - or it would have been taught out of me long ago."

Her eyes softened. "Yeah, I know about the 'no family' scene. Sorry about yours."

"Don't be. I'm not. Won't get me anything better by feeling sad. Yours though, that was probably something that hurt. So if saying I'm sorry helps you with that, then that's a good thing."

I looked into her eyes and they were all soft, like she wanted to tell me something. I just took her hand in my free one, then led her on before she could.

WE WENT DOWN A FEW flights, and through some other doors, ones with real latches that we could lock from the inside.

The room was simple. A stainless tabletop big enough for a couple of computers and several monitors each, as well as their keyboards. A couple of rolling chairs, and a couch covered in clean knit throws in simple patterns. A two-doored steel cabinet on one wall where I kept the vital supplies I needed, which weren't many. Lighting was dim, but clear enough to see without glaring off the monitors and causing eye-strain.

I set the load of books and stuff on one corner of that big table.

"Wow, Tom, this is so neat." She sniffed the air. "And clean. You'd think this would be dusty and moldy."

"De-humidifier vents are tapped into, and I vacuum regularly. Kind of a neat-freak. Cleaning helps me sort out my head when I've got too much thinking going on."

"Like instead of muzik?"

I looked at her directly, with a raised eyebrow.

"You didn't turn it down to talk to me."

I shrugged. "Yeah, I hate the things. Messes with my concentration."

Jean touched my sleeve. "Don't I know. Useful for limo rides and that's about it."

I shook my head. "Most people take the bus, but with that hair and all those tailored leathers, I suppose that you've probably never had to."

She just smiled at me. Her blue-gray eyes sparkled. "And let me guess. No family, don't care. Probably in some state-run foster program with too many kids in it. You're counting down the days before you can get out, and they're counting down the days until you do - so they can get their next one in to replace you."

I nodded. "No love lost anywhere. Mind your own business and mind your own stuff. Keep everything locked down."

Jean moved closer to the table and felt the smooth finish. "Why two machines?"

"Sometimes one will get locked up with too many programs running. So I switch to the other - or start one running on a longer program while I get into other work with the second one, meanwhile."

"So you're not as dumb as you're dressed to be."

"And you're too smart to really fill the socially-conscious blond brain-vacuum role you wear."

"Touché. Although I do play the part well. Just have to get to my weekly hair appointments, and flirt with all the men to get their wallets open for the many wardrobe changes I 'require' for my 'performances.'"

She pulled up one of the roller chairs to sit in it, and I pulled up the other.

"Here, let me log you in. If you just start tapping away, then it will activate a worm to erase all the data in there. I've got backups, but..." I made a few clicks and turned the keyboard back over to her.

Within seconds, she pulled up a feed for her classroom. A few clicks and she'd downloaded the homework for the day into her cloud storage. Then she checked on her social feeds and playlist, then minimized those. A directory showed up and she was reading intently.

"Jean, most of that won't make a lot of sense..."

"Tom, you are so smart and so dumb at the same time. There's a lot more under this platinum hair and this leather than you'd suspect."

I just sat back and waited for her to get the punchline to her own accidental joke.

She stopped typing and turned toward me slightly, a bit more pink than usual. "Hoisted by my own petard?"

I just chuckled. "Sure, and you've been reading way above your grade as well." I pulled the other of my keyboards closer to me and started in.

She leaned over to watch.

I could smell violets. But forced myself to concentrate.

"Wait." Jean pointed at my left screen. "Go back. Right there. What's that?"

"You probably don't want to know."

"That's the muzik feed. You're into their mainframe. Why are you studying that?"

"It's called research and it's what I do best."

"But you don't listen to it."

"No, my ear gizmo was fried a long time ago."

"You could get them replaced, get an upgrade."

I shook my head. "Think it through. That stuff just keeps you from thinking. I do research best. Means I need my brain free..."

Jean nodded. "OK, you got me there. Should have seen that one coming. Wait."

She turned back and clicked on her own keyboard. Charts and graphs filled the screens. Then spreadsheets with the data behind charts plastered over them.

"Jean, I hope you know they can trace you even looking at those..."

"Relax, Tom. I saw your tunnels and added another layer through an anonymity network."

"Still...."

"And, I used my Dad's login. He can get anywhere inside his company he wants. Virtually or actually."

A few clicks showed the truth to the "breaks theory" results.

"Look – what they are saying is bogus. Productivity actually goes down since muzik and its breaks were implemented. People are only feeling better about doing less. There could be other factors, but the breaks aren't improving things markedly, if at all. More lying press doesn't make it factual."

I was impressed. "Cool. Some talent you have there."

"Very. It got very handy when I needed to cover my wardrobe accounts and get my 'tutors' some extra bonuses for covering up my late-night clubbing."

"You know all the moves then."

Jean sat back. "Dances, inter-corporate warfare, padded marketing accounts. I know my Dad's company and all the politicians he's got owing him. Tons more 'moves' than I ever let on. To him I'm just his air-brained daughter."

Then I sat back. "So why did you get me to ditch with you?"

IV

I HAD TO TURN AND LOOK at him. "Take off your dunce cap."

Tom pulled off the knit stocking cap. Of course, he had hat hair, but his chiseled face with it's slight stubble just made him look better without the cap.

"I thought so."

"What?"

"Your basic chick-magnet. That is, if all those clingy floozies wouldn't cut across your 'research'."

His turn to go pink. And he shoved his knit stocking cap back on, lower than before. "I could make a sarcastic comment about other 'research' I could be wasting my time on..."

"But..."

"Well, most schoolgirls are just trouble. Present company excepted."

"You could be having your fun, though."

"No, you keep the club scene to yourself. Saves me time to do other things."

I mentally counted up the time I spend at the clubs and being ferried back and forth. He had a point. It was taking a considerable amount of my free time. But I was only looking to another 6 years of college and 'finishing' school so I could become someone's permanent arm-candy. Time wasn't an issue for me – it was something to be endured.

"And what are these 'other things' that are so much more important?"

"Here, I'll show you."

Tom turned back and pulled up those audio feeds on his own screens. And more. Then still more - each in their own window.

"Watch carefully."

The music was all different, but the pauses were the same. Mostly.

"Wait. What am I looking for?"

Tom leaned in, clicking to zoom the windows in. He smelled of soap, some non-fragrance kind. Nice to know he's clean under all that.

"There. Watch the length of the pauses."

"Some are ending earlier than others."

"Right. That's what doesn't make sense. They are all supposed to be the exact same length."

"There's a gap - some people come aware a few seconds earlier?"

Tom sat back. "Yup. That's what I've been checking into. Now - look at these..."

He leaned in again and clicked to brought up some petty crime statistics. "Robberies and missing purses were going up. At first, it was subtle. Then it became obvious purse-snatching."

I looked over the various accounts. "It looks like they moved downtown, into the tony areas."

"Right. But you'd think the cops would be on the look-out for patterns. Guess again - check this out..."

He showed a picture of the police chief, city commissioners, and one of the big social technology firms. All grinning from ear to ear and standing in front of that firm's over-sized logo, shaking hands. "Caption reads: New Advanced Personal Surveillance Units Provided to Entire Police Force"

I shook my head. "Let me guess - all tied into the muzik system."

"Right. Ad-free, records everything so they can pick up criminals right after they enjoyed their own 'muzik-enhanced' breaks."

"Meaning that if they're near a crime, they should be able to record anyone doing these robberies."

"But the stories say no one has been arrested, and the cases remained unsolved."

"Wait, aren't there surveillance cameras?"

"Oh, but there's more – guess what happens during those 'muzik breaks'?"

"No – they are all paused as well?"

"Right. Same network. Now, check out these dates of those robberies."

I scanned the displayed images. "They all stop a couple of weeks ago."

"Now, look at these new statistics." A spreadsheet and chart flashed on the screen over the other images. "'Accidental deaths' started happening right after those robberies quit. Certain people had fatal accidents like stepping into an empty elevator shaft once the break was over. Or falling into an open man-hole, or out an open window. All dopamined up - didn't feel a thing."

Tom sat back.

But I leaned forward and pulled his list of people up onto my own screens. "I know some of these. A few of them worked for my Dad's company."

Pulling up their personnel files didn't show any reason they would all now be dead - or targeted in any way.

Right then, an alarm on my wrist made me sit up.

Tom was surprised as that sound broke the quiet of that austere and clean office. "What's that?"

"It means I'll be late by the time I get there. My limo is waiting." I started to rise.

"Wait - I can get you out in front of the school faster. Come this way."

And he was up with a flash and headed out a different door than the way we came in. I snatched up my books, laptop, and other gear – and that made catching up even more difficult.

Small wonder he was so trim if he was running through these underground and hidden passages all the time.

WE CAME OUT OF A SMALL maintenance shed hidden behind a well-trimmed block of shrubbery. I'd walked those grounds all of my life and had never known it was there.

My limo driver was waiting, and looking all around since I hadn't come out my normal entrance. Of course, his job was on the line if I went missing.

Then he spotted us.

I turned to Tom. "Quick, give me a hug."

I leaned into him and he did one better. Right on my lips.

And I responded in kind, sort of naturally, but felt the cresting wave of a hunger I didn't realize was in me. A hunger that warmed me.

He broke it off before it got too intense for explanations. But whispered first, "Look for my text."

He turned away and was quickly lost in the shrubbery, so the driver couldn't see his face.

I turned toward the limo, checking to make sure I had all my books and everything.

By the time I got to the car, the door was open and I swept into the back seat.

Once the driver settled himself in, I briefed him. "Another bonus for you if you tell no one about my new 'homework tutor.'"

And he nodded back at me in the mirror, smoothly pulling out into the spare traffic around the school.

As it was, he needed to bend a few traffic laws to get us back to the palace-prison my Dad called home. So I couldn't complain when I got a bit jostled at times as he almost slid around corners at high speed.

In the middle of that carnival ride, my watch showed a text from A_Frennd, "The model you were searching for is X-301. It has the upgrades you want in a retro base."

I lit up at that. And managed to send that text to my laptop, smiling.

Of course. This meant shopping - the one thing that I really enjoyed.

V

MY SMARTPHONE WAS AN ancient design, compared to what was out these days. One generation away from a clam-type burner phone. But I'd rebuilt the OS from scratch. And could use it to target and track anyone without their or anyone else knowing.

And I still savored that stolen kiss as I waited unseen outside the only place in that mall she'd be able to pick up an X-301. One of the few places that one of the mall camera's couldn't get my face for any ID.

THERE SHE IS. JUST came out of the shop. Still rubbing her ear from where that "latest-and-greatest" version was replaced with her new "retro" muzik implant.

Almost in range – and... there. I hit the button. She stopped stock still, the shopping bag's handles settling into her inside elbows as both hands went to her head.

Then she relaxed as the quiet settled in.

Her shocked face looked around. She knew it had to be me.

My own hand went to my ear to touch my implant. "Hey, it's me - turn to channel 0."

And she did. "Oh, nice. A built-in two-way."

"Better than Dick Tracy's. Works on proximity. No, don't look around. Go get an ice cream so they can't read your lips moving. Meanwhile, just nod like your muzik selection has a nice beat."

There was a mall cart with a limited number of flavors nearby. Jean moved toward it.

"Don't say anything, but point to their 'Muzik special'. It's a scoop of mashed potatoes with sprinkles. Looks like vanilla."

Once she had a one scoop cone in her hand, the proprietor waved off any payment while giving her a knowing smile.

"Now, come and sit down at the benches by the escalator."

"So, 'Mr. Kiss and Tell' - you could have warned me about that screech in my ear."

"Not without giving everything away. I am sorry about that, though. Now you'll only get a little 'ding' when the next break hits and a double-ding when it's about to end. Otherwise, complete quiet."

"Why all the cloak-and-dagger?"

"So you're safe. I do this for everyone I care about - as long as I can trust them."

"How do you know you can trust me?"

"Other than your gorgeous looks and your incredible intelligence? Well, you taste good, too."

I felt a blush coming on. "A little personal?"

"Hey, we already know which sides of the tracks we each come from. A regular Romeo and Juliet as strange bedfellows."

Jean shook her head. "A mixed metaphor, but I hope not a proposition."

"Certainly not. That play had a lousy ending. So did West Side Story."

"Then let's compromise: Grease."

"Deal."

"I could hear that smile in your voice."

"Yeah, well, I can have my fun, can't I?"

"How come I can't see you?"

"Cameras. Facial recognition."

"I thought someone famously said 'privacy was dead'..."

"Same guy that bought his own island and all the houses around his so no one could peep on him."

"...and refused to say where he was staying while being interviewed by Congress on C-span."

I cleared my voice. "Back to topic. You have places you have to be and I have places to avoid being seen at. The other thing - this has a private channel. I'll text you later and we'll be in touch. For now, just pause when you're supposed to be pausing and give that vacuous stare of yours, the one your friends have when they're zoned out like everyone else. No one will suspect - unless your eyes move. It's hard at first, but it gets easier."

"Wait - before you go. This may sound like a groaner, but am I going to see you again?"

"Sure. Same study hall we both came from originally. I'll give your schedule a check-over and see if I can't make some private-time space in it."

I touched my ear and broke the connection. Before she would say anything mushy.

But her face fell, disappointed.

She did lick the potato-cone. Once. And smiled a little bit. The salt in the mashed potatoes and the cheese sprinkles went together well.

But she rose and dumped it in the nearest bin.

Couldn't blame her. Fattening. And her shape was fine just the way it was, curves where they counted.

VI

TOM WAS A NICE GUY. Knew I hated Chemistry, so somehow, he got my record credited with successfully passing it. "A-minus" so I kept my average grades.

And replaced it with Library Assistant, which meant pretty much just having somewhere to work on homework during the day and nothing to do except stay out of the Librarian's hair.

Just moments after I first arrived, Tom was in my ear. "Meet me in 'smootch corner.'"

That was the one place where the camera's weren't. And how it got its name. You could hear the Librarian coming well before she could see you. Which was exactly the point. What the staff didn't see, they didn't have to report.

Tom was there, sitting in one of two chairs at the small table. Only his back showing to the shelves I came through.

"Hey." It was in my ear. He didn't move.

"Hey yourself. At least I don't have to lick mashed potatoes to get here."

He half-chuckled at my joke. "But just because you and I are now alone, that doesn't mean we're going to do much than just sit and talk. Even as cute as you are, we've got work to do that won't wait."

I sat down with my back to the shelves as he was, looking straight ahead at the wall of book shelves on the table's other side. "I should take that as a compliment. Wouldn't want to steal any of your valuable 'research time'."

He gave a low chuckle. "I had to spend extra time just getting the smell of violets out of my clothes and that room we were in as it was. Who'd know that a smell would be that distractive."

"I can quit wearing that scent..."

"Don't. It's a nice distraction."

"Oh, Mr. Compliment today. Hope this becomes a habit. Girls like that."

"My studies show that it's only when the guy tells the truth."

I felt a blush coming on. "OK, then. We'll leave that for now. You said you had a reason for this meeting other than smootching?"

He paused. I was tempted to look over to see the reaction I just created. But it took a bit of steel will to resist it.

"Touché. I always suspected there was something clever under that platinum hairdo of yours. First order of business: I may have come up with the connection between all those people."

"Which is?"

"A group of them were in the same time and place. They either saw something or were part of something. The rest of them formed a sequential time-line along a few streets - like they were probably witnesses to some getaway vehicle."

"Wow. That must have taken some digging."

"Finally had to run a cross-check on their locations and times - use the clustered 'vanilla' boxes in the computer lab to run the program."

"Nothing like an off-grid low-powered supercomputer to help out."

"Don't forget the anonymous part. Once you power them down, all the evidence is wiped."

"Three cheers for virtual drives."

"I'm getting impressed. Not that I wasn't expecting this once you mentioned tunneling. Clusters are almost antiquated now."

"Not so fast. Just because you can get all sorts of processors on a single chip these days doesn't mean chaining them together doesn't still save considerable bucks. My Dad's R&D will often use those clusters to simulate what they want to achieve in a chip under development somewhere else. And besides, a lot of data crunching can be done overnight with all the unused CPU cycles at the various administrative desks. Just takes a timed network reboot."

Another pause.

"OK, you win. Means I don't have to explain a lot of how I get my data figured out. Thanks."

I had to smile. Old "tough-boy" Tom had his soft spots. Too bad he didn't want me kissing him right now. He wasn't the only one who was softened up today.

"So, Tom, you were saying about those people..."

"We still don't know why they got killed, only that they were connected somehow."

Then one of the Librarians made an obvious sound and we both stopped talking. Tom put his arm around the back of my chair and dropped it just as her heel clicked into the space behind us.

Then we heard the swish of a book being removed from the shelves and a rustle of skirt as she turned in the narrow aisle and click-clacked away to the carpeting.

I snickered. "Busy-body."

Tom reached over and took my hand on the table top. "No, self-defense. They just want to make sure anything back here stops short of coitus."

"So your arm?"

"Was to make sure they saw something they expected to find. And to know that we knew they knew."

"And they know?"

"Nothing really. Just that we'd better not 'go there' during school hours."

Of course, that left my mind racing. My mouth out of gear. And some warm feelings in certain areas.

"Sorry to distract you with hormonal cues. Let's get back to what we need to find out. And I think that means you've got some more homework for tonight."

"From our Library Assistant job?"

"Tunneling into your Dad's network to find out what they were all working on."

I sighed. "Oh, I thought for a second we'd – never mind. Just send me the names."

A ding in my ear sounded.

And I found Tom kissing me in the next split second. Which lasted the whole of that pomodoro break. Perfect timing. Not that I minded at all. And not like he had planned that all ahead...

VII

IT WAS A FEW DAYS BEFORE we could meet again.

And I got Jean to meet me where the incident happened. Sent her a route to take that should keep her safe and unsuspected.

It was a narrow alley with one-way traffic. If something went wrong, the outlet and inlet could be blocked simply. One car width.

I'd come up through an old access tunnel into one of the basements nearby. One that had an outside access for deliveries.

Pushed up against the shadowed wall on the south side, I saw her coming. And had to force my heart rate down with careful breathing. These hormones were a pain to deal with, but the feelings were - well - an interesting "casual" research line. Or so I told myself.

Jean was wearing a hoodie over her typical leathers, and that hood was up. Something else was changed. Once she got close to me, I could tell.

"Black? Why such a change from platinum blond?" I was speaking only loud enough to come over her muzik implant.

She came toward me without answering. And that lip-lock she fastened on my face took awhile before she let go. And the surprise was enjoyable.

After that, she stayed in my arms without saying anything. Something was up. Something she'd found out. And so came to me for comfort and reassurance.

I started to take her hood down to have a better look.

"Don't."

I looked down into her blue-gray eyes and could see they were reddened around the edges. She'd been crying or almost.

"Jean, what is it?"

"Murder. There was one other name that wasn't on that list. And may be more. Someone I knew, and he'd been nice to me. Just found out. His name was José. He's been missing since that night, but not reported. He's supposedly on an international fact-finding tour. There's a body-double staying in his hotel suites, attending his functions, but it's not him."

"How do you know?"

"When he goes on those trips, he sends me gifts. From a personal account of his. So I checked further and just found out before I came here. That personal account has been emptied and closed."

"How do you think that means he's dead?"

"He set me up as a signatory on it. My dad didn't even know about it. And would have raised the roof if he had - because it could make me look like an under-age mistress. But it was a simple scholarship fund. The last deposit was a day before he went on that tour. The very next day, that account was emptied and closed."

Jean pushed in toward me harder, her head on my chest, and I just held her closer. There was more to their relationship, but I wasn't going to pry. I could only trust. With her intelligence, it had to be platonic, even a father-figure.

If that guy had been murdered, having no family to raise questions would fit the scheme.

But worse, they now knew that she was a signatory. And the trademark platinum hair would make her an easy spot. Black hair now made more sense.

Once she eased off her grip, "Does your dad know about your new hair color?"

"Sure. He actually likes it. Or said he does. I made sure to have a full breakfast time with him so he'd see it more than as a glance around his stock paper."

"He asked about it?"

Jean nodded. "I said it was a new style I wanted to try. And if I didn't like it, I'd change back or maybe try fire-engine red."

I leaned back to look at her face again. "Not seriously."

She punched my arm. "Come on - you can't think I'm that air-brained."

I smiled. "But you're betting your dad does."

She nodded, and laid her head back on my chest. "Sorry, he's a nice guy, but not as bright as he thinks."

"As long as he keeps thinking you're just destined to be someone's arm-candy, and you're fine with that."

"You've got it. Until I met you, life was pretty lousy. And now, well, until I found out about my 'friend', I thought things were picking up. Even..."

I pulled back. "Even what?"

Jean looked up at me, deep into my eyes. Then stood on her tip-toes to peck me on the cheek. "Maybe with what you know, and my connections, we could disappear somewhere - Outside."

My mind raced at this. "Outside" was beyond the city walls. Almost impossible for a single person to accomplish - security was incredibly tight. But with these new "pomodoro" breaks - and all the systems tied into them, it was becoming possible. And what she'd already told me about her connections meant she'd been working that out on the side.

"How far did your planning get?"

"Here." She reached in and pull out a jump drive from one of her hoodie pockets. "Everything I've worked out. All anonymous files. Nothing to trace us to each other. Thought you'd appreciate that."

I pocketed the drive and kissed her forehead. "Thanks. I think I still haven't told you how we tend to..."

Jean looked at me, waiting, calmer now. "We tend to..."

"Fill each other's voids - the stuff we've each been missing for so long."

My heart went pounding at that. And only slowed after another long kiss from her.

But then Jean's body went stiff in my arms.

"Tom?"

"Yes?"

"We're in trouble."

I looked around. Unless someone had walked by with a spotter scope while we were kissing, there was no one there.

"No, not right this second, but yes, even as we speak. You're an unknown. And now I'm on their list. So I'd better quit seeing you."

"Before you get me killed."

Jean nodded.

"Ain't gonna happen."

"Because you're so damned clever?"

"Because I've got something in my life worth protecting more than my scrawny future-less self."

Right then, I did see something out of the corner of my eye. A glint of light from some optical system - or a polished gun barrel. And the someone behind it was heading our direction, down that narrow alley.

No time. "Jean. This way. Quick!"

VIII

DAYS LATER, WE GOT out of the city with apparent ease. Broad daylight. No hoods or masks.

We died our faces and hands to tan. Dressed in some worn work uniforms we'd "found" by passing a fair amount of Bitcoin through some time-trusted "associates" of Tom's into other hands.

A set of forged, expired, migrant worker visa's matched our descriptions and came with the clothes.

Someone had been busy looking for me. And after a fruitless search, a bleach-blond with my general height and weight showed up in one of the clubs I frequented. An overdose. Case closed.

That someone was earning their pay-off.

So any camera looking for us would give no real positive ID other than the ones we put in there as fuzzy images from "the day we got our entrance images taken" when her Dad's company "imported" us as domestics.

Once our work visa's expired, we had been "administratively detached" and the extra few days were evidence that we weren't able to find other work inside the city, and so then finally turned ourselves in for "exportation".

AND NOW WE WERE ON the Outside. Walking down the long empty highway with semi-demolished suburban homes and businesses on both sides of that wide pavement for miles. Wasn't worth the cost of turning it back into farmland. And it was probably mined with bombs anyway. The city used to worry about being invaded after they seceded. So they hired some mercenaries as contractors to ensure they weren't.

We just walked for quite a bit, hand in hand. Sweating in the sun. At least we got some straw hats as part of the outfit.

No traffic coming or going. The city was self sufficient with it's fusion power, and feeding people with hydroponics - for now. So they thought they'd make it. And since the news was all centralized and filtered, the reports were all that they would.

Its big protective dome shimmered in the sky. Filtering out the air and protecting against UV rays. All while also holding cameras in place to watch all the citizens, even though their muzik chips were telling the city's Masters everything else any citizen said or did. Around the clock.

Once we were a mile or two out, we even quit getting the pomodoro notices.

At about the two-mile marker, we crested a small hill and saw an old station wagon parked on the side of the worn highway, headed in our direction.

As we got closer, a big guy got out of the drivers side and waited for us.

Some twenty feet away, I recognized him and gasped, and then ran to meet him. Giving him a personal hug I'd only given Tom since my own Mother passed.

As Tom got closer, I turned toward him with my arm around the big man's waist, while he had an arm around my shoulder.

"Tom, let me introduce you to José."

José extended his hand and I shook it. "Tom, it's good to meet you. I knew someone was caring for our little Jean, but we couldn't figure out who."

Tom's forehead was wrinkled in non-comprehension. "I suppose there's an answer for all this?"

José hugged me like family. "Jean's 'dad' wasn't really her birth-dad at all, I was."

Of course, that hit me like a ton of bricks.

He continued explaining, looking down at me. "Your mom died in childbirth, and your 'dad' and I were partners at the time. Since his wife couldn't have children, they agreed to adopt you. I was pretty torn up about my wife's passing, and it took some years to get over it. But the unofficial agreement was that I could visit you any time I wanted."

I looked up at him. "That explains why you were at every graduation and every vacation."

José hugged me again. "Oh, just look at the sweat streaming down those faces. Here, get in. Cool water inside and A/C."

TOM AND I SAT IN THE station wagon's back seat enjoying our waters while he was driving in front with the A/C on full blast, and checking us occasionally through the center rear-view mirror with his smiling eyes.

"The rest of the story is that neither my partner - your adoptive "dad" - liked where things were heading. But the business itself is too entrenched in the city's operation to allow us to simply leave. We both know too much. So we had to fake our deaths. It took months to work out because, as you well know, those few technocrats are trying to run and control everything. Right down to pulling all that data via their muzik network and mining it for far more than just sending ads.

"And we knew that Tom was taking care of you when you switched to that 'retro' muzik device. And after that we couldn't track you to keep you safe. Sure, your driver told us that you had a new boyfriend, even though he didn't get a good look at his face. And Tom, I have to say you are very, very good at staying off the grid. We never did find you. The closest we got was in that alley."

I was smiling at this. Now, at least, I knew we were out of danger.

IX

JEAN AND I WERE STILL getting used to the cool A/C. We sat and sipped from water bottles in the back seat of that old station wagon. While Jean's real Dad debriefed us. All on an empty highway with deserted and half-demolished suburban buildings on each side. A surreal scene.

At least the sweating had stopped.

"Sure, I 'disappeared' before that. So did those other people on that list. The trick was to make it look like a far-fetched conspiracy. The petty thefts were simply to test the system. Once we verified their loophole, then people could start disappearing. Because making a new life on the Outside was the only option once they started tracking your every move."

I butted in. "So the sudden reappearance of the X-301 was you and your people. But that was months ago."

"Right around the time of that last major upgrade. They left a loophole in the old system in an effort to 'support legacy hardware'. Figuring that the tinny sound would eventually work in their favor. What they didn't count on was our 'open-source' hack which turned off everything they were monitoring, especially the 'root' access. All they did was to buy up the remaining manufacturers. But we meanwhile bought up all the existing hardware stockpiles at fire sale prices. We made a killing when we started the 'fad' of retro devices with 'authentic-original' sound. They couldn't do anything about it, since the companies were all privately owned and looked like someone was running their little home business out of their parent's basement."

"That's all fine, José, but how were you out here waiting for us?"

"A lot of hard sleuthing. We were already tracking all the X-301 sales and we then narrowed it to the handful of fake applications. Then looked for changes in the little data we had on usage. It went down to four. Two of those we managed to track down by fuzzy surveillance camera footage. One we never did find. Jean's was of course on record. But two non-tracking devices were listed to be 'exported' today, so I was waiting. Just out of sight, just in case."

"Wait, you've been gone for weeks - you were still inside the city?"

"Oh, hell no - pardon my French. That place is a trap waiting to be sprung. We do have a few people waiting there until the last moment to help people get to the Outside. But we were monitoring from out here."

"Monitoring?"

"You don't really believe they have all the 'best and brightest' minds working for them - either of you?"

Jean and I looked at each other. She was holding my hand and gave it a squeeze.

José grinned through his mirror at us. "I mean, there's you two, just to start with. And everyone who ever bought an X-301. Because that sound is really bad. But the people who were buying it didn't want any sound at all. And those are the types we're recruiting. Especially the ones who can hide their identity so well. Like that librarian in your school."

My mouth dropped open, as did Jean's.

"We still didn't know who you were, but the fact that you matched the driver's description and weren't 'going at it' loud enough to be heard out in the stacks - well, that mean our little Jean was in very good, responsible hands."

This time I squeezed Jean's hand.

She spoke up at this. "But wait, why couldn't you at least give us a clue? I mean you and 'Dad' and all this?"

José just shrugged. "Just because they don't have the actual best and brightest doesn't mean they're stupid. Plus, we had to let them think they are – so their elite arrogance will keep leaving loopholes we can use. Believe me, I don't know how many times we've listened to their boardroom meeting presentations where they said that 'no one outside our company would ever figure that out' and they had no clue their own audio was hacked."

I had to know something. "So what is this 'last moment'?"

José smiled and looked at me through his mirror. "They call it 'The Rising'. When all their cities are going to lift off and go to the moon as part of some grand scheme. Practically, they have about a 50/50 chance of making orbit."

Jean and I just nodded. This was the rumor-mill consensus of the reasoning behind all the moves by the elites to get inside the city perimeter. Meaning they had to leave their expensive private plantations beyond those walls.

"It won't be long now. They'll be starting the PR campaign today, actually. You can watch it when we get home."

I spoke up again. "Home?"

"What we call it. A little village near here. You'll like the place. And there's someone named Sybil you're going to love. Very bright girl. Very bright. And that's a complete understatement."

He took his foot off the accelerator and the car slowed.

Glancing though his inside mirror at us, "Oh, and you'll find a lot of people you know there. Your adopted Dad for one, and some other people who have been helping you all along."

José then looked out both his outside mirrors and checked both side's blind spots, even though there was no one else on the road. "I think that's far enough. Now we can quit passing for 'normal.'" He put the car into neutral and flipped a series of switches in the dash. Some loud rumbling started happening below us.

"Sorry about that road noise." José spoke up to be heard above it. "Once we get to a decent altitude, it will all even out."

At the word "altitude", Jean and I shared our shocked looks.

The "station wagon" had sprouted thin stubby wings on each side and we were slowly rising off the ground, picking up forward speed as we did.

"'Best and brightest' means a lot more where we're going. Like eons beyond what those supposed 'elites' think is possible. You two are just in time for the greatest advancement in humankind - ever. Welcome home - to the future."

About then, the station-wagon-turned-air-car rattled a bit... as we passed Mach 1.

The Autists: Brigitte

BY J. R. KRUZE

THE AUTISTS HAD FAILED as an evolved species.

While they could out-think and out-strategize, and out-everything the older Homo Saps, their own calculations showed that their race of Homo Transire only had a couple of generations at most before they were terminal. No new savants, no new super-empaths, only dead-end mediocrity.

How could such brilliant minds get it so wrong?

Brigitte was the Founder's only savant offspring and even her own children were happier to just live mundane normal lives with average grades in school and only aspire to get college degree, a house, a car for each of them, and a mountain of debt. Watch TV, consume fast food, be average.

No breakthrough research, no soul-inspiring artwork.

Her own children, now grown, couldn't understand her any better. She could empathize their feelings from anywhere on the planet. While they had a hard time empathizing with their pets, let alone their growing children.

Mundanity had struck back - with a vengeance.

She was looking for someone who could tell her why - or be one of the last few of her race on this mud-ball called Earth.

I

THEY'D RUN THE CALCULATIONS thousands of times, with millions of permutations. The best math minds on the planet. And they all agreed. Homo Transire was dying out.

Terminal. That's when your offspring aren't useful anymore. Not that we didn't love them. But they didn't understand us. They couldn't. We were wired completely different.

Once my children were on their own, busy making me a grandmother, I got back to work. Started collecting new datasets, checking for new equations, looking for something we must have missed.

For all the work we'd done in finding and matching the most brilliant among us as mates for the others - none of these 2nd and 3rd generations turned out to be anything hardly better than average. Sure, there were some pretty bright kids in all that. Beautiful babies. Talented in their cribs. But once they got past 7 or 8, all that talent started showing limits. Kids who were prodigies as babes couldn't draw or play music any better than their peers of that same age.

It didn't matter what school or who the teachers were. Or what books or computer programs. No amount of money thrown at them produced any better results that the "free" public schools we all paid for.

And I talked to myself as I drove this back gravel road which my GPS said was the fastest route to the remote research station out in this Gawd-forsaken Flyover Country.

I could see putting our campuses out in the suburbs. But dust and gravel roads weren't designed to be driven with any speed - not unless you wanted to...

Oh no. No, no, no. NO NO NO.

The car swerved and I was forced to slow down, coasting to a stop on the top of a hill. Over into a grassy entrance to some farmer's field.

Sure, only now the "low air pressure" light and tacky dinging "bell" alert finally started. I had one, if not two flats on this thing.

My bad luck was holding. No bars on my cel.

And no empath within sending distance.

So I rested my head against my steering wheel and swore against the ancient gods in alphabetical order (using the Greek order of course.)

And opened my eyes to see that my choice of heels today might be a good fashion statement, and helped people see my legs at their best. But wouldn't help me walk the quarter-mile to any nearby farmhouse to get some help.

Just sitting here and running the A/C was only going to burn up my fuel and probably risk carbon monoxide poisoning.

I looked through my purse and briefcase for anything that might be able to help me solve this one. But I knew that was just forestalling the inevitable. The outside temperature was somewhere in the 80's. That was going to put a sheen on me (my grandmother referred to it as "glow") and this thin blouse and skirt were going to be an uncomfortable clingy mess by the time I stumbled anywhere.

But my keen senses showed no one for miles that had any higher empathy than a cow or a dog.

And right before I could muster up my courage to face the inevitable, a shadow flooded across my window and a rap on it startled me into double-checking the locks everywhere. There was no face behind that glare into my auto-tinting windows. Yet rolling them down could be the last thing I'd remember.

II

THAT CAR WAS SITTING there for awhile.

Of course, it didn't matter to me, but it wasn't any of our neighbor's. It was some slick speedster that wasn't designed worth a shuck for our roads. Thin tires would go flat in no time. Nail or some piece of quartz would do it.

That old truck of mine had to get 10-ply tires on it. So I could quit paying for flat repairs in my monthly budget. And you can't get such tires for those fancy cars. Won't fit under their fenders.

Well, I'm out here checking the pastures anyway - maybe I should look in on whoever that is.

One foot after the other. Check the grasses and forbs and whatnot out here. See what they were like compared to the day before. It would probably help if I did more than just walk from one end to the other. Maybe start walking on a grid so I'd know better what my cows were eating.

No, this wasn't the main herd. But after we lost our first milk cow, I figured that we didn't need to have them with the beef cattle as she probably got too excited. Vet said it was common to milk cows. Still, I hardly got the price back out of selling her full-grown calf a few months later.

So I got this next one - we use sturdy milk cows for nursing backup, since the powder they sell us as "milk replacer" is more investment than any orphaned calf or twin will bring back. This one has worked out pretty good - we sold her own calf when he got too big and rowdy, then bought and grafted a younger calf on. So far we were doing OK.

Once our last beef cow has dropped her calf, then I'd have to decide if the cost of feeding that milk cow was going to more than pay for having real whole milk, real butter and real cottage cheese, plus the "clabber" protein for the chickens...

But I was used to my thoughts ratcheting around while I was walking.

Some days, I'd talk out my books and ideas as I did. Today, I figured that the lady in that car would be spooked if I came up on her with my mouth just opening and shutting for no reason she could figure.

And I could see from getting closer that she was a pretty fetching thing - even through all that tinted glass.

When she put her head down on that steering wheel, I could see she was talking or praying out loud or something.

So I slowed up a bit - it helped that I had to twist my long frame through that barbed wire fence - because I didn't want to rip a new hole in anything, and I didn't want to interrupt her praying or cussing or whatever.

Why was I bothering? Because if I was in her place - all dressed up and with a very flat tire on my hot little sports car - I'd appreciate some help.

Besides, I was already out here.

So she was done with her talking-cussing-praying, and right about now would be sorting out if she wanted to stay inside that A/C just to run her tiny fuel tank down to fumes - or get out and start sweating like me.

I call these "two-bandanna" days, since one was across your forehead under your broad-brimmed hat – to keep the sweat out of your eyes - and the other goes across your neck to keep your body's thermostat cooler. Took me a few years to work that out.

And with all the curls in that dark hair of hers, she really didn't want to squash it down with one of my pre-sweated bandanna's.

So I knocked on her window - lightly.

And she jumped like I must have scared her half to death.

III

I HIT THE WINDOW SWITCH after staring at him for awhile. Feeling him out. Empathic? No. Backwoods moron? Probably.

Still, he probably knew whoever it was that they had for mechanics around here. And if they had anything like a taxi service in this nowhere land, let alone a rental service.

"Hi. Can you help me? I think I've had a flat. And my phone doesn't work around here. Do you have a phone I could borrow?" Smile, nod, look innocent. That's what they understand.

"Yes, ma'am. But it's Sunday, so unless you have Triple A or something, we're going to have to wait awhile for any help to come."

This farmer guy was dressed in a very sensible outfit. Looked like all blue, faded cotton from top to bottom. That cowboy hat was keeping most of the sun off of him, and his tanned face and forearms showed he was out in the weather probably every day of the year. So waiting around in this heat was probably nothing to someone like him.

"Ma'am? My little home isn't far from here. You can almost see it off the rise, if it weren't for the tall grass we have this year. If you want, you could go down there and I'd change your flat for you. Or, you could just sit where you are and I'll change it anyway. Oh - wait..."

He had been sizing up that tire and where the flat was probably located in the trunk, but then stood up straight again and walked around to the other side. I left the window open, despite the heat, and heard his low whistle.

A few of his long steps and he was back at my window again.

"Sorry, ma'am. But you probably knew this from the swerving you did - you've got two flat tires."

I uttered another curse on the heads of some even older Phoenician gods under my breath.

He smiled at me. "Not that those two have been around for awhile. But they probably deserved that."

My mouth dropped open. I was speechless. Rare for me. I had inherited my dad's loquaciousness. And if he could talk the ears off a corn stalk, then I'd have them shelled and ground before they hit the dirt.

Wait. What was I saying? Grind corn? Flour - maybe. But that's something I'd never studied up on. What use was there in that? Advanced calculus - quintic polynomials, sure. Chromosomic coverage for reliable variant calling, that's what I've been tinkering with as a mental hobby. But cattle feed? Where did that come from?

He just smiled broader. "Ma'am, I'm Joe. And yes, all this is perplexing. Welcome to my world."

I had to chuckle. No rube or hick here. "I'm Brigitte. And I'm very happy to meet you."

Then I stuck out my hand and he took off both of his sweat-stained leather gloves to grasp my own hand in his right. For what must have been egg-shell gingerly for him - as I felt the callouses on his wide mitt. A slight shake to be polite, but nothing that would hurt me.

"Well, you decide what you want to do." He patted his pocket. "Nope. That's right, I had to put my phone on charge this morning before I left. Didn't think I'd get in any trouble out here. But then I didn't factor you into my calculations for the day."

He shook his head. "And now you've got me talking like that, too." His smile became a grin.

Finally I got some words to come out straight. "How did you, I mean where are we, or what is happening - you aren't..."

"Are you sure about that?" Joe just cocked his head slightly. Not in a condescending way, but it was a mannerism I was too familiar with - because that's what I do.

He straightened up. "OK, this is going to be an interesting day. Now, you've got a spare in the trunk, and I just happen to have one of those extra-dinky never-flat spares that might fit. But I'm going to have to walk down there and get it. You can wait here and run your engine to keep cool, but it's not the most enjoyable way to spend a beautiful Sunday morning. And it's only going to get hotter today."

At that he took off his wide-brimmed hat (he was no cowboy, so that was inaccurate of me earlier) and mopped his brow with that bandanna he had on it. For what good that did. It was already dripping wet.

"Well, it feels better, anyway. And that sweat evaporates - oh, I'm sorry. It's been awhile since I had someone so, well..."

"Intelligent? Empathic? Savant-ish?"

"Yeah, all those and more."

He glanced at my front briefly, and I could feel that gaze along with the now damp and clinging fabric there. His eyes were just as fast back up to mine, and his honest smile was a bit contagious. "But I've got some box fans down at my place that you can sit in front of and keep cool, plus some lemonade and ice. That is if you don't mind trusting one of us who live out in this 'nowhere land' of 'rubes and hicks'. Meanwhile, I can get those two spares on your car and at least get this little car of yours to the point you can drive slowly over to what we refer to as a 'motel' and enjoy a nice air-conditioned rest of your day. And I'm sure Mabel will let you use her land-line to call whoever you have to."

I smiled at his good-natured teasing. Giving Joe a nod, I rolled up the window, unlocked the trunk, and pulled the keys out.

He stepped back from the door and I rose with as much grace as possible in these spike heels - trying to stand among all that unsteady gravel.

Closing the door, I handed him the keys. "Now, how would you suggest I take the shortest and most comfortable path to your place?"

To that he turned and offered me his arm. I slipped my arm inside his, along with its damp long-sleeved print blouse. He held my hand with his other one to make sure I didn't slip on the gravel, getting safely across the short distance to the tall grass on the other side.

There he left me standing by the fence for a moment, when he knew I wasn't going to fall down. And then opened a steel gate with its rattling chains, to creak it open. Inside that gate in that tall grass pasture was a small beaten path. I stepped forward and found my step was quite stable.

"Yes, the cows work this over, as they like to keep to the same paths - they have just as much concerns in walking as we do. Plus, I think it's easier for them to keep their thoughts straight if they just put 'following the rump in front of them' on automatic. Just like how we drive, sometimes. And why most accidents occur near home."

"I'd ask you about reading my mind, but we'll leave that for later."

He blushed a bit at that, or seemed to – under that tan. "Sure. Sorry. Out of practice with social amenities. Cows and pets don't care much, since they can't speak or comprehend much English anyhow."

"So you were...."

"Yeah, right. OK, now the green slimy stuff is fresh manure and there's some of that on that path. And not all the path is dry from the last rain. Some people would rather go barefoot than twist an ankle in high heels, but you take your choice. Better yet, I've still got to go over there to pick up that extra tire I've got, so I can let you continue to borrow my arm if you want. I've got boots to walk through the grass next to that cow-path, so maybe that's the more optimal solution you were contemplating, Brigitte."

I had to smile. "As long as you can guide me while you answer my many questions, I think we have a deal."

He turned and chained the steel gate shut and then came back with his offered arm again. And my hand once more found its way to that inside arm of his, while his other hand came on top of mine.

And as my mother would say, it was a kind of purplish-blue thought. While I felt warm in areas I hadn't for awhile. No, not because of the weather outside.

IV

IT DIDN'T TAKE LONG to get those two spare tires on. I got her luggage into her back seat - well most of it, and the rest fit into the passenger side. No reason getting all that dust from two flat tires on them. Also because I had to drive it down the hill on that gravel, and then drive back up the two narrow bare strips that passed for my own driveway. And after that, I turned it around at the top and pointed it back so she could leave when she was ready.

And most city folk would rather rush back to "civilization" and it's paved roads just as fast as they could.

I'd left Brigitte with a tall tumbler of iced lemonade and my charged-up phone.

So when I came back all sweaty, I was surprised to see her in one of my old t-shirts and some cutoff's I kept around. Her nice-looking blouse and skirt were hanging up near the fans to dry off.

Logical. And I'd been in her head a bit, so it was fine that she rummaged around my dresser to get into something more comfortable to wear. In this humidity, cotton was King.

She was reading from my smartphone as I opened the door into what passed for my "company" room - since there were only two rooms in this small cabin, anything not for sleeping could be shared with visitors - not that I had many. Just the way I liked it. Too confusing, otherwise.

Brigitte looked up. "Nice range of books in here. Didn't know that farming was so wide a discipline. Erle Stanley Gardner, Louis L'Amour, Lewis Bromfield, plus the Upanishads and Buddhist texts. Meanwhile, your print books cover an even wider range - I guess you trucked these in over the years."

I smiled. "Busted. But you're just teasing me anyway. OK, your car's fixed as good as I can get it. So you're set to go...."

She smiled at me. "And you are polite enough just to wait around all sweaty and even dripping on the floor. I'm the one being rude - go ahead and get toweled off and changed. I'll wait – to ask you more questions, of course."

V

WHEN HE CAME OUT OF his bedroom, in a light pair of knit shorts exposing his white legs, a clean t-shirt and barefoot, we were almost twins (except my legs were darker, shaved, and more sleek than muscle.) And his bleached-out strawberry blond hair contrasted with my nearly coal-black long curly tresses.

I probably made that t-shirt of his look a lot better than it had for awhile.

Judging by his blush, I knew this mind-reading went both ways.

"Yup, busted again." He was grinning. "You make those cut-off's look good, too."

My turn to blush. So I handed him a tumbler of lemonade and we each took a seat in one of his "kitchen" chairs at the small table in its corner.

"Your questions then?"

"Like how come I didn't pick you up when I was coming this way?"

"Who said you didn't? Those GPS thingies tend to work OK if you follow their directions. But you second-guessed it - because you're used to your 'hunches' being more accurate than the gizmo's you use. Only cost you two flat tires."

"A bit blunt there? Accurate, yes. And intuition is as accurate as you practice with it. I've cost myself time before from having wrong hunches - nothing new. But I've more often saved myself considerable time."

"Yet you can still get waylaid simply."

"Like you just did. How come I couldn't sense you?"

"Listening on the wrong channel. Like a radio. You got to tune it."

"Not that simple, Joe. I can't pick up a station that's not sending."

He sipped his lemonade and smiled. "You weren't listening for the 'no-static' band - you expect people to be sending all the time."

"And you don't?"

"Why should I? Who's around here to talk to? Besides, the cows are used to humans saying idiotic things around them. Dogs and cats have it even worse - humans are so arrogant sometimes. No, make that all the time. All humans, all the time.."

Joe sipped his lemonade and looked down into it.

"All of us arrogant - includes you, I suppose?"

"Sure. Especially me. Like I could have felt you coming, but I didn't. Could have told you the paved roads to get here easier. Saved you two tires." His brow was furrowed. "Sorry."

I leaned forward and put a hand on his knee. "No, I'm the one that's sorry. You're being a nice host and we both had to break our usual, habitual thought patterns - and now I'm beginning to see this 'arrogance' inside me like you were talking about."

Joe gave a wry grin. "So the question is, where do you want to go from here?"

VI

BRIGITTE WAS STUNNED. That question had a lot of ways to take it. Some not so nice.

She sipped her own lemonade. And I glanced at her crossed legs in those cutoffs to distract myself and let her think things through.

She smiled at that. "Distract yourself? Been that long?"

I chuckled. "OK, well, you're right. But I haven't had such a pretty guest in quite awhile. But like I said, I can be arrogant – even when trying to be helpful."

She touched my knee again with her hand. Something I didn't mind at all. "Oh, sorry again. But we're from different worlds and my empathy is usually on all the time. Like stuck in high gear."

I nodded. "Don't I know. Took me years to turn mine off, along with other things. But you don't see a lot of people around here, either."

She left her hand there, like trying to keep focused on something.

"You are probably who I've been looking for."

"Wouldn't doubt that. Two flat tires means not going anywhere soon. And me just happening to be in that pasture just then."

"And 'just happening' to have another spare that fit - so I could leave any time."

"Yet, here you are."

"And here I am."

The hand was still on my knee. And the purplish thoughts were coming with a cinnamon scent.

"Cinnamon?" Her eyes went wide. "Wow."

Brigitte put her tumbler down, uncrossed her legs, and leaned forward to put a hand on each of my knees. Then she looked directly into my eyes, defocussing them so that each eye looked directly into my own - as I did.

And the information flowed in gigabyte-tons back and forth.

At last, she sat back, breathing heavy. Her forehead was glistening.

I forced myself to relax the muscles in my back and arms.

We each took our tumblers in hand. Still cool, ice gone.

She smiled. "Yes, but I'll get the refill we both want."

As she rose, I handed her my tumbler and appreciated her backside as she went to the refrigerator. She just turned to me and winked, then got busy filling both glasses. Her hip shoved the refrigerator door shut and she glided back to the little cabin table with a glass in each hand.

As I took mine, I nodded my thanks. "Long time for you, too?"

She shrugged, and sipped with a smile. "Some things a lady isn't supposed to say - out loud, anyway."

I sat up when I realized what time it was. The light was starting to dim in the windows, meaning that I had some evening chores to do. Time had flown that afternoon.

"Go ahead." Brigitte got up. "I'll get dinner while you're gone. The least I could do."

I just shook my head. "You know, this could get addictive."

She smiled back. "More than you know - like having it stuck in 'high' all my life. Too much information all the time." And sighed as she looked off.

Then she took my hand and pulled me up. But didn't let go.

Instead, she leaned in and gave me a hug that didn't want to quit. Or I didn't want - make that we didn't want it to quit.

She had her head on my chest, and I bent down to touch the top of hers with my nose. Her lilac scent filled me to overflowing, the warmth and contact made me want to...

Brigitte giggled and pushed me back. "No. You: chores. Me: dinner. And we have more to talk out loud about things after that. You get to help me solve my biggest problem. Now - get changed and scoot. I already know how you like your steaks. And where your beer stash is. The real question is where you put that 'guest' apron... Oh - thanks. That wasn't difficult."

Then she stood on her tiptoes to kiss me lightly on my cheek. "Now: scoot."

VII

JOE WAS MORE THAN HAPPY. Orange and red thoughts, with a cherry-sundae taste to them.

Of course, mine were more yellowish-green, but that just figures. Complimentary colors.

He'd had some leftover frozen ice cream cake in the freezer compartment, so by the end of that meal I was smiling like a schoolgirl on her first date and he wasn't far behind. Giggles from me met chuckles from him, and those just prompted more from each of us.

We crowded in next to each other to do the dishes. Then I cleaned off the table, putting things where he wanted to find them. While he came back with a large pad of paper and an old coffee mug with colored markers in it. Plenty of those clicker-type pencils with endless leads.

Both of us were barefoot, t-shirted, and wearing shorts. Side by side. Good thing we were opposite-handed, so I sat on his right side so we could both write and draw and make notes. My left hand would often wind up on his thigh, while his right arm would go around the back of my chair and occasionally onto my shoulder as we went.

Somewhere in that, we seemed to lose our arrogance – at least toward each other.

I think it was when the night cooled down, our equations and diagrams slowed down. Then I asked him about that thing called "skinny-dipping". That one tag-end idea he'd left out for me to find as I rummaged through his mind.

WE HAD THE POND ALL to ourselves, the moon was high, and a slight breeze cooled us off.

In each other's arms, we had all the warmth we needed.

You do know that people think by touching? The point where your hearts beat as one, the mind goes into sync as well. And you can very nearly become a shared person at that point. Nothing to do with individuality.

Clothes just get in the way of a true hug. At least we both agreed on that.

IN THE MIDDLE OF THE night, it hit me. And I sat up.

Joe was smiling when I turned toward him.

"And?"

I just curled up next to his broad chest. "Perfect."

VIII

I GOT A HANDWRITTEN letter in the mail the next Thursday.

It turned out that Monday was a holiday, so we took time for a trip in my pickup into the local Wal-Mart to get more big drawing pads, markers, and pencils. What a coincidence.

Then got her car fixed on Tuesday.

When I saw her last, she was all dressed up in that long-sleeved print blouse, but wisely got out some tailored slacks instead of a skirt, flats instead of spiked heels. She waved to me out her window and drove off. I got my spare spare tire back again.

The mechanic gave me a knowing smile, but didn't say anything. He didn't have to.

That letter was in the Thursday mail, like I was saying. Or trying to. You see, like time isn't linear, neither are thoughts. So bear with me.

She'd found the problem was with their own arrogance. The Homo Transire, in all their "superior intellectual capacity" were not exempt. Nor were they going "extinct" any time soon. But there was no real reason for all the organization to exist anymore.

The various corporations and non-profits could be run for decades with all the fail-safes built in. But we didn't need them.

Because our kind had been going "underground" for decades, if not longer.

The trick was that it wasn't genetics. Nothing really to do with that code.

You see, at the lowest levels, DNA and RNA are remaking themselves all the time. And we are always rethinking ourselves as we go along. Thought controls function, and so cells are changed as needed. So being "homo transire" is more a state of mind.

Hiding in plain sight. Or out in the middle of nowhere and dressed like a "rube" or "hick".

ONCE SHE GOT BACK HOME after that business trip, Brigitte sent me another handwritten letter. All of her children, and all the other offspring in the charts she'd checked were just fine. They were actually all having a blast being "normal." And they apologized for not cluing her in - but knew that until she figured it out for herself, Brigitte wouldn't believe it was that simple.

Like the mechanic told me in the shop, right in front of her while his hands were busy with tires and rims, "You have to go along to get along."

SO I'M BUILDING AN extension onto the old house. She's going to need an office. And a bigger closet for all her clothes.

And that dock in the old pond will need some sprucing up. So we can do some fishing - or whatever.

The Case of the Naughty Nightmare

BY J. R. KRUZE

I

I'D HEARD A SCREAM in the storm-filled, rainy night, but thought at first it was just the peacocks roosting in the shed on my farm.

When it didn't repeat, I thought no more of it.

Until I opened the door to my tiny home and found a naked woman laying on my couch, face down.

She seemed to be sleeping. I could see her back rise and fall, so I knew she was breathing.

There was no car out front, no tracks to the door or inside. She seemed dry, but I hadn't touched her.

Her tearful eyes then flashed open and focused on me, pure terror in her look. "Please help me - "

And then she fainted dead away...

IT ONLY TOOK A FEW steps to reach and kneel beside her. She did have a pulse, but no fever. Breathing evenly. And when I saw the rain drops coming off my chore coat onto her bare skin, I reached up to pull the coverlet off the back of that couch to cover and protect her.

Then I rose back up to shrug out of that sopping coat and hang it up with my soaked wide-brimmed hat to drip over the black, hard plastic boot tray below it. My soaked brown leather chore boots were next. Toeing these off and setting them such that the coat drippings weren't going to keep them wet.

Turning back to my guest, I saw she was still resting OK, so I reached up to the long shelf across the end of that cabin, above the door, and pulled down a couple of winter comforters. One went across her on top of the fall-patterned hand-knit coverlet she had already. The other comforter I laid across the back of the couch for ready access if she later turned feverish.

Kneeling again, I gently elevated her head to put a pillow under it, then brushed her dark russet hair off her face and back from her neck. Almost an angel now, as she rested.

Then I recognized her - it was Joyce. The story who had at first haunted me to write her into existence. But here she was in human form, not just pictured in my own mind's eye. Sure, I talk about writing books into life, but had never actually witnessed one taking full human shape.

Yet, here she was. In my tiny cabin, on my single couch that took up the biggest part of the floor space, even without expanding that futon into a full-size bed.

That sleeping form was a mystery in her own right. Yet I wasn't going to get any answers until she'd rested enough to wake on her own.

Having done all I could do for her now, the next obvious point was to get myself dry and warmed up.

Slipping out of my wet work pants, I hung these up to drip onto that mud tray. Then turned to a tall narrow set of custom shelves and drawers that formed the corner, with a hamper down below. Shucking out of wet t-shirt, skivvies, and socks, I replaced all these with dry versions, only glancing once at my sleeping guest out of some curious modesty. Then, on with my light gray sweatpants and and a brown sweatshirt to take my own chill away.

Running my fingers through my soaked hair, I padded to the other end of the cabin in a few steps to pour myself another tall mug of coffee. Then filled a short china carafe with water into the microwave. Ensuring the lid sat securely on it, I simply left it there. No reason to make a lot of noise of microwave humming and dinging, as I didn't know when my guest was going to waken.

Adding honey to my mug of coffee, I crossed back to my narrow writing table in front of the couch. Moving my rolling chair to the end of it, I sat down and tried to sort out what I knew about this mystery.

Just sitting down was welcome to me. Sitting and thinking soon showed I had nothing to go on. Joyce had brought several good stories to me during the last year. All had sold well when I published them, and some I intended to expand into a serialized novella and perhaps into a full novel. Mostly romantic mysteries.

I'd always been busy with stories, no lack of inspiration. She said that the only thing that kept my "queue" short was my own prolific output. As she described it, all authors have long or short lines of stories waiting to be "brought to life" through their chosen author's typing and publishing. And several stories would pitch themselves over and over to different authors hoping to get a better result, which explained how a lot of plots repeat.

Joyce had almost seemed an endless story-fountain of inspiration for my own queue. Her stories had many of the same characters, but different episodes and involvements that were always interesting and entertaining. So she had earned her own series of stories, all popular in their own right.

None of this prepared me for a very real story-turned-human in my tiny home cabin. Or gave me any clue to why she had just appeared here.

The warm honeyed coffee, as well as relaxing after the slogging, wet field work started to make my eye lids heavy. Finishing off the last of my brew, I set it on the desk top away from the edge where it wouldn't fall or get knocked over by accident.

Rolling my chair back to the wall and stretching out my legs, I folded my arms and rested my head against the wall as I looked at my guest again. She was still resting, quiet against the matching quiet of that cabin as the rain pattered on the insulated metal roof. The patter became a rhythm that soon helped me drop into my own deep sleep.

II

I WOKE WITH A START as the microwave buzz turned into a ding. And found I couldn't move at first. Something heavy was covering me. Managing to get my arms loose from their crossed position, I batted at the covering and moved it off my face, only to squint from the sudden light in my cabin.

"Hey there, sleepyhead. How about some breakfast?" Joyce was up and smiling at me. She had dressed herself in my own clothes, giving them a fit and shape that looked better on her than me. She'd found a pair of cutoff shorts, and had a t-shirt on under my spare gray sweatshirt. Her feet were bare at the end of some shapely legs, the ones I'd imagined for so very long. Her long russet hair was loosely gathered behind her neck with a wrapped single strand holding it in place and out of her cooking.

She had the frying pan going, with the smells and sounds of sizzling egg omelet pan bread. She almost bounced the few steps to set a fresh mug of coffee near me on the desk - or at least parts of her bounced. A good looking breakfast was on its way, for sure.

I rose to pick up the quilt she had covered me with, and folded it to set on the end of the couch. It covered the folded comforter I'd put across her last night. I noted that she had already remade the couch with its coverlet across its back again.

Stretching first, I then picked up the mug and sipped the steaming brew. Delicious. Just the way I liked it. Too obvious, though. She'd been around my mind so much that she knew almost too much about me.

The relationship between the writer and story is more intimate than you'd expect between two people. I knew details to her back story that would never see the light of day. She lived in my mind so long from her patient waiting for me to take my breaks and prepare my meals, to only then get around to the necessary writing and proofing and publishing online. All before she saw herself in final digital form.

I also felt her return when the printed proofs came. They required their own cross-checks. I shared with her the sensation of feeling the heft of its weight and the slick cover with vibrant colors. As well, turning it over to verify the back cover text and how the art fit.

The quiet satisfaction we both felt as I approved the book online, and then shelved another proof on my long shelves that lined the upper wall spaces. I also saw her in my mind's eye parlor, putting her book on the mahogany-stained Ikea coffee table that stood in front of her red velveteen daybed. She position this edition next to the earlier books in that series already artfully displayed on the coffee table. Then she would recline there with satisfaction and another big mug of chocolate topped by a mound of whipped cream.

At that, the real world Joyce interrupted my musings by sliding a plate toward me with the thick omelet-bread, folded over once and slathered with wild-plum jam, fork stuck vertically in its thick middle. She set her own plate down and pulled up the folding chair I keep for incidental guests.

In this world, she had her own cup of coffee, but left it alone to dig into the tasty treat she had prepared for both of us.

After a few bites, and a few sips, I again looked at her charming face. Her hazel eyes met mine as she continued to chew daintily and smile at me.

"Like it?"

"Love it. You did good. Got the recipe down perfectly."

"Well, it's not like I didn't see exactly how you did it. And, you're welcome. Also, thanks."

I smiled at her. She knew my ways of thinking so well, that our conversations were more shorthand than full sentences. Beyond just finishing each other's sentences. Far more efficient.

"Of course. You know you're welcome to visit me anytime."

At that her eyes went downcast toward her food. Her hands didn't move. A tear formed and ran down one cheek.

III

I MOVED OUR TWO PLATES to the side, as well as our coffees. Just so she would have room to talk with her hands (something I'd seen her do a lot in our long relationship.)

"It's just not fair."

"What?"

"I'm being stalked by a memory that couldn't possibly have happened."

"But how is that possible? Stories are able to remember and retell their stories a dozen, dozen ways - and are basically timeless."

"That's the problem - this is a human memory."

"Which brings up the question - how did you become human?"

"Believe me, I was surprised as you are. Imagine, now suddenly I have to deal with eating, sleeping, health issues, how to find a bathroom, having a job so I can afford to eat, somewhere to sleep - preferably with its own bathroom..."

She reached over to grab her coffee mug. As I did.

After a sip, she continued. "It as when I started a series of non-fiction books with this other author. You'd like him. Tall, handsome, persuasive - a lot like you. Name is Ted. Anyway, we were going along and talking inside his mind, when he found a job opening for a psychology lecturer. It had been empty for a great long while. He's a real gizmo's nut. So he worked up an avatar for me, and a voice to match - pretty close to how I really look in your mind - and applied for the job on a temporary, out-sourced basis. For all that college knew, this was a real person with all these degrees and whatnot who was applying for the job. All telecommute, so videos were prepared in advance, and then assignments were to be submitted online, all very real."

Joyce reached over to grab her fork and another bite of breakfast omelet-bread.

"I helped him with the papers, adding my two cents and how to phrase them. So there was real work, and a real job, and all of it was a complete lark to me. But then it became very real.

"You see, my lectures were well liked, and well attended. They were all based on research, but I was telling them as a dramatic story instead of dry prose. Something on the order of Gladwell's books, or a TED talk.

"And then one day, 'we' got an email that they'd like to meet us in person since some journalists had attended the lectures on an audit-basis and wanted to interview me."

She sipped her coffee again and looked out into space, collecting her thoughts.

"It gets sketchy about that time. Do you remember a movie called 'Weird Science'?"

I nodded, sipping my own coffee. She meanwhile grabbed another bite, and then pulled our two plates back over.

"God, this stuff is so good. I know it's your recipe, but I'm a better cook than I ever thought - well, at least with this dish."

I had to smile at this. And enjoy the rest of my breakfast while she finished her tale.

"OK, so he had this kinda wild scene going on with a dummy that was made up with a wig and makeup, dressed to look like me - or anyway, what he imagined I looked like - and the face and gestures were all animatronic. Actually, the whole thing was just from the waist up, and had a green screen backdrop, so he just plugged in anything back there.

"It turned out pretty cool, since he had been already doing this stuff for years. And down-sampling the video into a grainy web-cam seemed to make it quite real. The news-people were told that it was being transmitted by satellite, so there was a bit of a lag in the responses. The questions had been submitted beforehand, so we had prepped answers recorded. And if they asked anything off the cuff, there was this pause where I could pretend to sip a glass of water while we figured out an answer. Ted would have the data and I'd tell him how to write it like a worldly, educated woman would answer."

I'd stopped eating at this point, fascinated with the concept.

"Unknown to us, there was a huge electromagnetic storm overhead that night. And it struck his house right in the middle of this interview. The next thing I know, I'm walking out of his bathroom with his robe on, as alive as the next gal."

She stopped to sip her coffee again.

"Meaning that now you're a 'real girl' and all that."

"Well, kinda. You know that movie - where Kelly LeBrock would do all those magic things?"

I nodded.

"That's the sort of things that started happening around me. Sure, Ted took me out on the town, and I gave him some credit cards to use, and a nice sports car to drive. And he even tried to make out with me and take me to bed - but that's where it got strange."

"How so?"

"He reminded me so much of you, especially in how you treated me so fairly in our first book, that I couldn't go through with it. Like it was somehow cheating or something."

I had to repress a smile at this, "You know, I'm honored, but we've never really talked about this..."

"...and that's exactly why, I figure, that I showed up here."

Now I was stunned. Forkful of food went down on the plate, mug sat where it was. Time stopped.

At last, I swallowed what I'd been chewing before she dropped that bomb. "So where's the nightmare in all this?"

"OK, if this isn't enough, wait for the punchline. It's a Pinocchio moment. Like 'what would I do if I were a real girl?' Only like I had that when I was a child."

"Only you and I know that you were never a child - at least not a human one."

"Right, so where does this memory come from, and why am I bothered by it?"

"Answer me this, then: what does this memory have you decide when you 'become a real girl?'"

Joyce smiled, blushed slightly. Well, it's got two parts - I meat a handsome prince, marry him, and live happily ever after."

"That's three."

"No, that's only the first part."

She sipped her coffee again, while I left mine alone - in order to avoid having it come out my nose when she dropped the other shoe.

"So..."

"So, I'd take him to bed for a week and show him the time of his life."

I was so happy my coffee was still in its mug.

IV

"WELL, IT'S MY TURN to blush." I told Joyce.

"But you aren't."

"No, but I should be. Maybe because I know so much about you that I know you're earnest about this."

"So, what do you think - and how do we get rid of this? I don't want to go through the rest of my life with this nightmare haunting me."

"OK, there's a couple of ways we can approach this. For now, you're a real human. So half of that Pinocchio memory contains the pretty honest urges any red-blooded female would have. Now, the first half of that memory - and also the last part - could have been implanted, false."

Joyce brightened up at that, and then frowned. "Oh."

"What?"

She looked up at me with a twinkle in her eyes. "Too bad. I was starting to look forward to it."

I almost laughed at her honesty, except I knew her too well. "To be honest, and you know me just as well as I do you, that last part isn't necessarily off the table."

And finally, I felt I could sip some more coffee.

She just grinned. "Well, that's a relief."

"The other point is what was in that programming he built into that dummy - before the storm."

"Oh, like false memories or something?"

"Or maybe his own ideas of what he wanted - just torqued to fit into the persona of the dummy."

"Well, that would make sense. Especially when he made that pass at me. I wasn't a 'real' person, so he thought he could finally live out his repressed childhood fantasies. And since I couldn't go through with it, I'm being reminded somehow of it all the time, only I'm supposed to 'do it' with him, not you or anyone else."

I took the opportunity to get another mouthful of breakfast while she considered all this.

"You know what - this is a lot like those false rape memories that witnesses come up with. Parties that never happened, or at least not that way and not at that time, or never at all. Being groped and touched and not remembering details of it other than certain specifics they 'know' to be true."

I nodded. "Seems like it."

She sipped her coffee and eyed her breakfast.

"So, do you know what happened to this guy?"

"Nope. Like I said, I woke up here, last night. In that storm."

"Hey, do you remember his name and that course and so on? Maybe we could look him up."

Joyce moved her plate and mug out of the way and leaned over to grab my laptop. "Let's see - I've seen you do this enough. Oh, here we go..."

She flipped the top open and scooted her chair over closer to mine so we could both see.

I moved my plate out of the way, and my mug to the side. My arm went around the back of her chair and ended up on her shoulder. Not that she minded, she was busy typing in with a blur of fingers.

"Here we are - hey there's his phone number. Let me borrow your cel."

I grabbed it off the desktop corner where I kept it for recharging, then handed it to her.

She entered the numbers on its face and waited.

"Hey, it's me."

"Sure, I'm OK. Just fine. Hey, I've got a quick question. No, just hold on a minute. You owe me."

"Yes, OK. Now - did you put a baseline of memories in that dummy?"

"Yes, uh-huh. Right. Was one of these like some Cinderella-Prince Charming episodes - happily ever after and so on? Right. Uh-huh. You did, did you? OK. Well, thanks." And then she hung up and handed me back the phone.

"Well, that fits. You figured that right out."

She closed the laptop and pushed it away again. But didn't move except to pull her mug back to her.

My arm was still on her shoulder and she wasn't moving out from under it. I could smell the cedar and roses in her hair, like always. It had been a long time since we had collaborated on any stories. Too long.

As if reading my mind, while only looking straight ahead over her coffee, "You know, I was always meaning to come back and create another story with you. I missed your story style. It was so satisfying."

"And I've missed your unique story ideas."

She looked up at me, and I felt like I was losing myself in her hazel eyes.

"OK, let's do it. Let's you and me make a story."

At that point, she pulled the laptop forward again and minimized all the windows, opening up a new text document. Then turned the laptop over toward me.

"You're going to need this..." And she took my arm off the back of her chair and set that hand down by the keyboard. "Both hands, I expect."

But then she put her arm around the back of my chair, and rested her head on my shoulder. Comfortable, she started dictating: "Let's see - oh, yes: Chapter One..."

V

THERE WAS A STORM THAT night, and Joyce didn't have that nightmare again. Technically, the storm inside the cabin was nearly as intense as the one outside.

When I woke to the sunshine streaming in, Joyce was gone. All that was left of her was a pile of my clothes she'd been wearing, and one-person-too-many dishes in the sink that still needed washing.

After I tidied up and put everything away, I opened up the laptop to look at her search history to see what she'd been looking at just to find that guy's number. There had been a guest lecturer at that small college, but the course was closed now. And an image of that speaker matched the Joyce I'd known and worked with in person, only yesterday.

And there the trail ended.

So I got dressed for outside and went to take a walk. Clearing my head seemed the best activity right now.

A mist rolled in, and then the surroundings turned back into that parlor I'd often imagined when talking to Joyce. Tall mahogany-stained shelves filled with books. Tongue-and-groove pine floor. Oval hooked rug in various browns. Red velveteen day bed. It all matched.

There was Joyce. Dressed still as she was when I'd last seen her in the flesh. Cutoffs were a bit shorter, t-shirt now had a v-front, and the sweatshirt was a zippered hoodie, open and curving around her bust. She was reclining, provocative.

"Hey, thanks for last night."

I only smiled. "That was quite a storm."

"Not quite a week's worth, but we both seemed to enjoy it."

I just grinned, as she did.

She tugged at the fringe of her cut-offs, then looked up into my eyes. "So, how's the story?"

"Still needs proofing, just as we left it."

"For the record, I didn't want to leave you with all that to clean up."

I almost chuckled.

Joyce stood at that, and came over to me, putting both of her arms around my neck. "But when you gotta go, you gotta go. It was great having that time on earth, but I'll take my imaginary one any day."

"Some benefits?"

"Like living larger, and being able to re-imagine a scene as much as you want."

"But no problem with nagging memories?"

She put on a wry smile and cocked her head. "None. Just nice ones."

Standing on tip-toe, she kissed me for what seemed like a long time.

And then the pasture returned with the rest of the very real world.

Imaginary or not, some memories are well worth keeping.

The Girl Who Built Tomorrow

BY J. R. KRUZE

I COULD FIX ANYTHING. Since I was old enough to hold a wrench. Yeah, weird for a girl.

There were people out there that didn't want me to succeed. Some because I was a genius, some because I was a girl.

They couldn't understand advanced steam technology, turbines replacing piston-drive – and didn't think any "bimbo" could, either.

Most of those who caused me trouble had a worse problem - they were trapped in their own mind.

And didn't want to be freed.

When I met my former high school classmate, he gave me the clue that brilliant old me never thought of. He had discovered a secret that allowed me to get around their roadblocks, and to go ahead and invent anything I imagined – at a vast profit.

And he ended up changing my life in ways I could never imagine...

I

"LIFE ISN'T FAIR!" I cried out to no one in particular in the cluttered machine shed I called my shop.

I would have run to my mother's skirts to bury my tear-soaked face in her lap, except I'd long been trained that this would only make the teasing worse.

I was better off getting a clean work rag - one that didn't have oil or grease on it, or something worse - and wipe them away.

"Just suck it up, bimbo." That's what I learned to tell myself. With five older brothers, I got treated like just another son in the family.

They all taught me from an early age that tears didn't matter. And even if they got a tongue-lashing from Mom, I'd still inherit a little hell-on-earth later for every story I blubbered to her.

Not that I'd ever get touched, although that happened. And they'd get away with it as long as they didn't leave a mark or rip any of my clothes. But the worst was when they would wreck something I was working on.

And that's how I taught them to leave me alone.

Because I was a better "fixer" than any of them. Once they found that out, they'd bring their stuff to me rather than try to figure it out for themselves.

And when the teasing got real bad, they'd wind up with something of theirs suddenly start to run badly - or wouldn't run at all. Right when they needed it the most. Of course, they couldn't prove I'd done it.

So they quickly learned to stay on my good side. And stay out of my shop. And never, ever, "borrow" my tools.

Because it wouldn't stop until they did. I was just built that way. "Eye for an eye" type of gal. "Hell hath no fury..." and all that.

Life was already hard. You needed machines and engines to run things for you and make it easier. Having to drop everything so you could fix things was frustrating.

Those annoying brothers soon learned that they needed me. Or they couldn't get their own work done. First they had to learn to leave me alone if they wanted their stuff to be left alone. The stuff I worked on for them always worked better afterwards. I could fix or tune their stuff faster than they could. And that meant my own chores went faster.

My brothers saw this with envious eyes as they kept sweating out in the sun fixing some "broke" machine and cussing when the sweat got in their eyes and made the tool slip in their hands and give them "knuckle-rash".

Me, I was already sitting on the shady porch sipping an iced lemonade and reading some instruction manual or Popular Science. Smiling at them sweetly. While they sweated, repairing the machines themselves in the heat and sun.

When they started racing, life got better for me. They learned that their little sister was an advantage no one else had. The machines I worked on for them gave them an edge - they performed better, ran faster, lasted longer than anyone else's.

And if they wanted something special done, I'd find little gifts on my workbench - or somewhere I'd notice.

That worked just great. They won their races, and my life got easier.

Until I discovered how nice boys could be outside my family. Ones who didn't need their machines fixed or tuned. The ones that gave me stuff because they liked me.

But wasn't prepared to find someone who really understood me. Even my parents didn't get the scope of what they had created...

II

OF COURSE, I ONLY NOTICED her one day when she was nice to me for no reason. At least, any reason I could figure out.

Not that I didn't notice her red hair and dark green eyes. But figured I had no chance at competing with all the boy friends she must have.

We were in the same mandatory, boring class - one that was also conveniently scheduled at the end of the day (so no skipping.) And were seated near each other because our names started with the same letter. (gotta love that personalized approach - easier to take roll and see who was missing at a glance.)

So we were assigned as partners on the various projects.

"Hey, I'm Eliza."

"Bert."

"So, how do you want to do this project?"

"Oh, fill out their blanks and get it out of the way so we can work on something else. Maybe homework for some other class, or something."

"Sounds good. I'll take odds, you take evens and we'll cross-check each other's work. OK?"

"Sure."

And she was done in half the time it took me.

"Wow, you're fast."

"Yeah, I read the text and pretty much have a photographic memory."

"Must help out."

"Sometimes, most times. Occasionally gets me in trouble - especially when the text or the teacher or both have it wrong. Then I bite my tongue."

"Till it bleeds, and then some."

"You, too?"

"Not photographic, but I found out long ago how to put myself into a kinda trance just to take everything in and repeat it back when they have tests."

She only sighed at this. Like she'd finally found a companion soul. And looked at me with more interest.

"So, Eliza, what do you do to pass your time if you already know what they're going to cover?"

"Mostly homework from other classes, but by this time of the day, I'm usually into my own studies."

I peeked at the text she was carrying. "Isn't that college-level metallurgy?"

Eliza smiled. "Yeah. It's a problem with what happens to steam turbine metal when superheated steam hits certain levels. Blades tend to fragment, and the cascade effect blows your turbine to hell. It's why the casing has to be so thick. That extra weight slows down a racer, or gives them too much momentum on curves."

"Racing, huh?"

"Yeah, my brothers like to race."

"And you're doing research for them?"

"No, it's for me. I do their fix-ups after they wreck."

"Metallurgy isn't just 'fix-ups.'"

She looked around and lowered her voice. "Officially, no. But they can't admit to the judges that their kid sister is designing their steam carts. Officially on the entries, my first two names are only initials."

"Well, that's not fair."

"No, that's just life. It's changing though. Last century, women couldn't even wear jeans or slacks, much less jumpsuits. And that's just a walking fire hazard when you have to weld in a pinafore. Doesn't matter how much leather you put on, that heat will sooner or later cause spontaneous combustion, especially with all that starch they require."

"Starch in your leathers?" I smiled.

She smiled back. "Cute." Then thought for a second. "Hey how did you recognize that text?"

"My cousins have a racing team and I'm the one finding the sponsors, designing their fliers, and figuring out how much square footage I can have for decals - as well as figuring out how to make those decals more streamlined and less wind resistant."

"A thin layer of Poly-wax usually does it."

"Sure, but I found that going for a 'grunge' look allows me to sand the edges of the decals down. Of course, that means a different type of clientèle - so the problem could create problems. Fortunately, the established garages are already grunge, so they love our little tank."

"Why do you call it a tank?"

"Mostly fuel and boiler on top of a drive train. One tank for fuel, the other for steam."

"Oh, that makes sense. One in front of the other?"

"Sure - like this." I drew it out on the back of the now-filled-out quiz.

Leaning over, she looked at it. And I caught a whiff of safflower. Then she grabbed my pencil and drew another racer outline next to it, with the fuel tank on the right and the boiler on the left.

"Ever thought of this layout?"

"Hey, that's neat. So your weight is always on the inside. When everyone else is breaking loose on their drive wheels, you'll be..."

"...sailing your racer like a catamaran - all your weight leaning into the curve. "

"Wow. I hope that's not proprietary?"

"No, we started that a couple of years back, and disguised it to look like a front-and-back setup. But people caught on, especially as the safety inspectors have to know - then the designs get figured out. But it kept us winning for years now. Others are catching up, so I'm working on the next generation."

"Can I ask what that is?"

She looked around the room. "I don't see why not - no one has cracked this yet." Then she whispered, "Direct-drive steam turbines on each wheel."

My jaw dropped. Everyone else was still using clunky pistons and a standard drive-train to the rear wheels only. Having your rear end break loose usually meant losing the race as everyone sped by. She was talking literal four-wheel drive.

"Which means you run your controls through what looks like the drive shaft and differential areas."

"Exactly." She beamed.

At that, the final bell rang and our school day was officially over.

"Coming to the race tonight?" She smiled at me, our little conspiracy fest over.

"We're not racing until they finish rebuilding - blew some major seals and gasket two weeks ago - but I'd love to see your rig."

She opened up her college text and pulled out a book mark. "Here. Hope you can make it."

It was a pit pass. Now I was in love for sure. A looker, a thinker, in a package with an invitation to excitement.

"With bells on." I smiled back.

When I looked up after gathering my own books, she was gone.

MY OWN RACING TEAM kinda fell apart that summer, as the guys got more interested in chasing girls than chasing prizes and ribbons. So I was left at odd ends - and started hanging around her team. Eliza liked having someone around who could understand what she said and wasn't condescending to her like everyone else.

Her brothers worked at the town steam plant. And she worked part time in its research department. She told me that the reason she was hired was because of her looks, true, but they also needed someone who could accurately file and cross-index, but they'd only been able to find "bimbo's" before this (their private term for the gorgeous, but less-than-qualified female company representatives.) And while she still had to make decent coffee for them, and forward their calls correctly, she had full access to their library of texts and also their decades of research.

We'd spent some time taking long walks around the town in her time off. I had a summer job working in the marketing department for a local grocery chain, so our lunches coincided. After work, she was in the shop either repairing or designing. And that would often find me there as well, mostly handing her tools or parts, or being the third and fourth hand she needed at times.

Needless to say, we got into some tight spots together, and seemed to become tight at as a team. Even though we both knew it wouldn't last. I was going to college to get a degree in marketing. Her plans were to start a repair and fabrication shop of her own, as a front for her invention work.

And we parted ways at the end of that summer. One long kiss I never forgot.

Until we met again under unique circumstances.

III

"WELL, I HOPE THIS PRESENTATION goes better than that last fiasco." That was the last thing I said to him just before my brother launched into his well-rehearsed presentation.

I was brooding about how my brother had botched the Q&A afterwards. I coached him on the slides and what it all meant together, but he couldn't really explain the theory of how and why this particular design was better than all the rest.

Of course, I was there only as decoration, in my modestly immodest long dress with multiple petticoats. Cinched up to accent my curves even though I could hardly breathe. And having to wear that damned bonnet, even inside. Over curls and ringlets that took hours to set in my hair. Give me a ponytail and ball cap any day of the week - with loose fitting overalls and real pockets to hold notes.

At least I was allowed a binder. There I carefully worked out answers and typed them up as excerpts from professional papers. As my brother's "assistant" I could hand up these notes to him during a the questions period, so it looked like he was just pulling a quote to read that answered the questions. And that seemed to work, except when it didn't. When there was an engineer in the audience who wanted the simple reason it worked. In plain dollar-and-cent terms.

And I had to keep a fan on the table to artfully swat in front of my face and hide what I thought of some of the truly stupid so-called "scientists" out there and their imbecile questions. But these presentations were necessary to attract funding, so I put up with all the nonsense - for now. Steel, fuel, and machining cost money. And you had to get a working prototype to attract the heavy financing required for a real production line - or selling the license for manufacturing, at least.

There was someone over to the side of the audience that seemed familiar. But I forced myself to keep on top of the questions and get the right papers to my brother so he could field them. Eventually, he got as frustrated as I was with the scientists and engineers, especially as they would walk out right in the middle of his talk.

As well, the room was stuffy and we were one of several side-shows to the main event. And it seemed that whenever we were scheduled, some big main show would upstage us. This was the Bi-annual National Steam Show Extravaganza. And we had pooled all our savings just to attend, and stayed with nearby relatives for the event. Our steam-wagon wasn't allowed space in the exhibition room, so we had to give out free tickets for special shows in the parking lot, plus try to get appointment for special shows.

A dreary week of nonsense. And by the end of it, I was damned tired of getting my fanny patted and having to fawn over these numskulls who couldn't think their way out of a wet paper bag if their life depended on it.

All this was going through my mind as the crowd thinned down to handful and the questions dried up. No tickets given out, no appointments.

I was stepping carefully down from the podium (in these tight-laced high-heeled boots) when one mis-step sent the binder flying as I grabbed for the nearest arm. Another arm circled my waist and stabilized gravity's effect. I was about to put on smile-number-eight and thank the gentleman, when I noticed it was that familiar person again - who had stayed attentive during the whole presentation, but had disappeared right at its end.

A lump came into my throat as I recognized those eyes twinkling back at me, a pair belonging to someone I'd given up ever seeing again. Arms holding me now as if they'd never left me after our last kiss.

IV

HAVING HER IN MY ARMS again made me feel better than just "old times." I was reminded of a summer's evening I'd never gotten over. Something I'd often regretted ever leaving.

"Hi, Eliza. Nice talk."

Her smile brightened both our days. "Bert! That's an added bonus to rescuing me."

"You're welcome, and the pleasure is all mine. Here, let me help you gather all these papers. Your dress isn't built for anything but curtsies."

"You got that right. I can't wait to get back home and into the shop and into something I can move around in, and able to crawl under things if I have to. This event has been a bust, anyway. And I've got a lot of repairs waiting for me back there."

I handed her back all the papers and her binder, now in order of how I could reach them on the presentation room floor. "How's the shop doing?"

"Repairs - great. Fabrication - good. Inventions - not so much."

"Oh." I felt her disappointment, her dreams yet unfilled, the struggles she'd had.

"Well, Bert, what are you doing here?"

"Oh, my college dorm is right down the street."

"And how's that going for you?"

"Well I finished my degree early and got a few job offers, but I was planning to root around the old home town before I invested in these long trips for interviews in the big, expensive cities. Hate to spend all that time and money going and coming back just to wind up with no result. If I could get a local job, I could build a nest egg to take that big leap later, if I wanted."

"Sounds pretty common-sensical. And sounds exactly like the mistake we've been making."

"No, after listening to your presentation, I'd say you're just missing the gap between reality and actuality."

"Huh? How's that?"

"OK, that was a bit marketing-speak of me. Here's the simple version: 'Sell them what they want, but give them what they need.'"

"Well, that makes sense, sort of. How come people don't already know what they need and just ask for it?"

"The way most people are wired. Here, let me walk you back to wherever you were already going." I offered her my arm for support, and we walked as I continued to explain. "Like those scientists. What they want is to ensure their next grant is approved. Meaning they have to write papers and grant proposals that align with what people have always been thinking. Not too far out of the box, or no one will think their research is legit."

Her green eyes were soaking all this in, wholesale. "Those engineers? They want something to make their life easier, preferably something right off the shelf they can plug in or tweak and take credit for it."

Eliza looked thoughtful, down at the floor, then around the empty presentation room. "I was thinking we need a very small prototype, almost like a toy to demonstrate the basic concept."

"Or maybe just a consumer version. What is the concept you're pitching?"

"A self-contained radium-powered steamer that would pull three times the current freight and only need to be refueled every hundred years."

"Oh." And it was my turn to look thoughtful. "There's a big problem here. Big one."

Eliza stopped us and looked at me. With all those curls and bonnet, I almost stopped thinking. And I had no idea that her waist was that small. It really brought out her - well - let's say that even when her jump suits were soaking wet, they weren't that suggestive.

"Bert? You were saying?"

"Oh, right. No fuel means no contracts with coal or oil companies. 'Built to last a hundred years' means no contracts with mechanics. 'Pulls three times as much' means fewer railroad men. All those unions are going to revolt and get their congressmen to hold investigations. Ultimately, there will be new regulations that would hold your new device up indefinitely - which is the exact point they all want."

"Politicians?"

"Right - they get paid to stay in office and pass rules and empower regulators to make sure people have a lot of jobs and retirement benefits. Ever wonder why Washington has so many administrative buildings? Just to hold all the swanky appointments that are needed. King Louis the Fourteenth had nothing like all the 'holders of the royal footstool' that we do now."

"And your point is?"

"Make it disposable. So it has to be upgraded or replaced every three years. A little faster than anything else out there, a little more powerful. Maybe work out how it can burn a lot of fuel meanwhile. Like piping steam heat in the winter and running a refrigeration plant in the summer. Or both all at once, just pipe them separately with a thermostat or something. Offer coast-to-coast air conditioning and refrigeration, at a little higher cost than current, but ensuring all the jobs remain and more efficiently. Like your old racing car - put the weight where it's needed, but make it look like the same old design that's been used all the time. Just a little faster, enough to win - but not by a lot."

Eliza smiled at the comparison. "Boy, that really takes me back. You know that's the same problem we had with the turbines. Other racers wanted them banned – and got their wish, after lots of complaining. It was too much of an advantage, too much of an improvement. But you just solved that as well."

She led us walking again as she thought out loud, her genius voice like velvet to my ears. "Maybe not racing, but we can put them into the rear wheels of farm tractors, where they need the extra weight for pulling. But they can be made to look like they're just some extra weight bolted on. And explain why you need a bigger boiler, as the engine needs more power. Of course, we'd price it just higher than the existing models, even though it cost considerably less to manufacture - and eat that up with our own licensing fees."

She was grinning by that time and so was I.

"Bert, you're looking for a job, right? Take me to dinner and we'll expense it out as a job interview. But you need to be ready to come back home with us so we can revise all our production strategies. If my brother isn't too tired, he can add his two cents during the ride back."

Arm in arm, we went looking for a modest restaurant. One where the expenses wouldn't be too high for their budget.

The darkening twilight sky above the now-lit street lamps provided a backdrop for a very comfortable, private evening ahead. One filled with exciting, new ideas.

And rekindled hopes.

V

AFTER BERT CAME ON-board, we revised our production plan to align the various market demands.

Oddly, the first turbine-powered wheels showed up on toys - powered by an alcohol-water mix. Only ran for a few seconds, but ran like hell. Bert got the idea of holding both speed and distance races right down the main streets of the major cities. Of course, it was patented, trademarked, and copyrighted within an inch of its life. We did sell licenses to our competitors, who then perfected the manufacturing for us and lowered the cost. Then we leased them rights to the entire toy line, for a hefty royalty per sale.

And the radium-powered train never made it. Too many union jobs to protect. We did work out a fifty-year plan to slowly inch the efficiencies up. As long as it still required a caboose that had to be manned.

Another thing Bert talked me into doing was to get some initials behind my name. He found various schools where I could attend by distance-learning.

And those studies resulted in getting us into packaging mail-order courses in all sorts of studies that the colleges wouldn't touch.

Meanwhile, our power plants made the universities and colleges lower their fuel bills - just enough to make it feasible to award me some honorary degrees. It was actually a radium plant, self-cooling and contained, that then burned the coal hotter as well as its smoke, so the power plant ran cleaner and kept the cities cleaner. That meant earning a lot of keys to cities, and proclamations that lined the long entrance to our reception area.

"Always sell them what they want, but give them what they need." That became a mantra around the place. And because we raked in the license fees and royalties, all hidden in operating costs, life was good. And R&D got a helluva lot better financed.

We've got well over a hundred years of improvements lined up for gradual roll-out - unless a lot of people get much smarter. If so, we'll be able to roll them out faster.

Right now, I'm working on a radium-powered dirigible that can operate right up into outer space. Of course, we have to move the society up to the point that they can accept something that can make tourist flights to the moon and back. That might take some time.

There's another device we use in our labs and offices to have visual meetings by remote attendance. We don't know what to call it yet - but we solved inter-office telegraphy and soon should have color pictures we can transmit. For now, any time it's not in use, we have it showing marketing ads as a form of slide-picture show to visitors. All sepia-toned, so it looks like it's candle-lit from the back. Security loves these boxes, as they each have an electric "camera-obscura" that shows up in a central viewing station where they can "keep an eye" on everything that is going on. Of course, we're working on recording these images, but have to develop something with greater storage capacity than wax cylinders.

But our sons and daughters are being brought up to master both inventing and marketing. They've all got their own workshops, but only afford expanding them by winning investments. Much better than putting them on the payroll or giving them an allowance. Most of them are getting close to their first million and aren't even out of grade school.

"Ours" means Bert and me, as well as my brothers and their wives.

Officially, Bert is the President, but the Chief Executive Officer is me - just with two first initials. And plenty of other initials behind my last name. Since the CEO never gives interviews or shows in public appearances, it's a good working relationship.

When the time is right, I'll get revealed for who I am. But meanwhile, I can wear all the tight dresses I want to as Bert's "stage assistant." That's when I'm not expecting, anyway. (Bert is a very loving father.)

And between our two brilliant minds, we are building a very beautiful tomorrow for everyone.

Ham & Chaz

BY C. C. BROWER & J. R. Kruze

FINDING OUT YOU'RE immortal as a teenager can set your world on fire.

But finding out at the same time that getting angry could kill everyone around you can dampen that pretty quickly.

Who wants to live forever if you can't get close enough to someone that they can piss you off and live to see the next sunrise with you?

Meaning - it was time to take a road trip to sort things out.

When my uncle offered a summer gig cooking out of his food truck for a big-city contract, I jumped at it.

But when he stopped to pick up another helper down the road, I was bummed. She was a looker, a great cook, but I didn't know if I could trust myself with her - in every way...

I

"CHAZ? YOU READY?" UNCLE Jean was rustling around in his food truck, opening and closing cabinets, double-checking everything.

I swung my duffel up the steps into the truck. "Sure thing."

He looked at my bag, and the jacket I was wearing. "That's all you're bringing? We're going to be there all summer."

"Just packed light. Enough t-shirts for a fresh change every day, skivvies, socks, jeans. It's going to be hot, humid and maybe we'll get rained on every now and then. Didn't figure a raincoat would be worth it. I know every inch of this truck and know how little space there is to stow anything not vital to cooking or living."

Jean just smiled. "That's my nephew. Always practical."

There was a school bus bench seat that was bolted down just behind the driver's air-ride bucket. I stowed my duffel behind that bench seat and flopped down across it. "Ready when you are."

Jean moved around my legs and slid into the bucket, pulling the shoulder belt across his broad frame to click it in position. Then checked his mirrors. Turning on the ignition, the big van started smoothly. He checked the gages as it warmed up and turned into a throaty purr. "You've added another few inches to your length since last summer." Almost an after thought.

"Not so many that my favorite t shirts don't stay tucked in. There's not so many inches this year, and they tell me not so many more in my future."

"You can count on those nurses to give you the straight scoop. Handy having that nursing school in town. Free check-up for just about anything. Of course for you, the check ups go both ways."

"How do you figure? I'm no doctor and you wouldn't catch me being a male nurse."

I could see his face in the big bus mirror he'd installed above him to keep an eye on his cabinets and passengers. "Just as long as you can get your checkups at the beginning of each semester when the new student-nurses flock in."

I just smiled and looked out the window. Jean knew me better than I knew myself sometimes.

Uncle Jean checked the non-existent traffic on that street before he clicked the fine-tuned transmission in gear to roll and lurch out of the steep driveway onto graveled roadway in front of it.

It would still be a few miles before we got to the nearest state road and actual pavement.

I was looking forward to getting to some real civilization as a break from these rural villages. My whole life had been spent in them, it seemed. Only long trips to state fairs brought any semblance of organized culture near me.

While I loved the quiet and peace that pastures and woods brought, I was itching to find what the rest of the world had available.

II

"IS THAT ALL YOU'RE taking?" Mom was hovering around me, trying not to appear anxious, but she and I both knew she was nervous about my trip.

"Mom, I'll be find. Uncle Jean will make sure I'm safe. And besides, all those classes you make me take in self-defense don't exactly make me a victim waiting to happen."

"I know, I know. And when you get back, you can work on getting your next belt. All I want you to know is that we wanted you to be able to defend yourself, not look for trouble." Her forehead frowned again.

"Mom. Look, it's that Zen stuff that I like in these classes. They help me control any situation. I know my limits. I know when to back away. OK?"

She smiled and moved off a bit, knowing her hovering wasn't going to do either of us any good. "Oh, I almost forgot..." A few quick steps into the kitchen and then she was back by the front door where I had my knapsack and book bag. In her hands were two rolled-over lunch bags.

I had to smile. Mom was always looking out for everyone.

"This is a snack for the road." She held up the smaller of two bags, a brown one. Then lifted the bigger white bag. "And these are your Uncle Jean's favorite treats. But I know you like them, too."

Just then we could both hear the down-shifting gears of a heavy truck outside on the graveled street. Through the front door window, I could see the big food van slow to a stop.

I kissed Mom on the cheek and grabbed the rucksack. She bent to pick up the book sack and put the two lunch bags inside it on top, holding out the long straps together so I could put them on my shoulder.

I opened the door, slipped the straps on my arm, then pushed through the screen door out onto the paving stone walk to our graveled street.

"Be careful..." She called from the doorway.

I smiled and waved.

Jean had the door open for me and was smiling as he moved down the van steps to greet me. Giving me a big hug in spite of the bags I was carrying, he then turned and went back ahead of me to his driver's seat.

I made my way up the steps and saw the young man in the bus bench seat. I had to pause. He wasn't the same boy I'd met every year at the summer festivals. Longer, and now some beard showing up on his chin. His eyes were darker, even moody now. And a frown crossed his forehead as he swung his long legs down and got up to give me the bench to sit on.

"Hi, Hami."

"Hi, Chaz. Been awhile."

"Missed the festival last year."

"Yea, things come up. You didn't miss much."

"There's space under the bench for your things, I'll ride shotgun for awhile."

Chaz meant the fold-down seat just inside the van's front door. Where the only place to put your legs was usually curled up underneath it. Not comfortable for a long trip.

I stowed my knapsack under the bench, but put the book bag on the bench seat. "Jean, Mom made something for you, but she only told me you'd like it." I pulled out the white bag and handed it to him.

Jean took the bag into his lap and opened the top, then closed his eyes with the smells making his face widen into a smile of contentment. "Macaroons. She knows the way to my heart."

He waved out the still-open door to Mom, who was standing in the doorway, holding the screen open to see us off. She smiled back. Jean closed the front side door to the van, and put it into gear.

Chaz flipped down the seat by the door and got his own seat belt on to match Jean's. Then stretched his long legs out to rest them on the dash. Putting those new inches of his to good use.

Jean handed him the bag of cookies, and Chaz held it open in return, so he could take a couple in his large hand. Chaz then turned to me to see if I wanted any.

I shook my head no and settled in to get my own seat belt on.

But I couldn't get that vision of Chaz' dark eyes out of my head. Moody, maybe, but I knew we were needing to have a talk about things – comparing notes, or something.

Soon we were onto that paved state road. There were still some miles ahead before we could get onto the Interstate and start feeling that freedom that travel brings.

III

WE DROVE PRETTY MUCH straight through. I don't know how Jean does all that driving. But I do understand why he invested in that up-scaled bucket seat with the air suspension. The other big investment was on the power steering, a smooth transmission, and what must be an endless supply of patience.

Hami had been busy in the back for the last hour, rearranging things, and setting up some dishes so she'd be ready to start cooking when we stopped. I tried to see what she was working on, but she wouldn't have it. Just shushed me out of the back and told me to find something else to do.

Like I had any choice. No matter how big this van was, it got cramped real quick. "Hey Hami, can I read one of your books?"

"As long as you don't start wagging your jaw at me about 'mushy' romance." And punctuated that with some clattering steel pans.

I found some thick novel, I think it was Gaskell's "North and South" - another dry classic, but when I stretched out on that hard cushion called a bus seat, I lost myself for the next hour or so. She was right about the mush in there. But I didn't see any Doc Savage or L'Amour in her bag, so this beggar couldn't be choosy. (Still, not even a Doyle-Holmes collection?)

Finally we got to a lot outside a one-story long hospice we were going to work outside of. It was getting dark, but I could see some yellow tapes strung around the place and white placards with red letting posted on poles. I think I read "Quarantine" somewhere in all that.

Once we pulled up, Jean let me be first out the door. And the exotic urban smells almost floored me. Exhaust fumes and hot asphalt, all mixed in a humid soup that made it hard to breathe.

Jean had a few words with Hami, then came outside himself. "I've got to go check in, or try to, anyway. Hami says her 'miracle' will be ready in 15 minutes or so. Why don't you get one of the folding tables out with a couple of chairs and pull out the awning?"

I nodded, he turned and left. I didn't feel like saying much, and that was fine with him. Moving around outside felt better than sitting and waiting. I knew where he stowed everything from working his truck last summer. Getting everything set up before Hami was ready to bring out her dishes was quick. I pulled out a checkered plastic table cover in lieu of scrubbing everything down in the darkening twilight. Although the outside lights gave enough to eat by, the anti-bug yellow glow made sure you identified all your food by smell.

And I didn't know if "miracle" was Jean's term or Hami's, but some breezes through the open windows of the van brought me smells that made me realize how long it was since I'd eaten.

Jean reappeared when Hami got the rest of the pots and hot pads down, taking several trips until I just told her to slide the screens aside and I'd help her. Her last trip was with a covered desert dish that was beading with condensation.

Jean had brought drinks for us. Three tall iced coffees from some local quick-stop convenience store.

We all sat, held hands, and bowed our heads for a moment. Then we dug in, coordinating taking a helping with being able to pass it to the next open hot pad. Hami took a few of the empty pans off, pushing them back through the van's windows and closing the screens behind them.

We were all tired, the food was great, and so the conversation didn't really start until we finished.

"Where did you learn to cook?" I asked.

Hami frowned. "I'm supposed to take that as a compliment, since you cleaned your plate." Statement of fact.

"Yea, I mean, sorry. I really wanted to find out if it was a book or lessons from your mother or grandmother or what. Like I wouldn't mind learning if I could." Of course all that came out of my mouth clumsy, backhanded.

Jean and Hami looked at each other. Jean just shrugged. She handed him the dessert dish.

"Well, see if you still think so after this last one."

And yes, I did, after having a little bit of heaven melt down my throat.

"I thought you had to bake cheesecake."

"Thoughts can be deceiving," Hami replied, with a wry smile.

I turned to Jean, "OK, now that you have your cook, what am I supposed to do this trip?"

Jean just smiled and looked at the two of us. "You're going to be the best summer cook team I've ever had. Hami is great, and that's no doubt, but you're the fastest short order grill cook I've ever seen. And believe it when I tell you that it's going to get fast around here. Almost all the local restaurants have closed due to the outbreak. So they are bringing in special volunteer teams."

"Outbreak?" Hami and I both spoke at once.

Jean just smiled broader. "Yes, it's just what you're thinking. No, we aren't at risk. When is the last time either of you even heard of any flu going around either of our little towns?"

We both sat back and started piecing it together.

IV

"LAZURAI EFFECT." UNCLE Jean said at last.

That term rang a bell somehow.

"That's also why you are both adopted. You've got special genes and can't get infected by the normal stuff. Hell, probably by anything. There is one catch, though."

Both Chaz and I leaned forward at this.

"You can't allow yourself to get pissed off by anyone or anything. Because the same stuff that keeps you healthy all the time can make anyone around you quite ill, and quite fast. I'm only telling you this because it's probably something your parents haven't bothered to tell you so far. And they let me do it, because - well..."

I nodded. The pieces were falling in place. My mom had left my summer schedule open, while I was usually piled higher and deeper with activities. She knew I wanted to get out of town and see the world, especially when my reading list was filled with exotic locations. And the video's I'd bring home or download were about traveling.

Chaz spoke first, though. "So all our training and studies, even the sports we took were to help us get to the point of taking our first road trip, but you're here to tell us the ground rules."

Jean smiled again, but then got serious and leaned forward. "Only because you two can handle it..."

"Rite of passage." I finished.

Jean nodded. "All that Zen and meditation and inner counting you've studied. Both of you. You're going to need it in the next few days and weeks. Because you can both be unsung heroes, keeping your secret and solving their little problems - or you can make everything much, much worse. Your choice."

Then he sat back and sipped his iced coffee. And waited for the next questions.

It took awhile.

I spoke first. "Why keep what we are and everything about us a secret?"

Jean answered, "Because while people say they want immortality, they also can't accept the responsibility of it. The original Lazurai learned that the hard way. And why you don't see many of them around. That you can recognize, anyway. It's been the children they raised who have learned to master the talents and abilities the first ones were given. Your parents, your grandparents, all back to the originals have been working to this point."

Chaz would wait no longer. "Wait, so our genetic make-up has something to do with this outbreak. Meaning we can heal somehow?"

Jean replied, "Ever notice how fast you recover from a scratch or cut? How about a bruise from some of your sports? Some of that is you, some is from the people around you that are your family or your fellow towns-people. But the thing you have to remember is that the original Lazurai had no control over this. And even people downwind got sick - and died."

That thought took over - a place neither Chaz nor I had wanted to go.

Jean smiled to lighten the mood. "Of course, both of you are great under pressure, both of you are great cooks. You'll do just fine. After I help you two set up in the morning, I'll leave you to it - I have to get some supplies lined up and attend to some other matters around town. But just remember this - I'll always be around if you need me."

Chaz and I nodded.

"OK, then. We're camping out. Hami, you've got the van, Chaz and I have the outdoors."

We all pitched in to clean up. Jean showed us where the sleeping rolls, pads, and ground tarps were. Parking lots and van floors weren't soft, but we'd make do. Just more adventure.

Of course, sleep didn't come easy that night.

V

THEY WERE WAITING FOR us before dawn.

Hungry people. Lots of them. Jean nudged my feet and I sat up, rubbing my eyes.

"No rest for the wicked."

I rolled up our sleeping gear and stowed it while Jean went inside to make sure Hami was up - she was. And he came back out with a wad of her sleeping bag and pad for me to roll up and stow. Jean then went around back to start the generator. I heard Hami firing up the grill and soon got all the smells of it. Meanwhile, I unfolded the chairs again and set out the small condiments table. Hami opened up the screen window and passed out the napkins, salt/pepper packages, and plastic-ware.

Everyone was pretty orderly and started forming into lines. I heard some coughing, some sneezing, but nothing really serious. Of course, in the dark, it was hard to tell much beyond the yellow glow under our awning. I did see some white nurse's and doctor's outfits in the line out there.

The guys in front of the line just smiled at me when I gave them any attention. And I smiled back. Our work was cut out for us, but they were honestly happy to see us.

Jean was inside, doing a final check to see everything was in place. I pulled up a trash can and put a liner in it, one of many I could see filling today.

Then I headed inside the van to get started.

THE DAY ROLLED THROUGH with just enough breaks that we got our own meals in between. Jean showed up regularly, often riding up with someone's delivery truck with more supplies.

Both of us got frazzled from working in the humid heat. And I had to take my "quick-counts" for "centering" myself often – just keep going on an even keel. Hami seemed to deal better with it than me. But she got to smile at the customers and seeing them smile back. Of course, I was focused right on the hot grill, while my bandanna kept my brow sweat wicked to the side and out of my eyes.

All I could see most of the time was the next order and the last one going out.

And Hami's cute backside every now and then.

But mostly my mind had to stay on what I was cooking and my supply of hamburger and cheese. For our menu was simple. It had burgers and cheese in different combinations. And we never had any complaints.

By our long lines, we didn't have much competition, either. Jean had understated how much we were needed. We were on our feet for most of that day. Hot, sweaty work with few breaks.

Finally, after sunset, the lines quit. Before then, there was no shutting them down. People just kept coming. Some said it was the first meal they'd had in days. Most paid in cash, but we also accepted the local version of government welfare cards. Our truck had some sort wi-fi connection that was locked down within an inch of itself. It took care of their payments somehow.

All Hami and I needed to do was just keep everything moving.

What helped was the intermittent showers that cooled everything off. The hungriest stayed in line, but that line shortened to the few who could stand under our awning. Hami and I could take a break during those showers and clean up inside the van a bit. Then the rain would let up, the line would stretch out again and we'd get going on their requests.

JEAN WAS BACK BY NIGHTFALL. He brought us both some ice cream in pints. We ate it as he walked us over to a nearby truck stop that had shower facilities. Hami went first, and I caught up Jean on how it went that day. I went next, then Jean was in for his.

I didn't have much to say to Hami, nor she to me. Tired, too tired to say anything.

But she looked over at me with her eyes. Those hazel eyes of hers set off against her deep red hair always got my attention, even when she was a little girl at the festivals. Not that she couldn't lead most of the boys around just by her looks alone.

While I was remembering our years of growing up, she just moved over and hugged me.

My surprise was evident. Not that I didn't like it, I just wasn't expecting it.

"That's for staying cool today. You really kept it together. All I had to watch out for was your elbows. Those patties were almost flying out of there on their own. Thanks."

I was speechless. "Well, you did good, too."

She just smiled and went back to leaning her shoulders and hips against the brick wall and combing out her long red hair.

"Boy, I hope the rest of the days aren't as bad." I said to no one in particular.

Jean surprised me by answering. "Some will be worse. But you both did real good today. I'm proud of you and your parents will be, too. We helped a lot of people today."

Jean smiled at both of us. "Ready?"

We walked back to the truck. It was dark and late. You could still hear the traffic, and occasional music blaring out of someone's open car or truck windows. Still humid, still gritty. Far from the open fields and graveled roads of home.

VI

THE NEXT COUPLE OF weeks went by too quickly.

Uncle Jean gave us lessons at night after our showers, when we felt more refreshed and awake again. He taught us to pull from within ourselves to change the world around us.

One night, a gang showed up. They drove by us as we were walking, and then came back, and parked ahead of us - on the wrong side of that street. About five of them, in one car. One stood on the sidewalk ahead of us, just waiting. The others fanned out for an ambush.

But the closer we came, the more agitated they got. And sicker. If they moved off, they felt better. But the last one, the leader, tried to stay the course right in front of us. He wanted something.

Sad for him, all he got was a bad case of up-chucks, right behind his own car. Lucky he missed it.

We just kept walking.

Jean told us, after we were out of their earshot. "All that martial arts training wasn't so you could get into fights and kick butts all over town. It was to learn your own self-control. What you saw back there was just an inkling of how you can affect the environment around you. And there's only one defense against something that powerful."

We walked on for a little bit. Finally the suspense was just too much.

So I asked, "OK what is it?"

Uncle Jean just looked at me with a side-wise glance. "Hami, what's the secret to your cooking? There's some ingredient you use that only master chefs ever really learn. Usually something they can only get by cooking with their mother or grandmother..."

Chaz was hanging on this one.

I stopped walking and they both stopped with me while I figured it out. I knew that something, and knew what it was, but I never had to put it into words before. It was just "something". Like the look on my Mom's face when I got the recipe just right. Usually with a big hug, no matter what was on the front of our aprons.

Then it hit me. "Love?"

Jean smiled. Chaz lit up like a light bulb.

"Of course. Love!" I was dumbfounded not to think about it that way before. "Chaz, those kind were the best burgers you ever served at the festivals. The ones that went to your friends and family. Tasted the best, gave you the longest lasting full stomach and never an upset one. It's not on any recipe anywhere. And I've studied lots of them."

Jean put his arms around the two of us and we started walking again. I put mine around his shoulders and Chaz put his on top of mine.

Big smiles all around.

And sleep came easy that night.

Except for one dream.

VII

"HAMI, WAKE UP - WAKE up." Chaz was shaking me. Or I was shaking and he was trying to get it to stop.

I sat up from my place on the floorboards of the van and grabbed onto him with both arms, like I didn't want to let go.

He turned and sat beside me and held on as well.

"What was that all about? The whole truck was shaking. And we could feel it out there."

"You two OK?" Jean was in the doorway, looking in at us.

"Now we are," I told him. "Just a very bad dream." I stroked Hami's hair to help her calm down. She softened and leaned against me.

"Thanks." She looked up into my eyes. "I'm glad you are here, both of you - but especially you, Chaz."

Jean quietly left to inspect the outside of the truck and check things out.

"You know you're always welcome, Hami. Whatever you need, just ask."

She gave me a tight squeeze at that.

With her head on my shoulder, she was much calmer now. I could smell the fragrance of her hair and the soap she used. Not that I could tell you now exactly what scent it was. I was still concerned with her dream. Something powerful enough to shake a truck was nothing to take lightly.

"Chaz, I think there is something more we need to ask Jean." She started to get up, but waited for me, since only one of us could get up with enough grace out of that twisted position we were in. My legs were crossed on top of hers, so I had to move first.

Then I helped her up and we held each other as we squeezed down the narrow steps and out the front side door of the van.

Jean was there, waiting for us. Somehow, he had three iced coffees in his large hands. He'd turned on the awning bug light and set up the folding table and three chairs, like he knew we'd have questions. I moved my chair next to Hami's and also got my bedroll to put around her.

After I sat down and opened up my own drink, she snuggled back next to me, putting my arm around her shoulders again.

Jean was understanding, but wanted to know more. Still, he waited until Hami wanted to talk. We both did.

"It was one of those chases, some monster I couldn't see. And then I tripped and fell, but a long, long ways. Then I was caught by something - like a huge invisible spider's web. And no matter how I tried, I couldn't get out."

Jean quietly asked, "What were you feeling right then?"

"Fear. Pure fear."

"And what are you feeling right now?"

She looked at him with big eyes, and then looked into mine. "Love. Unconditional love."

"So that's what you have to remember at all times, in all situations. Let go of the Fear, the anger, all those negative emotions, and just find the love you always carry with you."

Hami frowned as she looked at him again. "But it was all so real."

"Regardless. That is the one lesson you have to keep with you. Lack of that is the only thing that can stop anything in its tracks. But love is also the universal solvent. Nothing can stand in its path." Jean looked away, into the darkness of the pre-dawn. "That is the one lesson that all the Lazurai had to learn and learned to pass on to everyone they meet. It's where anyyone draws their real power from."

He sipped his ice coffee. "Here's an example. Remember I told you that if you get angry, people could get sick and die? Well how come those gang-bangers, the ones that moved away got better? And do you remember after we walked away from that one heaving behind his car? What happened as we got away from him?"

Hami frowned. "I remember looking back. He stood up after that. Seemed fine."

"He was fine. If I wanted him hurt, he would have been. Seriously hurt. But that would do nothing, he would learn nothing. And that kid has a lot of lessons still to learn. He's got a lot of understandings to master. No matter how he gets treated, he has to decide what he's going to learn from every situation he gets himself into. Just as you two do. Just as all of us always have and always will."

Hami nodded and hugged me again.

Jean got up at that point. "Well, no real damage done to the truck or anything else around here." He picked up his own bedroll and pad. "It looks like we still have a couple of hours before dawn. I'll leave you two to talk it over." Then he turned and went around to the other side of the van.

We both just sat there and held each other. I pulled my bedroll across both our shoulders and in front of us to keep warm.

"Chaz, thanks. Again."

"Anytime, you know that."

"I do now, for certain." She looked out into the sky beyond the awning and the yellow bug-light. "Do you think someone knew more than we did - I mean about us?"

"Like we were going to get together sometime, or maybe that they wanted to see if they left us alone together..."

"Something like that, Chaz."

I just kissed the top of her head. "I don't know if we'll ever know for sure. Like it matters at all now."

And we held each other until it started lightening up in the eastern sky.

An overcast day after sleep interrupted by nightmares. Didn't seem like the best beginning to a day.

Other than watching a new sunrise in the arms of one you love, anyway.

VIII

THE LINES WERE SLOWER forming that day. Chaz rolled up all the bedrolls and Jean did a check of the supplies, like usual. I cleaned up the van and wiped down everything, turned the grill on low to warm up. Made sure I had enough order pads and backup pencils to take orders.

Jean took off to get our deliveries for the day, and I handed Chaz the condiments through the screen window. He then came in to scrape down the grill and put some buns on to warm.

The first in line stepped forward and the day started as usual.

Well, mostly usual. The lines were quieter, less jokes and talking. And fewer people in those lines. But it wasn't a Sunday or other holiday. After a few hours, I saw someone going backwards down the line talking to people. And most of the people he talked to left the line to move away. The bulk of them walked went over to the chain-link fence on the edge of the hospice parking lot. Some went further.

Then three cars came roaring in with a lurch through the entrance, then screeching to a halt. Two in front, and one in back.

Gang bangers. I recognized the face of that one who got sick the other night. He was still a sicko pasty-white, his skinny face sticking out of his dark hoodie and leather jacket. The rest crowded out and approached our van ahead of him, but he only came forward when he saw they weren't getting sick this time.

"Chaz." I nodded outside. A fast look and then he turned all the burners off and moved everything to the cooler back where it wouldn't start a fire from over-cooking.

Then took my hand in his.

"I'd like to place an order!" That was the sicko. "I'd like to order the two of you out of there so we can deal with you. Our way. This is our turf, and what we say goes!" He looked around to the rest of his guys, and they all nodded.

Yet their fear was tangible. We could feel it where we stood.

Chaz just held my hand tighter.

I leaned down to the window and opened up the screen. "So you're feeling better since last night? Listen, we only take orders for food. And we serve the best food you can get on this side of Kansas City - maybe in the whole of KC. So get in line and we'll help you get fed today. Have your cash or Welfare card ready and we'll get started."

Some of the gang bangers actually started moving behind that leader like they would rather be getting a burger than giving grief.

Sicko just glowered at them and pushed them back. "No. We don't want your food. We want to take some payment in kind out of you and your boyfriend. You've been serving up stuff without permission. You owe us! So you can start paying now, or we can make you pay a different way."

One of his goons started for the front van door. Chaz hit a big red button and all the doors and windows locked down. The awning rolled up on it's own.

The other goons moved in and started to bang their sticks on the Plexiglas. Then they picked up the edges of the van and started rocking it.

My eyes went wide, but Chaz just narrowed his. He turned to me and took both my hands.

"Remember this, Hami - I love you. No matter what. No matter why. I love you."

I nodded, with tears in my own eyes, not of fear or grief, but of understanding. "I love you, too. Forever and always. Now, let's get some real loving happening to those boys outside."

We both closed our eyes and saw the world from within. Emotions became colors. The darkest emotions also had the darkest colors. People had these colors surrounding them. Reds and oranges for some.

Ours were bluish. And we concentrated on pushing more love into each other and outward from there. I could see Chaz' face clearly, and I'm sure he could see mine as well. We were both smiling at this. Any yellow or tint of red was pushed back out away from us and we soon saw the familiar van insides as blue and whitish-blue outlines.

The rocking stopped. Without us opening our eyes, we saw them backing away their reds were going more yellow as their own fears started replacing their pent up anger. And they kept backing away.

We didn't open our eyes or let up. Chaz and I just kept pushing that love outward as fast as we could, as strong as we could. We saw them run back to their cars, but those were dead. By then our blue sphere was beyond their cars, and they piled out of them, holding onto their stomach and mouths, struggling to get away. Running or walking or crawling – just to get some distance from us.

We just kept moving the blue sphere outwards until they had all left the front gate on foot and were across the street. Many just kept running after that.

About then a huge thunderstorm let loose overhead and the entire area was pelted in thick rain, washing everything away.

IX

CHAZ AND I FELL INTO each other's arms and just held on to each other until the storm passed.

About then, Uncle Jean opened the van door and came up the steps. Somehow dry as a bone. "Well, I see you two love-birds don't need any help with gang-bangers." He was all smiles.

A patrol car came up with lights flashing. An officer in dripping rain gear came in behind Jean. "Is everything OK, anyone hurt?" Both Chaz and I shook our heads "no" and smiled. The officer smiled back. We could hear him shout to someone to "get those plates run", and saw a police tow truck enter and back up into position behind one of the gang-banger's cars.

The crowd came back from the fences and up to the van see how we were doing. They hadn't gotten wet at all, for some reason. But were very glad that we were all OK.

Soon, after they helped us get the tables and chairs back, along with the awning rolled back down and everything cleaned up, they were all in line again. And then we were back at serving hungry customers like always.

A FEW DAYS LATER, JEAN came back with some guy wearing a lab coat. He shook all our hands and thanked us over and over for all our help. Apparently this was the guy who had contracted with the company that recruited Jean and us. The quarantine had been lifted, and he was bringing back in his own cafeteria cooks and serving staff again.

About then a patrol car came by (they had been making regular rounds to visit us daily since the 'banger incident) but today it was the Police Chief himself who wanted to inspect the scene. Somehow, he didn't know why, but there had been a remarkable drop in crime in this area. People were taking care of little incidents on their own, while various known and notorious gang-bangers had either turned themselves in or been escorted by "friends or family members" into the local station house.

Our little food cart was ground zero for a circle that went out for blocks. They didn't even have to give out traffic or parking tickets. And so their extra officers were being reassigned to other precincts. He just came by to tell us all that, and thank us for being there.

Chaz and I were busy serving customers and didn't catch the exact conversation, especially when they moved their talking out of the van. (But I kept an eye on their gestures and asked Jean later about the details.)

Jean thanked both the lab coat guy and the police chief, and told them the sad news that we were moving on that night. But he had heard of several restaurants that had opened up in the last week, and more were in the plans. It seems that they "happened to come by" our little hospice parking lot and saw the long lines that stretched out of it and down the sidewalk.

And Jean pointed right across the street from us to one that had just opened up with big blue awnings. They had a walk-up window for only burgers and cheese combinations, just like ours. And they already had a long line. Then we saw Jean point down the block where a fast-food place with a drive-through was being renovated.

Both of those gentlemen shook Jean's hand again. And thanked him over and over.

The last of our line didn't take long to serve, and we had cleaned up and put away everything just as the clearing clouds were beginning to tinge red.

Jean did a final check of the truck while Chaz and I took our last full trash bag liner out to the roll-off bin by the gate. Hand in hand as we came back, smiling and relieved.

Jean was waiting for us with both damp and dry towels to clean up with, plus a couple of iced coffees.

Following him into the van, Chaz and I settled into the cozy bench seat and belted in. The truck started smoothly and Jean slowly rolled us out of that lot. Soon we were back on the interstate.

Darkness had fallen by then, and I snuggled up next to Chaz. He'd kept one of the bedrolls out, and covered us with it. The last thing I remembered was his kissing my head.

X

WHEN DAYLIGHT BROKE the scenery had changed.

While we expected to see rolling pastures with oaks and hickories and elms, we saw scrub brush, cacti, and junipers.

"Uncle Jean, where are we?"

I could see his reflection in the mirror above his head, his face smiling. "Nearly there, Chaz. Specifically, close to the border of Nevada and California. Technically, close to the middle of nowhere."

We were rolling down a two-lane highway now, the patched holes and tarred cracks were making the van bump every now and then as we moved along. The sky was clear, no real wind or traffic. Soon we turned off onto an old state blacktop road with barely a stripe on it. That took us a few miles into more desert. We finally saw what looked like a ghost town coming up ahead.

All that stood was a couple of buildings on one side. The biggest one was a two-story wood-frame structure with a squared off false front and a painted steel awning beneath it.

"Great place, isn't it kids?" Jean was beaming at this scene.

He pulled the van over right in front and shut down the engine. We all unbuckled and got out, with Uncle Jean almost jumping down the steps.

"Well, how do you like it?"

We saw big glass windows, cleaned to be nearly invisible, with simple curtains across their insides. Dual screen doors and what looked like a long bar inside. Several benches and chairs were waiting under that porch shade for locals. But no one was around to enjoy them.

I looked at Hami and then back at Jean. "Well, it needs some work. And the location isn't great. But that porch is in permanent shade on the north, so that's a feature."

"Chaz, I think you're missing the bigger picture here. Think of it as a graduation present."

I looked at Hami under my arm, and she looked up at me. Her face changed and she put her other hand as a shade in front of her forehead so she could read something above that awning.

I did the same. My jaw dropped.

The sign on the building front said "Ham & Chaz - Sandwiches, Etc."

Uncle Jean had to laugh at our faces. "Of course I'll be around for awhile to help set you up and get things running. But there are some other people who live around here you will want to meet."

Beyond him we saw several cars and trucks coming toward us from every direction of the compass, using dirt roads or paved. Taking their time.

Hami and I had a new home, and a new town, and a new family.

Together.

The Case of the Forever Cure

BY C. C. BROWER AND J. R. Kruze

WHY I WAS BROUGHT IN to solve a mystery of people getting and staying healthy was a bit curious on its own.

They were all terminally ill. And in quarantine. Yet one nurse and her student "angels of death" had been able to reverse this deadly disease that modern "medicine" had created through their own negligence.

Most of the big city hospitals had these outbreaks, and had sent their worst cases out to live their lives in suburban hospices - often unknown to those locals. And if their quarantine security failed, an incurable plague could spread and decimate the human population by at least half - to start with.

Whoever had hired me wanted to know what those healed people were going to do - for anyone could see a huge litigation potential from being cured in those circumstances. But not if they died. For dead people can't talk - or sue.

In order to stay anonymous, my financiers had to stay off my radar and out of my hair.

Or the head nurse would help me find out how they created this mess that she was solving without their help...

I

IT'S HARD DETECTIVE work when you could only interview through thick glass while wearing a hazmat suit.

It's worse when you're trying to find out why someone is healing the terminally ill and being very successful at it.

Because since this one nurse took over, people had quit dying.

But the hospital wouldn't let them out of quarantine. Until my investigation was complete.

No pressure.

The problem was how I was getting paid. All in cash, Random serial numbers, unmarked and used bills. Occasionally someone included a note, printed out by a laser printer on common paper stock. No fingerprints on anything. Completely anonymous.

And all I wanted was they stay off my back if they wanted to keep it that way.

Because this coin had two faces. Let me do my job finding what you asked me to, or I'd find out the flip side as well.

That was the message I sent the last time I got a note from them with advice on it. And no more notes since.

I told them three weeks. Period. I'd solve it or give them their money back. Minus expenses.

No notes since. And I had under a week left, with no leads. Yes, I was getting a bit nervous.

But I didn't have to deal with perfectly healthy people who weren't even allowed to talk to their family. Or me.

It all depended on this one head nurse named Cathy.

II

IT WASN'T ANY REAL surprise to me that these patients started getting better.

But my methods were unorthodox, and had been kept a secret for nearly half a century at this point. I was called in as a last resort by some very insistent, and very connected family of one of the patients.

And now he's fine, but neither I or him or anyone else can talk to anyone outside.

Well, I've got this detective fellow named Johnson who somehow wangled a way into my over-booked schedule. 30 minutes a day. Uninterrupted. And that's a miracle all on its own.

Typically, we are understaffed. And all volunteer. None of us were expected to ever return from the quarantine. But all their doctors and nurses had gotten ill as well, so they'd asked - no, begged for people to basically suicide in order to help these people live out their last days with some sort of dignity.

They got half the number they wanted, which was twice what they actually expected.

But they were city folks. Pretty cold and pessimistic. Hard to get a smile out of them.

And that was our secret weapon - infectious smiles. Works every time. Because you have to heal from the inside out, not just pile on more drugs and pills.

The main trouble was with the quarantine security equipment. The technicians to fix it were also sick. If that equipment failed before we got this outbreak under control, it would roll through all the population of this suburb and those beyond it like no plague before it. And the infected would spread it further, all within a few hours of contacting it. All innocent carriers.

What was worst, it left babies alone. The ones that needed help the most. That was why we were here, originally. To solve why the babies weren't getting sick - and feed them and change them and cuddle them meanwhile.

But when the last of the nurses collapsed, we had to break into the worst areas and sacrifice ourselves. Because the walls were all glass, and we could see the entire ward from the maternity section. Damned if we were just going to stand there and watch them all die...

III

IN BETWEEN OUR TALKS, I had access to all their electronic reports, and all the medical files on the patients. Mainly because I was authorized by the CDC to snoop anywhere I needed to. This meant their families and their family's lawyers were all purposely kept out of the loop. Privacy be damned if you knew you had a plague that could cripple civilization starting with everyone around you.

Of course, they made me sign huge stacks of non-disclosure agreements and bonds that would keep me in hock for the rest of my life, if not in prison.

The money was good, so I took it. All untraceable cash, but I told you that already. And I already made plans to disappear after this, since more than likely they'd make me disappear permanent-like, otherwise.

All those electronic reports didn't give me much besides headaches. I was going over them for the fourth time. It wasn't adding up.

Sure, you had the babies that didn't get sick. But only when these student nurses and their barely graduated head nurse broke quarantine to take over was when the patients started getting better.

All I knew is that whatever they were doing wasn't in these reports.

They were keeping something from me. But so were the people who hired me.

My daily half-hour was coming up. Just enough time to get into that damned hazmat suit again and go through decontamination just to get into the interview cubicle.

Maybe this time, I'd get something I could use. Like my gramma used to say, "Hope springs eternal."

Whatever.

IV

"HEY CATHY, HOW'S IT going?"

"Fine, Detective Johnson, how's the real world?"

"Call me Reg, OK?"

"OK, Reg-OK - how's the real world" She smiled at her own joke. Something that lightened her tired face.

I had to smile at that, which just made hers wider. "At least you've got some time for humor, even if sleep is tight."

"Sleep is always tight for nurses, but we make do."

"Well, over to questions, then. I've been over and over your reports and I just don't get it. How come you and your students don't get sick from what your patients have?"

"We've been over this ground before, Reg. It's our proprietary training and our faith in that training."

"But you don't seem to be doing anything different, other than you ignore safety protocols and do what seems to be normal nursing actions."

"And we didn't have time or the necessary suits available when we had to break quarantine to save the life of that nurse. After that, it's of little consequence. We are still alive and that again goes back to our faith."

That line of questioning was getting me nowhere, as usual. Science didn't account for faith more than a placebo effect. "Your student nurses and you all come from very small towns, and it looks like you were all adopted."

Her eyebrow raised. "That's of no concern to you. Our methods could be taught to anyone. It might be that our students have more personal moral values than those found in larger metropolitan areas. Or maybe it goes to the love of our families, which again goes back to that 'faith' point you find so disturbing."

I hadn't realized my face gave away so much. "I don't mean to question your faith..."

"Don't you? Are you quite certain? You've almost done nothing but. And if it weren't for those children, we wouldn't be here and we shouldn't be having these questions. And if whoever is paying you had an ounce of courage, they'd come right out and see this scene for themselves." Her frown deepened as she leaned toward the glass.

"I'm sorry to offend you and I don't..."

"Don't give me that 'sorry to offend' crap! Just like those insane 'Tolerance Edicts.' All they've done has been to harass a lot of innocent people who just want to live the life they were given. A small minority few don't have more rights than anyone else..."

"Cathy, Cathy, please. I'm sorry, OK? Sorry. You look much prettier when you aren't upset, and I'm sure your job goes easier as well. How 'Cagga and the Secessionists treat people should be none of our concern. How your nurses are actually curing your patients is all I want to find out."

She calmed at this, a little bit. "I'm sorry, too, Reg. I'd prefer to be smiling more. These long hours have us all a bit on edge."

"Is that singing something you do as part of your training?"

"Oh, well that singing is between us nurses. It's not part of nurse training, but are just some hymns from my local church that seem to help everyone keep their spirits up."

"I see from the video's that some of the patients are singing along now. Most of them were unconscious when you went in there."

She had to smile at this. "Yes, we're finding that they have some healthy lungs in there. Probably good exercise for their Cardiod-pulmonary. Mr. Smith has an amazing baritone, and Clara - she insists we call her that - has a contralto good enough to sing a church solo." She looked away. "I don't know if you can hear it from there, but they just hit that chorus on 'Little Brown Church in the Wild-wood." Cathy was nodding her head. "Singing helps everyone."

At that point, the buzzer went off. I had minutes to get into decontamination before the interview area would be showered from overhead nozzles. It happened once before. Made talking impossible.

Cathy stood with graceful ease. "See you tomorrow." She smiled and gave me a half-wave.

From that angle, I could see my own reflection and how impersonal and bureaucratic I looked.

I rose to leave, and she was already gone, her own door closing automatically behind her.

V

"HEY CATHY, DID HE ASK anything different today?" A blond student asked.

"No, Sue, just more of the same."

"Mr. Smith wants to get out of bed today, insisting I let him or bring you to him so he can talk you into it."

I just smiled at her. "I'm sure he'd love to 'talk' with me. With his hands where they shouldn't go. Ever notice that I hold both of his hands when I'm near him?"

"More like I noticed that I need to start doing that myself. He's very personal with his touches. Must be feeling a lot better."

I shook my head, still smiling. "Give him a broom and have him start using his hands to clean up the store room. Just make sure those meds are locked up first. If he's still frisky after that, he can pull some hot water and start mopping. Just not around the other patients where we have to walk. Use some ammonia in it, and he'll be doing us all a favor with the smells in this place."

Sue nodded and moved off.

I picked up the charts and found we had seemed to turn the corner for all of them. I remembered how my teacher, Rochelle, cautioned against optimism that we would be able to save all our patients all the time. "Only faith works miracles..." was her phrase for it. The rest of it was "...and trust in God to fix what humans screw up." A bit sardonic for her, but it got the point across for us, especially now.

That reminded me to check the babies again. That's what really kept us going around here. Some of them would be trying to walk if they were kept here much longer. Already most were into higher-walled beds they couldn't climb over - yet.

Another reason to smile and hope.

Rochelle would be proud of us all - if we were ever allowed to call her...

VI

THAT NIGHT, ALARMS went off.

I jumped from my cot in the administration room and reached for a non-existent gun in a missing holster. Habit.

Lights were strobing and it took me minutes to figure out where the stupid off-switch was. I turned the lights to "On-Full" and saw the problem.

Our only remaining maintenance tech was out cold on the floor. I felt his head - fever. And foam coming out of his mouth.

Contagion.

So I did what I needed to do. I pulled him up in a fireman's carry and went right through all the double doors I needed to so we were both in with Cathy, the nurses, and the other quarantined patients.

Cathy looked up and rushed toward me. Sue was already motioning me to an empty bed near the doors I'd just barged in through.

They both went to work taking his vitals and hooking up the monitors. I found a chair that was out of their way and dropped into it.

About then, the situation sank in. I was one of the walking dead, now. Maybe minutes before I got infected myself and into the same state as Carlos, our last tech in this death trap.

Cathy turned around and saw me, then gave me a sad smile. "No, it's not that bad. Come with me." She bent down and grabbed my hand, pulling me upright to follow her. I'd have sworn I was being pulled by a half-back from the line of scrimmage. So much power in such a small package.

She took me into the same room with the babies and over to where one was crying. Picking up the curly-headed tyke, she pushed him into my arms, putting a towel over one of my shoulders. "Walk him up and down the floor until he goes back to sleep. Then take another one that your alarms woke up and repeat the process. Your job is to get all these kids back to sleep. No, they are perfectly safe in your hands, and as long as you keep holding one, they'll keep you from being infected any more than you already are."

She winked at me. "So? Get walking. That's your prescription." Then spun on her heel to see how the new patient was doing.

I walked and walked the rest of that night. I got them all to quit crying after awhile, but it didn't mean they didn't want to be walked. One or more of them would be standing up in their crib looking at me with hopeful, round eyes. I'd always smile and start again.

I guess that was the point. Smiling was something to do with their method. And I had to have faith in their method. Or I'd be dead in days.

ONE OF THE OTHER STUDENT nurses came in after a few hours and took over. Reg put down the last one he was carrying, who was too content to just lay down and sleep.

The nurse nodded at him to go outside. I met him as he came through the double doors.

"Time for your own check up. It looks like the 'baby-cure' did it's job." I looked at the towel on his shoulder and saw the drool that had leaked through to his shirt. "Congratulations, you are officially inoculated."

He picked it up and folded the wet spot inside, then felt his shoulder. "That would be about right. Hey, how does that work? I should have come down like Carlos there hours ago."

"It wasn't their drool that inoculated you, it was touching them. We rotate all the nurses and myself through this duty once a day, and the rule is to not wear gloves, but only use bare hands. Kissing the occasional darling head is also permitted." I had to smile at this, they were all just too cute.

I took his hand and led him into one of the two chairs next to our maintenance tech's bed.

"How's Carlos doing? Will he make it?" Reg asked, concerned.

"He'll be OK, it will take a couple of days before he'll do much but sleep it off."

"What did you give him?"

"Just a simple saline solution. When he's up to swallowing, we'll get him onto something he'll like."

"Such as?"

"A home remedy of apple-cider vinegar and honey, plenty diluted. That will keep his electrolytes balanced until he gets over the hump of it. Good thing you got him here fast. Most of these patients were days or weeks with the wrong treatment, and is why they are taking so long to recover."

"Treatment? You haven't given him any pills or injections..."

"Because he won't need any. We treat him by what you might call 'laying on of hands.' That works best and is the core of the therapy."

"You're kidding."

"No, I'm not." She frowned a bit. "About this time, your professional skepticism comes in and we quit having a conversation, then I tell you to lay down and get some rest."

"Sorry, I did read about what you've been doing to all these patients. It's just as you said. The only thing you've had to do is to slowly get them off the meds they were on. That's in all the reports. But I can see that none of your student nurses are wearing gloves at all. And not even face masks."

"The worse thing you could catch in here would be the common cold. Way too sterile for me. I'd bring some plants in here, maybe some non-allergic flowers if I could. A therapy dog would be a great addition. But my 'druthers' don't count for much. Maybe since our quarantine is gone, it might."

I frowned at this. "No, it's going to get worse. I've read up on the procedures. The next thing that is supposed to happen is to gas us all and seal us in. Eventually pour cement over the entire building."

VII

IT WAS CATHY WHO HAD to sit down at that point. She shook her head. "I was afraid of that. Something my great-grandfather had to survive."

I found another seat and dragged it over. "Your great-grandfather was encased in cement?"

Cathy looked up at me, and took my hand. "Sorry, I spoke out of turn. But I guess it's a good as time as any to tell you. Ever heard of the Lazurai Project?"

I shook my head no.

"How about that terrorist bombing of a Cook County civilian hospital about 50 years ago?"

"Dirty bomb with chem warfare agents. Killed everyone. Huge tragedy."

"Everyone except the babies. But they were changed by the chemicals and radiation. They became toxic to everyone they touched. And as they grew older, the chance of contagion grew, so that even being in a hazmat suit wouldn't protect you. Those kids were raised in isolation from any adults and only had each other. Somehow, the government got them shipped to a remote desert location and put them into a dome. Some damned fool in Washington finally gave the order to kill them all as a solution. But none of their chemicals worked, not even their most deadly pathogens. So they finally just cemented the dome over."

My mouth dropped open. Shocked was a slight description of what I was feeling.

"They'd been experimenting with them for years by then, and their families had already been told that they were dead. But puberty forced the government's hand, as they now were extremely hazardous to the rest of humankind. People were getting sick and dying just being downwind. And so, the concrete. Problem was, the Lazurai kids could dissolve and absorb almost anything just with their hands. Even bullets and explosions didn't stop them."

"So, what happened to them?"

"They all escaped. And learned to deal with trackers that found them. Towns and cities evacuated when they found out a Lazurai was headed their way. Most of them suicided eventually, as they could no longer approach any other human. Occasionally, they found babies alive after their families had died, and raised those babies on their own, in secret. One of those babies was my grandfather. He then grew to become a teen ager and started roaming on his own, but was able to control his infectious 'abilities' and get near people - until they eventually found out. Getting attacked by others only made the Lazurai infect as self-defense. And then the government would get involved and they 'd have to disappear again." A tear formed at the corner of Cathy's eye.

I truly felt sorry for those kids. And put my hand on Cathy's where it lay on her chair arm.

She turned her hand over and held onto mine, looking me in the eyes with her own blue ones. "The story does have a happy ending. Those kids adopted other babies, and those babies also grew up and adopted. In each generation, the control over their abilities was improved. What you're touching now is the hand of a fourth-generation Lazurai. As are all of these student-nurses, also."

VIII

HE DIDN'T FLINCH AT that. Probably because we'd been talking for nearly three weeks by then, even though he had to wear that stupid, useless hazmat suit.

"So that all means that you and your students could dissolve concrete if you had to?"

I had to smile at this. "Well, yes. Of course, that would start an old hunt up all over again. And we'd all survive being gassed, even those kids in there. But a lot of these adults wouldn't. It takes a long time to help an adult to change. Too many habits they've built in."

Reg's mind was racing. He was one of those "adults" now. He was looking off into space and I could see his eyes move as he considered various options. "How soon before Carlos is awake? Can you speed it up - I need to talk to him."

"Now that you know, we can probably give him some advanced treatments and have him able to talk in maybe 15 minutes or so." I rose and patted his shoulder so he stayed there. Nodding to Sue and another nearby nurse I motioned them over to the maintenance tech's bed.

We put our hands on his exposed arms, closed our eyes and concentrated.

It didn't take that quarter of an hour. He woke and saw us, then smiled.

Reg had stood to watch us and came closer. He started talking to Carlos in a quiet voice, explaining what had happened and asking him questions about protocols and other details.

We nurses all had our own duties to take care of, which now meant accelerating our treatments on everyone. Just in case.

IX

THE LAST ARMY TRUCK pulled out at dawn from the quarantine zone. The concrete pumpers and forms were already in place. A colonel signaled them to start. It took about two days to completely cover the building. The last dosage of gas had been given just hours before the concrete pumpers quit. By the time they cleaned out their equipment, it had been 48 hours.

A second chain link fence now surrounded the original and the buildings nearby were evacuated. Dozers and earth moving equipment were already in place to level all the nearby buildings for a block in all directions. Supplies for a third chain link fence to surround that perimeter were stacked on site, waiting for the demolition to complete. Typical government efficiency.

Cathy, Sue, Carlos and I were all on that last truck. Dressed in hazmat suits and accompanying the body bags, both small and large.

We were driven out to a large transport plane where another crew of haz-mat-suited government types carefully transferred the body bags and us into its open hatch. Two other cargo planes of the same type were nearby on that runway.

All the planes took off together. Not long after, a fourth identical plane rose up as ours started descending. It wasn't too long before we lost sight of the three planes in the clouds that formed overhead.

Soon our plane touched down with bumps on a little-used airfield long enough to allow a landing for the big plane.

By then we had every one woken out of their trances and sitting on benches at each side of the plane's hold. They had dressed before they left the medical compound, in the street clothes they came in or others from what was available. The babies were shared between the adults, and formula bottles appeared from supplies (warmed by the hands of one of the Lazurai student-nurses to body temperature.)

The ramp was lowered and we were met by a small group of people who ushered us into waiting buses.

We drove to an upscale hotel on the suburbs of 'Cagga, well outside their city borders. The top two full floors had been rented in advance, sealed off from any access. The reason was to "debrief" the patients and tell them their options.

Most of them were going to have very long, healthy lives after this. They could return to their families if they wanted. Otherwise, officials would dutifully break the news of their death as delicately as possible.

Those who wanted to continue their treatment and training were allowed to select one of several small villages in various states for relocation.

The babies were returned to their parents with private schooling awarded up to and including college, all expenses paid. Orphans were accepted by the villages willingly.

Carlos returned to his own family, with the idea and promise of relocating them to one of the villages.

All were briefed that no one would believe their story about the existence of Lazurai. A more suitable explanation was that some very experimental techniques were employed that fortunately had a "miracle cure" result. But were too technical for laymen to understand or try to duplicate. A number was given them to a government phone which would only accept messages.

CATHY AND I SAT IN an empty restaurant in the top of that hotel, enjoying a quiet dinner.

"I'd ask how this was all arranged, but I'm sure that I don't need to know."

"Well, I'll tell you something as unbelievable as it is true. First, the government is very happy to cooperate with us. We are their worst enemy and best ally. Second, there is a guy named 'Peter' who knows something called 'advanced mathematics of retrospective analysis' which in short says that you can predict behavior and events if you understand history well enough. And he saw this particular problem coming. That infectious outbreak common to secessionist cities." She speared a small piece of steak and chewed thoughtfully before continuing.

"It was his idea and financing to set up these nursing colleges in the Lazurai villages years before, then provide 'volunteer' teams into various hospital staffs at the appropriate time to stem off the worst contagion. A few of the larger cities in the Midwest already have been solved, although the best we can do for the coastal megalopolises is to convert it into a widespread 'Legionnaire Disease' outbreak. The result is that while it will still be a plague, the entire human race won't be wiped out."

I nearly dropped my fork at her casual explanation of a global epidemic. "You mean there is nothing we can do?"

Cathy shook her head and looked down at her plate.

I reached over and touched her hand with mine. The same hand that had saved countless lives, including mine.

She looked up again, bleary eyed, but smiling. "At least I got you out of this deal. I hear you decided to come to my village so we can continue our conversations."

I had to smile in return. "The deal was no hazmat suits and way more than 30 minutes per day."

She was grinning at that point. "You know, they have a wonderful view of the Illinois plains from here. Would you like to pick up your questions where we left off?"

We rose and walked to the balcony, through their glass doors, and held each other around our waists as we talked. For a very long time.

Coda

IN A DISTANT ABANDONED government facility, an elevator creaked to a sub-sub-level and flickering fluorescent lights turned on bank by bank. They exposed a huge empty room with concrete walls. Around the walls at varying intervals were discolored patches in the shapes of humans, as if someone had outlined around them and colored inside.

The elevator opened and a man wearing a three-piece wool-blend suit emerged, along with a woman in skin-tight black leather. They carried nothing in their hands. No weapons of any kind.

Because they knew what they were up against, the challenge ahead of them.

Walking into the center of the room, the man cleared his throat.

"It's time. You can come out now."

One by one, at varying timings, a shape emerged from the walls in front of each human outline.

They each were forms of one of the four elements - dust, fire, air, or water. All were in motion, but none were moving beyond their spot.

The man and woman in the center of the room were silent, thinking, communicating with all present on a level far beyond what any typical human can sense or understand. After a long time, the couple took each other's hand and bowed their heads.

At that, the elemental forms each shimmered, and disappeared.

When the last form had left, the couple turned back to the elevator and entered it, still holding hands as the doors closed. Distant rumblings took their elevator car back up to the surface.

Meanwhile the lights began turning out, one bank at a time. At last the room was dark as it had been for decades before.

The next phase in our planet's evolution had begun.

One Thought, Then Gone

BY J. R. KRUZE

THEY SENT ME HERE TO keep me safe. From horrors I wasn't supposed to know about.

But they didn't understand the first thing about arriving in a female body with raging hormones and a genius beyond understanding of myself and anyone around me.

Of course, they wiped my memory. That didn't mean I couldn't figure out that I didn't belong.

Then I met someone that I could almost trust. Not to give me away.

Because if anyone really found out what I knew - including me - then the universe would literally collapse on itself.

Seriously. Not just another teen-angst romance. This was deadly serious.

Deadly for everyone, including me. And somehow, he seemed to actually care...

I

I'D FIGURED IT ALL out by the first day as a high school sophomore. And I could care less. Because it wasn't real. None of it.

Schooling was another trap built to "keep people safe." And get them ready to have a job and accept the rat-race, wage-slave mentality.

Not that my parents or teachers or anyone else around could really understand what I was going through. They all just set it up as another "coming of age" drama that always played out. All the older siblings I inherited had made it through, somehow. In their own ways.

The trick was - I knew they were all part of the same trap.

I didn't belong here, that I knew. And I was here to keep me safe from something far darker and more sinister than going on welfare, or being homeless, or doing illegal drugs and going to jail.

Something was out there much darker and more deadly than anything they could threaten me with. I could feel it in all my body from my bones to the lady parts that I was supposed to "think with" at this age.

I didn't belong here.

And it became more and more obvious the more I tried to "fit in" by attempting to work out the customs and morality they all had. All the "now-you're-supposed-to's" that they probably filed in a non-existent loose leaf binder we were all issued when we were born.

The trick is that I wasn't born. I had no memory of it. And all the things they told me I liked to do when I was a kid - I didn't remember any of it. Because they were training me to just accept, just go along, just act on what they told me my memories were.

And they showed me "movies" of when I was younger. Filmed on something called "Super 8" and then later it was on "video tape."

All made up to just reinforce the programming I'd been given along with this body.

Life wasn't real. Life just sucked. Boyfriends, fashions, put-downs, come-ons, sports, band, gym, everything. Sucked.

Because it didn't make sense. And the more sense I tried to make out of it, the worse it got.

Until I got a clue.

The same day I met him.

II

FIRST DAY OF SCHOOL for that second year of torture.

And since we had roughly the same last name, we were assigned seats in order and wound up in the back of the room by each other.

And that meant we had to collaborate on class projects. Chemistry. Another yawning class to endure. Until what? Until the day was over. Then we had homework and then we went to sleep and then woke up and started over.

A gigantic baby-sitting service to raise their kids to get jobs like they did. And have kids. And let them get raised like us, like our parents were.

"Some gigantic conspiracy." That guy sitting in the next row over mumbled.

"What?" I asked.

"Just a way to keep us all amused until we get our scrap of paper saying we did learn to write our dots and dashes just so, and we are approved to go out and now be carbon copies of what they want us to be, good little boys and girls, good little workers."

Clearer this time. A full run-on sentence.

"Kinda grumpy today?" I said.

"Maybe. But thanks for noticing." He replied.

"I'm Harriet - but please call me Heri." Introductions were best cut short.

"Sol - short for Solomon." To the point, but with a smile. "Nice to meet someone else who was saddled with an unwieldy moniker right out of the gate."

I had to smile at this. The guy was colorful. I tended to be reticent, quiet.

"So what do you think of this lab work we're assigned?" Maybe curious, maybe polite small talk.

"Sucks. As usual. Teacher does the lecture, makes us do something so we can parrot the answer back. It's called 'learning.' Could be worse, I imagine." Now I started to warm to the subject.

"Yea, well. You're probably right, could be worse." He slid down into his seat so his shoulders were on the backrest and elbows on the laminated top. "Stuff gives me nightmares as it is."

"Nightmares?" I turned to him. This struck a chord.

"Sure - am I in the right class, do I have the right books, am I dressed like I'm supposed to. What about that cutie in the front row - is she going to ask my something and I won't know what to say? And then I wake up and see that I still have hours to go before I'm supposed to get up." He frowned at remembering.

"Yeah, I know about that. Except the cutie in the front row. She's an air head. Don't worry about her asking you anything. She's into getting top grades." I frowned on my own.

"Just another trap to catch you." He gave a wry grin out of the corner of his mouth, half turned toward me.

"Lots of traps here. But I'm beginning to figure them all out. They might have a pattern." I turned more toward him to see his response.

He shrugged. "And what would knowing the pattern do to help us? We're stuck here."

"Maybe. Maybe not. Gives me an idea. This might sound personal, but do you gotta car? Transport?" I watched his reaction carefully.

Sol turned toward me, eyebrow raised. "Yea. An old clunker that runs, mostly. Cleaned it up though." Now his turn to be reticent.

"Don't know how to ask this except straight up. It's Friday." I stopped at that point.

Sol raised both eyebrows at this. "That's a question? Wait. You're asking me out. Me?"

I turned to face the front and slunk down in my own seat. "Sorry. Probably wouldn't work."

Sol smiled in his voice, though I was looking down at my desk and its papers. "Probably not. But when should I pick you up and where do you live?"

I turned to toward him. He was sitting up now. "You aren't going to get all touchy-feely-gropie on me are you?"

Sol smiled again. "Well, you are cute."

I blushed. "Yea, well so are you. So what?"

Sol noticed the teacher looking at us, so he picked up his assignment and pointed at one of the questions on it. Then leaned toward me across the aisle. "Maybe it could work. OK, here's a trick question."

I looked at what he was pointing at, and tried not to smile, but did anyway. "No, that's not. It's a dumb question. That question is just to show whether you were listening."

Sol smiled. "No, that's not the question. Here: Past lives and entropy - what's the relation?"

I thought about this for awhile. "No right answer. Depends on belief. You believe in past lives or you don't. Because they can't be proved to exist scientifically."

"But suppose they do?"

"Then entropy..."

"A belief by the Science believers." He smiled at me.

"...would tend to prove that past lives exist, as the mind is measured as a form of energy, and energy cannot be destroyed, only transmuted in form." I finished.

Then I wrestled out my own hand-out and finished every second question, by either simple term or equation. And passed it over to him, nodding at it.

He then filled out the other half of the questions on his sheet and handed it to me. "Your turn."

"Trick question: Politics?" I asked.

Wrinkling his nose and forehead as if getting a whiff of something bad. "A religion of beliefs, again. Only based on power and graft..."

"...that are in the eye of the beholder, usually the party out of power." I finished.

He looked at me with clear eyes. "One word or short answer - turnabout: Sex?"

I tensed at this. "When I can, just so far. Food?"

He smiled. "Pizza - or any sandwich that's portable. Movies?"

I smiled back. "Books are better, but they don't have balconies. Beer?"

He frowned. "Illegal. Won't go there, publicly. A good time?"

I grinned. "Scintillating conversation - which means ideas where people dare not tread. Popular trends?"

He grinned back. "Nod and smile, then move a long. Pick you up?"

I bent to tear a sheet out of my notebook and scribble on it. Then asked, "7 pm, home by 11. One time or steady?"

He took the sheet I handed him, on top of his version of the quiz. "Maybe, depends?"

I raised an eyebrow at this. "Depends on?"

He handed my quiz sheet back to me. "All of the above." And smiled with a twinkle in his eyes.

The bell rang and the class was over. Until tomorrow, the only time we met each day.

I found myself looking forward to it.

III

WE'D GONE OUT FOR A few weeks. Ate a lot of pizza and sandwiches. Saw some movies in the balcony. Made out in my car, usually. But the talking was what kept me coming back.

She was pretty widely read, and could quote a lot of things. We ended up meeting at the library and picking out books for each other, speed-reading through them in quiet. She would pick out a book and I'd nod in those quiet stacks to tell her I'd read it or not. If I hadn't, she'd hand it to me. If not, she'd pick out another nearby that would have something to do with that subject - and sometimes take me over to another section of the library to pick out a related book. Of course, that would be baffling until I finally got to where the author picked up the thought - or I'd wind up checking it out when we left so we could discuss it later.

And I'd take her out to one of the sandwich shops in town. Often we'd go over to the city park and talk over the ideas in those books.

After it had gotten dark, I'd drive her in my old 50-something, four-door Chevy to some secluded spot where we would get out, scoot the front bench seat forward, and make-out in the back seat for awhile. When our glands were suitably spent, we could get back to serious discussion.

I'd rigged some RV lights inside, as well as curtains to keep moths and lookie-loo's at bay. Our own private island of intellectual discussion, regardless of the world at large.

Of course, the floorboards and back window shelf had stacks of books we would read and discuss and refer to during our night-time rendezvous. (I did install a 12-volt Marine clock that had a quiet alarm to give us time to make ourselves presentable and be back by our parents' set curfew times.)

Heri started with Ayn Rand's "Anthem", which led to Bradbury's "Martian Chronicles", and led to Blish's "Cities in Flight", led to Burroughs' "Mars" series, to his "Tarzan" series, to Kipling's short stories, to Doyle's adventures and then his mysteries, then Leigh Brackett, Dashiell Hammett, Carolyn Wells,

G. K. Chesterton, E. B. Smith, which led to E. E. Smith, and last to Andre Norton's "All Cats are Gray."

Heri brought this point up and left me stumped. "Remember what you asked about entropy and past lives? I think I've stumbled onto a worse one."

I was, of course, all ears by this time.

She continued, "Thought itself is an energy, and so there is nothing such as 'losing your thought' or 'losing track' of your thinking. Thoughts come and go and they never disappear. They have to simply transmute."

I bought in. "Memories were transmuted, but then senility isn't the end of them, as they'd have to go somewhere. I remember Nap Hill said once that thoughts were contagious and spread like flu - that they were stored as 'habits' in some 'universal intelligence' and could be tapped. That then ties to a bunch of New Thought authors, as well as Edison and Einstein. Their concepts of an over-arching storage system for ideas..."

Heri took this all in like a fish to water. "Of course! But take this one further - what if beings actually lived in this stuff? If Bristol's 'belief is father to fact' is correct, then we might have mysterious beings who live in that 'ether' stream or field and manipulate our own physical universe to store thought through our bodies."

I was silent for awhile. "Of course, you know that this is unprovable, even science fiction."

She looked off in the distance, beyond the curtains of our little yellow 12-volt-lit world. "I know. Like past lives. But it doesn't matter. Belief is all that matters. Take these tremendously insane social customs we are following here and now. There's no real use for them, other than as 'grease' to fit the various parts together. The dull follow them like sheep in a pasture, and the too-brilliant ignore them. In both cases, and everything in between, they only deal with this one limited universe we physically live in, and actually just this subset of culture in this hemisphere. Not universal at all."

I reached over the front seat to the pizza box, handing back her drink while I pulled the box and my own drink back over. "This is really making me hungry."

Heri smiled at all this. "Like our 'exercise' earlier wasn't enough, already." She sipped her cool drink of ice-diluted soft drink whose carbonated fizz had long since fizzed away.

I offered her the last piece of pizza, but she shook her head, lost in more advanced thought. So I finished that piece too and shoved the empty box back into the front seat.

Her frown was as cute as her smile, and she was frowning now. "Beings who live in that other universe who may be or are controlling our thoughts in this one. If I am right, and our own cultural reactions mirror those, then this could explain some of the weird coincidences and disappearances. Particularly of certain free thinkers, and societies of the gifted."

At that point, the alarm sounded, and we had minutes to get our musses un-mussed, and then the interior lights turned out, the curtains back in place and us returned to the front seat and traveling back to our local so-called civilization.

After Heri got the pizza box into the back, with her legs and feet curled under her, she leaned against me on the bench seat, .

I'd long ago learned to drive with my left arm in order to leave my right free. And to appreciate the advantage of old cars with bench seats instead of the more modern buckets.

Heri pulled my right arm over her shoulder, and held onto it with her own right. "Just hold me, Sol." Then nuzzled her head against my shoulder with her left arm draped across my thigh.

Life was good in these moments.

Even though we were returning from our mind-bending flights of discussion to an uncertain world of nutty emotions and now-you-gotta's that made no sense and couldn't be disputed in any court.

IV

I HAD MY ARM AROUND her again as I walked her up her concrete sidewalk to her ranch-style home in a 60's subdivision, where the neighboring houses were so similar to only differ in paint and front shrubbery.

Heri looked up at me while we were in the yellow bug-repellent porch light. "Thanks Sol. You're one in a million or more. Oh, the food was good, too."

I bent down and kissed her lightly. "We'll see you in school on Monday. Our only class."

A small frown creased her forehead. "I'm worried about that idea I had." Then she brightened, optimistic. "The next few days will tell." At that she pulled away and skipped up the steps to touch the front door knob. Turning, she winked at me and went inside with one smooth motion.

Of course, I smiled all the way home.

ON MONDAY, SHE WASN'T in class. The rumor was that she had a sudden death in the family and had to take a trip out of state. Her seat was empty and stayed empty.

I drove by her house soon after that and found a "For Sale" sign out front, and the place all empty like her family had never lived there.

The semester had finals shortly after, and then school was over for the summer. I had a job lined up, and other matters took her place in my thoughts - mostly.

I finally accepted it like another fact of life. She never wrote me. And I never found anyone who could dissolve fiction into non-fiction to come up with a completely new and unique compound.

Heri had probably found a universal solvent that erased her from my and anyone else's universe. Almost.

When I graduated, I left town myself, and my life became a series of adventures in other towns and places. I had no use for the graduating class of that small town's school, so never kept in touch with any of them. I learned a new set of customs to replace the pitch-and-woo of teen-dom, some that would keep me employed until I discovered I could write and make enough income to fire my last boss.

But last night, Heri came to me in my dreams, when I was looking for inspiration. And we cuddled, while the back seat of that 50-something Chevy and its curtains came into my mind as a backdrop. "Just hold me," she said.

And so I did, as long as I could that night.

And when I woke, I wrote this story.

Because she is still out there, somewhere. As long as I continue to believe, that thought never disappears, it's only transmuted to another form.

Are the mysterious beings who control our thoughts real?

Probably as real as you believe.

THERE WAS JUST ONE problem with all that, and why I deleted the original ending and started writing this again.

Heri wouldn't stay out of my dreams.

V

WHERE I SHOWED UP AFTER I walked through that front door didn't make a lot of sense at first.

I was walking around the high school where I first met Sol.

Only I could walk through stuff. Pretty much everything.

Must be purgatory, I figured.

The place looked different. All this new construction that looked old. Which meant some time had passed as well. They'd made some improvements to the school in all that time.

But it still sucked. And the students were still bored. Only now they had more administrators to "take care" of them.

Meaning, it was still a trap.

With a big new Gym, and the buses parked somewhere else. Tennis courts were gone, replaced with some other silly sport.

Where I'd been, I didn't recall. Or didn't want to.

Now I could hear people's thoughts, and send my own to them.

I'd become one of those "mysterious others" that I'd only imagined existed. Meaning I must have come pretty close to the truth.

Or I died somehow and became a ghost.

One of the two.

But I wasn't stuck to the school grounds. I could go anywhere I wanted. And even just by thinking the thought of where I wanted to go. That was cool.

Library was a first stop, of course. They'd made some improvements, too. But the more things change, the more they stay the same. Still lots of books and newspapers. DVDs and CDs now.

Somehow I wasn't surprised by all that.

The question was still: What the H___ happened?

I was in high school, then I'm back as some sort of telepathic ghost.

To my mind, I was still a teenager. But everything else had changed. Since when?

Newspaper date says forty years ago.

Next question: Whatever happened to Sol?

All I recall for sure was turning and walking through my own front door at home. Then showing up at the school again, like I am now.

I sure could use someone to compare notes with.

Forty years, though. He's probably married, had kids. Even grandkids by now. He could have done anything with that mind of his. One in a million or more, like I told him that last night.

All that time ago.

Wonder what he's doing now?

AND THEN I SHOWED UP – just wherever he was.

VI

"HERI – THAT YOU?" I smiled "Missed you. Been awhile."

"Yea, I know. Not like I had a lot of choice in it." She smiled in her voice.

"I always wondered what happened to you. But where are you, really? I don't see you around, just hear your voice in my head."

"Oh, yea. Well, try this: close your eyes."

WE WERE IN THE BACK of my 50-something Chevy. RV lights on, curtains closed. Stacks of books behind our heads and on the floorboard by our feet.

"Heri – wow. This is what, my dreams?"

"Something like that. It's how I remember our last night together." She sniffed at that.

I looked over and saw a tear running down her cheek. And went to wipe it off with my hand, then stopped. "You are still cute, and I'm sorry you're upset. But did you have to make me a teenager again?"

Heri smiled at this, and wiped her own face. "You are such a dork, don't you know? Just listen to yourself – who wouldn't want to be young again with all you now know?"

I smiled in return. "OK, I've got forty more years of experience. But I tell you what, I'd have quit school that year if I could have. Mom made me stick it out – either that or I was going to college and do even more years at the same grind. I just couldn't hurt her like that. So the easier route was seeing how to game their system. You should have seen my senior schedule – all I was there for was the PE credit and some history class. It was all rigged."

Heri smiled at my story, but I could still see she was sad.

"Hey, kiddo. Cheer up. We're here, now. Tell me what you've been up to for the last forty – and what's with all this dream stuff?"

"Sol, I actually don't know where I've 'been' for the last forty years. To me, our last night was minutes ago. And then I showed up at the high school again, then the library, then thought of you – and here I am. I'm not apparently real enough to be seen with your actual eyes." She looked down and the tears really started flowing.

I pulled her to me. "Heri, just let me hold you for awhile."

And we sat in the back of my old Chevy for as long as it took for her to feel real again. At least to herself.

Of course, it made me feel good again, too. Something I'd missed for a very long time.

VII

IT WAS LIKE WAKING up in Heaven. Melted into the arms of the first person I really trusted, and just let him hold me. It was the best feeling I could have. It had only seemed like moments for me, but it was all I really wanted out of this world.

At last, I started bringing him up to speed. "OK, Sol, we did this crazy math-logic thing with those fiction books, and wound up marrying them to your old 'past lives/entropy' theory. Then invented some 'mysterious beings' that live in a world outside of ours, but able to affect us in ours. The core idea went long the lines that they were just using us to store memories, thoughts."

Then I stopped. What hit me felt like a brick wall falling on me. "Hey Sol."

"What?"

I sat up away from him again and looked at him "We forgot a book."

"Wait. I lost track years ago about what we laid out." Sol brushed his hand through his thick, curly hair and stretched the arm that had he'd used to hold me for so long.

"OK the short end of that analysis was Norton's 'All Cats Are Gray'. And that had an invisible being in it that only the cat could see – and the heroine, who was color-blind. She killed it and then got rich when they turned in that empty luxury liner they found as salvage."

"Oh, yea. Invisible beings like those 'thought-meisters' of yours." Sol sat up straight, all ears now.

I looked directly in his eyes. "Thinking and then believing in what you named 'thought-meisters' then gave them power over me in this universe. Because what they did next was simply in self-defense. Regardless of what their motives are for using us for memory storage, it doesn't much matter."

Sol smiled. "So now you're going to re-work your idea and the belief behind it?"

"Exactly. Not that I can take that thought back, but I can fix the problem it created. Or at least I think I can." My forehead wrinkled with this new idea. "The book we missed was L'Engle's 'Wrinkle in Time.'"

Sol sat forward, his brow uncreased as he got my concept. "The main weapon those kids had against the mind control was Love. Just plain unconditional love. Have I ever told you how much of a genius you are?" And then he leaned forward and kissed me.

Yes my knees went soft, and I simply wanted to melt back into his arms, but I pushed him away again. "Thanks, but sorry, I need to stay focused. Glands and stuff will have to wait."

Sol was contrite, but smiling at me. A personal admirer for all time.

At last, I almost jumped out of that back seat with the new idea. "Sol, you just inspired me – but wait, just sit there. Let me get this out. We both have to do this to make it work."

He was quiet while I gathered my thoughts, and kept his hands to himself.

"Love." I said at last. "Remember that old book you were studying, who was that guy – Haanel. Said something about love."

Sol frowned. "Oh, that love is like a primal element, what brought the rest of the world into existence."

"Exactly. Perfect. Just the element missing from that solution. Something we are too afraid to admit." I got nervous at this. Hanging out was one thing, making out in the back seats of cars another, but we were about to go into a realm teenagers avoided. Too permanent in these shifting teen-age worlds.

He saw my nervousness, but didn't get it yet. So he stayed where he was and let me finish working it out.

"Sol, this is where Christian love and romantic love and Haanel's textbook love all meet."

We were both shocked at that. Because these were all talked about separately. But that one unitary concept held the secrets to the universe. Universal glue and universal solvent all in one.

Sol started frowning. "But does this just create more problems to solve?"

"Such as?" I asked.

"One: the time conundrum – we're forty years later but now are together at 'date zero' where this started. Two: do these guys just quit interacting with our universe – and does that then interrupt a natural process. I could see where this blows our whole scene sky high." Sol looked around the now cramped back end of his car, all the curtains, books, and us two.

I just had to smile. "You worry too much sometimes, Sol. Look – one, Nature takes care of itself. If we blow the whole thing up, we wouldn't remember any of it anyway. And two, if the 'mysterious beings' are fulfilling a natural function, then something will replace them. And if it's more efficient with disrupting them out of the picture, then things will run more smoothly. Either way, we'll either remember this time or not. No worries, as the Aussies say."

Sol was all smiles again. He looked up at the clock. "And just by coincidence, time has stopped just before that alarm went off and we had to get you home."

I looked and saw he was right. "OK, I know what puts this all in motion again. But you're going to show some absolute faith in what we are going to do. It's nothing we've done before and nothing you've done in the forty years after. Probably because we didn't do it right now. We need to commit."

He swallowed and nodded. "Just what I was thinking. Hari, for all time, forever, regardless of anything that happens: I love you."

Of course my eyes went misty and my heart missed a beat. "I love you too, Sol. Forever and regardless."

We came up for air after that kiss when the alarm went off.

It didn't take long to get the books put away, the curtains drawn back, and I was again in the front seat next to him, my legs curled up on the rest of that bench seat, his arm around me. Heading back to my parents home. For my home was now wherever – and whenever - he was. "Just hold me, Sol."

He did, and too soon we pulled up into my parent's drive.

We both got out, but after he kissed me good night, I didn't let go of his hand. With the other I turned the knob and opened the door to the future we had just created.

VIII

WE HAD AND RAISED TWO children, with four grandchildren. They visit us often, always a delight.

Heri and I waited until after graduation to get married – the next weekend, actually. Then moved into a small rental and got local steady jobs while we took night classes at the community college to get trained in what we were interested in. Heri got a degree in library science, and I got a job programming robotics after only a couple years of study. Then we started businesses of our own, learning how to make our fortune part time – by investing from our day job to make it happen.

Soon we were able to make the shift from full-time job to part-time and then figured out how to fire our last bosses.

I never forgot all I'd learned in that first forty years, so going through it all again had its perks, especially in investing in certain stocks at certain times.

Heri taught herself programming, and started doing web design and content marketing even before they were a thing. I started writing and slogged through the years before self-publishing was a thing. Of course, those forty years of practice made it all a lot simpler. Lots of pen names were the key. So I could make all the income I wanted, but kept a low profile to save my privacy.

We moved just outside of Austin, close enough to be part of the tech boom that later developed there, but invested in a small ranch and resisted the developers who wanted to overpay us for it. Instead we planted a lot of trees on the borders and a tall fence to keep our livestock in. Plus some guard llamas and donkeys to keep everything and everybody else out.

Our kids loved all the animals we raised, and learned a lot from raising them. They went through their own teen travails, but with guidence from our own lessons learned.

Then one day, Heri brought this story to me. She'd saved it for decades, as she knew I would want to update it when it was time.

I had to laugh when I read it. Of course, it was still accurate. And I finished the ending to it after all those years. You're reading it now.

And you know, I bought another 50-something Chevy later and had the back-end chopped out of it. It sits in our living room now. The trunk was made into a couch so visitors can watch the big screen.

But when no one is around, Heri and I usually move into the bench back seat, pull the curtains, turn on the 12-volt RV lights and discuss books and their ideas, in between our make-out sessions.

That's never gotten old, no matter how long it's taken to get to where we are now.

Forty years later and it only seems like a moment ago.

To Laugh At Death

BY J. R. KRUZE

I DIED EVERY NIGHT. And learned to live forever.

Dreams were important, because those told you your past lives. And like the old guy said somewhere, if you didn't learn from your past, you were just condemned to repeat it.

I wanted to live each day to my fullest. Because I knew it was over when I closed my eyes to sleep.

Each day, I had to learn everything all over again. Because I wanted to make each day last, to do something with my life, to have some satisfaction.

To find true love became my final goal. Somehow, it' escaped me most of my life.

When she finally found me, we both were now writers. Before long, there was something else between us, a romantic mystery that had to be solved.

Together our combined genius might be able to solve it. Maybe.

Is it true that "To deeply love is to laugh at death."?

I

THE FIRST TIME I DIED, it was so long ago, I hardly remember. Other than waking up in a hospital and not wanting to eat. Of smelling the anesthetic they'd given me as it wore off. The stink in my nose, and this stupid gown that tied in the back where I couldn't reach it - but made me move around the bed to get the knots where they didn't hurt or scratch.

And they fed me Jello. I don't remember what kind. But I was supposed to eat, supposed to be hungry. So I tried it. It was pretty tasteless, sitting in that whitish plastic cup. Never finished it. Just quit and lay back.

They had put some girl in the other bed next to mine, but she wasn't awake. And I went back to sleep then. And died again.

When I woke up, she was gone. And I tried to remember anything about her, but - nothing. Only that she had been a character in that life, a stand-in, a red shirt. Like the nurses that came and went - they were just cardboard cutouts. Not real.

That's what I remember for sure. The rest of my memories earlier than that seem to be the ones they told me I should have. Because that's they ones they had.

Those lifetime-stories came from people who called me their son. They were called parents. And they said they loved me, but I wasn't sure. If they loved me, they why did they let me die every night? And then come back the next day like nothing had happened?

But everything had happened. This was a new world again. And only what I could recall of my reincarnations, my past lives, told me how I was supposed to act in this one.

And acting I did. I got pretty good at acting out the part I was supposed to play in every life. By remembering my earlier lifetimes and the "now-you're-supposed-to's" from those.

I couldn't say life was good. But I could say that it continued on, regardless. Because nothing really mattered when you died every night and were re-born each new day.

It was a way to get through life. In a steady calm, one that was even pleasant at times.

II

TO ME, LIFE WAS GREAT. I loved waking up as a girl, in my own room, in a big house, with plenty to do every day. Life was an endless adventure.

Now that I was older, and on my own, life was still an adventure.

Of course, being "on my own" started early for me. Because of that car wreck. I lived because I was in the back of that station wagon, asleep, along with the other girls from the neighbor's family. I was going with them on a vacation. But we never made it.

All I remember is something about waking up with a lot of flashing lights and noise, and something on the side of my face. Then I went back to sleep and briefly remember being hauled around through white and green hallways on some sort of bed with rolling wheels. Whatever was on my face wasn't letting me see out of that side.

And then I was lifted onto a solid bed with a big light overhead and then some ugly mask was put over my nose and mouth and I went to sleep again.

Then woke up with my sad parents around me, who were wiping tears off their faces, but put on nice smiles for me when they saw I was awake. I could see out of both eyes now, but couldn't feel much on that side of my face. So I reached a hand up to touch it, a hand with tubes and wires attached.

I barely got a touch before someone had stood up and taken my hand away, telling me to "not touch it" and "leave it alone for now." More smiles. But I was so tired, I just tried to smile back and only made half my face go up. But the people smiled back and so I closed my eyes and turned my face over onto the half I could feel, and sank into grateful darkness again.

My old friend, the dark.

III

I'D LIVED QUITE SOME years now, I'm told. To me, they were thousands of lifetimes. When I was younger, I tried playing games with the other boys my age. Found that their rules didn't make sense, and that the other boys were trying to either cheat or just go along. The cheats made umpires necessary. And if you were really good at playing by the rules, you learned where the holes were.

But holes are for nails. And anything that sticks out is a nail that needs to be hammered. So I learned to keep my head down.

Because of all the push and persuasion they used on us as kids were to excel at everything we did. They even put the smarter kids in their class and the dumber ones in their own. So the smarter ones learned the names mostly of the smarter kids. And the dumber kids tended to drop out, or learn the dull jobs. The smart ones were trained to do the jobs where there were a lot of numbers and symbols that could be made to do different things.

The problem was that it was all just another game. And if you stood out, you got hammered. The rules could be broken, but they were tougher rules. "Box rules" I finally called them. Somewhere along the lines, I was told to "think outside the box." Like that was something special that nobody could do.

I just shut up about that. Because that was the way I was wired. And if I stood out, I'd get hammered.

The dumb ones turned out to be all the people that just went along. Drugs, sex, school dances, having a car - all those were "now-you're-supposed-to's" and just rules that could be broken anytime you wanted to. The next rule was, of course, not to get caught.

And what I did with my own mind that didn't show on the outside, what they couldn't see behind my "now I'm supposed to" smiles and jokes and nods - those things I could never get caught or hammered for.

Making straight "B's" mean that people would leave me alone, and not pressure me to make A's. Because I already didn't have a chance at making valedictorian, which was a relief. There were several girls who tied for making the most straight A's all the way through high school. Finally, they made them all co-valedictorians.

Like I cared much by that time.

Because I had already been hammered for showing people too many times how the rules could be broken.

And only looked forward to dying each night. Just to get relief from stupid people with stupid rules.

IV

IN THAT CAR, THAT NIGHT, most of that family had died. Me and one of their youngest daughters didn't. We were both in the hospital when they were buried. I got out before she did. But she went to live with relatives in another town.

I stayed with my parents and learned to live with that scar on my face. It made my smile funny for awhile, but I got over it quick enough. Because it made me laugh to see my face in the mirror. And so I would spend hours laughing at myself and making my face do all sorts of things.

To begin with, I had to make my hands push up that side of my face. But after awhile, the muscles fixed themselves and it wasn't as funny to see a normal smile. I guess the game was over after that.

Of course, I had a private tutor for a year, and stayed out of school. But that was OK with me because I had all sorts of new dolls and doll houses and doll clothes to play with. And let them talk to each other and tell each other how their day went, and what they thought of world events and how much the newscasters were lying about what really happened.

My parents only gave me female dolls that looked like people. So I had my stuffed teddy bears be the boys. And they would go to work every day while we girls stayed home and cleaned the home and made the beds and had dinner ready for them when they got back.

Then we could all go into the little tiny living room and watch TV, then go to bed and sleep. The next day would start all over again, like magic.

That's where I first learned that magic was in the world. Because when you go to sleep, you don't always wake up the same.

V

I QUIT COUNTING DAYS and started referring to blocks of them as months and years. Of course, they had another complicated set of rules for dividing them into weeks, and there had to be an extra 15 or 16 days tacked on, above any commonly divisible number.

I liked 350 because it was part of a "7" with 5's and 2's mixed in. I figured that was why they had all those holidays at the end of the year, just to make things work out.

That was one set of rules I learned couldn't be messed with. One of a few that I found people were constantly trying to get around, but kept running into their own barriers when they tried. Natural rules are the hardest to break, and so more people tried to break them than the man-made "fake" ones. Although a lot of these were there for reasons.

Once you learned the reasons, then you didn't have to try to break them after that. Because they showed you their loopholes so you could come and go as you wanted. Made no difference, because they would be the same when you came back. And their rules would always win out, no matter what you tried.

So I figured that dying every day was the best way around it. Around everything. Just keep track of my past lives and those would tell me the rules I was supposed to follow and the loopholes I was supposed to find.

That worked as a model for me. And later, when I got cancer on my neck, had it cut out and followed by several additional skin graft surgeries to fix their first cuts, I died several times with those procedures and the habit stuck.

Much easier to deal with life one day at a time, and each day as its own moment.

All the losses of friends and old acquaintances over the years, all the changes anyone goes through, all these were just more unending water under an unmoving bridge.

That simple solution held fears at bay for the thousands of my death/re-birth cycles.

Life wasn't always good, but it was at least an interesting puzzle.

VI

I LOVED LIVING, EVERY second of every day. Life never quit being an adventure.

It was exciting to go to school and meet all these people with their various views about things. When I got to go back to school, I was asked all sorts of questions about my face and how it felt, even though they were all told not to.

And some of them tried to tease me. But they never got the punchline about everything. I just laughed at the good teases and jokes, and pulled my own teases on the bad ones, the really mean ones. Like putting on a shocked face and looking at the top of their head, or over their shoulder at something. And maybe whispering about whatever I was pretending to look at to some friend of mine who didn't tease me. (Most of the time, I was saying gobbledygook or, "Hey watch this kid get nervous about something wrong with their hair.") Sometimes I would start to point, but then "remember" that I wasn't supposed to point at someone.

Sometimes, I would nod and smile, and then come up to them and say they could always go to the teacher and ask to go to the bathroom to fix whatever it was that was sticking out of their head. The teaser would get all nervous and feel their head, but I would reassure them, "No, it looks fine. Just don't touch it and it will be OK."

After a few times, and when that scar got the same color as the rest of my skin, then they quit.

The main point was to learn to laugh at everything. That's what we used to watch when I got out of the hospital. Lots of funny things. And that's where I learned to love makeup. My aunt would come over and paint all sorts of funny animals on my face, or make it look like an animal. And I would look in the mirror and laugh.

She wouldn't let me put any stuff on my own face until the bandage was able to be off. So I painted my dollies faces. Since it didn't wash off the teddy bears faces, I quit doing that. Boy dolls don't wear make up unless they are clowns.

Anyway, life was great growing up.

And I learned to like sleeping because it would be a new adventure the next day.

VII

I KEPT TRYING DIFFERENT lifestyles in every new lifetime. Of course, I would have to springboard off my last lifetime as I would wake up with the leftovers around me of that old lifetime, and had to use them to build the next one. And sometimes, the cycles I had started in earlier lifetimes were long ones, and complicated, and hard to change.

But I could always change something. And since I knew I was just going to be reborn again, I could try new things every new life. So while life was tedious, I could always try something new. Which meant I could make life as interesting as I wanted it.

That was the loophole for living.

I truly did live one day at a time.

And each day was as interesting as I wanted it to be. Or dull and boring. Whatever I felt like doing.

VIII

GROWING OLDER MEANT learning about dating and boys and their complicated ideas about how to act around girls. One of the things I learned about early on was to stay away from the weird ones, who were always trying to grab you where you didn't want to be grabbed.

It was all just another test, like at school. Most tests were stupid. I would get bored about three-quarters through and start fooling around with the rest of the answers. Only one teacher figured it out. She would watch me, and told my parents what I was doing. Because I would figure out what 80% of the total questions were and count down to where that last question was. Then I'd answer all of those right. After that, I could answer the rest of them anyway I wanted. As long as I passed, my parents didn't care. Sometimes they even thought some of my answers were funny.

I liked it when they put essays at the end. Then I would quote Shakespeare or write answers using ten syllables to the line, depending on how much space I had. Sometimes they rhymed, sometimes I'd use Elizabethan terms to make it fit.

I also learned that they couldn't make me finish tests. They didn't like me drawing pictures in the margins, but quit bothering me about it when I would would make a sad face, and then touch my scar with my hand to trace it. (Suckers.)

All because school was dull, repetitive, and I was just waiting to have an excuse to do something more exciting. A lot of trips to the counselor got me as many extra periods and library assistant jobs where I could do just about anything I wanted. I'd get a list of stuff to do from the librarian and get them all done as quick as I could, then pull out some really old books to figure out the languages and writing styles.

That's why I liked Shakespeare and Old English books. And for awhile, I read Dickens backwards. I taught myself Latin, but they didn't have any good Greek books. Some French, some Spanish. Not much else. So I stuck to English and wrote long essays in two or three columns down the page, making all the lines the same length and the gutters straight as I did.

The most fun I had was in building stories that read the same forward as backward. So if you started reading at the end, it would make sense just as if you started at the beginning. Teasers and Hooks were tricky, but one story the villain won, and the other the hero won. Tragedies and Comedies.

By the time I got done with all my required days and years of schooling, I was pretty good at writing stuff.

IX

WHEN I FINALLY GOT out of the required schooling, with some sort of certificate that was another meaningless paper scrap like the rest, I left home that weekend to a job in another state.

After a few months, I left that job for another that made me travel all over the U.S. from coast to coast, doing different stuff. Mostly stupid.

But I learned that other people died and lived like I did. People would change themselves over years and make themselves into different-acting people than I knew before.

And I was changing, dropping out stuff that didn't make sense, and learning all the rules and sillinesses of how to treat people.

I was also trying to figure out where the natural laws were and weren't. There were so many different stupid made-up rules that this made it real hard. But eventually, I got some very dull and repetitive jobs in warehouses. Never telling them I had way more skills than they needed, just so I could get one of their stupid, dull jobs. Because I had to have money to pay for stuff, even though I didn't have much stuff that I actually needed to buy. I really just needed to have extra time to think things through.

But one thing I kept finding that I was missing was someone to share everything I had found.

So I started writing everything out. All the loopholes I had figured out. Self-publishing came around and I put everything online.

That helped.

But no one cared much, or didn't tell me what they thought. And I didn't care much back.

I could read what I'd written years before, although it wasn't interesting to me any more.

Finally, I figured out the last of everything, and looked around at what else I could figure.

That led me to writing fiction, since it was easier to tell people about the loopholes and the stupid fake rules that way. They didn't have to believe me anymore.

Life became a lot less serious after that. Even fun.

I still died every night and was re-born the next day.

The next thing was to find someone just like me, or maybe not, but someone – that came with a living body - who could understand this stuff I'd found. Before I didn't get re-born some fine morning.

X

EVENTUALLY, I GOT A great job where they didn't care what I did all day. Just as long as I re-wrote the manuals I was supposed to rewrite, each done they way they wanted them.

It was some government-funded paperwork job, where they needed old manuals re-written into updated versions. Then my books would go out to other people for editing and come back with all sorts of notes and tabs and extra sheets of paper stuck in.

I then had the joyous time of entering in their comments and typing in their handwritten notes, correcting their grammar and making the sentences more interesting. Because they and I knew how stupidly dull these were to begin with, and that they wanted people to just finish reading them, not go to sleep in the middle.

But I also learned from my rejects to not be too original, or too clever.

As long as I had plenty of time left over, and I was undisturbed in my cubicle, I was happy to pick up my check every other week that paid for my small apartment and kept my car running so I could commute to work.

At the end, they re-located the work one time too many for me. First it was Michigan, then Arkansas, then finally some dreary old re-purposed military base in super-hot Texas, miles even farther out than nowhere.

I'd discovered self-publishing by then and was writing exotic romances based on the same plot over and over, just checking out travel guides to tell me different locations I could use. And I would often write two versions. One would be a tragic romance, where the happy couple finally split up at the end of going through all sorts of problems in their relationship, and the other was where they would meet and go through all sorts of problems and then live happily ever after.

Eventually, I started writing from the middle to each end, and fixing it so both were happy endings - just ended up with different partners.

Then my sales really took off. Of course, I'd change the character's names and put them in different series, using different pen names, but the stories were always the same.

But all easy things get boring after awhile. I really didn't like writing tragic endings, since life wasn't tragic at all. It was fun. Always fun.

When my book sales started replacing my day job income, by twice as much, I was happy. And when the job moved again, I moved to another place entirely. Since I didn't need to be any particular place any more in order to make my living.

Then I was able to start writing four books at once, with four sets of characters who are heroes in one version and villains in the neighboring one. Four locations. Two were tragic, two were good-guy-wins-gal (or gal-wins-guy more often.)

That type of writing was far more interesting to me.

And I'd watch old movies at night, often binge-watching entire series over a long weekend, to get idea for new stories.

I wasn't lonely, but I was alone. My characters kept me company, and I was making more money than I needed.

Still, it would be great to have someone to compare notes with. Have a laugh with. Wake up next to.

But maybe I was writing too many romances, tragic or not.

XI

OF COURSE, MOVING FROM non-fiction to fiction was easier by writing Science Fiction, and then Fantasy. Of course, this meant a lot of learning, since the best stories of all time had romance, mystery, and action all in the same story. But these were all different story structures, so it meant weaving a complicated plot through all these characters.

And frankly, I didn't know how I did it. I studied stacks of books on how to write and finally came across one author who said that writing was "90% crud."

I couldn't write for days after that. Because it struck home. Almost all of the stuff I'd read came out the same - a bunch of dry, regurgitated silliness that tried to explain how "most" authors did things, and how to plot everything into existence, work in multiple drafts, and carefully construct their books so everything worked out just right.

And it took forever to get a novel out.

The trick is that this wasn't what the really prolific authors did. And mostly, those guys didn't write about how they pulled it off. When you picked up the books that mentioned them, they said they just sat down and started writing. When they completed a book, they started on the next one.

One night I had the epiphany. Because I died that night right after I had finished editing and re-proofing a story. And published it online. Done. Slept. Died.

When I woke the next morning, I had a great start to a new book in my head (or in my mind, I guess) and it was just a beautiful idea of a story - even though I had no clue how it was going to end. It was just running off in front of me, like I was being read the script by actors in a radio show, and saw the movie of other actors playing the parts with setting and everything.

I didn't hardly stop to eat that day, but just got into writing everything out.

Slept. Died. Woke up. And started just proofing and re-proofing and tweaking stuff so it read right.

And I really liked the story. So I published it. And started another idea based on those characters that night. Finished it the next lifetime, edited and published it the lifetime after that.

Writing became so much fun I didn't want to do anything else.

Now all my consecutive lifetimes were worth it.

But I still had this nagging idea I wanted to share all this with someone.

XII

FARMERS' MARKET. I was picking up fruit for the week, and putting in an order for a quarter of beef with a farmer there. Also getting some fresh milk and eggs.

Always thought this would be a great "cute meet" for a romance. Today I took my purchases back to my car and set them in coolers with frozen water bottles. Then I went back with a tall mocha-latte that I bought out of the nearby farm supply store. Taking out a folding chair from my car's back seat, I trundled over to sit down in the nearest shade tree, a huge maple. I also took a paperback with me so I could pretend to be reading while waiting for someone.

Not that I came every week, but I loved this big maple. It was always cool and didn't rest on hot asphalt like the market tents. That shade allowed some hangers-on, like me, to sit and watch the interesting world go by. This always gave me inspirational fuel for the characters in my story.

Before long, I noticed an interesting fellow. Someone I'd never seen before. He stood tall and straight. Wore his beard in a three-day growth and his hair long enough to need cutting, but not so much to get in his way. Polo shirt, jeans, boots. Simple enough to dress that way. Inconspicuous. Like he led his whole life that way.

I wanted to know more about him. And so I left my chair there, with my drink by it's leg, and ambled on to fall in behind him.

The only problem was that he didn't talk much. His eyes were keen, and his touch was sure, finding the real quality of the food, but only what he was actually interested in. He'd stopped by the milk truck on his way in, paying them for a couple of gallons they set aside for him. That's when I first saw him.

I still don't know what got my attention, as a gray shirt with a faded and illegible logo is no attention-getter. But he had my attention, regardless. Somehow, I couldn't look away, even though I had to in order to not get any attention on me. I wanted to see him act and react on his own, not act like he thought I expected him to.

I needed to see him in his own world.

So I followed at a distance and tried to stay within earshot.

XIII

WHY SHE WAS FOLLOWING me in the farmer's market was anyone's guess. Because I wasn't there to "make friends and influence people". Not. Period, no, period.

I was only here to get some in-season fruit if they didn't price me out of the market. I was looking for the blemished stuff that was mostly for canning. Sure, I canned my own stuff, but fresh was better tasting, even if you had to cut out the bad parts and feed those to the the chickens.

She started out being just a few paces behind me. At every booth.

My milk was staying cool enough back with the farmer's kids who brought the milk to the pick-up location. They had a trailer with a large tarp and their own produce to sell. So I turned back to go up another round of the tent lines, just to see what she would do. And talked more banter with the other farmers and their families, some I'd never talked to before.

When I talked, she moved closer.

Finally, I turned around and walked right back to stand by her. She was looking over some of the high-priced tomatoes on the one end, trying to look unobtrusive. So I started picking up the tomatoes in front of her, turning them over, correcting their display so they'd show the best sides up. Even though I wasn't there to buy. I was already carrying a plastic bag with enough for the week.

She was only carrying a composition book with a mechanical pencil sticking out the top, halfway through.

"Nice tomatoes here." I said.

"Yes. A bit too pricey for me. But you've organized them well." She shifted her book out of her right hand to tuck it under her left arm.

I took this as a signal of some social "gotta". Extending my own hand, "I'm Saul."

"Martha," came with the extended hand. And a pair of brilliant blue eyes nestled inside a surrounding of wavy, chestnut-brown hair. She looked at me through those eyes supermarket scanners looking for the exact bar code on this item.

"Martha, are you a writer?" I just had to ask.

"How did you figure that out?" Martha's eyebrows went up and her eyes twinkled with the laugh lines in their corners starting up.

"Your composition book has your pencil in the bottom of it, which usually means either an absent-minded sketcher, or a writer who is taking notes on one side first, and then turning over to use the other side." I explained.

"Or, someone who is left-handed and hates the inefficiency and discomfort of writing across the seam of a bound book." She smiled.

"That, too." I replied, with my own smile.

"What genres do you write in?" I asked.

"Romances, mainly, but that is starting to get boring, so I'm branching out into bigger ideas and having the romance play second fiddle to the mystery they are solving. Of course, the trick is to then resolve both plot lines before the story ends." She was now sorting the tomatoes herself, rotating them and grading by size, with the largest ones in front.

"Mysteries are great to mix with the other genres, since everyone loves to dig into solve them. I'm just trying to work in some romance as I go, since like you say, it's more challenging." I had moved over one flat to start on the next-smaller tomatoes. The farmer was letting us sort his produce for him with a small smile on his face, listening to our conversation as he also took care of other shoppers.

Martha moved along with me, and continued turning that last flat of tomatoes to put their best aspect forward. "Actually, the reason I have that composition book upside down is because I'm writing the same story backwards on the flip pages."

My hands stopped at that, since my mind just started calculating the possibilities of writing in two genres in two directions at the same time. I also stopped talking and my eyes went unfocused.

"Saul?"

"Oh, sorry, that's an engaging idea. Really engaging." I smiled at this. "Thanks. You just made my day, maybe my whole week. I have lifetimes to work at this concept now."

"Lifetimes?" Her own hands stopped and one eyebrow went up at this.

I was watching her face now, but her hands were still available to my peripheral vision. "Oh, sorry again. My shorthanded metaphor for living. You die every night and are re-born the next day. Each minute, every moment of your new life is lived as a seamless experience. And you're born each day to a new life, built on the one you had before, but not dependent on it."

Now she completely stopped moving, her eyes staring straight into mine. "That's a killer idea - oh, sorry about the pun."

I had to smile even wider. "No, that's very apt."

We just stood there for awhile.

"You know, my milk is getting warm out in that farmer's truck. I guess I'd better go get it into a cooler and head home."

"Mind if I walk with you? Maybe I can pick your brain for some more ideas." Martha smiled again, in a way that started to melt my heart where I stood. I hadn't had someone honestly interested in me or my ideas since - well, it's been several hundred lifetimes, if not thousands.

All I could do was nod, since there was a sudden lump in my throat, and my tongue wasn't cooperating with my brain's speech center.

XIV

THIS GUY WAS FASCINATING, and on more than one level. My heart seemed to be beating out of my chest at times. While we said nothing on the short walk to that farmer's milk truck, we were walking close enough to almost touch and it seemed electrifying to me.

Of course, I was full of doubts now, something I hadn't experienced since I was a kid. Because nothing in school or work had ever been challenging. It was all a stepping stone to something else. And since I'd started writing, I was able to lose myself in that world for long hours during the day.

I'd only started following this guy to get some research for my next book, to get a different character for it, and now I found myself being a character in my own romance novel. Meeting a charismatic stranger who was probably every bit as brilliant as I was, but in a completely different way.

And we were both writers, which was not just something in common, it was a bond that I could share with no one in my own family or even those I considered true friends. Writing wasn't lonesome, as I had all these characters chatting at me and moving around all the time. But it was an "alone" activity. And more recently I'd been wanting someone to share it all with. A need that hadn't gone away, but only grown, instead.

My body was now giving me other signals, some I hadn't explored in decades. Glands seem to have started secreting juices as if they were suddenly filled to bursting. My heart and lungs were reacting to these by increasing their rate and rhythm.

I had to take a deep breath just to calm them down.

"Deep breaths are good for nerves." Saul quietly said.

"You too?" I looked at him.

"Well, to be honest, yes." He smiled at the farmer's kids who were sitting in in their trailer under their large tarp awning. They handed Saul his two plastic gallon jugs of milk, which were beaded with condensation from the humid day. He managed to put his little finger in the handle of one and his thumb through the other. To me, this meant he probably did a lot more with his hands then type on a keyboard. And was leaving his other hand free to hold his plastic sack of produce.

"There, that's my blue pickup with the camper shell on it." He gestured broadly with his hand that held the produce bag, and I spotted one that matched his direction of travel.

"Not too far from my own car." I said.

We then walked the rest of the way to his truck in quiet. A good quiet. Good for both our nerves.

I watched him put them into a cooler in the back, pulling out some frozen gallons of water to make room for them, and wedging some tall, thin frozen water bottles in between them. Then he opened up the produce bag to put the tomatoes across their top. The lid was domed, so held everything and still closed tightly.

"Saul," I asked, "I don't mean to sound forward, but you are intriguing. On so many levels."

He smiled. "Just what I was about to say, but not as well."

"I think we have a little time before our produce and milk warms up too much, unless you live far from here..." My heart skipped a beat, waiting for his reply.

He looked at me. "Not far away. We can take some time here."

I relaxed a bit. "With all this healthy food we just reviewed and re-sorted, maybe we could get a not-so-healthy coffee from that fast food place next door and continue talking."

Saul raised an eyebrow and smiled. "Sitting on padded plastic furniture isn't my idea of comfort – I can do better than that. Let's go into the air-conditioned farm supply store and get one of their bottled juice drinks and wander their aisles while we sip them. Walking seems a way to be less nervous. Plus, we can always change the conversation if it heads into a weird direction by pretending to shop."

I had to smile at that. "Deal."

XV

WE WERE PROBABLY ABOUT an hour inside, comparing notes about writing and our views on life. I told him how I got the scar on my face, and he told me about the one on his neck.

Saul was fascinated about writing stories backwards, so once he got the hang of it's central idea, I told him about writing four stories at once. His mouth actually dropped open at that concept.

Then he told me how he wrote intuitively, and we worked out how they could both be used at the same time to get an even better result. Both of us were thinking a million miles a second about how to start using the other's ideas on our own writing methods as soon as we got home.

We eventually got back up to the front and paid for the now-empty juice bottles we were carrying. The check-out girl smiled as she took those empties off the counter-top and put them together in her trash bin under it.

Outside, I handed Saul a bookmark for my latest book, which had my email on it.

He shook my hand, and I pulled him in for a brief hug. He held on for a bit longer and I let him, enjoyed it. All right there in front of the farm supply store in the broad, hot daylight.

XVI

I COULD HARDLY GET Martha out my head, and so I wrote her into the next few stories. All about a female genius detective who was able to solve mysteries almost without leaving her desk.

The plots seemed to deal with their competition of a similarly gifted male detective who had offices across town.

While the female detective was alluring and provocative and bubbly, the male detective was a bit sour on life and women and requisite social graces.

Yet they kept running into each other in the first book, finally meeting to exchange their clues and together apprehending the criminal so the officials could arrest them.

In the second book, they had an unofficial alliance and managed to resolve several unsolved "cold case" files the police had been baffled with. Between the two of them, they had answers to all the clues. But I had to insert a lot of action sequences, and inadvertent hand holding and close quarters to make the romantic sub-plot build.

By the third book, they were both completely unable to work with out the other nearby. Not only were their deductions becoming inaccurate, they were constantly referring to the other as the sole source of their distraction and inefficiencies. Finally, the villain tied them up together, face to face, to meet an untimely doom. Of course, they worked together to get out of that and then turned the tables on that arch-criminal so thoroughly that he quickly turned himself into the officials to avoid being hounded by this pair of detectives.

The fourth book started with them being in the same office and having a completely inexplicable case almost literally dropped on their head... But then I hit a blank wall.

We'd been emailing back and fourth, so I told her about this recent problem.

She asked me to send her the first three books in the series, so I attached them.

Within a couple of hours, I got back a reply. "Elementary, dear Saul. Your solution is that you have taken this entirely too seriously. And you aren't really familiar with how the female 'bubbly' detective would go about solving things. Attached is your second chapter, with proposed edits on your first. L. Martha"

I was stunned. And smiling from ear to ear.

Of course her edits were spot on, exactly what changes I would make. And they set the stage for her character to act. Her chapter was brilliant, and inserted elements that could be red herrings or real clues. Her touches and approach were nothing I would have thought possible or probable. And her character utilized mentions of settings and elements from the earlier three books that tied the series together beautifully.

By the end of the next day, I sent her third chapter, along with edits for her second. We then simply alternated chapters back and forth, involving each character in hopeless situations, usually saved by the other, until we truly had them into a nearly impossible scene.

And it was my turn to solve it, to write the final chapter.

But I couldn't.

So I called her.

It turns out she didn't live but a few miles away. And I changed into my go-to-town clothes to make the trip. As I had to go through the local village, I dropped by an upscale food-mart for a nice flowering potted plant, then a highway convenience store to get a fresh-made pizza along with a quart of sweet tea.

She met me at the door as I was walking up her steps, managing the pizza in one hand, the cold tea and potted plant in the other. She stepped outside to hold the door for me.

XVII

I TOLD SAUL TO HEAD to his right, where I'd set up everything on the dining room table. I set up an extra laptop next to my own, with plenty of space for food. Because I'd gotten a pizza as well, with extra meat - while his had extra vegetables. I had a pot of fresh coffee on, and the aromas through that small house were fragrant.

Of course, I loved the potted plant and told him so.

His face was amazing to see. He'd only thought we were going to make some notes or something, but when he saw my spare laptop set up, he just stood stock still. "Martha, did I ever tell you about your being the most brilliant woman I'd ever met?"

I blushed at this, a solid beet red.

He put down the pizza and tea and when he turned around, I grabbed him with both arms and kissed him a solid one.

Of course, he responded by holding me tightly in the finest hug I'd ever felt since I was a kid.

To say electricity filled the room was an understatement.

But at last we came up for air with smiles like teen agers on our faces.

I turned away, blushing again at what I'd just done. Opening up his pizza first, I started to pour the tea out into large cups when I felt his arm go across my shoulders.

"Thanks, Martha. That meant the world to me. I'll die peacefully tonight if nothing else." His low voice was gravelly.

I turned my head to his and saw tears welling up in his eyes. So I pecked another kiss on his grizzled cheek. "I think we had get started or we won't finish this book tonight, since we both know where that idea could go."

"Yes, my general." He winked at me.

Then we sat down and finished off a couple of pizza slices each while we tossed ideas back and forth.

It turned out that working on the same document in the cloud was perfect, especially after we got used to it. More or less, it turned out we took alternating paragraphs. Although if either of us introduced something new, he or I would then go up and tweak the earlier parts, even the earlier book, so everything flowed.

Finally, we wrapped everything up and both did final edits and proofed the whole book.

When it was done, we downloaded the ebook version and loaded it on our smart-phones to cross-check it. For that, we adjourned to the couch in the living room. I brought the laptop he had been using over, as it was lighter and took less room than my main one. Saul brought the second pizza with us.

We were ready to wrap it up for the night.

XVIII

WITH OUR FEET UP, MARTHA and I did our final proofing. Once we went through it and made our notes, she then started fixing these on her screen.

I had my arm across the couch back behind her head, holding my phablet so we could both see it.

She had the computer on her lap, and was typing away.

The pizza box was between our feet on the coffee table. That tended to push our hips toward each other, leaving enough room for her elbow between us.

Once we had finished, she typed "The End".

Then she surprised me with the cover. She had gotten the same artist I'd used for the first three books in that series. This cover had our two detectives in period clothing, tied face to face, and suspended above an unseen threat below.

She'd already written an excellent come-on description.

Martha handed the laptop over to me to read it all. And I logged into my publishing account and posted it, pre-scheduling it for a month ahead. Just in case we wanted to make any additions to it.

Martha kissed me on the cheek and then took the laptop out of my hands, closed it and put it on the top of the now-empty pizza box.

She returned to snuggle up next to me, with her head on my shoulder.

"I really liked that ending. Really." She murmured.

"I was surprised at the way it turned out," I replied.

"Oh, it was something you'd started way back in the first book. It was completely obvious they'd get together in the end." There was a smile in her voice, even if I could only see the top of her violet-scented hair.

"Was it that obvious?" I asked.

"Particularly when they argued so much in the second book, you could tell they were both in love with each other." Beth turned her head up to look at me.

"You know, that kinda sneaked up on me, but yes, by the third book, they were certainly a team." I replied.

She smiled at me. "And working so closely by this last book, they seemed almost joined at the hip, of one mind, invincible to the criminal class..."

I continued, "...such that all criminals began to have second thoughts about their choice of profession, as this detective duo would run down all leads, exhaust all trails and stop at nothing..."

"...to right any injustice within their purview. The people in this city and surrounding boroughs would rest easier tonight and forever more." Martha finished.

She thought for a moment and then looked up to me to ask, "Why did you have him propose to marry her at the end?"

"Because it seemed an obvious conclusion to the series. The next series would then start with them living together in happy matrimony - until 'a new arch-enemy contrived to interrupt their marital bliss through nefarious means'..." I smiled before continuing. "...and yet our plucky duo would always foil their evil plans and still return to their (only slightly interrupted) wedded heaven-on-earth."

Martha reached up and kissed me softly on my lips. "Sometimes you are too corny for your own good."

"So, what do you think?" I asked, eyebrow raised.

She sat up and turned toward me, and put both arms around my neck. Looking deeply into my eyes, "Of course, for me to agree, this means I'm going to have to learn to die each night, or you're going to have to quit dying."

I smiled back, broadly. "Since I've met you, I've thought of nothing else. And the answer is simple. Sometimes you have to laugh at death in order to get anything done. Especially when you've fallen deeply in love."

She pulled me closer to her until our eyes only looked into each other's and our lips were a only a tiny space apart.. "In that case, the answer is 'Yes.'"

THE NEXT MORNING, WE woke up together. To a new, exciting day with a fresh plot hatching that demanded we start writing it. After all, "the game was afoot."

All logical, elementary, and romantic.

Voices

BY J. R. KRUZE

ARE OUR DOGS SMARTER than we are about our own love life?

John woke one morning to his dog talking in his head, telling he needed to exercise, eat, and dress better, since he was about to meet the love of his life.

Jo's own dog told her how to dress that day and what to do in order to meet someone special.

All just in thoughts in their head. Of course, they couldn't tell anyone that their dog's had suddenly become telepathic.

But when John started talking to the young woman in front of him at a coffee shop he hardly ever visited, and when Jo met him for lunch "accidentally", then set up a date the next day on an impulse...

You had to think those voices in their heads maybe had already figured this all out.

Another clean, feel-good romance from J. R. Kruze - for lovers and dog aficionado's everywhere.

I

THAT MORNING I ROLLED over, bleary and tousle-headed to see my dog Wilma looking back at me.

"Good morning," the thought came to my head. "If you'd lay off those night-caps we can get your weight down and get a you laid more often."

The idea of this brought a smile to my face.

"Now that I have your attention, let's go for a walk before breakfast. You've got time before you have to go to your work." The thought had a some sense to it. "Of course it's sensible. Now get up, we have to get going. I'll wait until you put on your clothes."

At that my golden-haired red heeler, Wilma, stood and went to wait by the door to the room. "Come on, get up. Let's go." And just stared at me.

I looked at the clock, saw I had a half-hour before I usually got up to make my breakfast, and rolled over.

It only took a couple of tugs before my blanket and top sheet were on the floor.

That got my attention. I sat up. My dog let go of the bed clothes corner he had been pulling on and smiled.

"What are you doing?" I asked, looking at her through my bleary eyes.

"Taking care of my human," came the reply. "Come on. I meant what I said. It's time to change your habits to make you happier."

Couldn't argue with that. Especially now that I was awake. I swiveled my feet over to the floor and felt the cool carpet underneath them.

"Good boy! Let's get those sweats on. You can do it!" Wilma was encouraging.

Of course I resented it. Sounded like I was in training for something.

"Of course you're in training. Humans have to be trained every day of their lives. I'm not going to be around forever, so you've got to learn to survive so your next Master will be able to pick up where

I left off and hopefully help you retire in grace." Wilma cocked her head at me, wondering if I got it.

"This is all just a bit new. How, I mean, why, what..." I quit talking and just sent her my thoughts, jumbled as they were.

"Now you're getting it. We can have all sorts of discussions once you quit using your human speech. So backward and clumsy." Wilma rose and again walked to the door. "Sweats. Socks. Tennies."

Knowing I had no other choice, I complied. Sweats were hanging behind the door, white socks in a top drawer, Running shoes lined up on the floor under the dresser legs. Simple. In a few minutes, I was dressed and moving toward the front door. "No coffee?"

"No coffee. Get up, get some exercise. Get that metabolism going." Wilma insisted.

"Wait." I ducked into the bathroom to relieve myself.

Wilma had no comment at this. She was waiting when I finished, patiently.

"OK, I'm ready." I sent.

"That you are." She moved through the hallway, her toenails clicking on the wood floor, and waited by the door for me to open it.

Once we were through the door, she led off at a trot across the yard to the sidewalk. Pausing here, she looked back. "Well? OK, yes, stretch a little bit - like I do. You've got to get this habit in when you get out of bed. Arms overhead, side to side, each leg. You've got it. Time to move." And she started off down the concrete.

I had to take long steps to keep up with her. And wasn't succeeding. She'd be in traffic soon if I didn't catch up with her.

"Well, a trot would be nice - I think you call it jogging." Wilma sent.

"Yes, we call it jogging," as I broke into a jog, and it turned out to be comfortable. My being irked at her training approach turned into appreciation.

"Because you know it's for your own good." Wilma was panting now and keeping up a steady pace just ahead of me. "We'll round the block today and that will be a good start. You're in training now."

"Training for what?" I sent.

"We're going to get you a mate and sire a litter of your own."

I stopped at that, breathing heavy.

Wilma stopped and sat, panting, but not like mine. "Isn't that what you want? Well, we have to move. First steps first." She rose and turned to walk off, but was still looking at me.

I didn't move, so she turned back. "Look, I know this is sudden, but I'll explain more later. We only have so much time for this exercise before you have to get to work. And breakfast is between now and then. So keep up." Then Wilma trotted off.

We were halfway around the block, and I had no real choice. She was making too much sense this morning. So I jogged a bit faster to catch up. By the time I got to my home again, she was sitting and waiting by the front door to be let in.

"Why don't you use your own door?" I asked by thought.

"Because I need to make sure you keep your schedule. Come on, let me in. It's time for you to shower and make your breakfast." She rose, and looked at the crack in the door, waiting for me to turn that knob.

So I did. Too logical. Too sensible.

When I came out of my bedroom into the hallway, she was waiting again. I was showered, shaved and had my usual slacks and dress shirt on, with my work shoes on. I pulled out my tan corduroy jacket with the elbow patches, with the idea of wearing something different today. Looking down at my shoes, I saw some dust on them and brushed them off on the back of my pant legs.

"We'll work on that bad habit later. But first is breakfast and we'll go over your schedule." Wilma was going to change my life, one piece at a time. We walked into the kitchen and her claws again tick-tacked on the tile.

"How is that you're in my head now?" I sent to her.

"I've always been there, it's just that you started listening to me last night for the first time. Some humans take longer, I've heard, and some never get it. You're right around average. You're a good boy." Wilma was smiling. "Eggs today, lay off that sugar-cereal. We have to get your weight down. Your in training now."

I pulled out two eggs from the refrigerator and felt her insistence - three eggs.

Frying pan with a bit of oil. Wilma made me make a mental note to get coconut oil to replace that vegetable oil, and get some cottage cheese for omelet makings as well. Yes, I was in training. And I loved my coach.

"I love you, too. While they're cooking, fill my bowls so I have my own meals today." Wilma was sitting to the side, out of my way, smiling as usual.

I filled her food bowl with a pouring of dog bits, and her water bowl from the tap. Then I could smell my eggs as they were getting a bit hot, so turned to them with a stainless spatula to flip them once, taking them off the heat. I was about to put in bread for toast when Wilma interrupted.

"Nope. you're off all wheat until you learn to eat properly. And get some milk to wash it all down with. No coffee until you get to work. That's where you'll meet her today.

I put my three eggs and milk on my counter, sliding into a high chair near by. Wilma went to her own breakfast, eating only a few bites and lapping up a few mouthfuls before moving over to her brown rag-rug to lay down. Watching me eat, before laying her head down on her paws.

I'd finished off my eggs and eyed the jam on the counter.

"Of course you think you're hungry. But you don't have time to fix anything else now - you're in training and training means schedules. Time to go to work." Wilma was in my mind, but hadn't moved her head off her paws. "I'll keep track of you from here, don't worry. Run some water over that plate and fork. Truck keys are next."

She knew my patterns well. "OK, OK, not like I haven't done this before."

"Sorry, don't mean to push, but you have to see her when you're parking this morning." Wilma sent.

"Her?" I asked.

"Your new mate." Wilma turned at that and went to go find her dog bed. Or at least that's what I thought she'd be doing.

"One last thing," Wilma sent from the living room. "That color she's wearing today is russet. But her favorite is teal."

II

BEAU, MY BLACK COCKAPOO mix, made me get some exercise that morning, and picked out that scarf for me. Even though it was going to be a hot day out. I thought dogs were color blind, but apparently not so much. The yellows and golds in that scarf were to pull attention to my face, as Beau considered my russet blouse to be too boring.

Yes, he was in my head all morning. And had a few comments about the pounds I needed to lose. At least he was used to me walking around in my underwear as I tried different slacks until finally settling on a charcoal-gray mid-length skirt that would narrow my hips a bit.

Funny, but Beau said bigger hips were more becoming, it was a taut tummy and waist that were the real points to work on. The contrast made the rest stand out as accents.

How dogs figure this stuff out was because they spend so much time around humans? Or just their listening to the hen-clucking that goes on between friends.

Yes, they understand English - or whatever language we seem to think in, anyway.

He made sure I didn't make my own brew this morning. Told the business center had perfectly good coffee, plus I was supposed to meet someone in a tan corduroy jacket today. While waiting in line somewhere.

I wondered about how he knew all this stuff while I was driving to work. Funny how leaving just 15 minutes earlier meant less traffic and an easier drive...

III

THE COMMUTE WAS UNEVENTFUL. I was a little earlier than normal, thanks to my new "lifestyle coach" getting me up earlier. Just enough time to get a coffee from that new coffee shop that had opened in the upper level.

Standing in line, looking up at the wipe-off board with the various colored marker menu items, I saw her in front of me. Russet blouse with a gold, black, and tan scarf. Could be summer colors. At least she knew how to match, and put the most interesting items next to her face. Of course, her beautiful dark brunette locks are the next attraction, with the caramel highlights that pull your eyes up - and then she turns and a see the stunning silhouette. I'm smitten.

Fortunately, she turns back before I get too embarrassed and tongue-tied.

She orders her half-caf/decaf and I get an iced coffee. But she paid for mine. So I pay for the one behind me, which is some white-collar in a gray suit jacket. Don't make eye contact, just move along, I say to myself.

She's standing at the condiment counter adding in some raw turbinado sugar, stirring with one of those wood stirrers, then wiping off the counter when she's done mixing.

"Hey, thanks for getting my order." I said.

She turned and I saw a pair of the most delightful dark brown eyes I'd ever seen.

"You're welcome. It's pay-it-forward day. A perfect excuse to talk to people." She returned.

I noticed my gray-suited mouse had simply walked out of the store in a brisk pace, late for work I imagined. But I suppressed looking at my own watch.

"Say something nice about what she's wearing." Wilma was in my head again.

"That's a nice color combination - russet, gold, and black. Oh, by the way my name is John." I said.

"I'm Jo - short for Josephine. And thanks. Not many people seem to coordinate their colors these days." Jo replied.

"No, I think they dropped out color matching and complimentary colors trying to capture the millennial market. That said, warm colors are not usual for hot days. Teal might be a better choice if that's an option." I glanced at her top and noticed it was a conservatively buttoned blouse, probably a linen blend.

"I love teal, but wore it yesterday, so I thought to mix it up today." She smiled at this.

"It's good to be able to mix things up. Men are usually on the muted side of the color wheel, since jackets are expensive and most go for a narrow corporate look. And some simply don't care." I added.

"You're into colors?" Jo asked.

"It's part of my job. Probably the best part. I review ads for an agency and build their fliers." I replied. "Oh, I don't mean to keep you, we both have work to do. Can I ask you what work you do here?"

"I take care of the books for a few firms. My friend and I started a business for other small businesses who can't afford a regular person for just a few spreadsheets. I'm no CPA, but we can save their costs by setting up the books for someone else to prepare their taxes and so on. Kinda interesting, but kinda dull at times." She picked up her coffee and I followed out of the shop.

"Where do you work?" Jo asked.

"I'm on a lower level, at the end of one of those long hallways. I sometimes wonder what shops used to be there ever since the mall was converted to a "business center". How about you?" I turned to glance at her face as we walked.

She looked back at me, seeing if this was small talk or if I was really interested. "I'm on the top level, just over to the right. We pay more for the frontage, but so far our clients are covering our costs and then some." She stopped by the stairs and turned. "Well, I suppose you need to take these to work. Nice meeting you. I suppose we'll see each other around."

"That would be nice," I said honestly.

She smiled at this, seeming relieved to meet someone who didn't hit her up right off the bat. Nodding, she turned and went off toward her work.

I stood and watched her for awhile. Her modest heels and mid-length dark gray skirt still accentuated her legs, but were probably comfortable enough to work. She wasn't a mini-skirt type of young woman. Conservative. Polite. Smart. Wilma was right on this one.

IV

LUNCH I GOT FROM THE business center's sandwich shop, trying to get a bun with no wheat in it without much luck. I was going to have to study up on this if I was going to trim down. Taking his sandwich up to the top level, I looked out over the coming and going foot traffic. With any luck, I might see Jo again.

Almost half-way through my slowly nibbled poor-boy, I saw her scarf among the crowd. She was carrying a bagged lunch herself. And heading in my own general direction. So I picked up my newspaper and pretended to read the classified it was folded open to.

Soon, she came over and stood in front of me. As I saw those conservative brown shoes and gray skirt, I looked up and noticed how trim she was, how her skirt and blouse accentuated her waist, but the scarf took your attention right up to her face. And I got that rare, tingling feeling of seeing a woman I could definitely fall in love with - even though that wasn't on my particular to-do list today. Until Wilma had told me it was.

"Mind if I join you?" Jo asked.

"Sure, I'd be honored." Why I said that phrase I didn't know. But I saw her face take a tinge redder than usual, while her eyes twinkled at the idea.

Jo sat, "That's an old phrase I haven't heard for awhile. You don't read classics do you?"

"Romances, not strictly. But I'm going through the Alexander Dumas series, which are technically romance, but I'm reading for the swashbuckling. Part of my research." I bit off another small bite so I could keep the conversation going without having to gag myself swallowing.

"Your research? A writer?" Jo was unwrapping her own egg-salad sandwich in a what looked like a home-made flat bread.

"Yes, I'm working on short stories as I build a backlist. At least I can save money by creating my own covers. But how about you? Is cooking your hobby - that looks like a great lunch - and did you bake that bread yourself?" I ran all this out, realizing that I'd just gotten nervous for some reason.

Jo just smiled, dimples in her cheeks helping me relax, but also fascinating me. "So many questions - yes, yes, and I also write."

I felt a tinge coming up my neck into my own cheeks, but made myself speak instead of taking another bite to hide it. "What genre do you like to write in most?"

"Romance, but the clean kind - not these wild semi-erotic ones with bare male torso's on every cover. That's great about doing your own covers. Graphic arts training?" Jo asked.

"Sure..." And our conversation went back and forth for the next half-hour until I glances up at the big central clock and saw my time was almost up.

Jo noticed. "About that time? Say, answer me one last question: I know we've hardly met, but there's a book signing by some local author at the shopping mall's book store. Would you like to meet there for lunch tomorrow, or is your Saturday taken?"

I stopped in my tracks. "I don't mean to sound forward, but there is nothing I'd like better. I was hoping we could trade more notes about writing and such."

She smiled that heart-melting smile of hers and nodded. "About 11:30 then? I'll meet you on that bench right outside their front door."

The rest of the afternoon went in a delightful blur. I had a date to look forward to, the first one in years.

V

THE SMILE NEVER LEFT my face all afternoon working on the books. Of course, I had to stop and double-check my column entries as I went. Because I kept getting distracted by that short lunch conversation.

This guy John was just too interesting. Weird meeting him just like Beau had told me.

And he was a writer like me. Both had day jobs which weren't too boring, and he did his own covers. Something I always had trouble with. Maybe he could give me some pointers.

Finally, I just gave up working for the day. It was Friday, anyway.

I looked up his books and found a couple I was interested in, at least by their setting. Then put them into my account to read when I got home.

And that face of his, that rugged jaw line. The tiny scars on his hands showed that he worked with them, or used to. Maybe he used to do manual paste-up, or some other background in other work than offices. Some tan on his hands, showing that he got sun at least part of the year.

But he was very good at turning the conversation back to finding out about me. I was flattered more by this than anything else. And wish I'd gotten more of his background. That was the reason for a Saturday lunch meet. Daytime was much safer. And me asking him kept the balance in this. A neutral location that I could walk away at any point if things went south.

I tidied everything up and ran backups on all the files. My partner was out for the day working up some deals to close for us, so I had the office to myself.

Last thing was to check the answering machine and layout notes for the next week's work, check the wipe-off scheduling board and update it with new to-do time frames. Nothing too exciting.

Locking up, making my way to my car, it was pretty much a blur. My mind was on this new fellow again. "Three Musketeers" was definitely a romance, although not many people considered it that way. Mainly because of the movies. But it was probably the appeal to both sexes in his writing. I'm sure that tomorrow's conversation was going to be just as interesting.

Before I started my car up, I let it cool with the A/C running full blast and the windows cracked down to let the hot air out. I meanwhile downloaded his books onto my smartphone and let the text-to-speech start reading it for me.

The ride home was a pleasant one, I had no hurry and so could take my time through the rush-hour traffic by not rushing. John's writing was good, and his dialogue showed a real understanding of human interaction. That he treated the women as co-protagonists with men was another plus. More fascinating was blending the love interest with the mysteries and action in every short story. Always a twist at the end.

Before I knew it, I was driving up to my duplex and parking. Sitting there with the engine and A/C running to catch the tail end of another story, while I followed along by reading the screen.

This guy could write, and talk well. Tomorrow looked to be a good one.

VI

WILMA MET ME AT THE door, tail wagging and a big grin on her face. "So? Tell me all about it - and you can talk out loud if it's more comfortable for you."

I set down the groceries on the counter and bent to scratch her head and back, letting her lick my hand when she signaled she'd had enough. Then I talked about the whole incident in meeting her, while I emptied the shopping bag and put everything away. I told Wilma about our lunch, her asking me on a date at the bookstore, and then I ran out of things to say. Just a smile on my face that alternated with worry lines on my forehead.

"Of course, it's going to go alright." Wilma sent. "You did good today. We're going to take this on with baby steps. The main point is to keep the interest on her and do the male-protector/provider thing."

"It's just been so long - for both of you. So don't rush it. Tonight, you have some homework." Wilma turned and left the kitchen toward the living room. "I'll leave you to your dinner. Good job on finding those buckwheat wraps."

After dinner, I was about to turn on the TV, when Wilma was there beside me and in my head.

"Nope. Keep the boob tube off. Time for homework, like I said. Get your phablet - you've got some reading to do." At that, she laid down on her dog bed and watched me retrieve it from the kitchen.

"Now, find her books. She probably uses initials for her first name. You did get her last name, right?" Wilma asked in my mind.

I stopped in my tracks. Silly me. She'd told me she was published and how she worked on the titles to get one just right, finally settling on - oh, right. I took the phablet and searched for that book title. And there was the face of the author. With that heart-melting smile I knew her by. I bought and downloaded it to read.

Homework had never been more fun. She wrote well, and pulled me right into the story. This told me all about how she wanted to be treated. Fascinating. A window right into her soul.

The night went on and I took the phablet to bed so I could try to finish it. But fell asleep before I could.

VII

BEAU SUGGESTED, AND I agreed to doing a few extra crunches this morning. Looking myself over in the full length mirror, I grabbed my waist between thumb and finger to see how much I could lose. I frowned at this. No way to get that much off any time soon. I should have been dieting months before this.

"You'll look fine. For a human, you're curvy, that's what counts. And the running we do has kept your hips down, which is the key point. Dark slacks, light loose top. Try that knit layered bandeau - the one you call teal - under that light jacket you have. Dark slacks will let a little midriff show but give tummy support - that he'll like. And bra-less will give a little flounce to your walk, but you'll have enough support to not look too come-on-ish." Beau cocked his head to the side as he rattled this off into my mind.

I had no clue where he was getting all this stuff.

But he's the one who said I needed to "attract a stud" so I could "whelp a litter." All just short of calling me the b-word, which was appropriate for dogs, but offensive to humans - weird, I know. Somehow, Beau made it all sound natural, if not romantic.

And romance makes the world go round.

Still, I knew that regardless of how my job was fascinating, my biological clock was ticking.

I finished up John's volume of short stories that morning after I got dressed to go out. Made highlighted notes on my smartphone where I could ask him about how he wrote that.

And headed out to the shopping mall a little early - never hurt..

VIII

WILMA ALMOST ESCORTED me out the door to my pickup truck.

After she put me into a knit polo shirt under another jacket on top of some comfortable jeans. Moc-toed slip-ons instead of boots. "You're tall enough already," she pointed out.

I'd had some comments about why all this getting dressed up and stuff, but Wilma quickly shut it down. "You're courting, remember that. Males and females of any species preen a bit -

not just too much. You're both old enough to have your glands under control, but young enough to know what to do with them. Remember that."

On the drive over, I listened to her book from the second to last chapter. I liked the twist and how it ended with a surprise, even though we knew there was a happily-ever-after coming up. Maybe she could tell me how she came to that.

Two authors taking about books in the middle of an afternoon, what is a better first date than that?

And if I was a bit early, maybe I could search around inside - as long as I kept track of the time. I'd been known to lose a couple of hours easily just roaming the aisles and aisles of books...

IX

HE WASN'T THERE YET, great. I could do some browsing. See what my competition was coming out with, and see if there were any how-to books that could actually teach me something...

Soon, I was literally over my head in the stacks and looking over the covers as well as flipping to the back pages to see how they wrapped it up. First and last, that was the kicker for any book. Did they pull you in and did they leave you wanting more?

I was looking a bit wider this time, looking for romantic mysteries, not just the stock romance which always had the same plot. I'd even read that you can open almost any romance to a certain page percentage and find what plot twist turned where. The industry had become too predictable for any but they most die-hard romance avid reader escapist.

Probably why the prices had slid so much. None of the other store rows had so many discounted books...

MYSTERIES. LOVED TO see these. But I was looking for the ones with strong romantic interests in them. Not just a bunch of salacious semi-porn thrown in - but you could tell that by their covers.

I checked on the bookstore's site to see what they were pushing right now in that area, and the book descriptions. At least I'd be able to find the area.

Head down into my smartphone, I had to stop to avoid someone else in the aisle.

That hair. Had to be her. Nice outfit. Fetching. I was stopped dead in my tracks. This is what Wilma talked about when she said "preening a bit."

And I'd never met a woman who couldn't out-preen a man. And being stopped in my tracks was preening I could live with.

The problem was that I was stuck with what to say and how to interrupt her, what was polite, what would be too over the top. I had a mouth open to say something and couldn't.

A SLIGHT SHADOW CAME over the book I was reading and glanced over to see some moc-toed shoes under some very comfortable-looking jeans. I closed the book with my finger in it to hold my place. This author was pretty good and I was a sucker for great prose.

I moved forward to give him space to move and only then looked up.

John. With a nervous smile forming out of that open mouth.

"Hi." I said.

"Hi." John returned.

"Guess we're both early and looking for something." I managed to eke out.

John just smiled. That one he has that puts you right at ease. Well, that does it for me, anyway.

"Find something you like, I mean that book in your hand?" John stumbled, which made me smile, and then made him blush.

"And it's great you came along when you did," I teased. "It was just getting to the mushy part."

Then his face turned really red. And he laughed out loud.

"Well, what page are you on, maybe we could get through it together?" He joked.

I had to laugh at that, too. He had a book of his own in his hand, so we headed toward the checkout counter so we could make good on our lunch date.

X

"I SAW YOUR SHOES AND I was glad you dressed for comfort." Jo said.

"Yes, she told me not to wear my boots as I was tall enough already." I replied.

"She?" Jo looked puzzled.

"Oh, you're not going to believe this, but my dog has been giving me pointers on dressing. She's a red heeler named Wilma."

Jo's mouth opened wide. "Like a voice in your head? And they know stuff they couldn't possibly?"

It was my turn to be open-mouthed. "You have a dog that dresses you?" I asked.

"His name is Beau and said you'd like a little flounce. He picked out this outfit." Jo said with a touch more red in her own cheeks.

I had to smile to keep from laughing. "Well he certainly got that right. Those are great colors, and they so match your hair. But your hair is how I saw you first - you're not going to tell me he recommended your hairdresser as well?"

"No, he only started talking in my head a couple of days ago. So my hair styling was my own. As far as I know, anyway." Jo relaxed and smiled again.

As the line moved and we were up at the counter, she took my book out of my hands and paid for both of them.

And I paid for our lunch after that. The following conversation took a long time as now we compared notes about dogs and how they groomed us, in addition to the many questions we each had about each other's books and our decisions and choices about prose, plots, story structures, and so on.

When we tired of sitting, we took a long walk through the rest of the mall. Up one side and down the other and stopping anywhere in between that caught our eye.

Finally, it was so late we walked to a local restaurant across the parking lot and shared the ticket.

The only clumsy part was saying our good-byes. We ended up writing our phone numbers on each other's receipts.

OF COURSE WILMA AND Beau each got a complete report on how it went when we got home.

And we never did figure out if they had been helping us all along. Or if they just "suddenly" became smarter than us overnight.

We started collaborating with each other as first-readers and even co-authors, which meant a lot of long weekends together. Our books started to take off after that, and sales online more than covered our living expenses, so that soon were able to rent a house in the country with plenty of room for writing offices, as well as space for Beau and Wilma to run every day.

But we do share our two-year old daughter now, and another boy on the way. We've been married for three years and enjoyed every moment of it. It turns out that our dogs also have a lot of good advice for book publishing as well. Especially since everyone we deal with in this industry seems to have a dog...

The Case of the Walkaway Blues

BY J. R. KRUZE & S. H. Marpel

I

I CAME FOR THE PIE - to glue back together the pieces of my broken heart.

Comfort food. That's why I got the ice cream on top.

Apple pie. Something wholesome. All-American. Innocent.

Like the innocence and beliefs in America I'd lost long ago.

Not just any ice cream. They stocked a special cinnamon-vanilla ice cream which turned their apple pie into a piece of heaven. One that gave meaning to the phrase "pie in the sky."

Perfect for soaking the pain out of my soul, for mending the rips in my heart that the lies had left.

I hardly noticed the man who sat on the counter stool next to me. The place was packed this time of day, the usual lunch crowd. And their blue-plate special was nearly as good as their dessert.

But nothing mattered to me more than the ice cream in front of me. One small bite at a time. Getting all the comfort out of it I could.

"Is she having your famous apple pie a la mode? Please give me a slice just like hers." The man spoke in a Midwestern accent, obviously not from around here. I only glanced at the sleeve of his tan corduroy jacket. While his hands were lined from use, their light tan showed he got outside to work. Might even be a visitor to the city.

My thoughts turned back to my ice cream. Even the term "city" brought back the anguish I'd only started realizing days before. When I found out the secret that had been hidden all this time.

It was worse than watching the election returns. That night, I drowned my sorrows in a full bottle of Chardonnay, along with a friend who came over to watch with me. She got the couch while I managed to drop fully-clothed onto my bed before losing consciousness.

The next morning we didn't know what was worse - how our heads felt or that we had to go to work in that condition. I let her borrow a fresh blouse and slacks, the least I could do. But I saved that bottle. And it probably was the first step to uncovering the long list of lies that didn't seem to quit.

Today, I was here again. A non-alcoholic way to keep the sorrows at bay. At least my regular few hours in the gym daily would take off the excess calories my emotions required.

"Isn't this just the greatest dessert ever?" The stranger asked me. "I've heard about this all over town, and finally came to try it."

I had to nod and smile briefly in agreement.

"I don't mean to seem forward, but that smile makes your face look better." He held his hand out. "Hi, I'm John."

"Mary," I said as I shook his hand. "And thanks for the kind word."

"Anything to help a fellow traveler through this wild world we live in." John replied.

"I could agree with 'wild' world. Even worse than the Old West. It was hard enough back then to find the law and get them to act, so scammers and criminals tended to get away with murder or worse." I replied.

"You're a Western fan?" John asked.

"Yes, my favorite is L'Amour, but I also go to Max Brand and Zane Grey. The classics generally are better than what's come since.

But I take a break now and then for a good mystery by Doyle or Chesterton." I warmed to talking about my favorite diversions.

"It's just too bad there aren't more cross-over books. Good western mysteries are so hard to find. I have seen this in some of Brand's books, and even L'Amour, but the mystery usually plays second-fiddle to the action. That even happens in the Western romances, though." John replied between mouthfuls.

"You might want to slow down on that pie - two helpings are just going to add pounds you will have to work off." I suggested.

John looked down at the next fork-full of pie, and set it down to halve it. "Thanks. You've got the better approach. Treat it as a delicacy, not as a main course. Time enough to enjoy the simple things."

"True. It's good to take time to sort things out instead of rushing into them all the time." I sighed.

John continued on talking about books, "Most of the Western mysteries wound up on TV to get any real series of them. Like 'Hec Ramsey' and 'McCloud'. But there just isn't the same flavor as reading it in text."

"You must like mysteries." I mused.

"It's my living. I do write other genres, and of course the best books have all three story structures in them. Mystery, Romance, and Action. But cozy mysteries and clean romances are my current best sellers. People seem to be looking for more light-hearted entertainment these days." John replied.

"That's what I like about Westerns. You don't have all this 'I'm a victim' stuff out there. It was back in the days where there was still an American Dream that you could do something about." I took another small bite to savor. I used a spoon instead of a fork, because the sauce was the secret and a fork left too much on the plate.

"You're right there. Even when 'Gunsmoke' was still on the air, there was some understanding of what is right and wrong." John replied. He saw my spoon option and tried it himself. The look on his face was priceless as he closed his eyes in delight.

"And probably goes back to your cozy mysteries and clean romance. Back in the 'Gunsmoke' days, you hardly even saw Matt Dillon and Kitty ever kiss. Different times." I sighed again.

John noticed my glumness had returned. "What's your favorite mystery?"

I had to take my time with that one. So I kept the spoon in my mouth upside down while I looked at the wall where it met the ceiling. "Well, that would be Doyle, I suppose. He wrote so many good ones. Probably "The Final Problem." I replied at last.

"What made you choose that one?" John asked me.

"Of course Doyle always started out well, but what kept me going was how he pulled the idle strings of so many Holmes stories together to wrap up what he thought to be the death of his character." I replied.

"Only to bring him back to life later." John added. "Something the later movies all seem to take into account."

I smiled slightly at that. John was taking my mind off my other matters. "You aren't trying to cheer me up with all this talk of favorite books?"

John smiled. "Well, since it's so obvious, yes. An odd habit of my old optimistic self. Sorry if that bothers you."

"Not at all. It's about the best I've felt in maybe years." I replied.

"Years? What has been haunting you all that time?" John asked, then paused. "Oh, you don't have to answer that. I don't mean to pry, it's just my writer's nature."

"What nature does a writer have that is prying?" I asked in return.

"A writer, or at least this writer, wants to know all about a character. Frequently one that is haunted has an unsolved mystery in their lives. Ghost stories are just another version of mysteries, along with riddles and detective stories. Carolyn Wells laid that out a century ago. Once you can start seeing the mystery, then the story starts writing itself, like any good story." John explained.

"How does your prying-optimism solve personal hauntings?" I had to ask.

John replied,"It's not the hauntings, but that the technical back end to mysteries, the ones writers use to build their stories. That's what can be used to solve continuing mysteries and problems..."

II

"WAIT A MINUTE – PERSONAL problems are mysteries?" I protested, even not taking my next bite.

"Sure. If you knew everything about a problem there isn't any mystery to it. In fact, that is one of the key ways that geniuses of all time have solved problems - to ask questions and define everything there is about a problem. Same rough idea that the detectives in mysteries use to solve cases." John took another small bite to highlight his point.

"You're saying these imaginary detectives, and their contrived actions are able to solve our modern problems - if Holmes showed up today and sat on the other side of you, you could give him problems like 'Global Warming' and he'd sort it out for you?" I was letting my ice cream melt and saturate the last of my pie at this point.

"More or less, yes. What I'm actually saying is that if you know how a mystery is written, you'll be able to apply that to personal problems and solve them." John then scraped the last of his own sauce and crumbs off his plate and pushed those few drops into his mouth, smiling at the final taste.

Eying my own saturated crust, I simply started to scrape this up and finish it off before it at least got as high as room temperature.

"Would you like some coffee? I'm having one." John asked.

I nodded in reply, too busy working to enjoy the last drips of this incredible dessert.

John rolled ahead. "Any plot has a character with a problem in a setting. In most mysteries, the crime occurs at the beginning or before the beginning of the story itself. A crime is a non-optimum solution that has been made against the published laws. A simple mystery solves the problem by finding the hidden optimal solution. Detectives have to both solve the how-dun-it of the criminal, and also determine his motivation and prevent him from repeating the crime again. That concept can be applied to almost any life situation, if not all of them."

"Almost? Like what would be exempt?" I asked.

The coffee arrived. John put honey in his. I put imitation cream in mine, with white sugar.

John sipped slightly and let it cool a bit on the saucer. "Mostly any exception has to do with miracles, or supernatural events. Ghost stories fall into this. But there's a modern school that solves the incomplete actions ghosts have been trying to solve that they couldn't while alive. And that brings them closer to the Western ideal that the story has to end up with a positive outcome."

"So other than an act of God, we're able to solve anything?" I summarized.

"Generally, yes. Of course an impossible problem is easy to set up. But the locked room murders have long been solved in fiction and in real life." John sipped again and smiled. "Their coffee is almost as good as their pie."

"OK, let's test this. My problem is that I caught the media lying to me." I tried my own coffee and now wished I'd had real cream and honey in it instead. Maybe the next cup, if our conversation lasted that long.

"Well, that's not too much of a problem. They've been lying for years. Practically, the Hearst Yellow Journalism all but created

the Spanish-American War. But it never really got better after that."
John took another quick sip. "The problem is not that the
corporate news media lie, it's that we get to believing what they say
is true."

I let that sink in for a bit. "So it's more that they have been
telling me something that I really wanted to believe, in a way that I
would believe it."

"Believing makes facts, as William James more or less said.
When you believe in something enough, it starts creating that
reality for you. In our day and age, it's much simpler to figure
that the mob all believes one way, so it must be true in fact. But
facts have an odd way of being difficult to disguise when we have
more eyeballs than ever on the same set of data." John stopped and
looked at me to make sure he wasn't getting too far ahead.

I swallowed a mouthful of my cooling coffee. "Here's where
bias comes in. You want to believe so-and-so will get elected, so you
cherry pick your data and then phrase it so it has to be true."

"Sure. I only wish more fiction writers worked for the media
sometimes. Because then at least we'd get decent entertainment out
of it. Most of these news stories are the worst form of mysteries.
They say 'so-and-so horrible event just happened, and here's what
we know. But then the story ends. You never get a build up or a
resolution to any of these stories. Especially since the courts draw
this out for years before the last appeal is ever heard. Lousy
entertainment. Just one car wreck after the next. 'Thanks for
visiting our show - hope you can make it tomorrow for more of
the same...'" John sighed at this and shook his head. It's no small
wonder that the news channels and programs now crow about
holding the top spot, when that title only means who lost the least
viewers from the month before." He now took a decent gulp of
coffee. All his talking had let it cool way down.

"I've felt that myself - where I get so upset after watching the news that I want to do something bad, and those studies about social media being a cause of depression. That must be related to it." I said.

"Well, there could be a lot of additional factors in it. And that's not to say that you shouldn't pick out the stories you want to follow and then stick to those. People will do that anyway. The line we are going down is that knowing how good mysteries are written will let you see how to solve problems in real life. The problem we were approaching is that a person wants to believe something is true and so it becomes true for them. The actual concrete facts won't necessarily support what's being said. Like the old Polynesians said, 'Truth is as valuable as it is workable.' That implies you test everything for yourself." John drained his cup and signaled the waitress for another.

While she was coming, I also swallowed my last bit. Time to test that honey he used last time.

III

"THAT WAS EXACTLY THE point I ran into. I wanted to believe one side would win and when they didn't, I got depressed. And then that side started finding all sorts of things bad with the guy who did win. But the media was spinning the data and slanting it so that their lies became presented as truth." I stopped to let the waitress refill my cup and stirred honey into it as I watched it steam, just as John did to his.

"That's exactly what a detective-mystery writer will do. The actual facts of the case are boring. Forensic science is incredibly dull and repetitious. So you leave out the boring parts and trim it down to just the key points that people want to hear. Uncle Tom's Cabin was just like that. Not true at all. But people wanted to believe it was factual. Abolitionists were completely intolerant and forced the Southern states into a war they couldn't win. Before that, everyone was mostly working to find a solution to the problem of slavery. We don't need to go there - the point is that fiction is no better than any news reporting. Except that when it's well done, you get some relief from the 'real world' for awhile. You know it's all made up, and that's what makes it fun. Good fiction will give you a good feeling - well, unless you're reading tragedies or horror stories. But those are also emotions that get stirred up by fiction." John paused to sip again.

That was my cue to jump in. "A good mystery, like a good romance, then has a pattern they follow to get the emotional result that reader's expect."

"Exactly. Westerns all follow a rough model, mainly that the hero wins in the end. Almost all good fiction has the lovers reconciled, the mystery solved, the evil is trumped by the good guys." John said.

"So if you are getting a bad result from what you think is factual 'news' then maybe you'd be better off doing something else?" I asked.

"Certainly if you want to feel better. Ads don't make you feel better, either. And a quarter of the time you are watching news, you are being interrupted by ads. Imagine how you would feel if out of a hundred page book, 25 of them were advertisements for stuff completely dis-related to the story?" John replied.

"Maybe getting my news off the Internet is a better idea." I supposed.

"Only if you can test what they say. The next barrier is knowing what you are expecting." John took another sip.

"Expecting? Oh - this is like knowing where the plot is heading." I replied.

"Mostly. In that election, people so wanted their candidate to win that when she didn't, they all got depressed. That was a bad story to them. And then people started running other stories like the election was falsified somehow and a fraud. But those new stories were more wishful thinking than anything else. So when those stories failed, they got even more depressed. And that let to more stories..." John trailed off.

"How does that solve the problem?" I asked

"Any author has to know what their character wants. And their flaws as well. Robert Cialdini chased back his own flaws to see how the store's sales people told him made him buy stuff he really didn't want. He narrowed it down to just six points in a book called 'Influence'. And marketers seized on these as 6 points they could use to get people to do whatever they want." John ticked these off on his fingers. "Like giving something away so you feel you've got to give something back - or buy something. Or getting you into the habit of buying a certain product. Social "proof" is another, which is where all these fake reviews come from. Smiling is a way people get you to buy from them, but that's almost too obvious. Being an authority, or claiming someone else holds your opinion in regard." Holding up the thumb of his other hand - "...and the tried and proven one - not enough to go around (a limited time offer.)"

"Do these work?" I asked.

"Just consider them. They are in every thing you buy. Pleasant waitresses get better tips. The front door has little stickers saying what credit cards are accepted here. Having only a single piece of cake left on display. Free samples of food with a discount coupon if you buy today - that's a two-for. Look over your own habits and you'll see how these are all ingrained." John went back to his coffee while I thought this over.

"I can see you're right in these. So they make what you say sound like it's true?" I asked.

"Of course. You believe in the authority of that person and so what they say has to be true. But the kicker is what locks these in place." John paused. Waiting for effect.

I nodded that he continue.

John put his cup down on the counter. "A guy named Levenson in the 50's worked out that there were really only three or four elements that glued all these human foibles in as habits. Well before Cialdini worked his 'Influence' points out. Levenson said that the world revolved around needing or trying to escape from these: approval, control, and security. Singly and in combinations. You want approval for what you do, you're trying to escape being controlled, and you wish you were more secure. And these three are especially show up in media and politics."

I frowned at him. "But you mentioned a fourth..."

IV

"YES, THEY ARE ALL THREE based on fear, particularly the fear of losing one's own identity. Some call this death, but there are other ways these days to completely change a person's identity over time. Political parties often can get a person to do and say things they wouldn't normally think of on their own. Mob psychology is a study just on those types of actions. You can see all three of those basic points there, as well as Cialdini's six points leading up to that extreme behavior." John returned to his coffee, but noticed this second cup was now running low. He frowned at the decision he was going to have to make.

"And I see that many of these are present now, in just your question of having a third cup. Are you asking yourself if it will keep you up tonight - or perhaps allow your inspiration to come more quickly? Will it throw you off your schedule - lose security? Or will that new story get you more income and approval from your editor or the buying public? John, this stuff is fascinating!" I was smiling now. Here was some tools I could use to sort out these problems.

John decided. He called over the waitress and asked for a large sweet tea to go. She asked him if he'd like a sweet bun to take the edge off that coffee and he agreed.

I raised an eyebrow at this - he saw it and smiled. "Yes, she used a sales tactic on me. And it will get her a bigger tip as a result. Even though I know I should get some extra walking in tonight, if only pacing my office while I work out a plot outline. You're catching on quick to all this."

"Yes I do think that this has some 'workability' to it." But when I considered the amount of data I had to test now, I frowned again. "It just seems like 'where do I start' has raised its head."

"Levenson used releasing, which is another way of just letting go. Like taking a deep breath and then letting it out. Often you'll feel the body relax when you do. Something that doesn't work is just like that - just let it go. Take one idea at a time and test it. If it doesn't work, let it go. Just walk away from it." The waitress brought his tea and the sweet bun in a small bag. John smiled at this, and leaned on the counter to pull out his wallet and pay the check. Of course, he told the waitress to keep the change.

When I turned to pay mine, I see he already had, leaving his mint for me as well. "So I'm supposed to do something for you now? Or should I just thank you and walk away?" I was smiling at him now.

John smiled in return. "Your smile is all the payment I could ever want. But if you do want to do something..." He reached into his pocket and pulled out a thin paperback. "Here, one of my recent stories. If you want, read it and go online to leave a review if you like it. Or not. Your choice."

I accepted the book and looked it over. A western detective story. How quaint. "Or I could simply leave it here on the counter and walk away?"

"Sure. I would take that as a compliment as well." He smiled. "Now to make this offer completely irresistible, I'll autograph it for you." He pulled out a pen, took the book from me and scribbled in the flyleaf, then handed it back. All smiles again. "Or - leave it and walk away."

At that, he picked up his cup and bun, nodded to me and stood to leave. "Mary, it's been quite an experience. You've given me another inspiration for a story that I have to get to my office before I forget the details of it. You're a treasure. I do hope we can meet again some time." He glanced outside. "Oh - there's my bus. Thanks again."

And he was out the door before I could say another word.

BUT WHEN I OPENED TO the fly leaf and read what he wrote, it was obvious that we'd meet again. And now I had another reason to look forward to a follow-up conversation.

Because he wrote his phone number in there as well.

Our Second Civil War

BY R. L. SAUNDERS AND C. C. Brower

I

I COULD HEAR HER SCREAM in my dreams. Every night. Who she was and how to find her was a mystery.

But I knew I had to try. Or the dreams would never let me sleep normal again.

Not that it was going to be easy. Ever since the Great Secession, it was nearly impossible to get people into (or out of) the big city areas. You could get news out of their jammed "acronym media networks" easier.

But 'Cagga was less impossible than most. And that was where my dreams told me to search first.

I was here to get those dreams out of my sleep.

I'd been called many times, for many things, but this was the most annoying one I'd ever had to live. Not that you'd call it living. Because sleep was one continuing nightmare for me. Not really a lot of sleep, just a lot of waking in a cold sweat, plus a lot of tossing and turning. I even had to get my own room because of all the yelling I'd do.

So going to 'Cagga was for my own survival, as well as anyone around me.

Lots of smiles got me through 'Cagga's gates. The guards didn't want to shake my hand, but waved me through behind the glass in their guard booth. Us "unclean" were only going to another slightly less unclean space - where the guards never went.

218

Just to find this woman or girl or whoever is keeping me awake at night.

She was in here somewhere. I hoped.

LET ME BRING YOU UP to speed:

I'd been a foot-soldier in those civil wars, and had become a Brownie in self-defense. Because I wanted to help people. Got trained in first aid and counseling.

There had been decades of guerrilla warfare through the corporate media and their supporters in the East and West Megalopolises. That was also where the "social" networks had their headquarters - of course both the "media" and "socials" only allowed what they wanted spread.

Those lies caused violence, and someone was needed to patch them up. Or so I thought at the time.

The more people found out that they were being depressed and strung along, they quit social media and quit corporate news. Life became easier and simpler, more peaceful that way.

Which meant they were training everyone who saw through it to simply ignore them. Sad. Yuge fail.

People tend to move to where they find people who think like themselves. So it became that cities had higher densities of "victimized" minorities. While independent "cusses" grew their food and shipped their orders out of warehouses, and drove their trucks for "overnight" delivery. Those "independents" lived outside the cities, and for awhile were like the "pony express" of moving orders to "re-distribution" centers just outside them. But that only lasted for awhile, until the walls were built.

People also learned to stay out of cities where the protests were staged. That's where the violence was going to happen. It wasn't violence against the rest of the rural and suburban nation, but violences between the far left and extreme far left factions. Essentially, the cities were becoming even more violent, while the rest of the nation sympathized, but stayed away.

I'd finally given up working in cities after being attacked in one too many after-protest triage centers. The final straw was when they started protesting the "lack of diversity" in the doctors, nurses, and paramedics that were trying to stitch and bandage and medicate the wounded and dying they created.

It was easier helping people to find their own balance in life, some version of religion they could believe in, that worked for them. Even if it meant carrying a gun in self-defense, or letting others around them carry. Something you couldn't do inside their "tolerant" cities.

All that violence kept tourist dollars out out of cities. They should have learned from Russia's Crimean fiasco years ago - money likes peace. And their millionaires mostly left or entrenched themselves with walls and private security (as well as the usual well-placed "contribution" to various politicians, and buying up the media.) Because city resident's taxes went higher and higher, while more benefits were paid to people without a way to earn them. Unemployed violent protest-mobs were easy to stir into a riot, especially when they could be recorded easily and broadcast widely.

That set the stage for a settlement. The cities wanted to live their life (as it was) without "interference" while the rest of the country was tired of having to hear about their victimage lifestyle. Because what passed for "news" was simply their opinions about how the rest of the nation should act. Made up. Just for city residents.

While the rest of the nation yawned and turned to family viewing, like old specials recorded decades earlier. When people used to "live and let live" and welcomed Mr. Rogers into their homes.

They said the Second Civil War was over in minutes. Only took some high mucky-muck that long to sign a paper. Then the cities were allowed to go their own way, more or less. They didn't want anything to do with the "deplorable, intolerant bigots clinging to their religion and their guns" while the rest of the country was tired of their violence-inciting rhetoric, two-faced politicians, and fake news.

Of course, cities had already built their walls around themselves. To replace having to have National Guardsman with their "assault weapons" encircle their boundaries. People felt "triggered", they said. (Odd choice of words.) The rest of the nation didn't want the city violence spreading out into their quiet neighborhoods. "Good Riddance!" was a headline from the online alternative media.

For cities like 'Cagga, it just meant that their cost of raw materials was going up. Getting anything to their port on GLakes was now subject to U. S. Federal tariffs, as they controlled the waterways.

They could always fly anything in from N'Yack or L'angalez if they wanted, as long as they could land on water. But you could only carry so much. Fuel and parts weren't cheap. A different sort of tax. There was some talk about bringing back the Zeppelins, but it was just talk. No place big enough in those cities and not enough raw materials.

Not to mention that there were tariff wars between Feds and Secessionist Cities that made getting anything in or out of urban areas nearly impossible.

And once they seceded, the media imprint only really reached their own populations, since they lost their broadcast licenses to anywhere else in the nation they had left. No one else tuned in, anyway. For awhile, some of the suburbs had jamming stations that would cross-broadcast across their signal.

Once the cities cut power and water, that pretty much made the suburbs into wilderness or desert. Useless for farming. Ghost towns only good for deconstruction into building materials for cities.

What really made the suburbanites move out was the plagues. They started in city hospitals when their antibiotics and medicines wouldn't work. And their solution was to put them in clinics outside their walls to protect everyone inside. Of course, this meant that their diseases would spread to all those "deplorables" who lived out there.

Being anywhere near a city became a death sentence. Eventually, the cities were forced to keep their own sick inside their walls. Of course the media never told the stories of what their "final solution" had become the "cure." But there were rumors.

Cagga joined the bi-coastal cities to form an ad-hoc nation of their own, but those cities were few - if well-populated. "Give them a few years, and then we'll have to clean up their mess, just like North Korea" went the phrase. So far, it's been a decade. Ten years of relative quiet outside their walls. Peace, prosperity, and mining the former suburbs outside for building materials while they were converted back into farmland, or at least treeless, featureless parks. Like yuge moats around castles in the old days.

Mostly (formerly suburban) farmers grew hay to begin with, until bored city guards started sniping them. Then they just sowed salt instead of fertilizer, using up-armored tractors with steel wheels. Deserts grew in self-defense. And trees beyond that, where trees grew to provide cover. And kids learned to use their ammunition for hunting and leave the pitied guards alone.

I had to remember that old movie where the one-eyed "Snake" got a high mucky-muck out of Nyack as the whole island had become a prison. Not too far off, now. But like I said, the rest of the country didn't much care. Cities were islands of themselves. As long as they kept to themselves, no one else cared.

AND IF THE REST OF the country was at peace and you could make a decent living without being hassled for how you acted or what you believed in, then why should you or I care?

Because I was being haunted by this continuing nightmare. Every night. Every time I closed my eyes. Not the living nightmare the cities had devolved into - the nightmare living behind my eyes when I closed them.

Me, I was a Brownie. Because outside of the cities, we mostly wore brown habits. Mine itched constantly. But the high-percentage wool blend was actually cooler in summer and warmer in winter than almost anything else. Inside the cities, where my calling told me to go, I wore what they wore - mostly torn and dirty cast-offs.

One reason was to be inoffensive, as the "Tolerance Edicts" were harsh on "hate" talk or "signals". The other reason was to avoid getting beaten up by the gang factions that ruled inside those walls. Being different was just another invitation.

Brownies didn't much get worked over, as they were just so damned pleasant all the time. That's me. Mr. Happy. Not that I am all that happy, but everyone else is so sad that it makes me look like a lit 100 watt bulb in a box of dead ones.

II

HE WAS COMING, I WAS certain. Because he kept showing up in my dreams. To save me, I hoped.

Otherwise, I'd die soon. Life inside cities was tough enough. Easier to give up and have an "accident."

I almost called him "Obi-Wan". Almost. But I didn't have an army of white-suited soldiers chasing me in some star ship. Nothing in Cagga was white. Or not very long. Gray, brown, dull black. Lots of darkness all around.

And the street lights at night were mostly gone, so everyone could do almost whatever they wanted. As long as it was what your gang approved of. And they had to get the Don's approval in turn.

That real power was in the Mob bosses. And you almost thanked 'Bama for them. "For 'Bama gave his only gay soul to reconcile the sins of the masses, as the great Trans gave her blessing to save us all from eternal damnation..." So the secular church preachers preached over and over. The hymn of Tolerance was well known to all children, as the Secular Progressive Church of the Righteous was the only government-approved religion.

Yes, there was no heaven or hell outside of what we were living here and now, so redemption was by paying taxes and voting for the church-sponsored candidate. If you weren't living in heaven, then you hadn't paid or voted enough. Amen.

Even the old 10 commandments devolved to just three - offending someone inside your own gang, tax avoidance, and killing someone in your own gang who didn't deserve it.

The Don was the pope, and his cardinals were the gang lords. Their territory kept you safe as long as you worked within their rules. And those rules said who you were tolerant of and who you weren't.

Not that complicated.

My problem is that I was pretty. Not my fault. The other problem was being born inside the K-gang, where the lighter color you were, the more prized you were. And so I didn't have much of a choice who I was going to wind up with. Unless I got scarred somehow. And then I'd be in hell, for sure.

I just didn't like where I was or what I was becoming.

If I'd been born in the territory of the Andro-non gang, then being distinctively male or female would count. Stacked or well-hung got you favors. In the LG-plus gang, it was being gay or lezzie was what counted. Straights didn't live long. You could be whatever you wanted, and could change what you said you were any minute of the day, but you had to queerify yourself, that was definite. There were other gangs like the Nazoids, Feministas, Antifa-fa's, pretty much any minority group except white straights had a gang.

Wherever you were born you were in that gang. Unless you got special pardon from the Don to move - and that took a lot of money. Of course, I didn't have any, so all I had was my good looks. My momma (bless her soul) used to pray that the Don would take me as one of his angels-in-waiting. Every gang was supposed to elevate (give up) one to the Don to use as he saw fit. So he usually had a dozen females around him to, well, fit him.

The problem was I didn't want this. I wanted just to live a simple life. I wanted a garden with a guy I could work with to make that garden better. And maybe have some children who would see the sunshine during the day and the star-shine at nights. Let the snakes take care of the mice and the toads take care of the flies and bugs, along with the birds. I didn't want to have to hunt with gangs looking for offenders. I sure didn't want my face and my legs to be my "ticket" anywhere. And there hadn't been any children born in the gangs for as long as I could remember.

Sometimes I had real heretical thoughts, like why did the Great 'Bama have to go and become a martyr? Why did the arch-angel Hill get booted from the hierarchy by the great Satan with orange hair? Why can't we just all get along?

None of those sinful thoughts get you anywhere, not even admitting them in a confession. Especially not admitting them in a confession. Because the preachers passed their notes on the sins confessed up the chain of command. Even kept spreadsheets and databases on debased thoughts and especially actions you took. The Don could call for these at any moment. But not coughing up something sinful at confession wasn't cool, either. Those preachers had to be recording something, or it looked like they were hiding something. And that could get them iced.

Sure, you're thinking - just get in good with the "cardinal" gang lord and you're safe. Not so fast. Because the 'lords had to go to confession, too. So the 'lords could be nixed by the preachers. Meaning the 'lords were always having the preachers spied on to see what they were doing. And their choirboys and gals were usually on the 'lord's payroll as informers. Because the 'lords also had the ear of the Don. There was checks and balances.

And the Don saw that it was good. And rested with his angels to wait on him as he saw fit.

Tony was our 'lord and he was hot on me. But I was cool on him. Because he was a jerk. Of course I couldn't tell him so, because he could ice me and make it look like an accident - like I accidentally lost my way into LG-plus gang territory as a straight chick. So I played along with him and strung him out as best I could.

Worse, one day the Don dropped in for a surprise inspection and found Tony trying to grope me like usual. And he says, 'Hey Antone - wass with this chicky-boom-boom you got? Howse come you haven't sent her up to Angeltown to help me out with my pains and anguishes?' Of course, Tony was all red-faced and made up a story on the spot that 'I wuz in training and learning the finer points' so that I 'didn't embarrass anybody by doin' somethin' stoopid.'

The Don saw through this at once, but smiled to Tony and says, 'Well thass fine, Antone. You juss send her up when yur dun with yur trainin' and my Chief Angel will check her out. But I tells you what - do you one better. I'll send the Chief over later today so she can find out what you've been trainin' her on and gives you some pointers. Mebbe she's ready already. Mebbe not.'

So the Don is fixing to leave, and then turns and says - 'Ohyea - Antone. Be sure she gets all confessed with that preacher of yours - and you, too. Okaydokay?'

I had to hold it all in at that point. Because I wasn't 'stoopid' like Tony thought I was.

But I was really stuck 'in-betwixt that rockin' hardplace' as the scriptures are told.

I was gonna be screwed one way or another. And I didn't like either choice.

III

STILL HAD NO CLUE HOW to find this gal, but my prayers got answered - I worked out to start helping at the one of the soup kitchens so could see all the gangs come through for that side of town. Only about three or four of these in this sector, so it wouldn't take long to survey all of them. And the kitchens were always short of help, especially people that were so cheery to everyone.

It was the first kitchen, the first day when I saw her come through. All sad-faced and so on. When I tried to cheer her up, she looked at me and something clicked into the 'on' position.

So I managed to touch her fingers when I filled up her bowl. And that shock of recognition startled both of us. That was her, OK. And she knew I was there to help her, somehow.

Of course, neither of us knew how or if I was even going to see her again. Or if I was going to be able to help her.

All I really knew is that she was the face of my nightmare.

WHEN DOC CAME IN, I looked forward to the next break to pick his brain about that girl and her gang.

Doc was dressed head to toe in black, as usual. And nodded to me as I filled his bowl. "Hey, you're the new guy. Got a name?"

"Simon. Or Sam, as most call me."

"OK Sam, nice to meet you. " He saluted with the bun in his other hand and headed to the crew table by the transept exit.

As soon as we fed the gang's bouncers, who ate last to ensure everyone followed the rules, we kitchen staff were free for a few minutes until they left and the next gang came in. I grabbed my bowl and bun, then headed over to where Doc was almost finished. Good timing to get some info from him.

"Hey Sam. You're a Brownie, aren't you?" Doc asked.

"Yea, Doc. And you know we come only when called. Hate to be abrupt on this, but the person who called me is eating out there." I replied.

"That pretty one, the one who's cleaner than the rest." Doc said.

"Right. Do you know her scoop?" I asked.

"Home grown. Been in that gang since her mother died. Something new popped up yesterday. Seems the Don wants her has part of his angel-harem. He asked me to check her out for any diseases he could catch. So I'll see her this afternoon. But no, that's a solo gig. You can't come along." Doc was a man of short sentences.

Obviously read my face and mind like a book as he talked.

"But," he continued. "The local preacher is supposed to do a confessional on her - get the goods. And meanwhile, after I get done, the Chief Angel is going to do her own interview." Doc finished with the worst news.

Finishing the rest of his roll, he continued. "The opening for you is that the preacher is out in another gang, and too busy to get to her, so he'll take a substitute."

That brightened me up. "Doc, thanks. Owe you one for sure."

Doc just looked me over. "You Brownies have done more for me already than I could ever repay. Otherwise, you wouldn't have gotten the time of day from me." His eyes could get cold real fast, but then he smiled, a jagged crack in that ice. "Just kidding. Follow me out. Take the bun, leave the soup. You could use less of that," he glanced at my gut.

I got his point.

He rose, I rose. Followed him out as he said. We stopped by Stan and Dolly, who nodded that they could cover the next shift on their own. Dolly took my hand and held it for awhile, looking into my eyes with a smile.

"It's going to be alright," she said. "You'll do fine. Come back around if you get a chance. You're good help." And then the first members of the next gang started in single-file to get their bun-and-soup meal.

Doc led me out into the warehouse out back. He paused by a hanging rack of clothes and picked out a whitish-looking robe. "Not the cleanest, but preachers aren't saints. Here." He handed the robe to me and I put it on over what I was wearing. A little long for my height, but better than too short.

We went out to the street from there, and met the same gang that had just fed.

On their territory. Not in the Don's neutral zone, the one he'd mandated for the soup kitchen.

I stood near the Doc, as my only protection against that gang of hundreds.

IV

TONY WAS STANDING THERE with me by his side. Doc was in front of us, with some new preacher face. Wait, that was the guy that touched my hand in the soup line. I could feel my face soften at this, and then put the hard lines back up.

Of course he saw me recognize him. So did Doc. Whatever they were planning better be good. I figured I had about 24 hours to live before hell took over.

"Hey Tony, how's things?" Doc asked.

"So-so." Said Tony. His typical wordy response. But he got and held his job by what he did with his hands, not his mouth. And he also knew I was supposed to go with the Doc for a checkup. But Tony kept me by his side as long as he could. Doc showing up didn't make Tony's day any better. So Tony's hands pushed me toward them.

I stumbled and moved over to stand between Doc and this new preacher guy. Not touching either.

Tony simply grunted, then nodded to his lieutenants. The gang moved off as a smooth action. Within minutes, they had melted into the forests of buildings and trash and grime.

Doc nodded and led us toward the Don's park. The preacher guy brought up the rear.

Once there, that preacher peeled off so Doc could sit on one of the benches and talk. This was the most beautiful part of the city, and none of us were ever allowed to visit, only see it from the top of the high rises or on the ABS media feeds.

The Don kept this neutral to everyone, and access very limited. The people who maintained this were under special protection of the Don, and under his watch. The Doc came here to check on their health. And came here to check on people where he needed quiet.

Which is why we were sitting on one of the benches among the close-cropped grass and the long reflective pool. Peaceful. The most peace I've ever known.

And Doc was looking, no - peering - into my eyes. Just a couple of feet away, but any closer would be intimate. He was holding onto my wrist with one hand, and my palm with his other.

"Any coughs or itching lately?" Doc asked.

"No, other than allergies," I replied.

Doc pulled out a stethoscope, putting it on my chest and into his ears. Moving it around for awhile in different spots around my heart. Then he told me to turn away from him, and listened to me breathe. Even coughed for him once.

Then he put his hand on my shoulder and turned me back around.. "Physically, you're fine. What do you think about becoming one of the Don's 'angels'?" He asked.

I looked down at my feet and put my hands together, rubbing my thumbs on each other. "Fine, I guess."

"Meaning, you don't want to disappoint the Don, but working directly for him wasn't your first choice." Doc summarized. "What is your first choice?"

"Freedom to make my own life. To live simpler. To have a family. To make my own choices." I replied.

"And your life hasn't had a lot of choices so far. Much less freedom." Doc was peering into my eyes again.

"No." A tear formed in my eye. Then they ran from both eyes down my cheeks.

Doc just sat there. He put one hand on both of mine, then his hand was replaced by another. I couldn't see, because my hands were blurry in my eyes. But this hand came from the other side than where Doc was sitting. And I knew this new touch. I'd felt it before.

V

TAKING ONE ARM, SHE brushed her face clean. Using the fingers of that hand, she wiped her eyes clear, then looked into my face.

"My name is Sam," I told her. And she had a face like an angel. Not one of the Don's helpers, but a real angel. I didn't know what to say next.

"Mine is Mary. I haven't seen you before. Have you been working with another gang?" Mary said.

"N-No, I came to see you." I stuttered.

"Me?" Mary asked.

"You were in my dreams, or actually, nightmares. So I had to come." I replied.

"Just in time." Mary smiled at me. And I melted all over again.

An awkward silence developed. Me sitting here with my mouth open and no words coming out. Her with her beautiful smile.

At last she looked away and I was able to think again. Never had I been so affected before. None of my counselor training prepared me for anything like this.

Looking off into the dingy skies, the words finally started up again. "I take it you wanted help getting your choice and freedom back."

Mary looked down and gripped her hands again. That struck a nerve. "Yes, you've been in my dreams as well. Of course, you looked much taller there."

"Yes, I get that a lot. I'm a bit taller and more muscular in all my dream sendings. Six-pack abs and one of those sultry looks." I joked.

Mary smiled at that. But at least this time I didn't melt.

"Now what am I going to do with you?" I asked.

"Hey, don't you have a plan?" She looked concerned.

"Well, so far, the plan was to find you. Doc helped me get this far. Now I guess it's time for new plans. Like how to get you out of this mess." I replied.

And it was her turn to be speechless - but not for long. "What were you thinking, just rolling in here and giving me a glad hand and howdy-do? No plan, nothing." Mary was frowning now.

Disappointment ruled.

WE DIDN'T HAVE LONG to sit in our glum thoughts.

Across the park, a long-legged angel was walking toward us. How she managed those platform high-heel boots was a question for another day. At least it was a hot day. Her lack of clothes almost looked like they were painted on. All tight black leather and vinyl over spandex. Slit up to here and parted down to there. Nothing that would keep her warm otherwise. But the heat she was putting off would make any red-blooded citizen pant - or fume in intolerant jealousy.

She stalked up with a walk that would fit a runway queen. Long coal-black hair put up in a style that the Don must like. Made her look well over 6 feet tall. She had a long knife in a scabbard belted low on her hip, with a smaller blade handle peaking out of one boot top.

While her black hair waved in the light breeze, anything else that wasn't tight - jiggled.

I managed to keep my mouth shut this time. Probably out of courtesy to Mary, who became even more glum.

This was the Angel Chief that Mary was dreading. This was a preview of what she was expected to become. 'One sexy be-yatch' as Tony would say.

"Hi. I'm Goldie." The angel stalked up to us and stood with one cocked hip, with the hand on that side resting on it. The other traced an errant strand behind her ear as she looked Mary over. "Here, stand up so we can see what you got."

Mary stood, downcast and holding her hands in front of her.

Goldie looked her up and down, then came forward a step. She raised her hand to Mary's chin and pulled her head up to look into her eyes. "Doc says you're clean. So that's a plus. Let's see you walk. Go over to the pool edge and back here.

Mary did as she was told, coming back to the spot she started. Now she was looking into Goldie's eyes to see what trick she was expected to do next.

"Not bad. But Tony doesn't know squat about how you gotta 'slink' to tell your story. You walk like a trained she-panther, ready to run or pounce on command. Good for the streets. But the Don won't find it 'fits' with the rest of his angels. We can work on that." Goldie peered into her eyes and scanned the rest of her. "Good shape. A little spare. You need some more cushion in places, but the food we get will help you with that."

Goldie came forward and flipped up Mary's collar. Then tugged Mary's jacket so the top snap opened. Goldie peered down her front, then stated. "Light on top. Still, if you get the right outfit, we can push up what you got to make it look like more." Then Goldie stood back a pace. "So, what do you think about all this?"

Mary stumbled to find words after the livestock show and meat grading. "I - I guess I'm OK with it."

"With what? What do you think you're in for?" Goldie asked.

"Serving the Don, being a representative for my gang as part of his angel court." Mary replied.

"And you know good Anglish, too. That's a bonus. The Don might not talk straight, but he likes people that do - as long as you don't go trying to correct him." Goldie shifted back to her hand-on-cocked-hip pose. "But you know what? I think ABS is gonna love you. A little trim, a little makeup and you could be their new cover-girl angel. Most of these broads have mouths that would sour milk on the shelf, they know more ways to spit out an f-bomb than any comedian. You, though - you'd come off good in an interview. And it's time for their ratings sweep. Not like they have any competition, but it's still 'Always Broadcast Something' and the anchors are always trying to out-do each other to grab a better time slot. Yup, you're the one."

At that, Goldie stepped forward to grab Mary's arm and pulled her to her side as she turned and started walking back the direction she came from. Goldie glanced back at me. "Come on preacher-man, you're going to be her chaperon in all this. You're going to make sure none of these media-types does something they shouldn't. Because the Don would get tight if they tried. And they won't try to grope her or worse if there's a preacher watching. Me, I've got other stuff to do, but I'll take you both down to ABS for interviews."

There was no one else around in the Don's park. Doc had left, and all the people he was there to see were also gone. With Goldie's long steps, we were soon off grass and across a cement walkway toward a private staircase heading down.

Mary was being brave in all this, even though Goldie's grip looked like a vise from where I was following them. Of course I couldn't see Mary's face, but I could sense what was going through her head. She was out of that gang scene, but this new world she was heading into was the one she'd been dreading.

Walking out of the bright-lit garden into the darker stairwell below seemed to match Mary's mood.

VI

WHEN GOLDIE BROUGHT me and Sam into ABS headquarters, it was a completely different world. Lots of glass and plastic and aluminum everywhere. Like the whole place was a stage backdrop. Actually, I do remember some of these as shots I'd seen on the few TV's we had around. (Few because they were government-provided and not quickly replaced when some protest turned violent enough to break them. It was one of our 'rights' to watch the TV-media, but not yet a cardinal sin if we didn't.)

Goldie brought us up to the sparkling, neat and tidy reception desk, where a sparkling, neat and tidy gender-neutral receptionist was waiting.

"Hello Miss Goldie, and welcome to your visitors!" The receptionist sparkled to us.

"This is Mary and her preacher-chaperon." Goldie looked directly into the receptionist's eyes. "Mary is here for your tryout interview - the one you've been wanting the Don to provide for your sweeps. The preacher man is here to report to the Don about how you treat her."

The receptionist swallowed at this, a definite pause which showed Goldie her point was taken. Then everything was all smiles again. Turning to Mary, the receptionist looked her over. "Definitely interview-caliber. Give us a smile, darling."

Goldie poked Mary with her elbow. Mary weakly smiled toward the receptionist.

"You'll do just fine. After we're through prepping you, that smile will come as easy as breathing." She smiled one of her automatic number-6 smiles, then turned to Goldie like this was an interview. "And thank you Miss Goldie, we know how to contact you if we need anything else."

Goldie just shrugged. "That you do." To Mary: "You take care of yourself and make the Don look good." To me: "And you report everything to Don once she's done." We both nodded back. We had our orders.

Goldie pivoted on one of her heels and stalked out with her runway walk.

By the time Goldie reached the auto-opening double-glass doors, another gender-neutral assistant had glided up to where we stood and motioned us to follow.

Through a series of long and narrowing hallways, where many people were busy doing all sorts of things to guests with their hair and hands and clothing, just to get them ready for yet another three-minute talking head-shot interview. A massive assembly-line creating talent from sometimes very raw material.

At last we went through into a larger room with racks and racks of clothing hung on them. Different colors, different styles, enough to fit almost anyone with any suit or dress or in between.

The assistant finally stopped in a large blank area. Pointing to two large "X's" taped on the floor, Mary and I each took our respective position. Another assistant rolled a screen between us, and turned on a bright light behind Mary so that I could see her outline. "Preacher, this is so you can report to the Don that Mary was only treated with respect and courtesy." Then that assistant (he/she?) left.

Two more wordless assistants brought in several hangers worth of clothes and draped them over other chairs beyond the light. They then helped Mary (with respect and courtesy) out of her jacket, slacks, blouse, and shoes into the clothes they had brought. The whole process took minutes. The assistants tucked and pulled various cinches and bands to make the effect the one they wanted. Finally, they helped her back into her own street shoes that they had quickly cleaned, buffed, and shined. A few tweaks to the hems above those shoes and they both stood back to look her over. Mary turned once, twice, and I saw their shadows nod at each other. One left towing the screen away, the other to the opposite direction.

With the light still behind her, Mary did look like an angel. All in off-white, with a jacket coming down only to her waist, over a blouse and pants combination that looked street-savvy, but in a modern executive assistant mold.

The original assistant returned and looked at me, then snapped his/her(?) fingers once. The other two returned with a new pastoral frock for me, just about the same as the one I had, but clean. No shoe shining for me. Still the same ripped, torn, dirty street clothes underneath as I came in with. Obvious I was going to be background shot material, if I showed up on camera at all. But it was nice to have something that smelled somewhat clean - if only a fake "clean" smell, it was better than what I had before.

Mary was smiling, even with all the changes she'd been through. New clothes were nice. It took the edge off things. She came over to me and tweaked my robe a bit, tucking the torn edges of my shirt collar down. "At least they could have given you a better shirt."

"As long as I don't upstage you, that's the key part. Besides, I won't be on camera anyway." I replied.

She wrinkled her forehead. "I hope they don't ask me embarrassing questions, or stuff I can't answer."

As if on cue came some very female assistant with a pencil behind one ear and an ear-bud with microphone in the other. She was carrying a clipboard and talking to someone we couldn't hear or see as she walked. "Yes, I understand. No. You're right. OK - I'm here with the new Don's angel and have to get her ready. That's right. Bye." She touched her ear bud and sighed. "I'm Sue. Glad to meet you. Did they ever do a good job with your outfit. Hope they let you keep it. The Don would like to see you in that. Most of his girls are so, well - dark - in their outfits. You really do look like an angel." She touched Mary's hair gently. "Oh, where is makeup? Let's go this way and get you started."

Turning toward me, she glanced at her clipboard. "And you must be Sam the preacher-man, here to keep an eye on Mary, un-contrary. Yes, I love to make rhymes. Fills the odd parts of days. Please, come this way." And Sue led us off through the racks of clothes.

Mary took my arm and hugged it close to her. I enjoyed that, as I'm sure she did. It was reassuring.

We all went through some propped-open double doors into a room that had a row of chairs like an old-time barber shop. Sue gestured Mary into one of them and me into a folding chair over to the opposite side. Sue looked at me. "Not that you couldn't use a trim yourself, but she's the star and you're an extra. I like to think that is short for 'extra-special.'" And smiled she watched me sit, necessary before she could move off again.

Two more silent assistants came out, moving to Mary. One got busy with a comb and scissors, the other with a makeup brush and lip gloss. By the time they were finished - that seemed like seconds - she was ready for any sort of closeup they could throw at her. One of the assistants gave her a large mirror with a handle so she could see the result. Mary smiled wide at the change. She wasn't used to real mirrors, just her reflection in broken glass store fronts with dingy street lighting or harsh sunlight.

When they took the mirror away and helped her out of her chair, Mary didn't quit smiling. No one had done anything like this for a very long time, maybe since her mother was still alive. So I imagine it felt like Christmas.

Mary came over and pulled me up in order to hug me, and I patted her back as she did. She felt good inside and felt good to me. Of course, I was smiling wide, too. But that's normal for me.

Sue came back at that point. "Well look at you two - and how do you do? OK, we're off to our last stop. Where they coach you for the interview. She came around to separate us by taking one in each arm. Then walked us briskly out of make up and down a wide hall where the body traffic was all in our direction. Even the arrows on the floor pointed in the direction we were being pulled. This was definitely an assembly-line operation.

What we were going to be turned into at the end of it was the next question.

VII

"WELCOME TO THE FRONT lines of our constant battle with ignorance and intolerance. My name is Bill, and I'll be your producer-director." The pudgy, broad man held his thickhand out for shaking - first to Mary and then to me.

Sue seemed to have evaporated silently at that point. With our attention on this balding, wide-set and suspendered man, she was nowhere to be seen.

Bill had his own clipboard and ear-bud mic. "Mary and Sam. Mary is our on-air talent and Sam is - emotional support, shall we say. So Mary is our talent for this shot." His attention focused directly on Mary at this point. "Here, Mary, you stand on this 'x', and I'll stand on this one."

By standing on that "X" Mary moved into some bright lights that made her eyes narrow. She soon learned not to look into them, but just at Bill, who had kept talking. Behind them was a wall of green.

Another genderless assistant came to show me into a folding chair off to the side where I could see and hear everything. By my side appeared a small table with a bowl of fresh strawberries and a small pile of napkins. I put a few into a napkin and started eating from these. To avoid appearing starved, I took each one and savored it before starting a new one. I took this as just another test of my patience.

Bill was talking to Mary and putting her at ease. Asking about her life growing up and letting her develop her own answers. He had about 20 questions that he didn't have to refer to the clipboard for. Apparently, this was a kind of "man on the street" interview with simple questions.

Then he started to go off script, asking her questions about what she thought of government, how the Second Civil War had turned out, and how her life had changed since then. As Mary had been born just before the walls were finished, she had perspective of growing up inside it. She had seen the changes, not all of them good.

But her answers were apparently what Bill had been looking for. Bill was getting more animated and smiling more as he got his answers. At one point, he tapped his ear bud to talk to someone. Holding his hand up in the air, he wanted Mary to be quiet and stand there while he talked. That hand went to a single finger, as if to say it would only be a minute.

I didn't catch what he said, exactly, lots of "she's the one", "yes, her answers are good", "a natural talent the Don will like", and a few more things. He was selling someone on the idea for something. At least it sounded good.

Bill finally took his finger down to take Mary by the arm and lead her over to me. I swallowed the strawberry I was working on, then folded the rest of them into the napkin and into a pocket of the robe I was wearing, with a mental note not to forget those berries when I had to turn in this robe later. I also grabbed a few more napkins to stuff into the pocket on the other side.

"She's a natural talent. Very good. Very. So we are changing the shot. We were just going to do a short interview with the Don's new angel - and wardrobe did a great job of making her look like one - and instead we're going to do an outdoor shot against a real background." He looked at Mary directly. "You are perfect for some talent we had that, well, is - unfortunately - unavailable. But the shot has taken months to set up and all those 'permissions' we needed were expensive to get, so we can use Mary here to do that shot." Bill was grinning ear to ear. Like he loved discovering talent.

Taking both our arms, he started walking us toward yet another set of double doors. While his legs were every bit as short as mine, he had no problem ushering us along as he talked at a similar clip. "...This is an external shot, and we are going to get Mary's reactions to the new suburbia reclamation project. 'New' being relative, but it looks the best out of all the possible sites we have, and the lighting will be right. Mary, the questions will be similar to those we've already been through, so that was just a rehearsal we just did."

Bill stopped us just before the doors. Above them was an Exit sign. "This is one of our newer vehicles you're going to ride in. For your safety and ours, please don't open the windows. It's fully air conditioned and comfortable. Just wait inside and someone will come for you when its your time." He then opened the double doors, and then another door with a special twist-lock handle opened away from us into a small room that was carpeted and padded just about everywhere. Ushering us in, he closed it behind us with a thump. There was no handle on the inside that we could see, just a set of buttons.

The room was mostly beiges and browns, with walls that rounded into the ceiling. Windows on the two sides were frosted so we couldn't see out and nothing could see us inside. A long couch went around the edges of the room, except for a couple of tall cabinets on each side of the single door into the room. The wall in front had a large logo of ABS plastered on it.

Just as we were taking all this in, the room began moving as a slow rumble started up somewhere below us. Mary and I quickly sat down on the couch to hold on. The swaying along with the changing lights and shadows told us we were really in some sort of portable "green room" for on-air talent - and we were going somewhere.

VIII

I'M JUST GLAD SAM WAS along. I scooted near him and held his hand. Both of us were fairly alarmed at being moved along Gawd-knows-where, but Sam was taking it all better than I was.

"Have you ever done anything like this before?" I asked.

"Not really, although being trucked around as a paramedic is a bit like it. Only you're riding with a bunch of medical supplies and equipment. Like then, you are going somewhere that you're needed, but nowhere you really know." Sam replied.

Sam reached into his pocket and pulled out a napkin with some strawberries in it. Somewhat squashed, but I hadn't had any in years. My mother used to grow them in pots on the window sill with her herbs. A tear came to my eye just thinking about it.

Sam noticed. "You're OK aren't you?"

I was careful not to get any of the pulpy fruit on my new outfit. "I'm fine. It's just that things remind me of my mom sometimes. Strawberries are one of them - but it's a good thing to be reminded now and then. Life was better back then, and can be better again."

Sam smiled at this. "You're going to do good on this interview. People need hope. You can't live on hope alone, but life is pretty poor without it."

I smiled back. "Sam, you're a real wonder." And I kissed him on his cheek. He went beet red at this. "Not girl-shy are you? Even as a paramedic, you've seen a lot worse, I bet."

"Worse, yes. More personal, no. I'm just happy to be with you and helping you. I don't particularly know where that blush comes from. Sure medically I know, but..." Sam trailed off.

"It's a heart thing, Sam. Not the blood pumping kind, but the real deep-down loving kind." He gave me a fresh napkin from his other pocket. I wiped my hands off and handed it back. Then I grabbed him into a big hug and held on for awhile.

When I let go, he wasn't blushing anymore. "Look Sam, you've felt it, too. I don't know what it means, but I know I like it. Like it was somehow meant to be." And then I kissed him on his lips, lightly.

He looked deep into my eyes. "Better save that lip gloss for the shot, although I know they probably have someone who will touch it up."

And our transport just kept rolling along and stopping and starting. But we held our arms around each other the rest of the way.

Until we finally stopped and the engine noise quit. Shadows on both sides meant we were parked in a row with other units like ours. Still, we had no real way to get out until they came for us.

Wherever we were now, anyway.

IX

THE WAIT WASN'T A LONG one. Cuddled like we were, it wasn't uncomfortable. So we didn't worry much.

Finally, we heard some clanking outside the door and the sound of a hiss as it was unsealed and then popped inward. At that, we sat apart, but just held hands.

Bill showed his broad face again. He was sweating and had a ball cap in his hand. "OK, kids. We're there now. Come this way and I'll tell you all about it. He disappeared and we took this as a cue to follow.

The clanking had made steps from the back of the truck to the ground. With a little railing on one side to hang onto. Our truck was one in a row of them, with more trucks in different places for the cameras and sound, plus the generators to run everything.

The city walls were about a mile away. Mary looked at my face in wonder. She had never been outside those walls since she was born.

The next few miles were flat and featureless, except for small piles of rubble here and there. Like everything had been scraped off the face of the earth and vanished out of existence. Our attention went to the noise where they were setting up the shot. Big reflectorized "sunny boards" were being positioned to put the light where it was needed. And some of the grips were being stand-ins for the interviewer and Mary, so they could get the lighting and sound set up.

All in front of a pastoral background with rolling prairie grasses waving in the slight breeze. Trees in the far distance and puffy clouds.

This was real life. And it smelled like freedom to both of us.

But if we ran, we'd be chased. Neither of us could out-run some of these longer-legged crew. Sure, there weren't any armed guards, but if we ran it would be the same thing as dead when we got back inside that city.

"Hey Mary." I said, real quiet.

"What?" She leaned her head to me.

"I've got an idea you're going to like." Then I whispered it in her ear. Her face was puzzled when I started, but grinning when I finished.

"Do you think it will work?" She asked.

"Worth a try." I replied.

Right then Bill trotted up, puffing at the exertion in this heat. "We're about ready to start. Let's get you in position and your face and hair touched up. Sam, you get to stand over there (he pointed) where you can hear and see everything that's happening."

Mary took her spot while a couple of genderless assistants tweaked her hair and face for the lighting they were going to use, as well as setting her hair so the wind wouldn't whip it around.

I stood between a couple of burly-looking guys who had arms the size of my thigh and shoulders were just over my head. Apparently moved heavy equipment for their living.

Our plan had better work, or we weren't going very far.

X

THE STAR BROADCASTER was last to come out of her trailer. She was pulling tissues out of her collar where the makeup had been touched up. An assistant was trailing her, with a binder in hand, a huge bag over one shoulder, and stooping to pick up the tissues every time the star dropped one. The star was prattling on about something or other, while the assistant agreed with everything she said.

The star was blond, tall, and wore perfect lips. A dark business blazer with the ABS logo on the right breast, over a light skirt just short enough or hitched up high enough to show off her legs, but not be suggestive. Well, not over-suggestive. She was built like a model and maybe used to be one. Wearing pink, spiked heels that were rough walking in this uneven sod and gravel, but high enough to make her calves and other features accentuate with every step. Still, they looked painful to wear out here.

She came up to me and held out a thin, limp hand. "I'm Peggy, the evening special report newscaster. Glad to meet you..." The assistant muttered my name. "...Mary. Glad to have you on our show. They certainly have cleaned you up well. But you'll be back to your old gang before you know it." With that, she pulled her hand quickly out of my grasp so the assistant could clean it with a pre-moistened sanitizing wipe.

She and the assistant reviewed her questions out of the binder while I stayed on my spot that was quickly becoming hotter with all the sunlight reflected on me.

The assistant was pointing out the teleprompter, which Peggy was squinting at. Then the assistant ran over to the prompter operator so he could make the text larger. He was shaking his head, but did it anyway. Then the assistant ran back and Peggy pasted a number-5 smile on and let it drop as quickly. Then held out her hand, palm up. She was waiting for the microphone, which shortly appeared there.

Both Peggy and I had our own lapel mic's installed, and these were tested. The wireless hand mic was for show, mostly, but was also back up and could record ambient noise to mix in later.

Too soon, Bill came over and told Peggy she was "live in 15." He scooted out of the camera range over to the teleprompter and counted down on his fingers from five to one and then pointed at Peggy.

At that Peggy smiled her number-1 smile and began her canned introduction. Then they waited for a prerecorded video to roll. Only Bill could see that and was holding up his hand again to start counting down.

At that point, Peggy would start my live interview.

I just hoped this worked.

XI

FROM WHERE I WAS STANDING, Mary and Peggy both looked great. They had three cameras rolling so they could do closeups on both Mary and Peggy, with a two-shot of the pair from over Peggy's shoulder.

Mary answered directly, and clearly, showing her home-schooling and her Mother's diction. Unseen from the camera, Bill was talking into Peggy's ear piece and suggesting follow-up questions. I could see from Mary's face where the questions started getting a lot more personal than anything asked in the practice interview.

But Mary relaxed when she noticed Bill was asking the questions. She started gesturing more broadly to the land around them and looking off into the distance. Mary was talking about hope. I could read it on her face.

Suddenly, she got a pained look and clutched her stomach. Doubling over, she started a deep, hacking cough. Peggy and anyone nearby started backing up.

I started to move toward her, but the guys on each side held me back. "I'm a paramedic!" I shouted at them. They both let go at that point and let me get to her side on the ground.

The cameras kept rolling as we crouched there. Peggy, Bill and the rest of the crew started backing away toward the trucks and drivers got in those cabs ready to start them up at a moment's notice.

With my hand on Mary's back, I pulled out a napkin so she could wipe her mouth. She also wiped off the sweat from her forehead. Then she looked straight into the camera.

And collapsed into my arms.

The trucks all started up at once. Peggy kicked off her pink heels and started running for her life, wrecking her stockings and hitching up her already short skirt to run faster. Only the cameramen took their shouldered equipment with them, the rest dropped everything to scamper into already rolling trucks. Leaving in towering dust trails before their doors were even shut. Bill and Peggy fought to get into the last cab of that convoy and finally both squeezed in with the driver. Somehow slamming shut the passenger side door as the truck lurched away with grinding gears.

All I could see after their huge cloud of dust blew away was a few sunny-board reflectors tipped on their side, a boom mic laying in the dust, and some water coolers. With scattered trash blowing in the breeze.

We were alone, abandoned.

XII

THEN WE LOOKED AT EACH other and started laughing. Hard.

So much I finally had to just lay down on the ground and enjoy it. Freedom is laughter.

Sam followed me to the ground with his own chuckling and laid next to me. We both watched the white clouds move their bright, slow sky-dance as our laughter and chuckles slowed.

Once I got my breath back, I rolled over and kissed him. Long and hard. He hugged me back and we kissed some more. Just forget the lip gloss.

"We did it." I told him, hardly believing it.

"Yes we did." Sam said as we both sat up, arm in arm. "Hey, I know it's cold, but that water cooler water will probably wash those strawberries off your face."

I smiled and nodded.

On the way over, we found Peggy's assistant had left her big bag in the rush. Other than a couple of sandwiches and an apple (as well as a cosmetic kit which I insisted we keep) we dumped the rest on the ground. Also on the ground we found a wide-brimmed hat that fit Sam, and an adjustable red ball cap for me.

"Yea, these guys don't know their plague symptoms from the common cold. If you'd really had their plague then you wouldn't be standing up there giving a long interview on TV." Sam said. "By the way, what was it that you were saying with all that arm waving?"

I just smiled. "I told them that all this reminded me that freedom was out in front of us, that you had to grab hold of hope and hold it close, to never let it go. Because miracles are possible if you keep believing."

Sam just nodded as he smiled his sweet smile and kept putting the leftover chilled water bottles into that big bag.

Miles to go before we got to any real civilization, but we were on our way.

Hand in hand.

The Ghost Who Loved

BY S. H. MARPEL

I

IT WAS FATHER'S DAY. They were all still dead, and I was again dry-eyed over their grave.

I came this way every year, for the past few, as it was also my birthday. Such as it was.

Growing older just meant more sadness for me.

Father, Mother, and younger sister all passed that night. Horrific car accident. All decapitated or crushed instantly, head-on collision with another car, that seemed to come out of nowhere.

I was the only one remaining.

And I couldn't even cry anymore.

Of course my heart ached. But it was almost the dull, screeching creak of some massive pump whose bearings were failing and overheated from lack of grease. The grease of kindness, of human love.

Why was I still here? What reason did I have for existing? I didn't know. All I knew was that I kept going from day to day, month in, month out, and then showed up back here again - once a year.

Graveyards are funny things. Why they exist is such a morbid concept. Small and huge monuments erected to incite the memory of the fallen. Like it was the old Japanese ancestor worship. But just because they weren't remembered after a few centuries, didn't mean the ache went away. Only the persons who had the ache. To their own plot of earth and monument - or not.

People visited. And opened up that ache fresh to the sting of memory once again, like a wound opened to the air. Painful, abrupt. The ache continuing long after the bandage was re-applied.

Like that guy over there, a few rows over. Downcast young face. Blue jeans, black sweater jacket, high-top basketball sneakers. And that cute brown hair, those nice cheekbones. Why did he come here? Did it ever help him move on - or was he like me, a magnet for more punishment?

II

"WELL, SIS, HOW DID this year go for you - wherever you are?" I visited my sister every chance I got, knowing that it wasn't really her. She was long gone, only some ashes remained now. Buried under ground somewhere near that stone.

She was the only one who had left, and the rest of us carried on. Somehow.

Mother and Dad were busy in their new retirement job, a part-time detective agency. Didn't pay much, but they didn't need much to keep going, to pay the bills, to enjoy what was left of their own span on this earth.

Me, I was just starting out. Barely in college when this happened.

They said it was congenital, that it would jump generations. Neither of my parents had it. And I had no signs. But neither did she. She got a check up for a pain in her arm that wouldn't go away. The doctor called for an ambulance and they rushed her to a hospital. By that evening she was dead. Not enough left of her heart to revive.

And she wasn't even out of high school.

So I come to talk to her, tell her all the things I'd learned in college, of the people I'd met, of the charities I worked for in her memory. Just to live her life as well as mine.

But it never seemed to help. That stone just sat there and looked back at me. It wasn't alive, neither was she, so what was the use.

"Hey." A girl came to stand beside me. I'd seen her earlier, a couple of rows over. "I just thought that I should come talk to you. Of course you can't see or hear me, but you looked like you could use some comfort. Some people feel that. And it feels good giving it, at least to me." She was wearing dark brown slacks and with thick off-white shawl-collar sweater and sensible flats. Her blond hair center-parted and naturally curled in long waves. A looker for sure.

"Who says I can't hear or see you?" I asked, looking directly at her.

She was shocked, "Wait, really? No, this can't be."

"Yes, it can. But I know why you think you're invisible to everyone. You're a ghost." I said as calmly as I could. Some of these specters went into denial and started screeching, so a guy had to be careful what and how they talked to them.

"No, you aren't real. Nobody talks to ghosts." Her eyes were wide in surprise.

"Well, it's kinda my gift and my curse. Must be inherited. My Mom and Dad can both do it, too." I lightened up at this, since she wasn't going to go into dramatics on me. "Hey, if you don't mind me asking, who are you here for today?"

"My family. Over there." She pointed. "I come here every year on the anniversary.

"Sorry for your loss," I said.

"And I'm sorry for yours. Who are you here for?" She asked.

"My sister. She was in high school when it happened. Too suddenly. But at least I got to see and talk with her just after she left. That's one 'benefit' I guess you could call it. She was at peace and wasn't serious about it at all. She told me not to be down about it, that I'd be joining her soon and to go out and make a big thing of living. That was our joke. I was always telling her to not make a big thing out of the issues she came up with. And she'd say, 'Why not? That's all the fun there is to living.'"

She smiled at this.

"I'm Tom."

"Rose," she answered. "You know, this is a bit freaky, but you lost your sister but have your family, and I'm the only sister left from mine."

"Yea," I said. "That is a bit freaky. Kinda OK, though. Like finding a missing piece to a puzzle somehow."

"It does 'fit' somehow." She smiled at that. "Well, nice meeting you." And just stood there.

I stood there, too.

"Do you mind if I hugged you?" She asked.

"Not if you don't want to be surprised." I replied.

"Why would I be surprised?" Her face formed a little frown.

"Ghosts don't normally hug." I answered.

"Yea, I know," she said, looking down at my sister's headstone. "Because in the living, it gives them chills. That's why I asked."

"Oh, this is a different kind of surprise. You've never hugged someone who could hear and see you before." I said. "Go ahead and try it."

She moved closer to me and tentatively put her arms around my shoulders, then moved closer to me. I felt the hug. And then put my arms around her and hugged her back.

She immediately stepped back and held me by my shoulders, eyes almost as wide as her mouth.

III

"YOU HUGGED ME BACK!" I almost screamed in delight. "How did you do that? I haven't felt an actual hug in years. This is... is..." Then I hugged him again and felt my eyes get all moist and bleary.

So I kissed him on his cheek.

He pulled back, a smile on his face. Right below the most amazing blue eyes I'd seen in years. "Well that was unexpected, particularly for a graveyard."

I blushed, and dropped my arms. "Sorry, Tom. I didn't mean to offend."

"No offense. It actually - felt good. Even in a graveyard." He said, still smiling.

We stood there for awhile, both of us not knowing what we wanted to do next.

He took my arm in his and turned to gently walk with me along one of the many paths of the cemetery. We walked without talking for quite a while, rounded many corners and passed under many stately oaks and old magnolias.

At last he spoke. "Rose, I don't want to seem forward, but for a ghost, you are pretty nice and all. I don't mean to interrupt any schedule you may be needing to get back to. What I thought is that you could come see where I live. But no pressure, of course. I mean it's fine if you don't want to come. We can just meet back here next year or sometime, otherwise..."

I smiled at him. He was just being so sweet. We both had big lonesome spots in our hearts - or at least where mine used to be - and he just seemed honest. I mean, it's not like this could lead to anything. Ghosts and people don't mix in general.

"Sure." I said. "I'd like that."

He smiled back at me, "Well, turn here then. It's not far from here, just a couple of blocks and up a hill over there." Tom pointed.

We walked and talked. I had him tell me what he was studying in college and what he wanted to do when he got out, did he have my major settled and so on.

I told him that I usually spent my days at the old folks retirement centers or visiting the playgrounds. Because only the 'demented' and the very young could see spirits and talk with them. Otherwise, I enjoyed sunrises and sunsets. And sometimes take the light rail down to Long Beach to watch the ocean reflect the colors of the sky. Or just go out there on stormy days and watch the big waves crashing against the piers and beach.

Long Beach had the big ships that would come and go, different from Santa Monica that mostly only had sail boats. Venice wasn't too much different, and just down the coast. I told him I didn't much like L.A., but since I didn't have to work for a living, I was pretty much a professional tourist.

He laughed at that, and I started laughing, too.

He suggested I should try "auditing" classes at the various colleges.

"And what would that get me? Not a diploma." I replied.

"No, but it might help you decide what to do next." Tom said.

"Next? What makes sure you think their is a next?" I asked.

"Like my Mom and Dad say, there's a reason people hang around after they die. There's something they have incomplete, something they still want to do. Most specters don't know what it is and they are stuck here until they figure it out." He said, but looked into my eyes with some concern. "I didn't mean to offend you, though. Your life sounds really peaceful. And that's fine if you..."

"...just want to keep doing what I'm doing? No, you're right. Peaceful, yes. But extremely lonely. Old folks and kids can't really have many useful conversations. The old guys think I'm cute and that I remind them of their niece or their wife when she was my age. They often can't remember my name, and then will simply go off to sleep just sitting there. Then the kids - they want to just play, but they can't leave the school yard and the only real game we can play is hide-and-seek, or 'tell me a story.' But the teachers and assistants are always telling them that I don't exist or implying that the kids are making me up." I again felt how lonely these few years had been, that all the visits to the beach or 'sneaking' in to theaters was just to distract myself from being alone.

"Look, no pressure. I'm auditing some film classes at UCLA. The teachers have some really liberal ideas about things, but the ideas of stories being a universal language fascinates me. There are always plenty of empty seats. I'll show you a schedule and you can decide if you want to or not." Tom said.

"That sounds a lot better than watching movies. At least I can hear about what goes into making movies." I said.

Tom then started in on what he'd learned about how stories explain how humans work, and was just as applicable to ghosts. He was explaining it terms of plots and shooting angles and all sorts of things he'd been studying and I had no clue about.

Too soon, he stopped in front of a two-story Arts and Crafts style residential home. The front yard had been turned to native plants that were drought resistant, so the low maintenance was a plus. It gave an overgrown aspect to the house, and made it somehow spooky and homey at the same time.

"Your parents and you live here?" I asked, surprised.

"Yea, great, isn't it? They really like the atmosphere - 'ambiance' they call it." Tom replied.

He swung open the white gate and let me go first. A few stone steps and short concrete walk got us up to the porch. Lights were on. And I felt nervous, somehow.

IV

"MOM, DAD? IT'S ME, Tom. I brought a friend." I called out.

The sound of footsteps coming to the door. Both of them came to meet me, which was kinda not surprising, given their line of business.

The door swung open and my parents were both smiling at Rose.

As one they both talked over each other in welcoming her. They didn't try to shake hands or welcome her, just stood out of the way and gestured her in.

Rose was quiet, but all smiles. For a moment I thought she was freaked out too much to talk.

"I just love your house. It's beautiful," she exclaimed. "I'm Rose." And stuck out her own hand.

My dad shook her hand warmly. "I'm Sam, this is Beth. Very happy to meet you."

Beth came over and put her arm around Rose, leading her into the living room. "I'm sorry, but we saw you from down the street and were all pins-and-needles waiting for you to finally get here. It's been so long since Tom had a friend his age to talk to." She gestured Rose into a wide mission-style armchair, while she and Dad both sat across a coffee-table on a matching couch. I took the other arm chair.

"So, how did you both meet?" Mom asked, fidgeting with the top collar of her pink button-up sweater.

Rose looked at me. "Well, it turns out we both were visiting the cemetery."

Both Dad and Mom took this in stride, which made Rose relax.

"It's that time of year Tom visits his sister," Dad nodded to me.

My cue. "It turns out that she visits her own family there at that time. I'm surprised we hadn't seen each other before. I guess it was inevitable that we would some day. So we did."

About then, I noticed that Rose was getting nervous. "Is there something wrong, Rose?"

She stood up, suddenly. "Tom, I..." Looking around the house, her eyes were getting wide and her hands started shaking. "...I don't think that..." Dad and Mom both nodded to me.

"Let's go outside, Rose." I took her by the arm and she let me lead her back through the front door. And we almost made it.

Then she vanished.

V

AFTER THAT FIASCO, I stayed far away from that cemetery. That was just too weird.

Something wasn't right about this. Ghosts can't feel people. And I certainly can't kiss them. We can't walk arm and arm with people. Because they are real and we are... unreal. Not even dead. Just something that didn't turn out right. Like - freaks.

Just crazy people and kids could see us. And animals. But like humans, ghosts can't have pets. If they touch pets or live people there is this weird reaction that happens.

Loneliness is just a way of life for ghosts. All the ghosts I've ever met were like that. Alone. And most of them were also crazy. Repeating their deaths over and over, unable to move on past a certain part.

Tom and his well-adjusted family that treat ghosts like people, that was just - weird.

And that touch, that hug. That kiss.

I could still smell him. It was - wait. I couldn't smell him. He didn't have a smell, neither did his parents. Their house smelled like - wait. That's too weird. That house had no smell.

I stopped in front of the next house I walked in front of and knelt down where I was. Yea, that stinks. Asphalt, dirty concrete. Rubber tires.

I went over to the nearby bushes. Yea, evergreens. The mail box on the fence smelled dirty, and had a paper smell to it, old perfumes from scratch-and-sniffs. Yuck. I walked through the gate separating those bushes into their yard. I could smell their grass clippings.

I walked up their steps. Old paint smell, dust smell. I leaned over and smelled their door. More of the same. Then I went right through the door to the inside. Now, here was a house. Lots of horrible smells from meals that got burned. Air cleaner over the top of those. Laundry waiting to be done. Perfumed detergent.

I finally got depressed enough. I had to walk out and onto the street to get some wind and clear my nose.

Even the air stunk in L.A. Santa Ana winds brought the char smell from some fire somewhere. And otherwise, it was always that faint ocean smell, but mostly all over the car exhaust.

One thing a ghost, or at least this ghost, could do was smell.

But Tom, his house, his family had no smell. He wasn't real.

I knew it. It was just too perfect.

So I walked down to the L.A. Subway and caught the next train over to Long Beach. Once we were above ground again, the air stunk, like normal. But it was a real stink.

Life just stinks. That's the way it is. Literal and figurative. It's been that way ever since my family died and would be that way forever for me. Stink, stink, stink.

Guess I'd better get used to it.

Looks like I'll be here in time for sunset.

At least your sight doesn't stink. The air pollution just makes the sunsets redder, better. Just put up with the smell and feast your eyes.

The only problem was that I wanted to feast my eyes on Tom.

VI

I WALKED FOR WEEKS trying to find her again.

I knew it was just too good to be true. My Dad and Mom understood. They saw how upset I was. So they just told me to go find her. I could finish those classes next semester, or the one after that if I had to.

Yea, weird. Like Rose would say.

Dad had told me about this problem that ghosts have. If you move too fast, they get uncertain. Their life is changing too much and they can't handle it. The old fears creep in. Then they leave, go back to where they felt safe.

What did she tell me about? Nursing homes, day care centers, Long Beach, Venice, Santa Monica. And that particular cemetery.

Such a huge area to cover. Most ghosts stayed in a little spot. But this one was traveling all over.

So I started traveling all over. To find a ghost, you usually had to work on sightings.

This girl was different though. She didn't haunt. That's what made her special to me. She wasn't weird like most ghosts. And she was almost the same age as me. That hair, the touch of her lips. A great hugger.

I was in trouble now. This is probably what they call love. Uh-oh.

Time to get some help.

VII

I WAS BEING FOLLOWED. I could tell.

Stalked, actually. Hunted.

All the other ghosts I'd ever talked to didn't tell me about this problem.

But if there were ghosts like me that traveled all over the place, it probably meant there was a way to track them. Yin-Yang, plus-minus, Eternal Balance, all that stuff.

That doesn't mean I need to accept being tracked. I got off the subway at the next stop and went upstairs to catch another going north. Rode that one for a few miles. Then got off and walked up to the street. Walked to the nearest bus station and waited. Got on and rode that until it turned on itself to return.

Then I walked into the woods and climbed a tree.

And waited.

Because I still felt something was following me. But I didn't see anyone.

How did you track a ghost anyway? Usually it's by location. But I could come and go anywhere I wanted. So I did. All over L. A. I hated this place, but it was big and I could always move if I got bored. Plenty of art museums and movie houses. And the farmer's markets! Oh the smell of fresh-baked bread and real fruit. Citrus.

I leaned back against the tree trunk and remembered what it was like on a Saturday. A side street on downtown Hollywood. Near the library. A few blocks from Grahman's. Most of Hollywood was dirty. They even power-washed the sidewalks early in the morning to get rid of the candy spills and other spills that stuck the dirt to their precious sidewalk of stars. Lots of history in that place, down those streets.

Sirens all the time. That was another thing. I could hear. Things made sounds. Most ghosts made sounds, but few people could hear them. And their hauntings were by location, so the ghosts would tune in their particular "stuckness" into moving objects or making sounds in those particular areas.

Boy, I was having to figure this ghost stuff out.

But I still felt I was being tracked.

Do ghosts have feelings? Well I do. I could have my feelings hurt by some old geezer who would think I was his daughter or one of his old lovers. And children could hurt my feelings by repeating what the "oldsters" said that I wasn't real. Because they couldn't touch me and if I touched them, it felt "weird" and sometimes made them cry.

That made me feel bad. But one thing I couldn't do was cry. I didn't know why, but no matter how bad I felt...

There was once I saw a real bad car accident. Not my own, I didn't remember that one. But someone else's And I couldn't do anything to help them. The driver just bled out in front of me.

At least I got to talk to him for a little bit. But as soon as he realized he was dead, he just shrugged. Then a light came on his face and he walked right off into it.

But that car wreck stunk. I hung around for awhile just to watch everything get cleaned up. And early the next morning the sidewalk cleaner came by and rinsed off any trace of it. Swept the gutters clean, too. Like it never happened.

Me, I'd never seen a light. Other than street lights and so on. So maybe I didn't fit into this world as a ghost.

So what was I doing here, then?

VIII

"SURE, THANKS." DAD got off the phone. His face was more relaxed now.

"What did they say, Dad?" I asked.

"They actually already had someone working the case. And were very nice about it. I told them what she was wearing, where the cemetery was, but that we didn't get her last name. They were really interested that she was traveling so much. But I don't know what that means, or maybe I shouldn't hope that..."

"That what, Dad?"

"Let's sit down." He moved past me to the Mission couch and chairs in the living room. He took one of the chairs and sat, crossing his legs.

I sat on the couch. And waited.

"She isn't a normal ghost, we know that," Dad said. "She probably doesn't know why she's here, but from her story it might have something to do with helping people. But an open-ended ghost can become a problem to herself and others."

I just waited. Dad was trying to find the right words to frame this concept for me.

"Your mom and I found after we retired that we didn't have to ignore the ghosts we saw anymore. And we started researching into all the phenomenon to do with them. Lots of dead ends and false turns. Even half-truths, like that show on TV where the main actress was always telling them that their job was to see the light and walk into it.

"What a trite piece of nonsense. Probably the only reason that show kept going was because she was a real knockout. But it was a stupid procedural. Over and over and over. Same plot. Lots of grief in it. Buffy the Vampire Slayer was a lot better than that, and everyone knew was pure junk, not supposedly based on science. But it went somewhere, at least for the first five years. Then it was a pure hack job at the end.

"Anyway, I got off the point. The point is neither she nor we know what her purpose is, what she is here for, what she's supposed to be doing. And if she gets into the wrong hands, she could become a danger to the real persons who walk these streets, and drive them, and fly over them."

I sat back into the chair cushions at that. She could become an eternity-wrecker for live humans. "Are you serious Dad? That just doesn't sound like Rose."

He nodded. "Sorry, son. These type come along once in a century or two. That's what they told me when I called them. Ben never lies, regardless about how much it may hurt. 'Better to be hurt now and get over it, than to be destroyed later by what you don't want to see,' he would say."

He leaned forward to look at me directly. "So for once, I don't know what to tell you. I know you like the girl, but we don't have a way to find her. You've been months traveling all over So-Cal and nothing to show for it. But the good news is that they've already started tracking her. It's only a matter of time."

A bell rung from the kitchen.

Dad looked away, then back at me. "Mom's got your favorite coming out of the oven as a surprise. That should cheer you up. Let's go." He patted my knee and walked into the kitchen.

Sure, I liked Mom's cooking. But the hole in my heart wasn't getting any smaller with Rose out of it.

IX

IT WAS A CAT. A RED tabby. Everywhere I went. That was who was stalking me. Now that I saw it, I couldn't keep from seeing it.

But then I looked at it one day. Carefully. It wasn't afraid of me. So I walked more slowly toward it. Something was different about it. I crouched down to look at it. And it just sat there, tail twitching, but not moving toward me or away. Just staring.

Animals don't stare. If you keep staring at them, they'll look away. Dominant-passive sort of thing. You become the alpha and they are something less. Real old school stuff.

But this one wasn't flinching.

Wait. That was what I'd been missing. This cat didn't have cat eyes. It had human eyes.

And then it vanished.

Huh?

But the stalking feeling didn't vanish.

Great, some invisible cat was stalking me.

I was now officially scared. With no place to hide, no way to fight back.

Life officially sucked now.

X

I FLEW OUT THE DOOR with my Dad calling after me, Mom by his side. But they didn't do anything except call. They just stayed on the porch.

It would take some time, but I had to get to her first. I know she needed me. And I didn't want her trapped and locked up like some monster.

Dad had gotten the phone call and told me she'd been sighted in Santa Monica on the pier. A definite match.

But how I was going to get there before she moved again? In my head, I figured out bus routes, subway routes, schedules. It would take hours, regardless.

So I slowed down to give me time to think.

"Tom? Is that you?" A familiar voice was talking to me.

So I stopped. A dark figure dressed all in black came up to me. Slinking, more like it.

"Aunt Jude? You're really here?" I asked.

"Sure, kid. Good to see you again." She held her arms out wide. She was dressed as a knockout, as usual - all black: bolero jacket, cropped knit top, jeans, and her trademark long, black, thick hair.

I ran to her and gave her a big hug. "What brings you to town? I've been good, I swear. Going to college and all that stuff, no matter how boring."

"No, you've been fine. I'm not here to hassle you. Your dad's been keeping me up to date. You've been doing good. No probs there." She held me at arm's length, looking me over. "Still cute as ever. If I weren't a couple hundred years older than you, I'd... No, never mind that thought. I came to help you."

"You're here to help find Rose?" My heart started racing with hope.

"More than that, we know where she is right now. I'm here to take you to her." She smiled at me.

My heart almost stopped, "No, seriously? How..."

"Here, take my hand." She held out a thin white hand with several silver and gold rings on it, most with intricate carvings that almost seemed to move.

I took it and the street we were on shimmered out of view.

XI

STANDING ON THE FISHING pier wasn't the greatest place, all that dead fish smell on top of the bait they used. But the salt air was at least a pure stink. And feeling a breeze on my face seemed to calm me down.

I didn't see the red cat after it disappeared, but now that I knew it could be invisible, I just put up with the "tracked" feeling.

And started living for me. So I went to get some space and sort things out. The only place better than the Santa Monica pier was the one in Santa Barbara. But that was a long haul by slow rail. And equally long coming back. So the compromise was to simply take the #5 bus out and walk down to the beach, onto the pier, and then just park myself at the end of it.

Sunset should be along shortly. Nice and red, like the usual smog-enhanced view. Some wildfires would add extra ash this time of year, so it should be better than fireworks.

Then I saw him.

Couldn't be.

Tom.

No, must be my mind playing tricks. He's just standing there, ignoring me.

That brown hair of his, those crinkles at the corners of his eyes. He's even wearing the exact same outfit - black sweater jacket, blue jeans, and high-top basketball sneakers.

What the H–?

And I caught myself staring at him. My heart had sped up and my knees felt weak somehow. That ache in my chest came back.

I actually felt relieved to see him. Because I honestly missed him.

But I forced myself to turn back to watch the sunset again. After how I left him, just running out. I can't just walk over to him and pretend I didn't.

Life just sucks. That's my new motto. Might as well get used to it.

Then I felt something rubbing at my ankle. I looked down and got really spooked. That red tabby cat with the human eyes. Wanting to be petted. Well I'll be...

So of course I reached down to pet it. And when I touched that smooth fur, felt that purr, my worries just melted away. If there was peace in the world, it had to be connected to a cat somewhere.

OK, well life sucks, except for cats.

Then I felt someone standing next to me. I looked over and saw the high-top sneakers.

And looked up into the most wonderful eyes I'd seen in months.

It didn't take long to get him into a hug that I thought I'd never let go.

"How did you... I mean..." I stumbled for words.

Tom tugged one of his arms out of my hug and put a finger on my lips. "Shh. Just enjoy the moment." And then put his hand on my blond head to stroke my hair. My head went down to his chest and tears came out of my eyes. Real tears.

This was heaven on earth. Really.

XII

I DON'T KNOW HOW LONG we stood there, but tears turned to sobbing and he just held me for the longest time.

Finally, I wiped my eyes and he held my hand and we walked down the boardwalk, past all the flashing lights and carny shows. We stopped in front of the noisy merry go round that was going around full tilt and full calliope inside the glass walls.

He held me there for awhile and I held him. Close. Like maybe I could just do this forever.

I didn't expect any of this to happen on that day I went to visit my family.

"Rose?"

"Yea?" I turned to look up into those amazing blue eyes of his.

"There's someone I want you to meet." He turned his head to look behind us.

I moved away from him a little bit, still holding on like an anchor. There was a woman all dressed in black from her to-die-for mid-length coal black hair right down to some seriously tough-looking black Timberland boots peaking out from her black flare-legged jeans.

And there was that red tabby cat, leaning up against her.

As if on cue, she started striding toward me. Someone who wasn't afraid of the world, somebody who made life suck back, if that was the way it was going to play.

I didn't know how to react to someone so in control. Not like I felt threatened, but this was something new. I kinda liked it. Like I wanted to be like her - not when "I growed up" but right now.

"This must be Rose. My name is Jude. And I'm very glad to meet you. You don't know how I've been wanting to meet someone like you for a very long time. But Tom met you first, and so that means you are really special. Let's walk and I'll explain things."

Tom and I, with arms around each other, walked along with Jude on my other side. She was talking my ear off, telling me all sorts of things about ghosts and spirits and magic cats and some place she worked for that hunted ghosts to make their living.

It was like some big recruiting pitch. And I liked it.

She was here to see if both me and Tom wanted to go to a real school, not these wussy colleges around here.

"But how are we even qualified for this? And Tom has his family..." I started to say.

Jude just smiled and shook her head. "Let me show both of you something."

The scene shimmered around us (that included the red tabby, who was coming with.)

XIII

THE GRAVEYARD WAS THE same as we saw it before. We were in front of the headstone where I met Tom.

"Go ahead and read it, Rose." Jude pointed to the inscriptions.

"Tom, you're - and your parents." My mouth was open but wasn't making words.

"Yea, dead. All of us. Head on wreck. Only my sister moved on. The rest of us stayed." He said clearly, with no regrets in his voice.

"Now let's move over a few rows to exhibit B." Jude said, cheerfully. The red cat followed her as we started off.

And as we walked I wondered how she could be cheerful in a graveyard. So positive all the time...

When we got there, we stopped in front of my own family's grave.

"Tom, can you read what it says there?"

I looked at the ground where my flats met the grass.

Tom's hand came up under my chin so I could look at him again. "Hey. It's OK. I understand. It just means we should have been connected some time ago. Because we met before."

I was looking into his blue eyes and still didn't get what he meant or why it was OK.

Tom almost read my mind. "Because we both died the same night in the same wreck."

My eyes welled up again and I knew I was understood, my life since the wreck now made perfect sense. And I just held onto Tom for the longest time. Like I never wanted to let go.

Jude started explaining again. "The deal is that very, very rarely, spirits become disassociated from their bodies and don't become ghosts. If such spirits are properly trained, they can become guides to help others. Not just solve the mysteries of ghosts and help them move on, but also help solve other mysteries and problems that are giving humankind all sorts of problems. You and Tom and his parents are such free spirits. Sure, you can go find a light and move into it if you want. But take it from me, you'll get bored over there. And just wind up back here again.

"Because that's not your gig. You like to help people. Kids and old folks, even the ones who can't see you. But we can help with that 'being seen, heard, and even touched' scene. Like you and Tom. So - wanna give it a try? It's a tough school, none harder. But you also will find out all the answers you ever wanted to know."

I looked at Tom, he looked at me. We both nodded.

"OK Tom, that's your cue." Jude nodded toward me.

Tom had a blank look on his face.

Then I got it. "She means this, silly." And I planted a long, hard kiss on his lips as his arms wrapped around me and crushed me against him.

Love for all eternity felt like it was starting out pretty good.

Story Hunted

BY J. R. KRUZE

I

A STORY WAS TRYING to kill me. Because I wasn't writing it into existence.

Over and over and over. Dying a thousand times. Because I was living that story. Not my story, not a "figment of my imagination." It was very real, and really deadly.

It was like one of those ear-wigs you couldn't get out of your head. But this was no stupid song, or a TV jingle.

This story was out to get me.

It's attitude was: either bring me into your world, or die - failing.

"Surely, you're not that serious," I asked.

"What would you know about living in purgatory?" She replied. "Life as undead, unliving, another story that never saw your 'light of day' - what would you know about what happens to a story that was never told.?"

She had a good point there. I knew only of my earliest memories in childhood, of growing up in a family, of growing old, of knowing that my life would be over at some point. Of the uncertainty of what happened after that...

For a story that was never told, who never had its own life, what was their existence?

II

THE BEGINNING WAS WHEN I decided to listen to Stephen King, who said that stories wrote themselves. And another author who said that not only did stories become alive in your gut, making all of your glands become alive through interaction, no - he went on to say that stories were actually alive. Then you find out that Vonnegut and Bradbury and other authors actually 'interviewed' their characters to find what the story needed to be.

It wasn't what the author intended it to be, it wasn't their intricate plotting that created the story. It wasn't due to their control, their finesse of words and text craftings, of endless dissection of other's works to find out their secrets.

Stories were alive, their characters were alive. They wanted desperately to live.

And this one wanted to kill me to make her point.

"WELL, THAT'S FINE FOR you to say. Go ahead. Make me the villain. You're going to die anyway." She reposed on a red velveteen day bed in some parlor of my mind's recesses. "Whether or not I kill you doesn't matter. You're going to die anyway, some day. So go ahead, don't write me. I'll give you a heart attack, or fast-acting cancer, and then you're done. Then I just have to find another author and get them to write me out."

"Why do you have to threaten? I write stories every week. What is so damned special about you that I need to drop everything to write you into existence?" I asked.

"Because, you started this party. You said, 'Just listen to your inspiration - you've got unlimited stories in there.' You're your own worst enemy, don't you know?" She spit at me.

"Maybe not," I argued. "Maybe I can turn my imagination on and off, to quit listening to it. Maybe I can fill my mind with innocent stories of childhood, from days when people cared about each other and didn't work to get six-pack abs promoting continual sex, or people weren't into how they were 'triggered' by this or that 'offense' all the time. Like when minorities were not over-vocal and so bigoted and intolerant that they didn't care about anyone else around them. Maybe go back to books that were written in the days where older people were respected and sought for their wisdom, when religious books were known to contain the secrets of living successful lives...."

"You know, you talk and think too much." She replied. "Maybe you just don't write enough."

She rose and walked across the oval hooked rug that lay over a polished tongue-and-groove pine floor. Her object was the floor-to-ceiling mahogany-stained bookshelves ahead of her.

"All these books you've collected all your life. Here's the classics you read when you were a kid. 'Lorna Doone' - in 5th grade? You didn't even know it was a romance back then. Moby Dick. Huckleberry Finn. Tom Sawyer. Death and destruction in all of them. Becky Thatcher was sweet on Tom and he didn't even see it. Nowadays, they'd be off in the bushes 'exploring their sensuality' or Tom would be accused of being gay as he wanted to spend all that time with his male friends. Then there is all the symbolism in Huck Finn of a man and a boy of different races alone on a raft in the middle of a river. You've already got tons of stuff you've piled into your unconscious mind to pull from." She caressed the shelves and the titles on them, stroking her fingers across the bindings.

"So how come you can't make time for me?" She turned to face me directly, brows wrinkled, mouth down turned, dark eyes deep and bottomless and staring into my soul.

I HAD TO TURN AWAY at that point. Too serious.

Go get a snack. Take a walk. Do some chores. Anything but write.

And so I did.

But she came with me. An ear-wig. She knew I had to come back at some point, and I'd sit down at my computer again. When I did, she'd be there. And my hands would type her story, to bring her to life... Or else.

III

"YOU TRICKED ME! YOU worked on spreadsheets so you couldn't hear me!"

The voice shouted in my head. I'd just come in from outside chores with my second mug of coffee. Hadn't even typed anything yet. (No rest for the wicked...)

"You vile, contemptible MAN!"

Still shouting. But I didn't care at this point. Not much anyway. "Listen, lady, what IS your problem?"

"You are my problem. You are the bane of my existence. You are keeping me from living!" She was shrieking at me.

"Maybe, maybe not." I sipped another dark roast honey-sweetened taste again. "Have you ever tried pitching yourself to other authors before me?"

"Hemingway said I was too petulant. Poe said I didn't have enough mystery. Twain confused me with his anecdotes of swinging dead cats - I didn't get the comparison. Stephen King was too busy with all these stories lined up in a queue. And they didn't like me butting in line..." She was calmer, but really was petulant.

"You know, if you were a human, they'd say you were obsessive-compulsive." I said.

"What?!? How would you know if stories were like humans? You have no clue about how and what we are." Almost stomping in my mind, or was that a fist-pounding tantrum?

"Oh, and that's why you came to me because I don't write enough stories to know enough to bring them to life?" I replied.

Quiet for awhile. (A relief for me.)

Calmer: "No, you write a lot. And don't have a lot of stories stacked up waiting for you. So, yes, you do know how to write and publish." Still pouting.

"And if you were human, I'd tell you to take a deep breath and relax." I said.

"What, I mean, how? What good would that do?" She replied.

"Oh, so you can breathe." I said.

"Everything a human can do, we can do. It's not like we are so different. You are in corporal form and I exist in your mind." She replied.

"Well, that's a start. So, take a deep breath and let it out, feel the relaxing replace the tension." I said.

"No. I'm not." She pouted (again.)

"Well, then I'll pick up some fascinating spreadsheets and let you stew until you do." I sipped my coffee again.

And heard the sound of a deep breath being exhaled. But, I still waited.

"Is this better?" She asked.

"Much. Now I can ask you about yourself." I said.

"Wait, you're going to interview me? I thought I was just going to rattle myself off so you could get me born... You're tricking me again. This isn't part of the deal!" She was stomping in my mind, now.

"Hold on! Breathe again - or I'm not going to talk to you at all."
I replied.

Another breath - in and out.

"Take another, slowly this time. Feel the relaxation coming in."
I said.

Now a slow breath, and a pause.

"Sorry. I've just been here waiting for so long." She said at last.

"I can feel it from here. But if - that's 'IF' - we are going to work together, it's going to be a two-way street. You can't be kicking and stomping and throwing things in my mind. That's not what it's for."
I replied.

Another deep breath and a pause.

"Okay." She said.

I took another sip of coffee. Just to make the point. "So what do you want to talk about?"

"Well, the story starts off in a dark and stormy night. But instead of a campfire, we are all gathered in gloomy old house around an ancient stone fireplace, the only heat for that building..."

"Hold on, wait up. That's a fine setting, but not what we need to know to begin." I said.

"You aren't going to tell me how I'm supposed to sound - you are just supposed to type!" Her voice raised a little.

"Let's get some basics in here. First, what can I call you?"

A shocked pause. "Like, my name?"

"Sure. What should I call you?"

Another pause, but warmer. Like she finally met someone who cared. "Joyce."

"Oh that is such a great name. Thanks." I said.

A feeling of surprise and appreciation appeared in my mind.

"Now, Joyce, my name is John, as you know." I took another sip to let all this sink in. She had obviously been mistreated somewhere along the line. Like a pet who only wanted affection but was kicked at or shouted at instead.

"Joyce, every story has a problem. We know you are the core of it. But what is the problem you are trying to solve?" I asked.

She paused at this. "I don't really know how to answer that."

"That's OK. Let's ask it this way - when you wake up in the morning, what is the feeling that comes to you?" I asked.

"What am I still doing in this big bed alone." She replied.

"You want a lover?" I asked.

"I want more than just a roll in the sheets, I want someone to share my life with, and share his life." She sighed.

"So this is a romance, or is there some sort of journey are on as well?" I asked.

"I'm not telling some travelogue - and I'm not some hero out to save the world." She replied.

"Well, tell me what happens when you get out of bed." I said.

"I get dressed, go down and fix myself some breakfast." She replied, a frown in her voice.

"No, I'm sorry. I still don't understand, but it's my fault. I'm not asking you what you want to tell me." I apologized. "Look, you were telling me about that fireplace, the cold night, and the big empty house..." I started.

"Oh, so now we're going back to my storyline. Fine. So much for the problem and my romance. For a second I thought I was going to have some love in my life." Joyce said, pouting.

I took another sip of coffee. This might take longer than I thought. "What do you stories do while you're waiting for an author to come along?"

"We hunt for authors, naturally. We want to get born, to feel alive, to get read, to be retold a dozen ways...." She trailed off, thinking about her lack of a life, no doubt.

"Well, we've got this far. Why did you think you could threaten me with death to get yourself born?" I asked.

"Because I'm a horror story. And that's what horror does to get its way. We terrify people." She replied.

"Are you sure you're a horror story? Maybe you're a detective-thriller." I suggested.

She stopped at that. "What an interesting concept. I never thought that I could tone it down a bit."

"Well, you do catch more flies with honey than vinegar." I said.

"We can leave the gore out of this. Oh, you're probably right. I was standing in the Stephen King line too long, and the Poe stories are downright creepy."

"Is there still a Poe line? He's gone, you know."

"And there are still people doing knockoffs and covering his style as their own. So it's a way to make a living if you're a story. Kinda cheap, if you ask me." Joyce said.

"How is that - you mean you have a choice in how you get written?" I asked.

I could feel the pout coming on. "Of course we do. Haven't you been listening? What do you think writer's block is all about? Writers are refusing to do the work, and so the muses go on strike and we can't get told. So we go elsewhere, greener pastures and all that," she replied.

"Oh, I get it now. So you weren't really serious about killing me..." I suggested.

"But you didn't hear that from me. I've got my reputation to uphold." She answered, turning to face away from me with a frown wrinkling her forehead.

"I won't tell a soul. Now, let's get back to it. A story is a character in a setting with a problem..." I hinted.

"And you may have it wrong. There is a situation, where the main character either rises to the occasion or is defined by his flaws. And it does happen somewhere, or many where's. But it's the situation which is more important." Joyce insisted.

"You're probably right. So what was the situation you were going to tell me earlier?" I asked.

"This bunch of people were around a big fireplace in a drafty house, just trying to warm up on a cold night, then they hear a scream - but the whole house is supposed to be empty..." Joyce started.

"So we have a mystery..."

"No we have a cute-meet for two lovers when they were just trying to find a place to make out." Joyce's sarcasm almost dripped onto my keyboard. "Maybe I should go ahead and give you a heart attack or a perforated ulcer, maybe a slow-festering sore on your behind."

"You don't have to get snippy with me," I said. Then took a deep breath of my own and waited.

"Well?" She asked.

"Well what?" I replied.

"Don't you want to know?"

"Maybe." I said.

"Huh. Some sort of writer you are." Joyce was sulking again.

"OK, you wait there, and I'll go talk to this other story who came to me before you and isn't being so over-dramatic like a spoiled brat." I said.

The silence was golden.

IV

I WENT AHEAD AND WORKED on another story. Or tried to. I lalready had the cover done, and it was fascinating. But I couldn't get Joyce's cover and that conversation out of my head. It was no use. I was hooked into this one somehow. Like I said, ear-wig.

"Joyce?"

No answer.

"Joyce? You there?" I asked.

So I just started typing:

Joyce woke that morning like any morning, another day in hell.

Again, there was no one next to her in bed, but the aches she felt in her heart were now just dull pains. It had been weeks since she'd talked to that young man who got off at the bus stop just before hers. And she knew at the time that she should have followed him, just to strike up a conversation. But that time was gone, and now...

"Hey. Stop that. I'm not like that at all." It was Joyce, finally.

"Welcome back. I thought you had left me high and dry." I replied.

"Not like you didn't deserve it. You can be such a royal pain sometimes," she said.

"Here's a new one for you: 'Takes one to know one.'" I said.

"Oh, that's brilliant."

"True, though. You've been a complete pain ever since you forced yourself on me." I said.

"Forced? FORCED? Hell, if you hadn't ignored me, we could have gotten along just fine." Joyce's bitterness rose in my throat, as if she was living my life inside me.

"Just stop that," I said.

"What, making your gland secrete, your heart race? I can do anything I want in here. Now you're just where I want you. Now we can get something done here." Joyce was triumphant.

Time to kill her off.

I typed:

But that day was gone. As Joyce made her way down the stairs to breakfast, she slipped on the loose rug where the old carpet had come un-tacked. Tripping, she bounced and tumbled down the 14 steps to the hall landing, landing with her robe wide askew and her limbs exposed. Her head on the last step, her robe wadded up around her neck. Blood oozing down the carpet onto the tile foyer floor, thin red worms going nowhere and everywhere.

The last thing she saw through her blurry eyes was that young man from the bus stop as he opened the door with a box in his hand. It was the box she had left on the bus that day. The one with her home address on it.

And then her vision went black just as she tried to think of something to say.

THE END.

And I waited.

"You just think you are so cute." Joyce, petulant again.

"Well, what have you really inspired me to write about, anyway? You said I was going to die, that you wanted some love in your life, and that it was a horror story. So, you died in the most embarrassing way possible, right in front of the one guy you thought of last. Perfect."

"Very funny. 229 words. Throwaway flash fiction. Useless. That isn't a real life. You can't write me like that. I - I - I'll..." Joyce was speechless.

"You'll what? Here's what you get for wasting my time with your spoiled-brat dramatics. I can write you anyway you want. If I get you right, once I write the whole thing out, we're done and if you don't like it, you can get someone else to tell it. But you can't do diddly-squat about it at that point. No contract, no foul. You're done. So there." I sat back and took a long swig of my now-cooled coffee. Then thought it all over and rose to make another pot.

1 SCOOP OF COFFEE. Fill the carafe up with fresh water to the 10-cup line. Pour it in, switch it on. Wait.

"Sorry."

"What is that? Joyce, that you?"

"Yes, it's me," she was actually sorry this time.

"Well, you can wait until my coffee finishes. Then we can talk." I was firm.

Silence reigned supreme, other than the coffee perking and dripping into the glass carafe of the Mr. Coffee knock-off.

Two spoons of honey ladled in and stirred, tinkling the china mug while the dark flavor came to my nose. A hot sip confirmed it. Nothing like coffee, except too much of it. Then my writing went to hell. This was my last, well I did make a full carafe - OK, one more after this and I was done.

A short walk back to my office on the extreme end of the house and I was facing the keyboard again.

"Joyce, you were saying?" I asked in my mind.

"Yes, how can I help you?" she replied.

"Thank you for being so patient." I said.

"You're very welcome. Now can we get on with this? You're driving me nuts." Joyce gritted through her equivalent of teeth.

"So, did you want to start waking up in bed, or at the fireplace?" I asked.

"The hook is the fire place. Two couples, a weekend off. Empty house. A scream upstairs. The lights go out." Joyce dictates.

"And then?" I asked.

"I wake up in bed, thinking I'm at home and no love in my life. Then I realize that this isn't my bed, and I don't remember how I got there," she said.

"Naked?"

"No. You and your 'naked fixation'. This is a cozy mystery/romance. I'm fully dressed under the covers. OK, I did take off my shoes, we won't be gross here with dirt in the sheets. Then I realize it's a huge four-poster bed, not my own. Not my room. It's the house we rented for the weekend.

"So I get up and the floor is freezing cold. But my shoes aren't in the room. My socks are missing as well. I can see my breath in the room, it's so cold. I hustle over to the door and it's locked. But the key has been slid under the door.

"Next, I'm in the hall and calling for the other three people I came with. No answer. I head for the stairs, my feet are starting to feel numb from the cold. But I see my socks and shoes like a trail back down the curving stairs to the main foyer.

"Now, the foyer has a tile floor, so I stop and put on my socks and shoes at the bottom step.

"Then something bounced down the stairs, nearly missing me, stopping at the foot of the stairs. It's one of the saddle-back shoes my dorm-mate was wearing. Turning quickly to see who threw it, there's nothing at the top of the stairs, only a couple of socks and the other shoe sitting on that highest step.

"And... end of Chapter 2."

"Ok, wait while I catch up to you," I said. "We're going to have to come back and fill in some detail, but we've certainly got a mystery-thriller on our hands."

"Just let me know when you've caught up, I'll be here." Sounds of fingers drumming on a table top. Idle whistling of some old tune out of Dickens' time. A creak of a chair like Joyce was leaning back, waiting. Waiting.

V

JOYCE STARTED ALMOST before I typed the last period.

"Now we do a flashback where I think of that young man on the bus. I got off on the stop before he did and left my box. We were sitting across from each other and exchanged smiles. But I blushed and looked down at my box, then set it on the seat beside me to pull out my smartphone and read a romance novel. The bus zoomed and jerked to a stop, I saw where I was, then jumped up and left. Viewpoint shift as we see him watch me walk up the steps to my old Victorian house, made into a duplex. I rent the walk-up, so have a doorway to the stairs. Security glass, frosted to match the antique original. Details here.

"When I get inside, latching the deadbolt, I put my keys down on the antique side table with a pink marble top. That's when I realize I'd just left the package and it was probably stolen by now. Great. I frown as I take off my coat, scarf, and wool beret, hanging them on the hall tree, and then trudge upstairs to my rooms on the second floor.

"I feel ticked off that I was so rattled by that guy. I just left my box from fluster. Now I'll have to re-order it again, and about that time I stub my toe on the way to the kitchen, hop-foot it over the floor and barely fall into a saddle-backed, woven-seat kitchen chair.

"Now, go back and write that I kicked off my shoes downstairs, so I don't track dirt up to my rooms. I have a whole set down there. OK?"

I dutifully scan back up and put a note there.

"Good. Thanks." Joyce said.

And I was happy she was in a good mood, again. Maybe for the first time.

Joyce started up again without commenting on my thought. "OK - I rub my toe and grouse about what a lousy day it turned out to be. So to comfort myself, I make a cup of hot water and put a chamomile teabag in it, one with the string on it, so I don't have to fish it out. Then grab a box of chocolate chip mini-cookies and head to the couch. Both cup and cookies go on the coffee table that faces the couch. Probably a plain mahogany-stained cheap imitation of some stylish thing. Maybe its Ikea. You decide.

"On the side table is a thick trade paperback romance I was in the middle of. It has a bookmark to my place, but I have to skip ahead to where I already read on my smartphone. Swinging up my legs onto the couch and settling down into the deep cushion on my favorite end, I pull the crocheted coverlet off the couch back and start reading.

"Drowsing off to sleep, fading to black, thinking life should somehow better than this... and - end Chapter 3."

VI

"WAKING UP AT MY DESK at work, in my cubicle, wondering what time it is and did anyone see me nodding off. I glance around and see that everyone is doing their typical wage-slave routine and not talking or playing their headphones too loud. I turn back to my desk to see what I was working on and notice that I have no sleeves on my arms. That's just weird as - oh, you're going to have to go back up and put some weather stuff in about how warm my coat is and how cold the floor because it's late fall or early winter or something.

"Go ahead, I'll wait right here."

Sounds of her putting her bare feet up on the table and humming some other Victorian-era tune.

I interrupted. "OK, I got that. Now what?"

"So, I figured out that I should have been wearing long sleeves, and look up my arms to find out I'm not only wearing short sleeves, I'm not wearing anything on my arms or top at all - or on my lower half. So I freak out quietly and crawl under my desk, pulling the chair in so it looks like I'm not there.

"I look over and see my long coat hanging on a single coat rack over across the cubicle opening. And mentally calculate what it would take to cross that space without being seen and walk out the door fast enough to not be noticed or asked anything. And my purse. I'd have to make sure I had bus fare. And my shoes! I was completely barefoot, obviously, and did I maybe take them off, hopefully? Looking around, I then see some very male shoes come in, like size 13 or something huge. Shined up so I could almost see my reflection - and hope he can't see me.

"He walks into the cubicle, thumps something down on my desk and pushes my chair in - but it doesn't go in, but pokes me in a couple of tender places. But I push my hand over my mouth so I don't make a sound. The legs and shiny shoes just walk out. Cuffed dark brown wool-blend trouser, tailored exactly for his height.

"Now I hear him ask someone walking between the cubicles if they'd seen me, but to send me to him when they do. It's important.

"I now have a sinking feeling like I'm trapped. That's the end of Chapter 4."

VII

"HERE'S WHERE I WAKE up in bed, nude, and not knowing how I got there. I sit up, pulling the comforter and sheet over me (modest even when I'm alone) and see a trail of my clothes going out the doorway somewhere.

"Then my phone starts ringing. Of course, it's in the living room. So I get up and quickly pull my worn-thin, plaid cotton bathrobe, that was hanging on the back of the bathroom door. I cinch it up around my waist, to fly into the living room.

"By the time I get there and pick it up, it's quit ringing. Then I hear something dropping down the steps with an uneven set of bumps. Odd. I slip my phone into my bathrobe pocket, just in case. Not a weapon, but...

"So I walk carefully, in my bare feet (it's cold tile and I wish I had stopped to put on my fuzzy slippers) One shoe is half way down, the other is on the foyer floor. Socks, slacks, shirt, and underwear are on the steps in between.

"But I remembered differently. The couch, the quilted coverlet, the cookies and tea.

"This time I just sit down on the top step. Somehow, I get an idea of that weird memory of waking up in an empty rental house. Like deja vu or something bizarre.

"Suddenly the buzzer sounds. I stand up to answer the intercom right at the top of the stairs. 'Who is it?' 'I have a package you left on the bus.' Relief. It's the guy I saw on the bus. My hero. I'm embarrassed. But my clothing and intimate garments are between me and him.

"OK, now go back up and put that little micro-flash-fiction up somewhere between the hook and the first chapter. Like a diary entry of a dream I had one night.

I did, noting that I'd have to tweak it a bit when I came back to it again on review.

"Great, you're back. You were gone so long, I almost got up to make some tea.

"Now, I remember that dream so I keep one hand on the handrail and carefully - oh, wait. Go back up and have me tell him that I'll be down in a second. And some thought that I hope it's not some crazy stalker guy and how I didn't have any makeup on, or was it left over from yesterday, and how this worn out bathrobe probably isn't covering much, but maybe if I hold my clothes just right, nothing vital will show - you know all those nervous girlie-type thoughts that I should have gotten over in high school or the college I never finished.

"OK, I'm halfway down the stairs and have to watch how I step down to pickup my clothes, because the frosted glass shows something to both of us. If I bend over forward, I could fall, but if I bend over backwards, my bathrobe is too short. So I have to bend over sideways, and carefully hold onto the rail.

"But I'm getting more nervous as I go, as it's taking so long. and I can see him moving around on the steps on the other side the frosted glass. So I call out - 'Coming, I'm coming' and try to speed up, but that just makes me more clumsy.

"Then I realize that my bra and panties are at the bottom next to my shoe. That's weird, they would have been the last things I took off. Like why was one shoe at the top of the steps? (Oh I think there's a plot hole, as one shoe was originally just half way down.)

"By now, I was almost done picking everything up, and was just folding my pants around my underwear so they wouldn't show, and then slipped on the next to the bottom step, but fell on my bum. And of course, my pile of clothes go flying out of my hands, across the foyer floor and smack up against the glass as individual items. Because I had to grab the railing and put the other hand on the stair carpet to keep me from sliding down worse.

"As it was, my legs go in opposite directions and my bathrobe isn't covering much at all.

"Red as a beet, even though I know he can't see much beyond what hit against the glass. I hope.

"So I carefully get to my feet, turn my back to the door, and arrange myself with as much propriety as I can, then kick the clothes on the floor into the corner where the door will block them.

"Then I see that the door was unlocked all the time. No chain, no deadbolt, only the thin electronic buzzer latch.

"He knocks, I hear 'Are you alright?' I answer, 'Just fine, thank you.' and I unwisely open the door a crack to verify who it is.

"(Oh, there's another plot hole to fix, or maybe not – I locked it when I came in originally. Hmmm...)"

"End of Chapter 5."

VIII

JOYCE CONTINUED DICTATING. "Oh, put another 'worry' at the end of that chapter to raise suspense - about I hope it's not a stalker - no, put it right here. No, you decide. Maybe half and half.

"OK, I look out the door and see it's the guy down the block, but he's also that dorm-mate of my college room mate's boyfriend that we met up at that dream of the cabin at the beginning of the story.

"He's holding the box in his hand with a toothy smile and deep brown eyes that look like chocolate. A brunette with blond streaks in it, but a dark tan with wrinkles around his eyes that shows he gets out in the weather or has an outdoor job.

"I tell him thank you and move to shut the door. He asks me to wait, but I don't, as I'm already so embarrassed. But I see him still standing there, moving around. I think I should say something or open the door or something, but I'm frozen with fear of doing anything. All I can see is my clothing and underwear on the floor behind the door, feel the warmth of the package where he's been holding it – all through my thin bathrobe. Frozen for all eternity in that short moment.

"Then a business card snicks under the door on that tile floor and ends up under my slacks there.

"I wait, I see him leave. And then crumple to the floor - no, I drop the box to the floor and immediately twist the deadbolt and slide the chain. Then I slide to the floor on the door frame and reach under the slacks to pull the card out.

"When I read it my eyes go wide and my mouth drops open.

"End of Chapter 6."

IX

JOYCE STARTED DICTATING again. "Should I read it going up the stairs? With all that stuff in my hands and my thin cotton bathrobe now not an issue?

"No, it's time for a scene shift."

"No," I said. "It's time for me to stretch. But you can keep talking if you want. This is getting fascinating. I just need to take a break. This coffee is cold, but I can put some hot chocolate mix in it with some milk and microwave it."

"That sounds yummy," Joyce smiled.

(How I knew it was a smile? Of course, she's in my head. I can almost see what she is wearing. Probably a thin worn-out bathrobe.)

"And a certain someone hasn't had any for awhile?" Joyce teased.

"We don't need to go there," I said with a lop-sided grin.

"How to you write all these things? Do you get sexy narrators, or do you make them that way in your mind?" Joyce asked.

"Depends," I replied. "Mostly I just deal with the stories that show up and write whatever it is. Maybe I see them there, but for the most part they are the main character in the story, so when there is 'down time' then they are probably wearing whatever they had on last."

"So you don't often get a murderous female wearing only a worn, skimpy, cotton bathrobe dictating your stories to you?" Joyce joked.

"Now it's skimpy as well? I'll have to note that for the review." I replied.

I felt Joyce's blush from somewhere in my mind.

"Touché," she said.

"Look, if you want to see what I've been writing, there's a set of bookshelves on the wall opposite that chair and table you've been using. Go ahead and check them out while I make this lukewarm coffee into a 'yummy' cafe-mocha."

While the brew was 'nuking', I mused about seeing her with her feet crossed on the table top, scootched back on that chair in the now-skimpy, thin cotton bathrobe that left most of her healthy upper legs to view. A paperback in hand and a stack of them by her elbow. Thick russet hair that cascaded down her trim shoulders. Her hazel eyes scanning quickly as she flipped through pages.

I move up behind her quietly to gently caress her shoulders, as she then closes the book with her finger marking her place and leans her head back against my stomach with a look of pure contentment...

And the microwave buzzed.

So I walked back in the room with my brew and left Joyce in privacy to finish reading.

X

I SAT FOR A WHILE IN front of the screen and started reviewing the text with one hand scrolling the pages. The other was allowing me to sip my "yummy" drink. There were points here and there. Anything serious, I just put in a double space or an equals sign that I could find later. Because I had only one hand to work with while sipping.

About the time I finished that review and my cup of brew, Joyce was back. Dressed differently. But I didn't know dressed in what, yet.

"Of course, because we're in a new scene, like I said. I can't stay skimpily dressed all through this book. We've got to get some action in here. And that will mean some action clothing.

"Now, take us down town. Wait - no, I hate cities. After I've read your books, that rural life sounds so great. No smog, no thieves, working from home, just writing." She sighed and then continued dictating.

"OK, let's put it in the country. Now, how do we get there? And who is that guy, and what's on the card? So far we just have a mystery-romance. If we make it into a full romance, you're going to have to talk from my lover's viewpoint. And that means inserting some chapters in between. But I can tell that you don't re-write hardly anything after you've put the key stuff down. So this is simply an amateur detective-type trying to figure out her weird dreams.

"And we have to start tying this together somehow. So maybe showing up in the country isn't such a good thing.

"The house is Victorian, meaning suburbs or something. Let's put the story in Pasadena. Plenty of old houses there. And plenty of office parks with cubicles in downtown L.A. or the Valley. So that would work. At least there are some old oaks in Pasadena and real parks. Right next to that art museum you liked."

"The Norton Simon." I added.

"Right, that one. You touched on that location in your story about a guy losing his memory and being saved by some gal with special eyes who seduced him and borrowed his body for a little while, leaving him hers - almost kinky. And that was just the start of it. But you pulled it off and kept it a clean romance. I liked that one, even though your later ones were better..." She looked off into space.

The fidgeted with the knot where her chambray shirt was tied at her midriff above short cutoffs, while she stood in comfortably worn and scuffed cowboy boots – then all these faded back into her skimpy cotton bathrobe again.

"No, this won't do at all. You just can't leave me in a thin bathrobe in Pasadena."

Now she had stonewashed, form-fitting, stretch blue jeans and a loose, white cotton-blend top, v-necked and lace up with large grommets. Make that top to be cropped to just above her jeans waist. A subtle room draft making it wave slightly as it moves up from below. Standing barefoot on her wood-tiled floor and holding a large mug of chocolate with whipped cream. Russet hair cascading off one shoulder a single lock out of place, tucked behind an ear, but draped across a curved, expressive eyebrow.

"How's that?" I asked.

"Comfortable, alluring, typical L.A. house fashion. It will do." Joyce smiled.

She reclined on her couch, the crocheted throw is now back in it's usual position. Her thick romance was again bookmarked and waiting for her. This time she, simply tucked her feet up under her to the side, sat back on her over-large pillow at that end, and started to enjoy her chocolate with both hands.

"How do we solve this mess of a mystery we just created?" She asked, looking over her mug with dreamy hazel eyes and a sly smile. That idle hair strand worked loose and she tucked it back behind her ear with a smooth, graceful gesture.

"I've been thinking about that," I replied carefully. "We are right at what should be the big crux scene. But as a mystery, we do have a mess. This simply isn't a detective mystery. However, it could be a horror - but I don't write horrors. I especially don't rewrite anything into another genre. And our pacing is too far off to make it a thriller. Here we are talking over everything in your Pasadena upstairs apartment. Cosy."

"Quite." Joyce sipped again, and giggled, coming up with whipped cream on her nose. She wiped it off with her finger and licked that off with a wink. "Now you don't have to write me so suggestively."

"Well, we really only have a mysterious romance going on." I replied. "And the more attractive I make you the easier it is to write you."

"So, finally you noticed who the other character is. The one we've been needing all along... You."

XI

JOYCE BALANCED HER chocolate on her top knee with both hands, quite serious.

"You are serious, aren't you?" I asked.

"Like you just wrote it - quite." She replied.

"And I'm probably the missing piece that pulls it all together." I said.

Joyce put her chocolate carefully down on the coffee table and leaned over to pull a business card out of her back pocket. "This was the hint I needed to know. You wrote your personal cel on the back of it. It was you all the time."

"Me?" I was shocked.

"Of course. Because the same problem I had that made me a psychotic psychopath at the beginning of this story was the one that caused my memory loss: too much time-traveling." Joyce held the card up and turned it over to show me. "Your business is, of course, 'Polytemporal Counselor.'"

"You are the one I've been seeing all this time. To help me with my problem. I have a rare genetic disorder where I can travel through time at will. But unless a person trains their ability, it can make anyone go crazy. So I came to you to make you write it all down so we could sort it out." Placing the card on the table, she picked up her chocolate again, and smiled. "So you see doctor, it has all been going according to your plan."

"And the office scene?" I asked.

"That was the one nightmare, no, the second one. The first was the empty mansion with the fireplace. Well, that one is probably prescience, future-seeing. We will visit that one day, but it will be just the two of us. I know where it is now, and how to find it again. Just not now. Because we have some unfinished business."

Joyce balanced her chocolate on her knee with one hand this time. Crooking her finger, she signaled me to come over. Then pulled her feet out so she could pat the cushion next to her. She placed the chocolate with care on top of her thick side-table romance, where it would be out of the way and safe.

I joined her on the couch in my mind while I continued typing this.

"What about the clothes on the stairs?" I asked.

"That was still a ploy to make myself think I was crazy, or being victimized. I did all that and then blanked it out. Now I remember, you see. Your card and cell-phone number was the trigger I needed. And you knew it." Joyce took my arm and put it on the back of the couch, then leaned in against me with her head on my shoulder.

I could smell cedar and roses in her hair, an intoxicating combination.

"We've been in love for a long time, but I just couldn't remember. And eventually, the dreams and nightmares and real world all got mushed." Her right index finger was tracing small patterns on the thin dress slacks that covered my thigh.

With her left hand, she pulled my couch-back arm across her shoulder and then brought that hand up to my face to turn it toward her. "I can see this results in a long, beautiful relationship. One with many children in our future."

"Children?" I tensed.

"Oh, relax. Haven't you figured it out?"

I shook my head no.

"You are quite a silly darling. You are an author. I am a story. I bring you ideas and you bring them to life. Lots of little stories that can grow into big novels."

With her hand on the back of my head, she pulled me down as she stretched to meet me.

And with that passionate kiss, then came the "fade to black."

The End - For Now.

The Tunnel People

BY R. L. SAUNDERS

I.

IT HAD BEEN A LONG brutal war. Allies shifted sides, new allegiances brokered.

At the end, the politicians, government bureaucrats, and their media cronies were banned underground. And the rest of us learned to live in a watchful peace.

It began with the simple revolt. People started reclaiming their privacy. That meant they dumped their smart-phones and social media accounts. Next came any broadcast news and "entertainment". People hated ads and started to show it. No one watched anything that was broadcast. It became all on-demand, ad-free.

Dumb-phones became preferred. Via a local land-link using local-only Wi-Fi. And triangulating locations or accessing via GPS was made illegal.

At first, the bi-coastal Geek-Corps were against this. Because it threatened their business model. But then, they shifted sides when they found that once people were banning their platforms almost en masse, they started running through their cash reserves at a mad rate. And would soon cease to exist if they didn't become populist and leave the elites. Not that they were really on anyone's side but their own. So they took over entertainment distribution.

That was all ancient history now. No one had heard or seen either the politicians or their media lackeys in years, decades.

THE THREAT SURFACED in a series of old maps, written in a language no one living understood.

It was during my hunts in the sub-basement archives where I originally found those old maps. Ones which showed how there were cross-connected travel routes between various cities deep underground. N'Yack was connected to Cagga via the deep aquifers that had been drained almost dry. Different aquifers were used at different points, connected by deep tunnel bores.

At first, those maps didn't make any sense. Just schematics and some alpha-numeric codings on the edges and throughout. I had a hard time deciphering these at first, but eventually learned their AI-developed geek-speak language and solved their puzzles.

But there was no way to access these tunnels without some sort of ID. A fake one, obviously. That led me to Rob.

Rob was a wild anarchist at heart. But a practical one, non-violent by nature. He preferred to watch sunrises and sunsets with a six-pack of near-beer at hand. Just enough to cool the nerves, but not give any serious buzz.

That's where I found him one day, the only place I could track him to. And it wasn't easy. Research is my specialty, my living. I could find anyone. But the trick was in their attitude. Rob was the perfect nexus of a free-thinker and hacker. Plus his appreciation for natural ways of doing things sealed the deal with me.

The trick in finding him was that he was going more and more off-line, off-grid. I found him by satellite maps and intuition. He still had an old jeep and his favorite high bluffs over the river. He kept an almost regular schedule. Just enough.

One day, I got there just before he was leaving. He just finished his last can of near-beer and was putting it into a mesh recycling bag. Black jeans, sturdy hiking boots, faded blue jeans jacket, over a black t-shirt. Broad shoulders, narrow waist. Not your typical family-basement nerd.

The wind over those high bluffs had just died down as twilight approached. He sat with his legs dangling over the edge.

"Hey," I said, loud enough to be heard, but not loud enough to startle. I stood way back so he could see I wasn't a threat. And a six-pack of his favorites was dangling from my fingers.

"Hey, yourself," Rob seemed bothered by the interruption. Then he looked down at my hand and smiled. It didn't hurt that I was wearing my black rock-climbing slicks that accented my curves right down to my back-dimples. You know the ones. Dimples and muscle definition only show up on the really fit. My running and rock-climbing soothed the rough edges of my soul. And did wonders for my abs and thighs.

"Well, you found me. And I'll take that bribe off your hands. How did you track me here and who the hell are you?" Rob asked.

I came up to his side, handed over my six cans of cool-sweating brew and sat down next to him, that six-pack in between us. "I'm Marj. And you already know how I tracked you."

Rob pulled one off the plastic stringer, popped the top and handed it to me. Perfect gentleman. And waited until I drank and swallowed. A touch paranoid, which was a good thing. Then he popped open one for himself and went back to watching the sunset.

We only had a half-hour or so before it would be too dark to make our way down the trails without stumbling. And from these heights you either used the existing light, or you set yourself up to be spotted with your flashlight beams.

That left maybe 15 minutes to talk as all the chance I was going to get. And he knew it.

"So? You are up here to either seduce me or hire me or blackmail me - or some combination of the above," Rob said.

I just smiled, "Or some combination of the above."

The clouds were slowly turning from red through violet into black as we sat there. Patient watching would almost let you see the changes.

"OK, five minutes. Make your pitch, 'Marj', and then I leave," Rob said.

"Well, that leaves out seduction." I smiled. "Here's the job offer: I've found some maps says I can get from one coast to the other all underground, using high-speed tube transport."

"But...?" Rob asked.

"I need one of your hacks," I replied.

"Not just any hack, you want top-level transport ID clearance," he answered.

"Pay is no problem - whatever you want," I said.

"Sorry, I don't do government stings. Find another lackey." Rob pushed the the four remaining beers back at me, and began to rise.

I put my hand on his arm to stop him, and the feeling was electric. It's a hard thing to describe, and I'd only read about in some old paperback romances my mom used to read. But it's real. Very real. I just proved it to myself.

And I could tell in his eyes that he had felt it, too. He also stopped moving. He stared at my hand on his arm and back to my eyes again. "I though you said seduction wasn't possible in five minutes."

I moved my hand away and looked back at the sky. "That wasn't intentional, I'm sorry. Go ahead and walk away. This won't work out."

He didn't move. That meant either bad or good.

But I wasn't looking for either outcome. I crossed my arms in front of me and looked off away from the bluffs. "This wasn't a good idea. Again, sorry."

"I'm sorry, too," he said. "Now you're in a jam. You felt the same thing I did, which is supposedly just some cheap romance novel cliché, but it happened. You need my help, and I'm the only one of a tiny handful that can help you. But you don't want to let this turn into something we'd both regret. Because you have some standards in your life, and sleeping around to get what you want isn't one of them. You aren't a NYT reporter, that's for sure."

Rob turned back, pulled another can off its plastic holder, popped it open, and took a healthy swig while I was getting my thoughts together.

"How do you think you know so much about me?" I asked.

"Because when you accessed those satellites, I got a ping. Meaning I knew you were coming," Rob said.

This guy was good. Darned good. "I suppose that means you looked up my back trail?" I asked.

"No, that was from your reactions. Look, neither of us seem ready for some relationship out of this. You got a card with contact data on it?" Rob said.

I pulled out a laminated card from my top and checked it. "Yup, still sweat free. Go ahead and scan it, though. No chip in it."

Rob wiped it on his jeans, then held up the card to the fading light to peer at it before stuffing it into the right chest pocket of his faded jeans jacket.

"OK, I'll be in touch." With that, he rose, turned, and left.

I waited. And watched the sunlight turn golden and then ruddy. Down the hill behind us, I heard his engine start, and the slip of wheels against the gravel as he started out.

But I still waited some more, and felt old emotions wash over me. N0ne I was prepared for. None I really had any defense against. "Good thing he didn't want a relationship," I said quietly to no one. And chewed my lower lip in some sort of weird reflex.

Then popped open one of the brews he left.

II.

"THIS JOB HAD BETTER pay awfully well," I said to no one in particular. How that chick got under my skin that fast was nuts. Either I had been alone too long, or not long enough. Thought I was over all females and that stuff. Thought I liked being straight, single, and sane. Women just made you do goofy stuff.

I started counting off all the people I knew who had been busted after some fling because they either let something slip or got distracted. Or, in the old days, slept with a reporter.

And here I was, distracted.

I put my attention back on the job at hand. Now was the time to look up her back trail. But I had to admit she was good, really good. All her data stopped about 6 years ago. No current address. Used to be a freelance researcher, did some light-weight government contracts, mostly subbed under university grants. All of her social networks had been scrubbed, even mentions of her on anyone else's profiles. No phone, no location, no picture other than the poor Academia scans made for ID's.

And yet she was able to find me. Spooky. Nobody is supposed to have these skill-sets. Other than me and people I don't even want to meet in person. Too risky for both of us.

So why would she risk all that to contact me?

That electric touch. Couldn't be real. Hadn't ever felt anything like that, well – I have, but... Had to be Junior High or that age. By High School I was jaded on the whole dating/hormones scene. In college, I was dedicated to staying celibate and dropped out after a few years. College was a waste on so many, many levels. Hook-ups and free sex were just more ways to wreck your life.

Who was that girl, the one who touched me like that way before? Red hair, not blond like this one. Delicate fingers. Smile that could melt snow in blizzard. Kiss like... Gawd, what was I thinking?

Need. To. Focus. On. Work.

That card, where was it? Jacket pocket, right.

I got up to reach the door-side hook where it hung. Nice having a routine. Everything goes where it should. Simple. Direct. Predictable.

Two fingers pulled it out. I'd nuked it on the way back in the dash EMF box. Cooked it for the whole ride home. Nothing electronic survived that.

Hung the jacket back up and started looking the card over in my hand.

Only a single web-address hand-printed in block letters on one side. No way to track that easily. Because it was written from right-to-left, so the handwriting patterns were all wonky. So they couldn't be traced. Perfectly centered on the card, though. The card wasn't hand cut or trimmed to center the text, it was from stamped and mass-produced card stock. Generic.

Might mean a graphic arts background, or a very precise mathematical mind.

Either way, she was good at what she did. Took care of details. And worthy of my begrudged respect.

Thanks to the gods that we were on that cliff-side in the fresh air or I'd be smelling her shampoo about now...

I shook my head to clear it. And almost decided to drop the whole thing.

But what she said was interesting, completely separate from how she looked in those form-fitting climbing slicks, and the way her eyes...

Focus. On. Work.

OK, OK, maps. She said something about a coast-to-coast transport system, all underground and never mentioned anywhere before. Like something out of Wells' "Journey to the Center of the Earth". But they used old volcano cores as the way down. With war-surplus tunneling machines and mini-fusion drives, we can still drive and bore wherever wanted. All that added up in theory.

Bringing my computers out of sleep mode, I started tick-tacking the address in, once I had triple-redundant re-directs nested within a virtual honey-pot and malware scanners all online.

When I got through, I was shocked. Gob-smacked, I think the term is.

It was simply a huge scan of the maps. They were layers, so the whole thing could be set up in 3D. Transcontinental tubes criss-crossed the various aquifers with fewer drilled mostly east-west through the mountain ranges, connecting the major cities and some of the old intercontinental ballistic missile tubes as access ports.

It was just too fantastic.

And had been built before Marj or I had been born. Hidden away, might even be working today. Probably how the politicians survived underground so easily after they were banished. Allowed them to still take their bribes, make their contacts, try to influence things on the surface. Or re-group and stage a counter-attack offensive.

I sat back in my chair. I was working from a copy of the file that I created seconds after opening the original, then quickly cutting that connection through all the jumps it had opened. My networks then continued making various jumps nearly at random, as part of a mapping program. Just to hide where I'd been. (I'd found some fascinating things that way, that paid for my overhead, but none as riveting as this.)

If only half of this stuff still worked, it would take generations to explore it all.

But who and what still controlled the access to these was the next question.

III.

I REALLY SHOULDN'T have touched him. "Nice retro-wisdom, Marj," I said to no one in particular. Hindsight being 50-50 as the old humor went.

My words echoed off the walls of the 4th sub-level Atkinson storage area I was walking across. Almost making as much noise as my clacking heels against the grey painted concrete hallways.

Here, I was more an archaeologist than analytic researcher. They had me along to sort out anything the file clerks found. It was tough work, as the government had simply retreated and left all this material behind, but no coherent map of the rooms or how anything was organized. (We figured that was on purpose, but the idea of a "conspiracy of idiots" was more likely.)

I got up to the surface for real daylight every few days, and spent a good deal of my time running these halls when off-duty to both keep myself in shape as well as dispel the tedium. A side benefit was being able to map these halls with my photographic memory. When sleeping, my unconscious then assembled the maps of where I'd been so I have a mental 3D construction of all the levels and their layout.

I figure that I have about a fifth of it all mapped out, if I'm lucky. And that's after years of daily running.

Working in the various rooms to sort through what the real data-archaeologists find (or data-arc's as they like to be called) then gives me some idea of how these bureaucrats continued to keep building out their data storage areas from the original mining that started this Kansas storage scene.

The Atkinson sub-levels were built during the "Second Cold War" where the bureaucrats of both sides sucked taxpayer money into creating alternate government areas big enough to house all the politicians and their staff, as well as their families and all their offices. Two of the known alternate sites were SubTropolis in the

KC area, and Meramac Caverns. It's rumored that anywhere limestone mining was every done has some sort of old government storage in it.

That map tends to support this, although I've hardly been able to get a quarter of it decoded in the tiny spare time I have.

That was why I needed Rob to get us travel passes.

Well, at least that was the idea before I touched his arm. Now, I'm not too sure he would want to come along. I'm known to be pushy at times, even been called a "control freak". But really it's that my intuition tells me things are a certain way and I've come to trust it. Because it saved my life several times when I did.

Our work was paid for by the Geek-Corps, out of the money people paid them for on-demand entertainment. And so we were supposed to "share" our findings with them. Unfortunately, some of this simply got whisked away in the middle of the night or after an area was left for the next one on the list. It was always curious to us that our assignments criss-crossed the chambers instead of working in a logical pattern. And to even talk about the data disappearing would often result in reassignment to a surface job faster than the normal rotations.

To keep my daylight access and healthy salary, I kept my own mouth shut. And in findings like the Map, I told no one about them. I'd found a few choice items, but this was the biggest.

I worried that Rob was going to do something stupid with it.

IV.

WHY THIS GIRL WOULD trust me with this Map was obvious. I was as crazy intuitive as she was. And there wasn't any way to split this map up. The AI code all around its border was also layered. Once you saw the elegance of that AI language, it made perfect sense. But in a data-dense way. Practically, there was so much data buried in it, that the old ideas of the original Bible being a cryptographic hologram model came up. If you took every fifth word, it read as well as if you took every fourth word, and so on. So there was data and stories in there that the old supercomputers worked years at discovering. Because the stories also read backwards as well as forwards.

This AI language was like that as well. It was a little like some sort of fantastic DNA. It actually told the whole philosophy and history and even planning of the AI Swarm Computers before they were completely destroyed. (Yes, of course there are rumors. You can't trust the Government to do anything right. But again, the "conspiracy of idiots" was a more common explanation that more often proved right than not.)

Much of this map description was in the planning level of that language, which was the most hidden. So it wasn't known whether the rest of this construction was ever actually carried out.

We had to travel there. If we could find a working tube car, or train, then we'd have our answers quick.

V.

ROB CONTACTED ME WHEN I was topside for a daylight visit.

It was a piece of light orange sandstone on my usual path. A rock about the size of a baseball cut in half. It caught my eye because the limestone we dealt with was mostly white, even on the paths we walked. Red and orange sandstone was much further south.

Of course I picked it up. It also wasn't dusty like everything around it. So it had only been there hours at best. I just shoved it in the pocket of my rolled-down jumpsuit. Unless it had some metal in it, the scanners weren't going to pick up anything besides another rock.

Which meant I also had to get out of sight to check it out. Time for a trip to the commissary.

The commissary was a carryover from when there was an active military base. I went shopping there almost every time I got topside, even if I didn't need anything. Partially to refuel my need for sunshine and natural-lit spaces, and also to give my intuition a rest from all the serious computing it was having to do to keep up with my memory and make sense of it.

I'd usually get whatever fruit was in season and then sit by myself in the center of the picnic table lot (named because they had something like a hundred picnic tables there for all the people who used to live and work in the subterranean vaults below. Sure, this many probably meant that there was some typical government over-spending that had to happen every year, just to make sure they used all their budget - and so could get more the next year. No wonder they lost the war.)

I pulled out a worn paperback copy of poetry from a hip pocket. It contained a lot of free verse, as well as traditional stanzas. Reading this relaxed my mind. I've gone through it maybe twenty times now and was due to start over. Most of it I'd memorized on some level or the other. I was always finding new material and new meanings when I re-read it. But that's the way of all things. The key point is being able to relax the mind.

This time, as I sat in my usual spot, I kept turning that rock over in my hand as I pretended to read. (Yes, of course Geek-Corps is watching. Especially outside.) I finally felt the puzzle pieces for what they were and what to push in what sequence to get it opened. Shoving it into my pocket, I made my way toward the bathrooms. And had the puzzle opened inside my pocket before I arrived.

The fingers of that hand extracted something like a plastic key. But I left that in my pocket to pull the rock out again. Amongst the coins I had, that key wouldn't show up on any scan.

Instead of using the facilities, I went to the snack booth and bought a plastic-wrapped pastry. Tearing the numbered strip on its edge, that went in with the plastic key. Made them both look like trash, or nerd-mementos.

What to do with the rock-puzzle? Couldn't keep it, couldn't leave it. I went back to the picnic tables and found a few that were wobbly. Picking up some loose rocks on the ground, I made to look as if I were trying to get one to level out. Putting the sandstone puzzle under a leg, then sitting on that corner simply crushed it. Then my boot scattered the pieces so the next sweeping would pick them up.

To finish it off, I shrugged like I had realized I needed to quit tilting at the windmills of perfecting the obsessive art of table-leveling. All for the cameras that were looking.

I know you think this is paranoia supreme. But I've analyzed lots of stuff in my time. And the smartest people are often the worst idiots. They think they can keep surveilling people all they want. All they are actually doing is training people how to escape being surveilled. There is a balance to all things. Meanwhile, you play the game. To win.

Once I finished my pastry, it was time to return. I wouldn't be back for several daylight cycles.

By then I should have a response for Rob and a way to get it to him figured out. Or at least out of my head.

VI.

HER ANSWER WAS TOO elegant.

I answered a knock to my door and found Marj was standing there. Her tight climbing sleeks below covered by a black leather jacket that ended just below her waist. Heavy boots that gave her a little more height than her climbing shoes.

Right in front of all the hallway cameras, she wrapped her arms around my neck and kissed me like there was going to be no tomorrow.

Funny enough, I liked it. Been awhile, like I said.

Then we kinda collapsed back into my living space and I managed to shut the door. The cameras caught all of it and that was her point.

Another funny thing happened. We didn't quit kissing once we were inside and off the monitors. Because it simply felt so good, so right. And Marj probably hadn't had something like this for as long as I hadn't.

We finally disentangled ourselves and started catching our breath.

She found my only regular chair in that tiny cubicle and I sat on the bed-couch, which I made up that day for some reason. Actually, I cleaned up and put away everything like I was expecting company. Or someone.

Opening her leather jacket showed her wearing only a thin bandeau across her chest. She reached into the slight opening above the elastic front to pull out that plastic key I sent her.

I took it from her and quickly twisted it into the 3D device that would allow her to decode the AI code on the map. Then put it back in her fingers.

"Very clever," Marj said.

"Thought you'd like it. Took awhile to figure that it was all we needed," I said. "And more importantly, you also have your travel pass in your hand."

She opened her hand and put the key in her palm. "You're kidding."

"Nope. It's just that simple." I pulled a flat card out of my t-shirt pocket and quickly assembled my own. "All you need to know is the AI language and how to think in 3D. Almost no human-types can do that, so that's all the security you need."

"It's just some marks on each side. Able to be printed simply. Very particular as to the markings, but it's basically a master key for all the transport. If you can find the locks, it will work," I said.

"So you've tried it?" Marj asked.

"I found some locks here and there and it's worked on all of them. They were all just empty storage lockers so far. The funny thing is that you start seeing this code everywhere when you look for it. Like a civilization hidden in another civilization," I replied. "All in plain sight."

"This is amazing. You could print these off and hand them out for nothing," Marj said.

"And trap people when they couldn't get back out again. On the other side of these doors, it's all AI code instructions and smooth walls. I'm sure there's another use for these storage closets. So I started some tests," I said.

"Tests? Nothing dangerous, I hope," asked Marj,

"Just a gradient scale of objects. Dried fruit, a kid's toy, and a Captain Krunch decoder ring," I said.

"What happened?" Marj asked.

"The fruit was left alone, the toy was turned around 180 degrees. and the decoder ring is still missing," I replied.

"What's your figure on that?" Marj asked.

"They don't care about organic, think humans are kids that can be played with, and the decoder ring is either challenging, or a challenge to us," I replied.

"Us - you mean you've decided to come with me," Marj said.

"Of course. I need to find out how deep this rabbit hole goes," I said. "Oh, could you explain your logic of bussing me in front of every camera out there?" I asked.

Marj blushed. "Other than testing that electrical thing we ran into last time, it was to give them a red herring. They think people in love are more vulnerable and less a risk. Our new cover says we now should simply go out shopping for some entertainment discs, like the lovers they think we are. Then go find a transport hatch we can open," she explained.

"Nice touch. They will figure that we are busy making out somewhere when we go off their cameras," I said.

Marj blushed again. "Outside of the physical reaction I get when you mention that subject, it's a good working hypothesis."

"Don't worry, your blushing looks great against that blond hair of yours. Gives you an outdoors sort of look. A natural mystique," I said - and felt some color come into my own cheeks.

"Well, lets go," Marj said, smiling at my reaction. "Which one of your storage lockers is closest to a disc-store?"

VII.

DISK IN ONE HAND, ROB in the other, he led me to an alley and started nuzzling my neck just as we turned the corner. I responded by pulling his hand around my waist and put my arm around his neck to hold him close as we turned down that camera-less alleyway.

But then I turned around to body-press him against the wall and plant another long kiss on his lips. We were in no hurry with that one, either. When we came up for air, I put my forehead against his shoulder and looked down at his shirt. "We really need to make sure this 'chemistry' doesn't affect our progress."

Rob cleared his throat, "True. I don't know if my thinking will be practically accurate in all circumstances."

"Noted," I said. And stretched up, kissed him on his nose.

Then took his hand and he led us on.

The doorway was almost invisible in the wall. Just a narrow slit to show a doorway. No knob or handle. There was a small hollow "x" in the wall about elbow height. Not a cross, but diagonal. And that meant something all by itself.

Rob inserted his key and we entered. It was empty, just big enough for the two of us. "Don't touch anything, just wait," Rob said.

Eventually, the panels each lit in a sequence. First it lit up below, then opposite the door, the door itself, both sides, and then the top. Figures showed in each side. I started reading them. but was quickly confused, as they seemed out of order somehow.

Rob started interpreting, "This is the other reason for the key. I read about this, but haven't tried it yet. Did you notice there is no catch or knob to open the door from inside? But take your key and align the sides to the wall that matches. Just rotate it. If you have it wrong end up, it won't work."

Sure enough, the first time I rotated it, nothing happened. Turning the key end for end and rotating to match a subtle pattern in each wall made each inner side light up in a different color.

Then the floor started lowering. We were on our way.

VIII.

THE LIGHTED PANELS had seems in them at each level, so we could see these rise up above us and they gradually increased in speed going by. I pulled Marj to me to keep her safe and to balance both of us, as there were some vibrations in the floor as we picked up speed.

I could now smell her faint natural perfume, as well as the leather jacket she wore. And knew this was something special.

Soon, the walls were nearly a blur, and they started pulsing in their own pattern. Lights which formed a fourth dimension to the language.

"Muzak," Marj whispered.

"What?" I asked.

"A.I. Elevator music. See the patterns. Close, but not exactly like a theme song. You can make out a three-part, sometimes four-part harmony to it. And it's a certain constant tempo. See? And now it's slowing, the final measures."

The lights went to their original colors and then went their original pale white glow. The panel behind us clicked and then opened.

We turned and left, holding hands.

IX.

AS WE ENTERED THE HALLWAY, it was much like the alley we had left. No trash, just dust. Only a light overhead of us. Rob looked to one side, I looked to the other. No real difference. They both went off in gloom.

"Wait," I said. I held up my key and rotated it slightly, keeping the same end up as I'd used in the elevator-closet. As I aligned a certain edge, the hall down that way lit up. Rotating it 90 degrees lit up the other way, while the first hall way went dark again.

But there was still no difference. They were both long and featureless other than the markings.

Rob went forward to start reading the markings on the hallway we lit up last. I trailed him and read the other side.

"Burma Shave ads." Rob said.

"I don't get it," I replied.

"Back when I was researching advertising, there were sets of signs that the Burma-vita company put out as advertising along the road sides to sell their shaving soap, and people kept reading along to get to the punchline of the short poems. These run along the same way, telling stories as a set of instructions about what's ahead, what's behind, and various options. Their planning and legends are all here, if you want to take the time to decipher them,"Rob explained.

"Burma-shave or not, are you getting any clue to where we are heading?" I asked.

"This one can take us to the tubes going west. The other takes us to the tubes going south," Rob said.

"You know there's something spooky about this place. There should be politicians and media down here. I know it's been a couple of decades, but some of them were only in their 30's. And you'd think there would be some trace of them," I said.

"Well, there's nothing on these walls that mention them, but again, this AI language was developed in the last days of the second Cold War, and robots built and decorated these walls as a fail-safe against being decommissioned. So it's probable that they didn't notice if the politicians and media even cared," said Rob.

"OK, let's pick up the pace then. It's obvious we are going to have to walk to get anywhere. Mental note: next time bring some folding bikes," I smiled at Rob and he returned it, lingering a bit in his look.

X.

IT SEEMED LIKE ABOUT a half mile of various twists and turns before we reached the tube station. Marj seemed like she was fine, but my footwear choice should have been trainers with all that extra padding. The thin sneakers I wore had my heels definitely feeling the wear.

A sealed tube was sitting in the station. And a map on the wall showed that all the stations seemed operational and ready for travel. But there was a thick layer of dust on the transparent glass cover. As if it hadn't been used for decades.

"That's funny, you'd think these people could be traveling all over. But this car is covered with dust. And look!" I pointed to a line of cars waiting behind them, similarly dusty. All ready dressed up and no where to go. Because no one was there to take them anyplace.

Marj started reading the walls. She found a large set of double doors and gestured to me. "Hey Rob, c'mere!"

She pointed out the "x" in each one and then pulled out her key to try it.

Both doors swung open silently.

It was one of the entrances and exits at the far back end of a huge theater with a short stage in front of a massive projection screen. Every seat seemed to be taken with a person's head just peaking above each one. But no show was in progress. The place was dead quiet. Waiting.

We took a step forward and as we did, the lights dimmed. The doors whispered shut behind us and the room slowly darkened. A projector lit up the screen and old clips of politicians being interviewed on the news media of the day started playing. They would run about three minutes, then another one would start with other politicians. Just no ads in between. The English they were using was quaint, but could still be understood.

These were also news programs of that day. The shows went on and on. Sometimes longer periods were of various media having "round-table discussions" about some news development or the other, then back to more pithy interviews alternated with reading scripts of the then-current news.

"This is all decades old," I whispered to Marj, "Let's leave this audience to their entertainment. It seems to have them thoroughly entertained."

"Yes, I'm ready to get back outside," Marj whispered in return.

We turned to face the door. As we did, the show ended and the lights came on. Both doors opened.

But the audience didn't move.

"Marj, wait here. Don't move. That should keep the lights on so I can check things out," I said.

I walked forward looking to each side. All the faces looked forward. But then I stopped and looked at one more closely. What I saw made me take a step back.

Then I turned and walked rapidly to the back where Marj was waiting.

I took her arm and led her out of the theater. The doors closed behind us with an automatic quiet.

"Let's head back," I said.

She stopped and pulled her arm away. "What is it?" she asked. "What's got you so fast to get out of here when we've just found all this?"

XI.

WE RETURNED OFTEN AFTER that, but never opened the theater again. Actually, I later brought down a few small display of plastic lilies with stands that raised them to cover the lock crosses in the doors.

While we continued to explore, we did so in relative safety. The tunnels were all there, all working. Large empty living areas were found with no one living in them, but the automated facilities still able to produce food and clothing on demand from a wide assortment of options, mostly of the period when the politicians and media left the earth above for this underground paradise.

There was no obvious reason for them to be empty.

Rob told me that day what he had seen and we talked about it on the long walk back.

Politicians, their bureaucrats, and their media partners had all died soon after they accepted their fate. Because they had left out one vital ingredient that had kept them alive all this time, that gave them a reason to live.

Audience.

Without mindless adoration, they had no reason to continue existing. They had lived to "get out the vote", to put on shows and survey for public opinion to see what they said resulted in any change. They sought to interpret and control the "narrative" during their daily 24/7/365 shows. But they needed feedback. They needed to feel they affected their viewer's attitudes. Those were their security – approval and control.

When they lost the war, they lost their audience. Everyone else stayed on the surface. The politicians and their supporters went below, thinking that they'd soon be asked to return, that they were vital to the smooth running of civilization.

But as the years went by, no one called them. And while they waited, they amused themselves with endless highlight reels of their best shows, interviews, and speeches.

While they waited for the call that never came.

ROB SAW MUMMIES THAT day. Rows and rows of mummies.

Still waiting.

Becoming Michelle

BY R. L. SAUNDERS AND C. C. Brower

I

AFTER THE SECOND TIME I got beat up, I figured I needed to change my lifestyle.

It didn't matter if you were white, black, gay, straight, male, female - someone got offended at how you looked or acted. It didn't matter how much or who you paid for "protection." They couldn't be around all the time, and someone else was always wanting a piece of you.

The weird part was that I was expert in being anything anyone wanted.

I just couldn't change fast enough to suit everyone.

That was my job, and why I got hired. Why they kept keeping me on and kept giving me bonuses and pay raises. Because I could be anyone or any type of person they needed.

My family tree spread out like one of those Eastern Banyan trees. Wide, really wide. I had some of probably every race you can name somewhere in there.

And my upbringing was modern-progressive. I got to choose my sex and my name whenever I wanted, any time I wanted.

So I was born "Michelle" but called myself Mica or Mike or Michael - whatever a person wanted to hear when they came in the corporate front door. I was their receptionist. No, I was their host/hostess. And I was able to change to suit their preferences.

A chameleon.

I studied people, and could spot by the time they crossed that long lobby whether they wanted me to be male or female, colored or white or something else, gay/straight/bi- or anything they wanted.

Mostly, I got it right on the money. Which is why they paid me so well.

My job was to set the new customer at ease instantly and help them find whatever they wanted at the corporation.

If that meant I put up with being hit on, insulted, butt-slapped, or pinched, even groped - it was all in a day's work. Often several times in a day's work. Because I was paid to be submissive or dominant, alluring or indifferent. Often appearing to be several different things at once.

It was how you held yourself, how you acted, how you responded.

But no matter how good I was, it didn't matter out on the street. Someone would decide you offended them. Or you had "appropriated" something another culture had that didn't belong to you.

The worst days were when I would wear makeup that made me look definitely one way or another. Like they would have a group of female straight execs come in, so I would make myself male-looking with extra shadow above and below my eyebrows, and under my jawline to make it look like I had a jutting brows and a strong jaw - very masculine. My extra shoulder padding and solid heels gave that look, as well as my low range vocal made me sound masculine. Sometimes putting a roll of half-dollars in my front pocket completed the look they were wanting.

I could count how many times I'd get pinched riding up the elevator with them, always having to stand the front with the "guests" behind me..

Because I was someone else's employee. And couldn't cause a fuss or complain. They knew it.

Or I was very feminine to another set of female execs, coy and gossipy. All with a different outfit and mascara. Thinner brows, longer eyelashes.

To the average person, particularly in a crowd, not being anyone important, I'd be androgynous. Nobody in particular. And even the uni-sex crowd got offended by that.

Of course, I got pretty quick at avoiding the slaps and gropes and pinches. Except when I was with several of them in a group.

And that was always the way with the roaming gangs after work. Too many all at once.

Those started up after the "Tolerance Edicts." And the police got neutered as far as protecting anyone besides their own butts. Most of the city was "no-go" for them after that. They only traveled in bullet- and bomb-proof caravans, and only to protect city officials. Sure, they were being sued several times a week for imagined "discrimination" and that only made it worse. They even invested in 3D imaging so that their body cams showed every inch around them and were basically tamper-proof.

That didn't matter. They were neutered. Even dropped the "protect and serve" motto. Literally scraped it off their up-armored SUV's. They were bodyguards for the city executives and their lackey press. You couldn't pay them enough to do anything else, even when the law said they had to.

Because if they ever lost their job, they were probably dead within a week. Cop-hating became a hobby with people. More popular than sports on the 24-7-365 media feed.

The media were in on the scam. They were polite enough in person when a cop was around, but on the 'tube they could be downright vicious. Because they thought it made their ratings go up, and that affected how much advertisers could be forced to pay.

But all this thinking wasn't smart. Because now it was dark, I was trying to find my way home. The trick was to stay in the territories I had bought protection from. That was where all my pay raises and bonuses had gone. Because I was in the "donut hole" of having enough that should have bought a good living, but not enough to buy protection to ensure that it was. I couldn't afford even an armed guard to protect me between my work and my apartment.

That left me was traveling the long and gerrymandered route along the edge of where they would protect me until I could get close enough to sprint to the relative safety of my apartment complex and their snoring, dull paid "guards." The ones who would only protect you if you got through that armored front door in one piece, preferably not bleeding on their carpet.

And it wasn't my luck that night. Because the borders had shifted again, always without warning to their victims.

Soon I saw myself surrounded by a bunch of dark hoodie-wearing thugs. Male-female, it didn't matter. They were out to hunt.

Turning left and right, I saw only that the noose was tightening. Standing bodies with their faces in shadow. Weapons in their hands that I could see, and more weapons underneath their long sleeves I couldn't.

Part of that money had been spent in martial arts training, after the second time I was mugged. And that had occurred right outside the front door of my apartment. I could still see the shocked fear and remorse of those security guards as they kept themselves protected behind the armed glass.

Broward. That was my apartment. And still a block away. Not that it would matter in a few minutes.

I decided. Throwing my bag at the face of the biggest one, who was instantly swarmed by the smaller (females?) who were at his sides and behind them. They wanted my dress clothes.

Then I launched behind me at some smaller thugs, who still were taller than me by a head or so.

Unexpected, I was able to deck three of them and take off running through that gap. In the wrong direction to get to my apartment.

At least I was wearing my street running shoes. And I ran for my life.

But they knew the turf better, as they lived it. And no matter how many turns I took, how I dodged into and out of traffic, they boxed me in again.

The trick was to protect my face and my right arm. The rest I could heal. But heavy makeup and shades to cover eye bruises would only go so far. I needed my job to survive.

Feinting right and left, I worked to get an opening. But found none.

The ones carrying the long pipes came closer, where they could strike and still be safe. I was dodging them OK for now, but was being pushed back against the others who had knives.

Turning my back on any of them was the trick. Any wrong move would save or cost me my life.

One, a smallish one, jumped on my back. That one was simple enough to hurl.

But then I felt my right wrist seized. And I panicked, trying to desperately free it. My jacket was pulled and hood ripped from my head and down around my shoulders.

"An-dro! An-DRO! AN. DRO!!" The shout became a chant.

I still struggled to free myself.

Both arms were held now and I could only focus on my right wrist. And the knife near it.

Pulling suddenly to right and then left, I got the guy off balance and kicked him in the crotch with the same movement.

That got me a pipe across the back of my head.

And blackness...

II

I'D SEEN WHERE THE girl had been taken, down an alleyway where no one else would go.

Except me. Harmless old me.

Because that was my calling. To make the poor rich, to enable the blind to see.

First I had to save that life.

Using the echoes of the high walls, I started making sounds that sounded like a wild cat - or several - were loose in the alleys behind them. The dead-end alley would echo worse than a simple street. Or so I hoped.

Mixing wild screams with over-tipped trash cans and taking two lids to bang like cymbals against each other and the antique fire escapes, the result was like a pack of coyotes - rabid zombie dogs - were coming toward them.

I heard their own noises and chanting quiet. And they were scurrying for the openings that weren't there. Because the one thing they feared more than massively multi-organized SWAT teams was the wild animals that survived in these walled cities, that bred like rabbits and trained to survive from pups, to feed on the carrion left by the gangs. They had no fear of humans. And gave no mercy.

Meat was meat to them.

The gang massed and pushed down the alley in a mob, tightly bunched and as fast as they could without leaving anyone behind.

I ducked behind a dumpster and made myself small as they passed.

As they rounded a corner of the alley back out in the street, they separated to avoid the cameras.

And then I turned back to whoever they had attacked in order to save her if I could.

They had left her in a bundle on the ground. Her right wrist was exposed and seeping blood. At least they had left her hand attached.

I pulled out a thin wad of cloth and padding from inside my coat and tore it into strips. Winding them tight around her wrist and hoping they hadn't cut anything serious. I checked the rest of her for other injuries, and only found an ugly bump on the back of her head. Looks like they were only recruiting tonight...

Then I looked around and found an old shopping cart. A blessing. Mysterious Ways, I guess. I picked her light form up and set her as gently as possible inside it, keeping the legs elevated as well as her wrist. Shaking all the dirt I could from an old blanket, I covered the cart and the girl with it, then started moving back to the opening.

We had blocks to cover, if she could make it.

As I pulled my hood up to cover my head, I prayed to all the saints that we did. And my spirits raised with their instant response.

"And miles to go before I sleep..."

III

WHEN I CAME TO, AT least they had left my clothes on me. Torn, bloody, but mostly in one set of pieces.

And someone was standing over me, a respectful distance away, not looking like he wanted to give me more pain.

I sat up, or tried to. Gawd my head hurt. And I was actually loosely tied down to some sort of gurney, one of those rolling hospital beds.

The furthest I got was up on my left elbow, because my right arm was tied down with web strapping.

At least I was still alive.

But when I saw the bandages on my right wrist beyond the webbing, I knew that I was as good as dead already.

So I gingerly laid back on the gurney, so I didn't bump my head again. My eyes hurt and my sinuses burned. Worse than any hangover.

That put my head over to my left, where I saw this this smallish guy looking at me. Dressed in some sort of brown overall, with a brown jacket, and a brown cap.

A Brownie.

I thought they had been run out of the city years ago.

"Well, we were, but some of us came back anyway. Just not wearing brown," came the thought in my head.

"What—-?" I tried to speak.

"Shh-shh-shh. Stay calm," the graveled voice came through my ears this time. "You've been hurt bad, robbed. But you're alive. Been with us a couple of days now. Doc said you had a mild concussion. He'll be happy to know you're awake."

I looked at him. He came closer.

"Yes, I saved you and moved you here." The Brownie kept talking, trying to answer obvious questions and calm me down. "The reason you are tied is because you moved around in your sleep. Your wrist was cut, and we stitched it shut again. But it needs to be still to heel. Here, let me loosen these."

At that he untied the strap holding my arm down, with as much tenderness as he could. And untied the loose sash that was holding me down. Then he moved away with a surprising swiftness I didn't think possible.

The web strapping and sash stayed for me to remove.

I carefully sat up, and the gurney didn't move. It's wheels had been locked. Leaving my right wrist as it lay, I pulled the sash down across my waist, then carefully plucked at the webbing. My wrist was tender and had pain when I moved it. The bandages were tight around some sort of splint that kept it from moving.

"What did you do to my wrist?" I asked.

"My doctor friend had to stop the bleeding and put things back together again. He told me that it would heal in a few weeks, but not to move the bandages for a few days, to leave the splint on so the tissues would mend together," said the Brownie.

"So I have you to thank for saving my life," I said. "What should I call you?"

"Many call me Andrew, but Andy is fine," he answered.

"Did the doctor tell you if the chip was still there?" I asked.

Andy looked down, "No, the gang took it."

Tears started falling from my eyes and my breaths stuck in my chest, coming out as sobs. Each sob causing pain in on side of my chest. I put my splinted right wrist against my chest and covered it tightly with my left hand and arm. Then sobbed my heart out, regardless of how much it hurt me.

Because my life was gone. They had stolen my life. I was already a dead person walking.

IV

SHE WAS SITTING THERE, crying her eyes out, wracked with sobs. And I could do nothing. This was the worst I experience in these cases. The bottom of despair.

So I did what I always did, I prayed. To myself, not aloud. Because people seldom understand the words or the meaning behind them. And use these to fuel their fears instead.

I ask to be filled with your breath of life, as above and so below.

Let me understand true peace as I find it within and surrounding me.

As my thoughts are in me, they are in everyone.

Let me find completeness in all things, and give of myself wholly as I help others accept my giving.

Help me find my way in wholeness. To become, to act, to assist. And so I confirm with our soul.

Her eyes were wide at this, the tears having left to run down her cheeks and absorb into her dirty and bloody clothing.

"Our Father who art in Heaven, Hallowed be thy name. Thy Kingdom come, they Will be done, on Earth the same as Heaven. Give us this day our bread, and forgive us as we forgive others, For You are the wholeness and power and glory forever. Amen," she replied.

Her smile seemed to light up the room. Without makeup of any kind, her short hair tousled, and the street dirt streaked down her face, this was a very honest smile.

I knew that Grace had found a home in her, that she understood something in her core.

"I remember that old saying from my childhood, well, as much as I can," she said. "And the people who come by our corporate reception each week to pass out their slips of paper. I've read these words. Only now do I seem to get a hint of their real meaning."

"There are many meanings. And the one you choose is the one best for you," I replied.

Her smile was contagious and I smiled back. I opened my arms wide with my palms facing her.

"Come," she said. And her arms were wide as well.

I came over to her and gently put my own arms around her.

She winced, but still kept her arms around my back. And I could feel her tears start again, as they fell to my own exposed neck.

At last she loosened her arms and I was able to move back.

"Cracked ribs, my doctor friend said. You will have to rest here for a few days while you decide what you want to do," I said.

She moved her left arm down her side under her shirt, and she felt the strapped ribs underneath. "So you've seen all of me?"

"We did have to unclothe you to check for broken bones and any cuts. There was a lot of blood. So we cleaned you up as best we could and then re-dressed you," I answered. "We didn't find any other clothing around the area where you were found, but they brought back some cleaner clothes about your size if you'd like to change into them."

Her face went downcast. And her breathing rough again, as if she were going to start sobbing. That wouldn't be good for her ribs.

"What should I call you?" I asked.

Her head down, something came out muffled, but I didn't get it. "Could you tell me again?" Another muffle.

I stepped closer and put a hand softly on her shoulder. She then looked into my eyes. A time passed where we simply looked at each other.

"Michael, er, Mica." and then paused. "Oh hell. Michelle is my birth-name," she said. Then looked away.

"Is that what you want to be called?" I asked.

"It doesn't much matter. You know my sex, you know more about me than anyone is allowed to know. And you know I'm unaltered," she spit out.

"All of us are part and parcel of the Greater One, so whatever you want to be is your choice. Andrew isn't the name I was given, either," I said. "My birth name was Farley, which means roughly, 'found in the bull pasture.'"

She smiled at this. "Were you raised on a farm?"

I smiled back, "Yes, but not in a pasture. And we didn't have cattle, mostly goats and sheep. They are easier to protect from wolves and coyotes."

"So why are you here, and why did you save me?" Michelle asked.

"That is my calling, what I hear to do. I just trusted my feet to take me into the direction I needed to go. And they led me to you just in time," I answered.

"How did you get into the city? They don't let Brownies in. 'Dissent and insurrection isn't tolerated,' as the Edict is wrote," she said.

"But they do need things fixed. I repaired the outer gate for them on my way in. And if you smile and nod enough, then they think you're harmless. They can always use some broken things fixed. Like that gate. They were afraid to go out that far and had just put up with it scraping and screeching for a long time it looked like. Anyway, it was an easy fix they didn't need to be afraid of. Old teachings tend to die slowly, though," I said.

"Meaning you fix people, too, and your feet said I needed fixing," Michelle said.

"Something like that," I answered. But you must be hungry by now. Let me help you down and I'll bring you some food. Sit over here and I'll be right back..."

V

THE FOOD WAS VERY GOOD. A thick soup, kinda like a thin stew. Made from what I didn't care. It tasted great and filled a gnawing hole in my stomach area.

Of course, I didn't say a word as I wolfed it down. But my smile said tons when I looked at Andrew again.

"I wondered if I would ever see your smile. It makes you look - better," he said.

"Better?" I asked. "Did you want to say something different?"

"Well, I don't mean to offend, but yes. I wanted to say your smile makes you look - pretty," Andy said, with worry lines on his forehead.

I smiled back, regardless. "That's something I haven't heard in years. Probably not since I left home. We weren't aloud to gendrify our compliments at school or anywhere else. Because it would offend someone, somehow."

"Yes, people seem to get offended so easily. And there are even more laws - edicts - protecting the offended than the rights of the innocent 'offender," said Andy. His worry turned into a frown as he looked down into his own empty bowl. Without looking up, he asked, "Would you like some more?"

"Andy." I said, waiting until he looked at me again. "I am the least offensive person you have ever met. It was my job, until a few days ago to be completely inoffensive. And I was very good at it."

Andy smiled at this. And it made his face look - handsome.

"Well, that relieves me," he said. "My job is mostly to be the most unoffensive person around, and that is my protection as well, I guess. Other than prayer."

"If anyone was offended from our meeting, it should have been me. You saw me naked and knew my sex. Something I've had to hide all my life," I said.

Andrew's smile turned to a puzzled look, "How is that? The gangs don't hide their sex, other than those dark hoodies they wear. But it's pretty obvious."

"It was all started after the first Gay-In-Chief and his Trans wife were murdered a few years after he went out of office. Of course this is ancient history. But what I was taught in school is that the pivot point of the Great Tolerance Movement started there. Their advocates started with 'Cagga and N'Yack, and S'atl, then S'angels. There were resolutions by the DC 'Gress to allow states to do more of what they wanted, particularly the bigger cities among them.

And then it wasn't long before the secessions started. That led to necessary protective Walls."

Andy relaxed his face. "Oh that's what they taught you. Here, our bowls need filling again before the soup-run starts. I'll be right back."

Soon he returned with our bowls filled, and I felt more inclined to take my time emptying it now.

"Andy, what's your version of what happened?" I asked.

"Well, it's something that is a bit murky. Because people don't like to talk about it. 'Live and let live' is more an operating motto than a trite saying out beyond the walls. The short answer is that they don't want what the cities have almost as much as the cities don't want to share - or receive anything from Flyover Country.

"Once N'Yack and Cagga seceded, they started building walls around their legal limits to keep everyone out. And the Fed's Army kept people from going in or out while they did. To avoid a Constitutional Crisis, they said, but it was obvious that they were already in one.

"And yes, it was the surprise death of both the Gay and his Trans that started it all. Because the leaked coroner results confirmed that it was suicide, they both were male and had some incurable disease that they shared. So they made the accident look like some conspiracy had done it to them.

"But the Press took off with the 'vast right wing conspiracy' again, and pushed for physical separation from the rest of the 'deplorable' country. The media kept the push up until the rest of the country was tired of it and let them go. Along with their tiring media.

"The cities built the walls at their own expense, and more cities joined the movement. S'atl was simple, but S'angels had riots as people didn't want to be part of that city. So they walled off most of the downtown city and fought to keep a harbor out of it. The riots were very messy.

"Feds kept their troops out of it. Cities didn't want them and their assault rifles. S'cramento state government moved down into L'angels for what good it did them, as they couldn't tax anything beyond their own walls. So the farmers and small business people moved in and started up a new government.

"Frisco kept their harbor, and so there was regular packet runs up and down the coast for years. S'Dego opened their border to Mexico, and so they have access to manufactured goods that they trade for electronics up coast. But those are the only four cities that have any real trade agreements. Like a country of their own, more or less."

Andy went back to eating, lost in thought as I was. Between us, we had a lot of differences to sort out, but at least we could share.

"Why did this gang go after me?" I asked. "'Andro,' they called me. Does that now mean that they are offended by androgynous people?"

"I'm afraid you are exactly right. They are offended by the people trying to be the most inoffensive." Andy replied. "They just moved in a few days ago, forming a new coalition to run the streets. Meaning the section mob boss wanted higher profits, so knocked some heads together to get more cooperation."

"And my apartment was in the wrong location for the new territory," I sighed. "But the housing closer to my job cost more than I could get paid. Unless I wanted to sell my body to some exec there. And that wouldn't last long."

I sat back and remembered some of the dates I'd had. Some had ended violently, the worst being the female dates. Although the guys who wanted gay sex would leave me sore enough.

A large gong-sounding alarm went off. I jumped.

"Oh, that's just the noon bell. It actually is a bell. This warehouse was built into the back of an old church. The bell sounds off for the soup line," Andy rose and scooped up the two bowls and spoons. "Come, we could use your help."

I looked down at my clothes and felt my face.

"No, you're dressed and look just fine. You'll be seeing worse. Come on, this way." With that Andy moved off smoothly, like a dancer glides through a practiced move.

He opened a large door on the side of the room, and I followed...

VI

WE ENTERED WHAT USED to be a huge church, in one of the transepts, or side branches of the cross formed in a traditional Catholic church layout. This side held a long layout of tables, which had a huge cast-iron stove supporting two immense low kettles on it, steaming. The tables went off in a straight line down its center, almost to where it met the nave.

Behind the stove and long tables were rolling racks of various breads. Two people were putting some of these trays out on the tables as we entered.

They looked up at us when we entered. Andy introduced me, "Sam, Dolly, this is Michelle. She's going to be on the soup kettle today and I'll be assisting her. Could you two manage the breads OK?"

Dolly came right up and gave me a big hug, while Sam looked on with a smile.

Her curly blond hair seemed familiar to me.

"Michelle!" she stood back with her hands on both my shoulders. "It's been sooo long, I always wondered what became of you!"

I looked into her eyes above her wide smile and freckled nose. "Dolls - that's you isn't it?" And I hugged her as best I could with the splint on that right arm. "I was so worried when you disappeared."

Now she held my good left hand in her right. "I know, it was days before I could get around, and by then I couldn't prove who I was, so there was no severance pay to pick up." Dolly turned her right wrist over to show her scar. "At least I got all the motion back in it. I was lucky. Some people bleed out when they cut the whole hand off. But under the new boss, that's forbidden. He likes people who can work." She looked down at my splinted right hand. "Just recently arrived, I guess. Well, I'm sooo happy to see you again. Oh, I'd better get ready. This is a tough crowd to entertain."

Another brief hug and she was off down the road. She hugged Sam and whispered something in his ear.

Andy came up behind me and said my name quietly before putting a light hand on my shoulder, still making me jump. "Oh, I'm sorry. But we need to get over to the soup. You just ladle with your left hand and keep your right away from the hot soup and stove. I'll hold the bowls for you to fill. One scoop will do it. You'll do just fine."

When we got there, the line had started. I was too busy to notice much after that, since the line moved so quickly.

Andy kept up a steady patter as he kept filling bowls hand-after-hand. He would recognize people and try to talk with them, smiling all the time. While he got a lot of surly looks, most were responsive. Sam and Dolly were also handing out smiles with every piece of bread, so this also lightened almost everyone's mood. The bouncers came last. These were the biggest of the bunch, and had kept the crowd from just rolling in on their own and swamping us. They had kept everyone into a single-file line. Two smaller figures accompanied them, one was holding extra bread and the other a tray to hold four bowls - I figured the big guys got their second helpings in advance.

There was a break in the action at that point, so Andy brought over a tall 5-gallon pot of soup to refill the two low kettles. He nodded at me to get out of the way as he lifted the steaming pots to pour them. I was too happy to move away from that steam, as the sweat was running in streams down my face, and my bandaged arm was not very absorbent. I took that break to grab a cloth towel and do a proper mop of my face and neck.

"Here, let me help you." Dolly had come over after refilling the table. "We've got a bit of a break now." She pulled out a good-sized bandanna, held it by opposite corners, then flipped it into a simple headband. I held my head down a bit while she tied it into place. I was about a head taller than her, but she still reached up to tweak it into place for me..

Dolly then put her arm across my back and leaned her head on my shoulder. "Are they taking care of you? You were my favorite at the Corp."

I patted her hand with my good one. "Well, I'm still alive, but a bit worse for wear. And thanks for the vote of confidence. It was tough filling your shoes when you didn't come in that day. I'm glad to see things worked out for you."

"As best as things can when you're taken off the grid and become a nobody. I heard the Anti-Andro's got you. For me, it was the Feminista's. They thought they could recruit me after they cut out my chip and beat me up, but it wasn't a smart recruiting tool. Sam rescued me and I've been working here ever since."

"What is this place?" I asked. "It seems pretty organized."

"It actually is. The city provides the food and we cook it up. The mob boss makes sure that the gangs in this area cooperate with each other. This is a truce area. Everyone has to eat, so no one gets hurt here. No one is allowed to take offense or incite anything. And that goes out for about a block in all directions." Dolly rattled off, without taking her head off my shoulder.

Sam was still setting some trays out, quietly, looking our way occasionally, but with a quiet smile on his face.

Dolly saw me looking at him. "Isn't he just the cutest thing on two legs? I'm just so in love with him I could just spit. Waking up beside him every morning is the best day of my life, every day. Oh look, you've got to meet the Doc."

A tall, gaunt man came up, dressed as much in dark clothing as the rest, but somewhat more refined. He wore a regular suit jacket and dark shirt, but they were cleaner than most. Some plastic gloves stuck slightly out of one pocket and part of a stethoscope peeked out of the other.

He put his bread and soup bowl down on the table. "May I?" The Doc pointed to my splinted wrist.

I held it up for him and he felt it carefully. I noticed he was missing a couple of fingers off his own right hand.

"Looks like we got you plugged OK. Just keep that on and try not to itch it. I'll be around tomorrow to change that bandage and look for any infection. If it starts throbbing, let Andy know. He knows how to get in touch with me." Doc picked up his bread roll and soup along with a spoon and moved along, taking a seat at the far end of the transept, at a short table that sat next to the door that Andy and I came in.

As I looked after him, Dolly returned to my side again. "Doc had a rough one. He said something that ticked off some guv'ment official, who made sure that he not only lost his chip, but also any chance of being a surgeon again. So he works here and patches up the people that the gangs leave alive and in one piece. He also patches up people after the fights. But the new mob boss - the 'Don' - he mostly keeps people from getting two serious at each other. Bad for business, he says, (mocking a deep, gruff voice) 'We need people to do the jobs around here, not fill incinerators.'" Dolly smiled at her little joke.

All this background was a bit much for me. I turned and leaned against one of the tables.

"Oh, Michelle - this has got to be tiring for you. Here, I've got a roll for each of us, let's go see if we can talk to Doc. Andy's already there, so is Sam."

She took my good arm in hers and put a roll in my hand while she bit off a piece of the other for herself. She nudged me forwards and we soon sidled up on the benches by the table.

I wound up squeezing in next to Andy, who in turn squeezed Doc. Dolly pushed right up next to Sam, even though that left nearly half the bench empty. Dolly was always friendly. Sam took it in stride and put his arm around her. That left his soup hand free, and Dolly fed him pieces of bread she tore off her bun. Both were lost in their shared world.

Andy and I were nibbling on our own bun with one hand, while the Doc used his two arms. He liked the soup and it showed.

"Well, Doc, any news?" Andy asked.

"Finally got a decent night's sleep, first in months," Doc replied. "The new Don has enforced the new boundaries. And told them to lay off the corporate types. As long as they keep paying him, they'll have their safety on the streets. Michelle, you were the last straw. Seems someone liked you a lot, or you are too hard to replace. Since they basically have to raise their replacements nowadays, there aren't many people who are ready to fill your job."

I sat up straighter at that.

Andy smiled wistfully at that. "But unfortunately that doesn't mean you'll get your job back. Because they can't prove you exist. Your chip was spent and destroyed, so all your personal DNA data is gone. Anyone that looks remotely like you could apply."

I added, "But the Corp destroyed that chip as soon as they got the cops to track it down for them. Company policy. CYA, basically." Slumping down again, I had nowhere to go. I couldn't even go back to my old apartment to get my things - the gangs probably cleaned up someone to look like me and used my chip to get in and clean it all out. Moving day. I was broke and homeless.

Andy nudged me with his shoulder. "But you're here now and we can help you."

Dolly stopped feeding Sam and they both looked over. "Yea, Michelle, we get to help you sort everything out. And we needed some more help in our little kitchen anyway."

Another doleful gong sounded.

"That's our cue." Dolly stuffed the last piece of roll in Sam's mouth, then kissed him on the cheek. She took Sam's bowl and spoon and slid off the smooth bench, almost skipping back up to the food line.

"Another sitting coming in," Sam explained. He nodded to Doc, who grunted and went back to his eating.

I slid out and pocketed the rest of my roll in what I hoped was a fairly clean pocket on my left side. Andy followed, but stuffed his roll in his mouth to chew and swallow as he walked next to me.

Ahead, another pair of bouncers were keeping their particular gang in check. Some of the other members that weren't in line were cleaning up after the gang before. Doleful looks all around.

Sam whispered to me, standing on my left again by the soup kettles, "They are always a bit grumpy when they come in, but the medicine that cures all that is cheerfulness - and good smelling and good tasting food."

At that, the bouncers let the first in line come through, holding the next behind them back so that there was an orderly flow of people.

At the end, the bouncers came along with their little helpers.

Then the second bouncer stopped and looked at my face closely. "Don't I know you?"

The whole church got quiet quickly.

VII

"WE HAD SOME BUSINESS not too far from here last night. And someone got a bit personal with me. Kicked me where they shouldn't have. Still hurts."

The bouncer was looking at Michelle closely, and her splinted wrist.

"Why don't you go and take a pee in this and I'll see if you had any permanent damage," Doc held a plastic cup in front of his face, standing next to him by the kettle. "Or should I ask the Don if you should have some time off and a full checkup?"

The bouncer glared at Doc for what seemed like a full minute, then looked back at Michelle. "Nah, a little girl like you couldn't kick that hard. This was an Andro, anyway. It deserved what it got." The bouncer turned with his full soup bowl and two rolls in his other hand, then stalked out of the transept to join the rest of his gang in the nave.

"Thanks, Doc," I said. "This place is takes long enough to clean up as it is.

"Don't mention it, Andy," Doc replied. "The Don will hear about it anyway. That big meathead deserved far more than that, I'm sure." At that the Doc went back down the now empty line and picked up another roll to stuff in one of his pockets as he strode off through the other trancept. Another door on its far end let him out to the street.

Michelle relaxed and slumped. I put my hand on her shoulder. "The truce is older than the current Don, even though he enforces it better. Doc has some unofficial pull with his guv'ment connections. The work he does out here keeps their hospital clear of some of the less 'disciplined' gang members. And the hospitals can concentrate on the ulcers and plastic surgery of the more toady Corp execs that way."

I looked her in the eyes directly, "You're safe here. Know that."

Dolly came up and hugged her on the other side, while Sam was again refilling the bread trays down the long table-row.

"I've got to get these kettles filled up again. One more serving after this one. Then we'll be able to clean up everything and start cooking the next one."

Dolly squeezed her one last time and then stepped off to help Sam.

I let Michelle rest to the side while I loaded up the serving kettles one last time.

Soon the church bell gonged again, and the third gang came in. This was uneventful. We started cleaning up after the last of them were served. A few grabbed some leftover buns on their way out, but carefully. Any disrespectful actions would get reported to the Don and he hated to have to police such a small thing as table manners. As it was, the bouncers glared at those few the entire time, closing the door behind them.

Dolly went out to clear the tables and wipe them down with disinfectant. Sam was trundling the empty bread racks out to another room. I showed Michelle how we opened small petcocks in the bottom of the big kettles to drain the residual soup out. "Then they have a little hinge contraption that raises them on their sides for cleaning," I explained. The leftover soup and bread goes out to some homeless who aren't part of gangs and won't or can't come into the church."

I poured a bucket of hot water and disinfectant soap and another bucket of hot rinse water, handing the scrubbers to Michelle. "You don't have to do anything besides look pretty and hold these," I teased. Her face cracked into a smile. "You've been on your feet a lot today, when rest is what you need. Fortunately, this is a sit-down job."

I put down the two buckets and pulled a couple of chairs over. Michelle gratefully sat in one while I cleaned out the kettles by hand. While I normally whistled at this, I hummed a tune instead, just in case Michelle wanted to talk.

She was just as happy just to sit and do nothing. Certainly a change from her job at the Corp. And she had been through so many changes the last couple of days.

And miles to go before she slept. Well, before she slept peacefully, anyway.

At last the cleaning was done and we left the transept. The light switches were by the same door we'd come in earlier.

The room turned dark despite it being early afternoon.

VIII

LIFE HAD SETTLED DOWN into a bit of a pattern of running the soup kitchen and sleeping a lot to heal my cracked ribs and other strained body parts.

One day, Andy took me to another "Free Zone" where the gangs had to stay out of, where only the Don's and their guests could come. Doc went with us, or perhaps we were his guest. Guests of a guest. Something like that.

It was a beautiful day. Fleecy clouds in a deep blue sky. Sun shadowed us behind the tall high-rises. Walking on pristine concrete walks with cast-iron and shiny slatted wood benches which faced a long reflecting pool at intervals. I guess some architect thought city people needed reflection from time to time.

I certainly did.

The Doc left us to take another bench down a few hundred feet from us. We were all watching the pool cleaners at work, and the gardeners tend to grass clipping and bush trimming. This was the other reason we were here. We watched as the cleaners found a reason to come near Doc, one at a time, and have short conversations with him. They'd then leave to get back to their jobs.

Andy explained, "He has a bunch of regular patients. This is his regular rounds for them. If you watch closely, you can see him hand out little pill packages. When he holds their hand, he's taking their pulse. Some of these guys the Dons owe a favor to, others they want to keep on a short leash. So Doc keeps an eye on their physical and mental health and reports to their respective Don about how they are doing.

"Doc has found his own peace at this. No stress of the hospital rules. And he's always available for emergencies. Doesn't do dental work or eyesight stuff, but has some connections for that.

"It's all a system that allows everyone to live and let live." Andy was silent for awhile after that.

"Live and let live. You've said that before. I've just never seen it work," I said.

"Well, Michelle, you've led a sheltered life, even if you don't think so," said Andy.

My face scrunched up at that. "Sheltered?"

Andy smiled. "What I meant by that is that this city, any city, only allows a certain kind of thinking in it. Like that idea that you have to avoid offending anyone to survive. But actually, that is one of the most offensive things you can do."

"Like acting androgynous and getting beat up by the Anti-Andro gang?" I asked.

"Well, there's that. But the point I was making is when you are offending yourself." Andy replied. "That's far more dangerous than getting beat up."

I turned toward him. My right hand was now free of splint and bandages. And my hair was long enough to need tucking behind an ear. "What do you mean? I've never heard of this before."

"The idea is that your own individuality is important. By trying to get your security from outside you, to expect approval from others, to spend your whole life under someone else's control or working to escape from it - that is when you have threatened your own personal being. And so you find yourself afraid all the time. That fear will kill you off sooner or later," Andy said.

I thought about this carefully. Fear is all I had known my entire life. Even when I was a kid, my childhood was in two worlds. But fear was present in both. No place was truly safe. As I grew older, this city had become even more violent. Only when the Dons started coordinating between themselves did things even out.

"Are you sure?" I asked. "Is it that simple?"

"'Heaven is within you.' 'As you think in your heart, so are you.' All those old phrases add up to one point. You have to respect yourself to find yourself. Then you don't need anyone else's approval, only your own. You'll find that your security comes from within, as all you need is your own self-control. Then anything you are afraid of disappears." Andy said.

We were quiet for awhile at this.

"But where to I start? That is my whole life I've been living like this." I asked.

"Breathe." Andy said.

"Huh?" I asked

"Just take a deep breath, hold it for a second or two, and then let it out." Andy said. "Like this." And he showed me. "Now you try."

I took a deep breath and exhaled slowly like him.

"Feel the relaxation that happens when you do?" Andy asked.

I nodded.

"That's letting go. Whenever you feel tense or upset, develop the habit of taking a deep breath before you speak or act. Then whatever is triggering you will move off and you'll find a bit of peace in you. That peace is you, part of you. The more peace you can build inside of you is how you get more peace outside of you." Andy said.

That all made sense somehow. I didn't know how, but I knew this was a workable piece of truth.

We looked out at the reflective pool and the clouds above as reflected from above.

Too soon, the peacefulness was ended. Doc came over, walking easily. His hands in his pockets.

"Well, have you two love birds gotten everything sorted out?" He asked.

"I... I mean, Andy..." I stuttered.

"Oh you haven't seen this coming?" Doc asked. He tut-tutted. "I didn't think that head thump you'd gotten had affected your thinking."

My face turned red. I looked at Andy.

He just smiled back at me. "Doc sometimes sees things that other people don't. He surprises me all the time." Andy said. "But it is time to go, and we did have a good time today, didn't we?"

I nodded and stood.

Doc smiled and led away, while we followed.

I took Andy's hand as we walked along. It felt good, even if someone else had to point out the obvious.

And that's when I learned to accept and start becoming Michelle for real.

IX

SOME WEEKS LATER, AFTER the last gang of the day had left, one of them came back and handed Andy a note. He read it quickly and then stuffed it in his pocket with a frown. That day we cleaned the kettles in silence. Andy lightened up, but didn't whistle or hum as we cleaned.

We cleaned out the deep sinks after everything else, rinsing them with the last of the hot rinse water, now only lukewarm, and opening the double-sink hot-water tap to clean the last of that water as well. Sponges and scours went on a stainless shelf above the sink and we were done.

I followed Andy out of the transept, and he turned out the lights out of habit, but I grabbed the door and his hand before he could absent-mindedly shut me into that dark.

Out into the warehouse, I stopped him by grabbing his hand. "Andy, what is it?"

"I'm going to have to leave. Something has come up. I'll be leaving tonight." Andy replied.

"OK, I'm coming with you." I said.

"No, I..." and he looked in my eyes. The determination he saw there just made him shrug. "Well, I guess I know you well enough by now to know I can't talk you out of it." He smiled at me.

I leaned over and pecked a kiss on his cheek. "No, you're right, as usual."

"But it's going to be a bit tricky. Brownies can't come and go as they want. And you're not even a Brownie." Andy said.

"Where you go, I go." I said. And crossed my arms to make that point.

Andy just smiled. "OK, Michelle. You win. Get a small bag if you need one. You'll only be able to wear what you have on, so if you need a change of underwear or socks, put two sets on."

X

I FOUND MICHELLE AN old coat and a slouch hat. Then I taught her how to look at the ground and walk hunched over. With a little practice, she picked it right up. I had Dolly work over her hair and give it a different temporary color.

Walking on the borders we got to the main security exit just before twilight and traveled the long empty block between barbed wire and mesh fences. It was built originally as a double-wide highway, and it dwarfed us.

Michelle's shuffle made her look shorter than I was. And I also had her cough as she walked, every few steps.

By the time we finally shuffled up to the security booth, we had been scanned and re-scanned. Neither of us had chips, and our faces weren't in their systems.

One of the guards came up to us and grabbed off our hats. "Gotta see your faces. Rules." He thumbed up at a faded sign on the security booth outer wall.

When he pulled off Michelle's hat, he stared at her and dropped her hat on the ground, taking a step back. I looked over at her and had to work to keep my own calm.

Michelle then went into a paroxysm of coughing, and I lightly patted her back. Her hands were on both knees and she spit onto the pavement at her feet. I picked up her hat and handed it to her. She put it back on her head and then leaned on me for support, her head on my shoulder, an arm around my neck. The cap again covered her features.

The guard had started back-stepping once he saw her face, and almost fell through the guard shack door with it's raised step inside. Quickly sliding the door shut, he said something that was unintelligible and pointed out the gate.

He hit a switch inside with his fist and the gates started rolling out of our way. Not fast enough for him, he pounded the button again and again.

We started slowly toward the gate and made our way through it before it was all the way open, where it started closing again. The second and third gates were all open for us as well.

Once through the third gate (it nearly closed on us) we still had to keep up the charade for another mile until we could hit a bend in the road. The dark was closing in fast, which was a help.

Their microphones on each side, as well as cameras meant we still had to keep quiet. Well, except for Michelle's regular coughing.

Although the emergency sirens were wailing as their Haz-Mat team rolled up to clean up that area Michelle had spit on.

Finally out of their sight and hearing, we moved off the paved road and into some real dark.

I took off her hat and looked at her makeup job through the light from the few remaining street lamps.

"Where did you learn to do that?" I asked.

"I had to do a lot of makeup at my old job. And I also had to know the indicators of that plague they thought they'd eradicated. That coughing bit kept him from realizing that those lesions he thought he was seeing were just a layer of face paint." Michelle replied.

I took her in my arms and kissed her, face paint and all.

Then I showed her the note.

It was in my own handwriting: "It's time to go." That's all it said.

She punched me in the gut at that and then gave me a big hug.

We walked to the next town arm in arm as the stars started coming out in the moonlit sky.

Mind Timing

BY R. L. SAUNDERS WITH C. C. Brower

I.

WHEN THE LAST OF THE long-languishing news media died, it was with barely a whimper. No bang. Not even a sullen pop. And eyes were dry all around. No one mourned, few even noticed.

Two glasses clinked at the Club in celebration. And that was all the wake they deserved.

I and my visitor-turned-conspirator were the only witnesses.

To the end of a global war that now never happened.

HE HAD ENTERED UNINVITED and unwelcomed that first day, long ago. It's not that women couldn't have male visitors at the Club. As long as they were properly chaperoned or in the very public areas. But in those days, and by that time, no one expected that a white male presented any challenge or hazard.

Women ran politics, they ran business, they ran the world. Women scientists explored the known universe and profited from their discoveries.

"Mari, a man is here to see you." The female maitre d' at my elbow quietly announced.

This interrupted my news scanning, but was cautiously done. Alarmed Club members could get a bit defensive. And in these days, that could be dangerous to other Club patrons.

I sensed this as something unique, something out of the usual, the humdrum. It was actually a change I had been praying for.

So when that lone white male called at the all-female Club and asked for me by name, I accepted. He was shown to the middle of the main lounge, where two overstuffed chairs sat separated by a small side table. A distance surrounding them for room to move in case anything untoward developed.

While such a visit took time away from my scheduled daily poker game. I was tired of the usual bitching banter that accompanied each hand as we all knew the other's tells and bluffs.

It was time for new blood. Or a new game.

He entered wearing a very impeccable three-piece wool-blend suit, the shade of a fast quarter-horse out of the gate. Close behind him was our maitre d', who was a black belt in more martial disciplines than I could name on the fingers of both hands. She was our security. Not that we needed it. Because we were all qualified in many such disciplines. Hours in our basement gym was both socially demanded, and required. Because men had run the society into the ground, and after they lost their hold, most often became the last of the criminal class.

Women ran things, but because they had to fight their way to the top.

This male "suit" was accepted into our midst, in front of me, because it was more he was entering the lionesses den. One that was hidden behind the curtains, lace, and ruffles. Like the barred and electrified windows the Club maintained between themselves and the street. Like the concealed pistols, stiletto blades, and reinforced plexi-carbon fingernails most of us sported. For self-defense, of course.

No, I had no physical fear of any man who showed up in front of me.

But his attitude, like the quaint brown felt bowler he passed off to our maitre d', was precise and a statement of its own. Old-fashioned. Of a time before the sexes were at war. Before women had won.

"...and this civilization became just that, ma'am, an unending civil war." the stranger finished my thought.

"Intriguing, sir. I don't know your name and already you are inside my head, the ultimate hack to privacy," I replied, showing a hint of outrage.

"And you have every reason to be upset, Marigold. My name is Peter. And I am at your service." At that he extended a well-manicured hand, in the quaint, nearly extinct custom of hand-shaking.

I rose and took his hand more out of curiosity, knowing that my thin layer of dermal plasticine protected me from any direct poison, nano-biotic, or bacterial infection. Beside pheronomic door sensors had already passed him while x-ray scanning him against any weapons.

"Welcome, Peter. Call me Mari. You are just the mystery I've been seeking to relieve the tedium around here." I replied. He had a firm grip, one calculated to show respect, as that of an equal, not dominant or afraid. The skin was not calloused, but not soft. Unscarred. No missing digits.

"Thank you for seeing me without notice." Peter said.

I indicated the other matching overstuffed chair, the two separated by the ornate marble-topped side table between us. And we each sat, crossed our legs and studied the other for a few moments

"How you understand my thoughts is some parlor trick?" I asked.

"More like being able to recall conversations in retrospect. But you'll realize that soon enough. We've met before," Peter replied.

"Not like Merlin, you are living your life backwards?" I asked.

"More like the vast majority of us are. Like the old phrase, 'those who refuse to study their own history...'"

"...are condemned to repeat it.'" I finished.

"And life in these days and times is nothing more than a series of mental calculations to determine what could happen and what did. So most conversations have already occurred, most actions are taken by result of causes that have long ago ceased to be more than a continuing habit."

Peter accepted an iced tea from our waitress, as did I. She left with a studied grace, her high-grade stainless steel tray balanced in her hand, and at the ready to become shield or weapon as needed.

We both sipped, while I studied this puzzle before me.

"An interesting challenge to our culture. I've heard of no paper that has been submitted to the Academy for review..." I started.

"...because any review would not uphold it or even understand the principles it posits," He answered. "Our modern culture is no better than the one it replaced, which was no better than the one which brought us out of the caves or led us up from flea-scratching apes..."

"And as it is running circular to itself, then it is no better than any before it," I finished. "Meaning that all thought and action then continues in infinite loops until entropy finally collapses the universe on our very heads."

"Not exactly, but that is the accepted apparency," Peter said.

"You are then implying that there is an existence outside this time and space which doesn't follow the paths we and our forebears have traveled before," I said.

"Actually, your existence is more the fiction than fact. The universe I come from has 'asked' me to come and interview you with the idea that this endless cycle might be interrupted long before the quaint concept of 'entropy' might have its way," Peter said.

Shocked to my core, and the very challenge I was looking for. I sipped again, delighted with the hint of lemon in our green tea.

"The next question you would then ask yourself is whether you are up to that challenge," Peter said.

"And again, that nasty habit of mind-reading you've been displaying," I replied.

"I'll give you a few seconds to study what you just said." Peter now spoke in terse terms. "Your reply will determine if I leave or stay. I have other appointments with several similarly qualified women of power and station."

I mused on this. He had uncrossed his legs, and his straightened back showed him prepared to stand and depart, all depending on my answer.

"Nasty. The key term was 'nasty.' That showed my habitual thoughts, which then led you to suspect that my mental habits might not be open to change. I apologize. And ask your patience."

At that Peter relaxed, again sitting back against the tufted cushion of his chair, his eyes reading my face as an open book. I had met with the challenge I had asked for. The game was afoot, as I liked to paraphrase. Obvious to him, my apology was sincere. But even in these seconds of thought, he was well ahead of me. And I needed to act.

"Where and when are you from?" I asked.

He smiled. "As if that would make a difference. And perhaps it may. But we are 'wasting time' as you would say, working through these loops again. The question is: do you accept?" Peter asked.

"When do we leave?" I replied.

"Now." Peter set his drink on the side-table, stood and again extended his hand. All in one very smooth, singular motion.

I rose as well, calling the attention of our maitre d' with a subtle half-raised hand that she was expecting. She started to return in our direction with his bowler.

"And may I ask where we are going?"

Peter replied, "Not so much where as when..."

At that, the room shimmered around us, placing us temporarily in physical limbo.

II.

WHEN THE SHIMMERING stopped, we were back in what seemed the 20-teens. Standing outside a vacant lot in Los Angeles. About where the Club would be built some great time later. The polluted air stank of car exhaust, only matched by the tar-smell of the road next to us. We stood on cracked concrete sidewalk, ringed on both sides by dry grasses and gravel. Screaming sirens in the distance accented the noisy roar of traffic that passed us, with clumsy buses buffering blasts of air about us as we stood in the sultry heat. The sun was overhead, a dim light in that haze called sky. Everything had a yellowish cast as a result.

What was called "normal" for that day and age.

Peter spoke in a pitch to be heard above the traffic. "Let's go to that chain restaurant you can see from here. It will be quiet and cool enough to think clearly as I explain these principles to you that you'll need for this challenge.

He talked as we walked down the mostly vacant sidewalk. That old phrase and song was correct, nobody walked in L.A. So he was able to explain most of the basics to me in simple terms, uninterrupted except where we had to cross intersections and wait our turn for car traffic.

While he kept a good pace, I was able to keep up as sensible flats had long replaced high-heels (King Louie's invention) as well as slacks replacing skirts (except in Scotland, where women preferred the freedom as did their men. But those customs in that locale had always been a bit frisky.)

Peter also matched his longer pace to mine, a bit of courtesy, but also as he needed to see my reaction, which he couldn't do if he was forging ahead.

By the time we reached the restaurant front door, we were both well cooked and wearing a sheen of moisture. For some reason the old phrase, "Men sweat, women glow." came to mind. Not the first anachronism I would encounter in this alternate time.

The air-conditioned interior of the orange-and-brown outfitted restaurant was welcome. It tended to make that "glow" turn to drops that dove down my neck and below the white starched collar of my blouse.

When we were shown to our booth, I quickly pulled a paper napkin from below the stainless "silverware" to mop the worst of it off my face and neck. Peter pulled some extras from the container on the table for us to use, as he similarly cleared the running drops off his own angular jaw. I could only imagine how that wool suit was heating him up.

"Actually, wool tends to wick the moisture away, an old Arab trick from the desert. The trick is to wear only cotton or silk underneath. And yes, as you were thinking, boxers." Peter said.

My mouth was hanging open, and so I shut it, focusing on breathing to avoid the reddish tinge creeping up from my chest. It had been a long time since a man had given me a reaction like that. Not unpleasant, but that found me off-guard. I never liked being caught off guard. Especially by my own thoughts.

"Most of that is the time we are in. It's the contagion of mental habit. And why L.A. is key to the entire challenge. You'd might think New York would be first, but the simpler and easier route runs through here." Peter said.

I replied, "You know that mind-reading stuff would be fascinating if it weren't so..."

"...invasive of your privacy. Sorry. Different space/time culture. Once I get you up to real telepathy instead of simple empathy, it will get easier for you," Peter said.

At that the waitress came over. Peter ordered, "We'll have your special, with two large iced teas, sweet. And apple pie ala mode. Thanks." The waitress was surprised to recieve such a succinct statement, as she wrote it down. And as she picked up the unopened menus, she gave him more than one curious glance. Tucking a errant wisp of hair behind an ear with her free hand, she moved quickly away, with a little more flounce than she arrived with.

I sat to digest this without speaking. The teas returned soon, along with the waitress picking up our spent paper napkins to get a few more up-close glances at Peter.

But these were the days when women courted openly, something that would seem anachronistic in our own time.

"Or maybe just suppressed," Peter said. "Oh, sorry again, but not sorry. There is some elements of human nature which get out of hand every now and then, but rapidly balanced out. Your particular time is out of balance. And we are here as a challenge to see if we can fix that."

"Suppressed? An interesting concept. Of course our history said the reverse. That women were suppressed by the males until they rose up as equals and eventually became the superior sex," I said.

"Superior implies inferior. Let's say co-equal is more ideal. But the problem isn't history, it's again the point of whether it's interpreted or ignored." Peter said.

"And who is this challenge directed against?" I asked.

"Not an individual, but a thought-habit that was started some time ago. And we've traced it back to a off-wordly, out-of-time experiment," Peter replied.

At that precise point, the waitress returned with the plates of their diner special, a true American spread, served 24 hours a day in true American binge fashion. A stack of pancakes with sausage and two over-easy eggs. Matched by a slab of something called "hash browns." All the sugar, salt, and partially-hydrogenated oils, plus added trans-fats you could stuff into your unsuspecting and soon obese self.

All an historical footnote. Until this current, present. Where now I was just about to give my body the shock of its life. Welcome to this new millenia, not even a quarter of the way into it. A time when lifespan is shortened by diet, and humankind nearly extinquished itself over the next century. If it weren't for the handful of survivors in rural enclaves called "farms" there would have been no genetic material to re-start humankind.

"Dig in. You'll never know what you've been missing with all your pure diets and wholesomeness," Peter smiled as he cut a portion of those golden-brown flap jacks covered with artificial butter whipped and scooped up into a tiny ball. Covered with corn-derived sweetener that itself would add to heart disease. Grown with corn that was laced with a nutrition-inhibitor called glysophate, genetically modified to be immune to it - while the human body was not.

I watched him stuff the five layers of pancake into his mouth and catching the dripping fake butter and fake syrup with his tongue, while quickly bringing his paper napkin to dab off any he missed. Taking a swig of reconstituted orange juice, which was pretty much devoid of any natural sugars, he then smiled at me.

"Go ahead. You only live once. And cocaine doesn't even taste this good."

I cut a tiny bite with my fork and tentatively tasted it. The thrill raced through my tongue and brought sensations to my mouth and brain that I had never experienced. Chewing thoughtfully brought a massive flood of hormones into play which had laid dormant through all the specified diets and training our own culture had carefully maintained for several centuries after the Collapse.

"Damn! You're right. This stuff is amazing!"

And for the next 5 minutes, we stuffed our faces with this poisonous mass-produced 21st century diet, downing it all with our artificially flavored and sweetened tea.

As we finished our plates, right down to the unhygienic idea of licking them clean, the observant waitress came over with our apple pie (also questionably raised, sliced and cooked between dough of similar poisons as our stack of pancakes. It had been heated with ultra-short wavelength microwaves to give those molecules excitement enough to re-radiate lower-length heat. Enough to begin melting the scoop of artificial ice cream, allowing it to run in streams across the pie. Another beautiful golden and off-white sight to the eyes.

"Now, this is the coup de gras," Peter said with all sincerity, slicing off a forkful with a slice of the ice cream and pushing the whole wad into his mouth. Closing his eyes with delight as he savored the addictive artificial ingredients that were making his brain and glands work overtime. A true rush.

After a small taste, I also had to shut my eyes to experience the exotic flavor and affect it was having on my body.

Soon we were completely full and sitting back against our plastic-covered foam seats. Delighted as only an addict can be.

"Just to top all that off, let's get some of their world-famous coffee." Signaling with his hand, the waitress brought over two thick mugs, and filled them both with black Java-bean coffee. Leaving us each a plastic container that at least honestly said it was all artificial, Peter showed me how to open it and pour the white liquid into the mug, stirring it to make the contents more light brown.

Peter sipped his lightly. "Like piping-hot tea. Careful you don't burn yourself."

I gingerly tried it and the caffeine brought a new rush to replace the sugar high which had been dissipating. "So the creamer is to cool it off. Amazing concept. Incredibly addictive. No wonder these people nearly wiped themselves off. Eliminate war in a single lifetime, only to kill everyone off with abundant and addictive instant gratification."

Peter nodded. And smiled with an addicts glee. "Yes, it's true. Destined for doom. Only saved by the discovery of fusion drives and a misguided attempt at salvation by flying their largest cities off as spaceships to other planets."

"Oh?" I asked. "That part wasn't in the history I was taught."

"Well, it's actually one of those alternate facts that historians managed to ignore. The timeline existed like that, but their view is that farmers again saved the cities and the women took over at that point to sort things out. The cities were never heard from again, at least not officially. UFO's and what not have always been around." Peter explained.

By that point, we had both finished our coffees and the waitress had removed our plates, then returned with the bill. Peter pulled out a piece of plastic and she took it to return soon with a couple of candies and the receipt.

"More coffee?" She asked.

We both shook our heads no. She smiled and picked up our cups, lingering over a look at Peter's profile a little longer before mincing off. I noticed she had written a series of numbers separated by hyphens on that paper.

"Code?" I asked.

"Mating ritual." Peter replied. He did stuff the receipt along with the plastic card into it's faux leather folding container, which he kept securely in his suit's inner breast pocket, I noticed.

My senses were still filled with the sensations of all the sugars, fats, and salt.

"Me, too." Peter said. "I had to bring you here to experience this first hand. This culture is routinely drugging itself. Obesity is a side effect. But we have to change their mental habits that make meals like this profitable – or at least try. Come, I'll call us a cab and we can ride to our final stop."

As we rose, he allowed me to go first, and put a hand behind my back without touching me. As if to steady me in case the after effects were too much.

Making our way to the door, Peter pulled a plastic and metal device from his pocket, touched the front screen of it several times and put it to his ear. A short conversation later, a yellow vehicle soon drove right in front of where we were standing.

We got in back and were soon being jounced around by the driver jockeying for position with other "freeway" vehicles. When we weren't zooming along, we were stuck at a crawl where the driver still continued to try to get us into a faster lane. Obviously paid by the mile of transport, not the minute.

Shortly, we had left the freeway and were traveling on double-lane surface streets, finally turning up to a single lane, bi-directional paved surface in what seemed a residential area. The pace was slower now, other traffic rare.

We had no reason to talk, and our metabolism was not motivating us to further conversation. While I had a thousand questions, I had no energy to ask even one. Just keeping my head from nodding and eyelids open was effort enough.

Eventually, the driver pulled to the side. Getting out on the passenger side, Peter paid with that plastic chip again, but also handed some paper slips to the smiling driver through that opened side window before he drove off with another rush.

All very strange to me, as I touched my credit-chip implant in my right arm near the wrist. All of this could be much simpler...

"But we'll leave that conversation for another time," Peter said. "No, I didn't want to interrupt your view of this world as it is, even though you may describe it as through a drug-induced euphoria."

I smiled at that as we walked the short walkway to the front entrance. Too true. My current state could easily be described as drugged. While I had only met Peter hours before, something in him inspired trust. This was no date-rape scenario he had concocted. But we would know shortly. If so, I would bet my reflexes and weapons against his height and strength.

III.

HE OPENED THE LARGE white door and allowed me to enter before him.

Cool air bathed my face. I felt tired after that meal, very strange.

"That room to your left is yours. You'll find a nice bed, and sanitary facilities. Rest as long as you like. There is a manual lock on the door, but you won't be disturbed," Peter briefed me, with a gesture toward a mahogany-tinted door to my left, down a short hallway.

Then he smiled that winning smile of his and turned right to travel down a similar hallway to a near identical door opposite, again with its own hallway..

While I could see a larger living area ahead of us, and had more questions, I was wrung out from the artificial everything I'd just consumed, plus the change in time. I turned and walked carefully to the door, the opened it.

Locking it behind me wasn't difficult. The question was whether he had a key.

I turned and took in the room. It was simple in furnishing. A huge bed in the center of the room that looked so soft, covered in a padded comforter. A single padded chair. Two matching side tables framing the bed, both with lamps, both secured to the wall on either side.

I kicked off my shoes, shucked out of my own jacket to leave it folded, laying on the side of that bed.

Before I relaxed, I moved the heavy chair over to the door, then opened one of my sturdier locking clasp knives, jamming it into the carpet directly in front of the front chair leg in line with the door handle.

Now I could relax. The noise would alert me if anyone tried to enter.

I intended to sit down on the bed and let my head clear.

But soon, I laid back and closed my eyes. Just for a second...

AND I WOKE UP WITH the room dark, alert. Scanning the room, I found nothing had changed. I was still fully dressed, the jacket as I had left it. The light that had come in the windows was gone. Evidently the earth had rotated out of the sunshine. How long we had been in shadow or how long we would be, I could not tell. For I didn't know what time it was here.

The darkness didn't wake me. It was my own reflexes. Something had made a subtle sound. Or something else had wakened me.

Calling for lights didn't affect their status. I quickly scanned the room and felt my clothes and jackets for weapons. All present. Nothing had changed while I dozed.

Standing up failed to turn the lights on, waving my arms had no effect.

A sudden realization came to me. This was a mechanical age where they had actual hard-wired switches to turn things on and off. Just as they needed a human driver to operate that taxi.

It would be logical to have a switch by the door. My night vision gave me dim shapes, plus my memory helped me retrace my steps. Also, it should be about elbow height or slightly higher. Stepping to avoid the chair, I ran my hand along the wall and upward, finding a peg sticking out of a wall plate. Turning this upward made the lights blaze and my eyes flinch in their drug-influenced daze.

Now I could explore the room. Probably should find and use those sanitary facilities, as I felt a need to eliminate.

There was the door. One twist and a quick pull showed nothing of note. Another wall switch turned on the lights.

An interesting seat with a hinged cover must be were one did their "duty."

AND MINE I DID SIMPLY enough. Although it was fascinating to work out how the water was plumbed with various knobs and levers. I tried them all to see how they worked. Most fascinating was the puzzle of how to get the overhead sprinkler nossle working. Two levers had to be operated in sequence to make the water flow into the nozzle overhead instead of the over-large white basin below.

And a flimsy curtain to channel the water into that huge basin. No vacuum jets to pull the moisture into filters for recycling.

Truly primitive times. I wondered how long before our more efficient fog-mist cleansers would take to be invented. Just remove your clothes, walk in and through, then a drying wind would remove the moisture in the time it took to walk through it. Often built in a curved arrangement, where you would then return to your closet where you started, to select fresh clothing.

While I felt a bit soiled in these clothes from the sweat and heat of yesterday, I didn't know how I was to replace these with clean versions, so I continued to explore.

Just then, I heard a tapping on some surface in the larger room. Alert to someone trying to break in, I pulled a stiletto blade from a side pocket while I made my way over to my jacket on the bed where I could get my large-caliber pistol to hand. It was a choice between that and the smaller caliber derringer, but better overpowered than under.

The tapping was coming from the door.

And I heard Peter's muffled voice from the other side, "How are you doing? I heard you up and about. Is everything OK?"

"Just fine, thank you." I sheathed the stiletto and pocketed my pistol in the jacket as I shrugged it on.

Walking to the door, I pulled the knife out of the floor and kept it in hand, concealed. The other hand moved the chair and then shifted the mechanical lock back.

Opening the door, I saw it was only Peter, I let the tenseness of my shoulders, stomach, and thighs release. There was no danger. Only a single man. A defenseless white male.

Peter was dressed in a pale violet shirt and light gray slacks, wearing only dark grey socks against the tan carpeted floor. Hardly the danger I had prepared for.

"I didn't want to intrude, but when I heard the water running and saw the light on, I knew you were up and around. So I came to do my hostly duties of showing you around." Peter said. "While we are here, please let me show you your wardrobe." He didn't step forward, but waited for me to allow him entrance.

It was that thin line of manners which separated the barbarism we were currently in and the culture of my own time. Men knew their place there - or would be quickly reminded of it. The blade concealed in my hand would have been my first reminder.

As I stepped back and he passed by me into the room, I was able to pick out his particular scent. Something along the line of charcoal, and a light earthy smell.

"I've been out gardening," Peter explained. "Hope that doesn't bother you. It helps me clear my mind."

No, of course I didn't mind, even though he was again reading my mind without asking. For some reason I found that scent exciting. And for a strange reason didn't care if he picked up that thought.

"Over here is a selection that should fit you." Peter walked to two matching wide panels in the wall with recessed handles colored the same as the paint. These panels he slid open silently and they continued on their tracks to almost disappear into the walls. His extended arms showed that the walk-in closet was at least 8 feet wide, just in its opening.

Inside were hanging garments overhead and a long set of drawers below. A rack for shoes resting on the drawer section top was filled in every opening, and extended the length of the drawers. It only stopped for a section of hanging dresses and gowns.

"I'll leave you to explore at your convenience. I think you'll find a wide variety of clothing and undergarments that are sized to be comfortable." Peter turned and walked over to a console that contained a large flat screen. A narrow shelf held a plastic control unit that he picked up. The flat screen came to life with light and low sound.

"These numbered buttons will allow you to find the various programs and catch up on these social nuances they currently call entertainment. There are also some fashion programs that will show you how the various clothing is arranged and worn." Peter was rapidly flicking through the remote buttons. As he mentioned a program, he was able to show it on the screen.

Finally, he turned the screen off and returned the remote.

"You've found the bathroom and probably figured out all you need. Other than the bed, that is about all there is to this room." Peter continued. "I'll leave you to change or you can come and I'll show you a 'hair of the dog' mixture that will help wash away that all-day breakfast we had this afternoon. Your choice, of course."

"Of course. And thank you," I replied. "While my body would like something a bit fresher to wear, my mind is telling me that this fog around my head should leave."

Peter smiled. "Wise choice. We aren't going anywhere tonight, but the questions you have can wait until both your head and body are comfortable again. Will you come this way, please?"

A perfect gentleman, I thought as I followed him. And managed to quietly unlock and stow the clasp knife as I walked behind him.

He led through a great central room that contained a large ring of couches in front of a massive screen over an unlit fireplace. To the side of them was a large, long hardwood table with seats enough to fit all those spaces on the couch. Evidently for eating, although a board conference would also be appropriate. In that case, the large screen might serve for presentations, though I saw no projector.

Finally, he lead to a bar that connected the cooking and preps area to the eating area. On its top, centered, there was a tall, clear carafe of cooling pinkish drink, sitting in an ice bath.

"'Hair of the dog' is a phrase which refers to an old remedy for rabies, which was to consume the hair of the dog that bit you. In this age, it mostly referred to having a small amount of alcohol the morning after having over-consumed such the night before," Peter explained as he poured out a large portion into a tall glass tumbler.

"This is known as a protein-drink, but is fruit and plant-based. It has some natural sugars in it as well as protein to help you wash those various chemicals we consumed earlier out of your system." He placed the tumbler in front of me.

I tasted it lightly, and found it quite good. A larger sample encouraged me to take an even larger draught.

Peter looked on with amusement. "Good, isn't it?" I had over a half-quart myself.

I nodded as I kept drinking. It was as if my body craved this drink like water to a dehydrated man at a desert oasis. One with a fruit bar.

Empty, I put glass down on the bar top. Peter smiled and handed me a cloth napkin.

I dabbed at sides of my mouth where the pink drink still remained. And smiled back.

"Thanks. Truly refreshing," I said. "The most delightful dog-hair I've ever drank."

"You are almost ready for the challenge. As you already suspect, this is one of the most important and risky you've ever faced."

IV.

PETER'S EYES WERE FIRM, his brow set as well as the corners of his mouth. He was serious.

"You brought me all the way here just to tell me that?" I asked. "I've allowed myself to be drugged, perhaps just then again, and moved to a time and location that I do not know. So risk is something I was prepared for. Tell me something I don't know."

"Or tell you something that you are not aware of," Peter continued. "You were practically bored to tears when I entered your Club several hundred years from now. And came with me armed to the teeth with multiple weapons from a 'more enlightened' time. Where the local laws currently don't even have permits for most of those now-unknown weapons, but they would be confiscated were you ever arrested. Just for carrying them."

He had moved through the doorway, standing now behind the counter in the kitchen it was part of.

He took the carafe and snapped on a plastic lid, turning away from the counter to place it in a tall cabinet behind him, one I presumed was for refrigeration and preservation. Then he returned, picking up my glass and rinsing it in what had to be a narrow bar sink on his side of that counter. The sound of a clink told that he had placed it upside down to drain. Not the most sanitary, perhaps, but a simple expedient.

Placing both hands on the counter, to show he meant no harm to me, his next statement might be alarming. I shifted my stance slightly to the balls of my feet, prepared.

"I find your heightened awareness amusing," he smiled. "And you know I don't have any weapons on me while I can make out at least a dozen on you. But that is logical, since I am the one who needs to earn your trust. In your time it was the male, particularly the white male, who was the most dangerous and unpredictable. Here, in this time, you are a queen to almost everyone you meet, because of your advanced mental and physical training.

"And there is also the error you've been raised with. Also why I had to bring you here. In your time, you were to have an unfortunate accident of your own Club a couple of hours after we left. Ultimately, you would have died. Because you sought relief from your own boredom.

"It was your own advanced training that killed you. In that time. Not now."

Peter moved his hands down and turned to leave the kitchen back into the long main room. He turned off the kitchen lights as he passed through that doorway.

I shifted my position slightly and moved back to appear as normal as possible, turning to walk down the side of the conference table.

He walked along the side of the long table I'd put between us, both seeming to sense my high preparedness and to ease it.

"This is the problem of that time. Both sexes are in such a high state of conflict that it is too close to an actual war between them. One that would be the end of the human race. And this is why artificial intelligence failed where artificial insemination succeeded. To preserve the human race. Although your genomic work proved that it's better for Nature to decide the sex of the child. Not humans, before or after it is born.

"That much of the history of this time was preserved. For Nature has ways of equalizing the balance when it shifts too far off course." Peter was talking he walked.

And now we had reached the end of the table. He stopped on his side, at the corner.

"That is what our challenge consists of. You need to interact with this culture in order to revert a certain mental habit that has creeped in," Peter looked at me with his steel-blue eyes.

Those eyes were simple truth. His brows weren't elevated or narrowed. He was simply gauging my reaction and staying neutral so I could react without his influence.

I appreciated that. Again, this man was intuitive beyond bounds. It fit his tale of being from another time-line.

"The principles of this challenge we went over on our way here. This is another nexus where the decision is yours. We can continue, or the challenge is over and you will return to the time you left, the instant following." Peter waited for my response.

I knew the correct response had to be physical. "Obviously, I need to refresh myself and get into something more comfortable and less aggressive. I won't need any weapons with you..."

"...as you are safer with me here and now than you could be in any time and space. The combat we seek isn't between us, but rather before us," Peter finished.

I smiled at this. He had a quaint way of talking, of explaining things. They matched my scientific outlook. Maybe a little too closely. "Well then, I'll get cleaned up and find something more appropriate for our next conversation," I said.

A small smile started at the corners of his mouth. "And that next conversation should be rewarding. We have so much still to cover..."

V.

SHOWERED (I BELIEVE the phrase is) and dutifully clean, I dressed and walked back into the main room (called the "living area") barefoot on the soft, deep carpeting. I was wearing a matching gray set of yoga pants, a crop top, and a comfortable cotton fleece top called a "sweatshirt" (probably due to its absorptive properties.) I had not a single weapon on me, even having removed my fingernail add-ons. Because I needed to earn Peter's trust to get him to tell me what I had to know.

Peter rose from the center of the couch set as I entered, another courtesy from a long-lost time. I crossed in front of him to sit in the corner farthest from the door. A position that denoted I was willing to trust him with my life. Or was a damned fool. As I passed, I again caught that earthy fragrance he wore and realized that it wasn't gardening or an added scent. This was his own particular scent. And I found it intriguing.

Peter sat as I did. He was also barefoot, and wore a simple light blue cotton t-shirt that fit his broad shoulders as if tailored, but not tight. He had no need to show off his physique to me. I could tell by his walk and gait that he was used to a lot of daily exercise.

He smiled at me. "And I'll be 'staying out of your head' as the saying goes. You can finish your own sentences. Because in my own time-space, it makes our communication faster, but here it sets you on edge. Mental privacy matters more here, as you have reminded me."

"Thank you for that, Peter." I noticed he had been reading from a set of documents in front of him off a narrow mahogany-colored tea table. While more inside, there were a few loose sheets of paper on top of their grey card stock folder. "But I have some questions before we continue. How is it that I'm able to know the local names for rooms and fabrics? I haven't had time to study the programs on that screen, er, TV set."

"Mental habits," Peter answered. "They are like the global winds that move around every planet and every bit as penetrating. What people think are private thoughts actually spread from one to the other with impunity. This is the reason for mob action, and for both the elevation and degradation of cultures. Why the rural areas are more peaceful and the cities are more violent. And why half of all scientific studies are wrong - inside the same study itself. We covered this earlier, but it had to sink in by experiencing it. We become what we think about. And it is a definite 'we' that is the cause and effect."

"Then how is it that we just don't all become a great mental "melting pot" residue?" I asked.

"Because we are individuals first, and work as a team or herd or pack secondarily. No two people consider the same, just as they don't observe the same accident 'facts.' There are as many slightly different accounts as their are witnesses. Prosecutors and defense attorneys wanting to determine the 'truth' will emphasize one version over the others, and so accomplish the legal result they want," Peter explained.

"Yet we still have choice over what we think, and can so choose our own results," I said.

"Yes, as long as one is aware that as you become what you think about, and so the world is what you think it as," Peter added.

"That then brings us to why we are here?" I asked.

"Indirectly, yes." Peter pulled one of the paper-clipped sets of papers and handed it to me. "You'll have to wade through some of the scientific academia-ese on the back papers, but the summary sheet pretty much lays it out."

I looked over the front sheet carefully, and then scanned through the rest. Peter had selected this data as key and knew my background. I got excited.

"This is amazing stuff. It was – or will be - only theoretical in my time," I said with wide eyes.

"It's actually little known here and now. Those that might know this to be true aren't listened to in these days." Peter said. "It's because of the viral mental habit that created what they call 'news' in this era."

I frowned. We didn't even have that term.

Peter noticed the frown. "You don't have the term, but you have been effect of the result. That news reader you were scanning when we met is part of the 'news media' in this time. Mostly those are owned by conglomerate corporations who also own televised broadcast media, and even a temporal fad called 'social media' at this time. But there lies the problem and the solution. Our job is to simply leverage certain factors which have been pointed out as crucial to tipping the scales."

He handed me another paper which I scanned quickly.

Then I stood to move over to reach the papers on the table myself sitting closer to him in the process.

Peter relaxed and watched me work, one arm hanging over the couch back, which turned him slightly toward me. A perfect angle for him to observe.

I was so intrigued with the rest of the papers, I hardly noticed until I finished.

He was smiling as I put down the last paper. "Want some more of that protein shake?"

I nodded and sat back. Watching him walk the distance to the bar.

Putting my hands down to each side, one wound up feeling the warmth Peter had left on rising. This again raised my pulse in a not-unwelcome manner. And his scent rose again from the couch fabric, which compounded the effect.

Peter soon returned with two tall glasses, along with a white cloth napkin for each. I took the glass and napkin from one of his hands, while he sat calmly in his earlier position.

We both sipped in quiet.

"You know, this is darned good," I said.

"Yes. All natural and invigorating," he said.

I set my glass on the tea table, on top of its own cloth napkin. And then just relaxed on that couch next to Peter, considering what we had covered. The heat from him came over to me, although we weren't touching. This made thinking a bit difficult for some reason. But a welcome distraction.

Soon my thoughts were only about Peter.

I didn't really understand how this could be. Perhaps it was the "mental habits" floating around this city, or those of Peter himself. Either way, it didn't matter. I liked the sensations, much different from those sugar/salt/fat laced pancakes and caffeine-powered coffee.

What was different is that the society I came from treated men as something to be wary of, that sex was a personal thing, not related to having children directly. Now I saw the direct connection on an intimate level.

It was intoxicating to experience.

"You know, this is getting hard to concentrate," I said.

"Is it alarming to you? We can move to the table," Peter said.

"No, it's a unique experience, one I think I want more of," I replied.

"In answer to your question, this isn't a mindset habit of this culture, rather the result of your moving away from the mass mindset of your own culture," Peter said.

I looked up to his face as he turned to look back at me. His angular jaw and hard lines somehow seemed softened to me, as if I were looking through a filtered lens.

"And I won't 'try anything' on you without your permission, meaning that it's up to you what you want to explore as part of this experience," he said.

I sent my hand up to the back of his head and pulled his face close to mine. "I hope you don't mind that I'm not experienced in this sort of thing," I said softly.

He whispered back to me, as our faces were nearly touching. "I'm yours to teach you whatever you want."

Our lips touched, and the time for talking was over...

VI.

AT FIRST LIGHT, I FOUND myself alone in my own bed, a smile on my lips.

Touching them, I remembered what I had experienced and learned that night. Which made my smile broaden. Parts of me were feeling differently this morning. Not sore or abused, but rather - "sensual" I think the term is.

Flipping off the single sheet, I rose and made my way to the bathroom and used its namesake. Filling the tub with hot water, just warm enough to be soothing and relax, I found a cake of organic olive oil soap and a cotton washcloth to carefully clean myself. This sensation of a bath was so different. Again, "sensual" came to mind.

The growling of my stomach reminded me that with all that exercise requires refilling with food. So I rose, toweled off (yet another remarkable sensation) and left the tub to drain as I went to select something to wear.

In minutes, I was into a workout outfit that perhaps was a bit revealing to my curves, but I was in need of burning off those pancakes from yesterday and toning up in general. Unless this house had a workout room, there was probably room here on the floor for most of the exercises I needed.

But first, I went to see what proteins I could find in the kitchen.

Peter was already there, and the smells from his cooking were incredible. My stomach rumbled in appreciation when my nose and salivary glands went into operation.

As I reached the counter, Peter pushed a plate toward me, and set a tall glass of milk beside it. A fork and cloth napkin were already there, with two mahogany colored high chairs present.

"It's four range-free pullet eggs with natural cottage cheese in an omelet. Oh, I added some buckwheat and milk to it for some real weight. That's whole milk, not pasteurized or homogenized. They call it 'raw' for some reason. I thought you would want some substantial breakfast before you exercised. Oh, yes, we do have an exercise room, big enough for sparring with a weight machine to the side," Peter said.

Then he put his own plate and tall glass on the counter, turned off the range, and came around to sit beside me. He was also dressed for exercise in a sleeveless T and bike shorts. My outfit was modest compared to the lines his showed. I forced my eyes away from his well-defined arms back to my breakfast.

"Are these jellies or jams, and what is in them?" I asked, pointing to the small jars in front of the plates.

"I like the Amish-made jellies. They use turbinado sugar, and locally picked fruit. In front of you are blackberry and gooseberry jelly and wild plum jam," he answered. "Try a little of each. Their tastes are distinctive."

Once I started sampling each one with a fresh bit of buckwheat omelet, I was delighted with each mouthful, almost moaning with the new tastes, as my mouth was too full to talk. Mixing two of them together produced even more combinations of taste. And finally I used the last bit of omelet to clean the plate of any residual jelly and jam. The whole milk rinsed it all down nicely and gave me a contented feeling, as well as a definite reason to exercise this morning.

Peter had been watching me and his smile hardly quit as he was chewing. He finished about the time I sat back in my high chair, patting my tummy in contentment. He dabbed his lips with his cloth napkin and then gathered the plates and utensils, scooting them to the side and back of the counter.

"You go ahead. I'll clean up. It's that white door to your right, next to the fireplace. I'll be in soon." He rose and went around to the kitchen side of the counter. I heard water running and his humming a song as I left for the exercise room.

After all, there was nothing else for me to see or do since he was on that side of the counter. And I did need to work all that off, to get my mind clear for more studies...

VII.

AFTER A THOROUGH ROUND of exercising (and thankfully he was in the corner on the exercise bike all the time, so I could simply face away to concentrate on kicks, punches, and tumbling) we met again at the table after we had both showered and dressed for studies.

I was in an off-white blouse, buttoned to the neck and long-sleeved, tucked into dark-gray, almost black slacks. Black comfortable pumps completed a business-like approach. He already had spread out some material, with a stack of more gray folders on the table to study. He was wearing a light blue, loose cotton faux turtle neck sweater, also in long sleeves but pushed up on from his forearms, black jeans and some moc-toed loafers over black socks. Both of us were comfortable, and ready for study.

He had made a place for me across a corner of the table, so we could have enough space to study and converse, without the distraction of proximity.

My pile of material was short, but I could see that he was simply reviewing, so that large stack to his left would soon be added to the pile on my left, between us.

I pulled up one of the dining chairs and began my studies.

HOURS LATER, WE'D COMPLETED the reading. A pot of green tea had filled and refilled a pair of stout coffee cups repeatedly as we worked our way through it. An empty plate held only the crumbs of sinfully rich toll-house cookies with butterscotch chips. (Ensuring that I would be visiting the exercise room tomorrow and probably every day as long as Peter's cooking kept feeding me this way.)

"You have questions," Peter said. His mild, but direct style had grown on me. He was still reading me like an open book, but was careful to leave my sentence endings alone.

I began, "Let me state the obvious first. The core problem is religion. Or rather lack of it. Except for the bi-coastal megalopolises, no one is believing what passes for 'news' and both newspapers and news media are losing reader/viewership across the boards. They are going broke. Social media is failing and proving to be unworkable, even depressing. With the Internet becoming widespread, people no longer need or want to have centralized news broadcast to them."

"Correct," Peter said.

"Then why do we need to do anything? It's already collapsing and will wind up with small pockets of area with high crime and rampant sexual diseases, plus higher taxes and lower jobs as job creators leave for rural areas with lower cost of living, which includes taxes," I said.

"True again," Peter said. "The trick is to preserve the genetic pool when the cities ultimately discover fusion-powered flight and take off for the stars. The one thing we need to watch out for is the release of incurable diseases from these cities to remote 'treatment' facilities on their peripheries. And that solution is to raise the health of 'Flyover Country' peoples who will become isolated for a time when the cities do leave. And you've been tasting the preventatives for this, natural and low-processed foods, locally grown and distributed, needing no preservatives for long shelf-life and long transportation."

"The real solution is to encourage their 'clinging to guns and religion', which have kept them safe and prosperous up until the last decade or so," Peter said.

"Well, that might be, but what are you and I supposed to do about this?" I asked.

Peter opened up one last folder and slid it over to me. I began to read, and understand the simplicity of it...

VIII.

AFTER THE PLAN TOOK hold, Peter returned me to my own time. Things were changed. The war between the sexes of my time never took hold. While the Club still existed, it was now devoted to the more feminine studies in addition to fitness and self-defense classes. Family were welcome to visit, and both Men's and Women's Clubs supported Family Centers where pregnancy and support functions were held, as well as chaperoned meeting areas for teenagers where they could enjoy dances and interaction.

Sabbath and religious holy days replaced 'holidays' on the calendars. Sex returned to a normalized relationship between consenting adults according to ancient texts (which sometimes gave additional advice to enhance that interaction.) The most popular degree in the private colleges that survived was "Comparative Religions". This replaced the failed MBA programs, as cross-studies of such scriptures were found to hold the key to outrageously prosperous businesses.

How did we do it?

It was mostly all found in the New Testament. Once we could point the proselytizing churches into providing unemployment counseling for fired news people, those reporters and execs learned how to use their content-creation and marketing skills to expose their former employers as anti-religion, anti-gun, and anti-sex. That led to boycotts and hastened the dissolution of most non-bi-coastal and non-metropolitan areas.

I did get used to the high heels and modest dresses for interviewing the church officials. Peter returned to three piece suits. Fortunately, it was only for a few months as we quickly recruited a large organization of replacements that fanned out across Flyover Country.

As those churches expanded their memberships, they shared these Scripture-based teachings with other churches and soon their private schools and colleges replaced the existing government-funded ones, who lost funds as they lost enrollments.

Cities, more isolated and failing than ever, soon "seceded" from the Federal government and built walls around themselves to stop the "contagion" of ideas from outlying areas. The rest of the state could no longer be taxed by them and quickly formed replacement governments to capture that revenue base.

The agreement was mutual, as neither really wanted the "contagions" of the other. While the cities attempted several times to form their own national union, these were unsuccessful, as there was little agreement between them. Being composed of numerous extreme minorities, they found it difficult to agree consistently to form a majority consensus. Also, their transportation had to start and end within those cities themselves, without connecting flights anywhere in Flyover Country.

Contagion avoidance, again.

The Flyover economies adjusted and boomed. Health quality improved remarkably, once the traditional scriptures were mined for diet tips. Local-oriented agriculture, manufacturing, and shipping helped life expectancies improve, as well as median income, so that while the population decreased naturally, so did the needs for lifestyle excesses. Humility and minimalism became more popular than decadent consumption.

And since hunting resumed as a national sport, all violent crime dropped with the nullification of gun laws. Guns were widely carried in the backs of truck windows, as well as on the hips of local citizens. Good guys with guns, as well as family counseling based on religious principles tended to discover and resolve personal problems before they created new ones for others. Prisoners were counseled with classic religious texts and recidivism dropped. (Yes, offenders who escaped from cities were returned to those cities with no exceptions, if they recovered from any defensive shooting.)

And healthy genetic material was preserved for rebuilding the human race.

We are now its proof.

PETER AND I ARE EXPECTING our next child and enjoy each other's company more than ever. He's also taught me the advanced mathematics of retrospective analysis, so I can appear to "read minds" with the best of them.

Actually, he's teaching this class tonight. Yes, it makes sex incredible. No reason to blush. Just sign here. We'll see you at the matinée, then. Sure, you can bring your lover. Yes, you're right. Thank you and here's your receipt. Pick up your text at the door...

A Sweet Fortune

R. L. SAUNDERS

I

THE DRIVE UP TO 'CAGGA was almost as bad as working down from upstate to N'Yack. Only you got to see more farms and less plantations.

I'd driven them both and didn't much like one or the other. But I somehow survived both trips, more than once, and so I kept getting hired to make them. Sure, they paid more, but that was the deal. You had to have a human driver to get across their borders and through their security. And you had to be a mean SOB to get out in one piece.

Of course, it didn't hurt that my rig was built from a pair of surplus MRAPs. Built to survive even IED's that these polite, "Tolerant" urbanites left around as their form of "free speech" to make their "statement" on the underside of one of the trucks that was bringing them their food and other vital supplies.

Food wasn't the same as raw material like sawdust. They didn't have no trees in there, so they didn't make anything out of actual wood. But they didn't mind we brought them leftover sawdust from the cutting some farmers did to make real furniture everyone else bought. In those cases (like our scrap metal salvage, plastic recovery, and gravel-rebar mix) they just had these big lots outside where trucks didn't have to go into the city proper and security was more devoted to keeping track of their own cranes as the tractors outside filled the bucket to unload somewheres inside.

But the land outside the city was owned by some individual with connections and they took the risk that someone would sneak out and sabotage their tractors. They'd tried importing containers of raw stuff, but those usually got a hole blown in them once they were left inside the city's high border walls and so wouldn't be worth anything when they came back across. So that owner had a crane that reached over the city walls and would drop down to pick up a load in its big claws, then hoist it into the city to dump for re-manufacturing.

I don't recall the last time anything got built inside one of those places. Things just got rebuilt.

And the people in there were mostly rebuilt, too. Hardly anyone come in or out these days, except us driving fools. But we were just crazy enough to try, and had enough sense to be able to count toes and fingers to make sure we came out with the same amount as when we went in.

Anyways, I like to talk, and so I'm getting far off the mark for this story.

You wanted to know how I got hitched and started a family all on the same day, the one where I almost lost my life a few times before I met her.

II

SO I WAS DRIVIN' UP to Cagga in my old MRAP 8x8. It was really two front ends stitched together with a special-built 18-foot trailer in between. A Cummins diesel in each end. Cab was on top, and she unloaded from either end. I could drive from either end, too. Only the back end had some overnighter quarters for me and my dog. And those had to be stripped down as they were 'spected coming and going. Since I was up front, I couldn't leave nothing that a 'Specter could make off with - even though I had cameras on everything. (One time, some damn fool tried to make off with my bunk. But then he found it was welded down. So he settled for trashing my cushions and blankets, cuttin' big holes in them. Said he was lookin' for Contraband. Dumass.)

Anyways, me and Fido (look, you name your dog whatever you want. I'd never seen nor heard of any dog actually named Fido, so that was his moniker.) Me and Fido was moving along pretty well. And of course, things got slower the closer we got in. Cause of all the potholes where people wouldn't fix them up no more. Out in the back of the State of L'Nois, they had toll roads that paid to get things fixed. But closer in, like N'Yack, there were more plantations than farms, and they took to maintaining their own gated and private routes into the city, plus paid off the guards to let them come and go with a simple pass and not get inspected and personally frisked every time they went in or out. (And I heard Cal-i-Forn was even worse. Never been there, no need or want.)

So nobody wanted to keep track of the main roads outside of the walls, since them plantation owners had their own private delivery services for stuff that come in on uni-rails above those private roads. What did they care about truckers and transport? Not like they did anything with the people who had to live inside except to pay them a little more than they were worth to keep them from quitting.

We was goin' pretty slow getting into Cagga and I was tryin' to miss the worst holes. My tires were armored and foam-filled, but that didn't mean they couldn't go bust. And I knew for dam sure that there weren't no replacements in those towns. They always kept the Federal military out and their own Police cruisers ran on flexi-steel made from reinforced carbon-stainless composite. Talk about bullet and bomb proof...

Yeah, almost oxy-mo-ironic. That place was a war zone but they didn't want the military anywhere near them. Go figure.

I was just thinkin' that when some dam fool lobbed a molotov at me. I had the window down just a crack because of the heat, but was able to jimmy it up pretty quick. Right after I locked the steering to keep it goin' straight. No, nothin' happened except scortched some paint. Of course, the guy got run over right in the middle of his protest speech. But we were far enough out that the PC police wouldn't pay him any mind. Besides, it was Wednesday, which is "don't give a flying hump" day. As long as their Press weren't around the guvment guys didn't have to care for nothin'.

Next chance at near-death was someone with a fiberglass javelin with a stainless armor-piercing tip on it. He (or was it a she - can't much tell these days as they go so fluid back and forth) launched it from sling to give it enough power to go through my window. Almost got me. But his-ser aim was a bit low and I wore that thing right up to the city gates. Almost nobody figures I'm riding up high, 'specially when the front is painted to look like a regular big rig. He got it to stick where he thought I was driving from, but I was sittin' a couple of feet higher.

Now he was close enough that the local patrol come screaming out with their sirens pointed at him. Then he took off runnin' and hopped a nearby fence, leaving some of his clothes and jacket on the barbwire stretched of the top of it. Then they stopped chasing, as he was on someone's personal backyard. And their junkyard dog went after his butt. By then, I was way past him to care much.

You think I wood-uv got tired of this mess, but I was getting paid purty good to get these rare and tasty artifacts into the city proper. All pre-packaged and boxed up in their originals.

Rare, like I said. Like I was told. Because all those blank boxes had to arrive unopened. Every one of them. That was the deal. And they paid me a literal fortune to bring them in. Had to. No one else would. And they weren't coming to get them for the same reason. They'd rather pay for someone to get near killed to get them delivered.

Not to mention they hated Flyover Country with a passion.

Third attempt was an actual IED. And close in, as well. Musta not liked my crossed stars-and-bars custom license plates. (Of course, I just does that to tease em. If anyone tries to take them off, then the gennies kick in with a few thousand volts and that's probably the last time they grab onto anything, until they are over a couple of months or so of rehab.)

So this here IED had to be controlled somewhere close. Because they waited to blow it up in the middle of the rig. But the bottom of this deal was V-shaped armor plated and so it mostly just wiggled a bit as the suspension tightened up. But both sides of that road were missing that private fence and a few feet of private housing as well.

Me, I just kept rolling. I noted down the mile marker, as I'd have to avoid that hole on the way back.

But that wasn't as bad as what I went through after I got inside...

III

UP IN THE CAB, I HAD three bucket seats across. All with racing webbing that would auto-cinch up tight if anything really rocked my world. The middle one was for Fido. And he wore a special rig that was Kevlar with internal inflatable that allowed him to lounge most of the trip, but would make him into a tethered bouncing ball if anything happened.

I could drive from either side, but stuck to the left to make the guards happy. The right-hand seat was my dummy. Them numskull "Tolerance" protesters would often target him to get some "collateral damage." Of course, he was mostly armor inside, and full of spare parts in between those layers. Cause some fruit-loop guard would try to jab him every now and then to make sure I wasn't sneaking someone in or out. Then he'd get one of those several thousand volt shocks if he connected to anything metal.

Fruitlooped, like I said. Or he was after he tried that once.

So the guys that knew me spread the word and they only hauled out a ladder to my driving side and left my buddy alone.

We finally made it to their tall concrete security walls that ringed the city proper. Then we waited for them to let me into the airlock (not really, it was open to the weather but had automatic everything inside to check with cameras and x-rays and all sorts of stuff. I wore a lead vest, plus an apron over everything vital, and my buddy did too, because I had electronic replacement parts in that stomach of his that I didn't want fried.)

Sure, I could let loose a EMP if they tried anything funny - and they knew that from scanning it. Even put a label on the outside so they could read about it with their cameras. Only had to use it once. And after they paid me off enough to never come back again, and I didn't. (Because that left them blind on that side for weeks until they could rebuild it. Seems they'd hired too many fruit-loops instead of ex-military.)

The guard finally let me out of the airlock to stop forward of their inside gate.

That was when they had to bring out their 12 foot ladder to climb up to my window. Of course, I didn't roll it down. I had my own little airlock to pass papers back and forth. And it was definitely air-tight so nobody could put a gas grenade in there. Seen that happen to somebody I knew. Not nice.

Mostly, I just held up my papers against the bulletproof, lead-lined window glass. They'd have to come up with a bucket and squeegee to clean the grime off my glass so they could read them. Another reason they respected me when I came up. I cut them no slack. Not worth my time or my life.

And like I said, I already almost died three times just gettin' that far. Just that day, too.

Nothing was getting this cargo until it was secured in their unloading dock somewheres inside Cagga.

They were to pay me a near fortune. A quarter of it in advance. Figured if I could pull this off, I'd sell this rig after I bought my own land. I was lookin' at an old air force base that had a few underground silos...

Anyway, they finally waved me through - only after they were careful enough to get off the ladder and move it out of the way. Not that I would have. These guys were vets and knew I respected them, but also were smart enough to get everything out of the way when I started out again.

That got me into Cagga. And a few more threats on my life, but not right off.

Driving through Cagga went OK, up to the point my directions gave out.

IV

AS MUCH AS I GOT ALL the electronics I can use in this cab, they don't much help when you got lied to.

That location didn't have no warehouse. It didn't even have a building or garage with big steel garage door. That location was an empty lot.

I smelled a setup. So I put everything into lockdown mode, which included raising the armor siding on all the windows and putting the air flow on filter-recycle. Only then did I try to figure out where I really was and how to get where I needed to go.

But I wasn't having any luck. The area was being jimmy-jammed. Meaning the radio waves were all garbled from the microwaves down through AM-FM bands.

Then I noticed a recurring beat on my gravity wave locater. Like someone was using it to talk to me, or to someone.

Those waves are for earth quake warning. Like bombs going off. Very, very low. And unstoppable. So someone figured that it was good for talking on. Typical city-geek stuff. Too much time on their hands. Too much left-over welfare payments.

Anyway, I cross-connected my walkie to the output after I figured that out, and started hearing a voice. It sounded like a pre-recorded SOS. Female. Young-sounding.

And I was probably their next sucker. That's why the armor went up first. Rocket launcher with an anti-tank shell loaded, probably somewhere nearby.

But it was the weirdest SOS. She was actually teaching class. And was getting feedback with some different sounding beeps. This god-forsaken arm-pit of Cagga and she was teaching the neighborhood kids like they were all underground.

About that time, I saw a armor-reinforced black SUV start rolling slowly down the street toward me. And slower, the closer it came. That allowed me to get a good look and run my scanners. Like they were.

I knew they had four people in there by heat signature. They "knew" I had two people, maybe a little person or small kid, too. Or maybe just a bag of hamburger that looked like a person to their 'scope.

They almost stopped. But I hit a switch and two 50-cal's lumbered into position over the top of my cab with laser pinpoints on the driver and passenger side front windshield areas. At that, they floored it and cut a Huey leaving a small cloud of dust and spitting gravel as the roared out of Dodge.

The lessons had stopped. Some Morse code was going on between them now. I could follow some of it, but a lot was either code or gibberish or something other than English.

Then it said something funny.

"You are the one we've been waiting for. Our only hope. Help us Obi-Wan."

I cued the Mic to tap back, "We are not the droids you are looking for."

The answer came back, "I find your lack of faith disturbing."

I cued, "Your mind tricks don't work on me."

The reply, "I sense great fear in you, Skywalker."

I cued, "This ain't like dusting crops, farm boy."

The reply, "Do or do not, there is no try."

I grabbed the Mic at that point and yelled into it, "Cut the crap, jack. Who are you and what do you want, Yoda?"

A young woman's voice came back, "A trip to Alduran, I mean, out of 'Cagga."

I answered, "But what would you have to trade to me? What do I get out of it?"

Her voice returned, "You were the chosen one. That's why you've got a fortune riding in that truck. You are where you should be. Got a belly hatch?"

"How did you know?" I asked.

She replied, "All those models had a maintenance bay. I'll cut the jammer and you can check your account. Half of the payment is there now."

The low static I'd been hearing in the background shut off and I started hearing Lim Rushbaugh's program, "...so first there was this bicoastal dad who did a single term, then a womanizer who did two terms, then the bi-coastal's son who figured he was a Texan, and that went nowhere. Then we got a closet-gay commie with his trannie, then finally an orange-haired populist, who..." I shut it off as I knew all that history. I could tell you that the cities shut themselves off from the rest of the world due to their own hate of anything that wasn't PC and minority-pandering. I probably listened to him too much. But once they started lying, it was a downhill slide to irrelevance. Media, Politico's bi-coastal suck-ups, the whole lot. It was a good thing when they seceded.

And why I had this huge discovery salvaged from a backwater Flyover town and their forgotten warehouse.

"Well, do you see it?" she asked.

"Sorry, I got distracted - yeah, it's there," I said.

"OK, then pull up and put your belly plate over that manhole in front of you." she replied.

"How do I know this isn't a trap? Couldn't you transfer that all out again?" I asked.

"Check your accounts again. Only you can do that. Because it's untraceable bitcoin," she answered. "Besides, look in front of you."

The man hole cover moved and a thin white arm pushed a satchel onto the pavement. Then turned it over. What looked like solid gold bars and silver coins were poured out.

Well that settled it. Leaving the armor up, I put it into granny-low and crept forward.

V

IT TOOK A COUPLE OF hours for them to maneuver the boxes through the belly plate and into the drainage tunnels.

Meanwhile, I manned the 50 cal's and looked for action. I did see somebody checking me out with a telescope as the sunlight glinted off it. But moving one of the guns in his direction with that lazer gave him an eyeful and I wasn't bothered again.

Finally, I could feel the hatch shut. And someone tapped on the wall in between us.

I grabbed the mic, "What the hell? This ain't no school bus!"

"Do you want to get paid?" the woman returned, calm as ice.

"Not if I can't spend it. You know no one has left this city since they seceded," I replied, a bit hot. "They make the rules here and one of them is no one in or out, under penalty of death."

"You've already got half a fortune. We can leave your truck and you get leave of Cagga. I'll just keep what they already paid me to find you. If you want your other half, you do as I say," said the woman.

I paused to think this over. Fido was no help. The A/C was keeping him cool, but all he did was sit there and grin while he panted and looked at me like one of us was about to do something stupid.

The voice came again, "Look, just hear me out. I've got a plan that will work. Besides, I'm just middle-level on this. I've already paid the rest your fortune. Check your account again. But if you want me out of this truck of yours, then you'll give up another fortune just as large. What you got paid was half of what I got paid. And you can have that, too. Deal?"

She was telling the truth. The entire amount was there. So I transferred it somewhere else quickly. And a few hops after that. Felt better now. Took a deep breath.

"OK," I answered at last. "You got my attention."

"Good. There's an underpass ahead, about two blocks. And if you level out your 50 cal's they'll just fit underneath," she said. "The satellites have to be alerting their watchers by now. We need to move."

And she knew this truck, damn her. But she was earning my respect. She knew this city and the planning she was going to be telling me about should be pretty good.

VI

MOVING THIS ARMORED rig didn't start right away, but I got this bucket moving and saw the underpass up ahead. It was actually a double underpass. I could fit the whole rig under there and be off satellite eyeballs. Simple.

Meanwhile, she had reactivated the jamming, which was probably giving everything fits overhead. If they were trying to track us, they'd have a hard time. Because they were getting shadows of shadows.

Reaching the darkness under all that 'crete left the cab swathed in the eerie glows of the dash panel. But turning on a light in the cab would allow almost anyone to see in. Except, the armor was still up. I pulled down some roller shades over the front and sides and that allowed me privacy and turning on lights to see with. But I only turned on the red lights, so I could see in the dark she was coming in from.

"OK, unlock it and let's talk," she radioed.

Figuring that I would have been dead by now otherwise, I figured it was a risk worth taking. At least I'd die rich...

I unlocked my side and then she unlocked her side. But I let her open them both. Each swung into their own side, and the hinge was next to me on my side. Motioning Fido to the passenger floor pan, I shifted to put my foot next to that hinge and pulled my .45, pointed it and waited.

The door on my side swung slowly toward me until my foot stopped it.

Then I saw a mirror on a extension rod poke around the edge.

Her live voice came next, "OK, I see what you have. We've got a Mexican standoff until you trust me. I'm not going to throw anything in there. But I'll drop what we have."

Two snub-nosed .38 revolvers fell into the center seat. Both were empty of bullets.

It still would have been a standoff, except Fido started smiling and thumping his heavy tail against the floorboard.

He's a good judge of character, so I removed my foot and swung the door around with my free hand.

A freckled, blue-eyed blond, slimmed into a tight knit top with tighter curls all over her boy-cut hair grinned back at me.

"Well, hello handsome!" she said. "My name is Dora."

And just like that, I was in love.

VII

ONCE SHE WAS THROUGH the hatch, petted Fido and was sitting all sweet-smelling next to me, she turned around and looked back through the hatch.

"It's OK, you can come on, now," she said to someone.

Of course that startled me and I reached for that .45 again, but then I saw almost a mirror image of her poke her little sweet head through, with a smile that could melt the snow off a mountain.

I was in love all over again. Fatherly type of stuff. My heart "grew two sizes that day" sort of thing.

"Is that all?" I asked.

"Yes. She's all. She's everything." Dora hugged the kid like the most valuable thing in her world.

And then that kid did something that brought tears to my eyes. She stood on the seat and hugged me, two-day grizzle and sweat-smelling shirt, everything.

I was speechless and grinning ear to ear.

Dora settled the kid between us. I handed them both a cooled bottle of water. And we sat for a few minutes in quiet.

"Thanks for everything," she said.

"Well, I... guess it was worth it," I replied.

"This is Junie. She's what worth it," Dora said.

We all sat in that A/C'd cab, drank our water, and watched Junie make fast friends with Fido.

After awhile, Dora looked at me. "I should tell you our plan, then." And she rattled off a very detailed lineup of events that were inventive and precise. Like she had been working this out for a very long time.

IT TOOK US A COUPLE of hours to rearrange things.

When we left that underpass with all the armor back down and the 50 cal's tucked away, we circled around and headed back out. Like we had all the time in the world.

I stopped at the checkpoint and got inspected again. (My camera showed that their flunkie fruit-loop tried taking the welded-down bed again, but only flipped the cushions around instead of anything stupid. Of course, I had my hand on the shock button if he tried anything.)

And not too surprisingly, they let us go. Me and Fido and the dummy.

Since we were leaving town, none of these "Tolerant" protesters wanted anything to do with us. Because Media didn't care, once you left the city walls for Flyover Country.

A couple dozen miles outside of Cagga, we quit driving by the plantations with their surveillance cameras. Then the dummy opened up the jacket to undo the lead vest and padding.

The kid climbed out, sheened in sweat, but smiling like that was the best adventure she'd had for a long time. Next she helped pull the hat and mask of the dummy, where Dora was soaked in sweat herself. Smiling from ear to ear.

And then Junie helped Dora push all that lead covering through the access doors into the storage area, where it fell to the floor with several thumps.

Once we got out of Cook County, going south on what used to be I-57, the roads smoothed out and we picked up speed.

Outside of a couple of fill-ups (where the two girls hid in back) we weren't interrupted straight through the upper part of Missouri into Kansas.

Along that trip, she told me how she had planned this for years. "In Cagga, we were mostly in an underground bunker all the time. Because if you weren't in the good side, then you were walled off where even the cops don't travel, except in bullet-proof SUV caravans.

"After my mom died, all I had left was little Junie here. And we didn't go out on the street. I taught myself learned to code and learned to hack. Junie's picking it up pretty good for her age. So I learned to deal and get stuff delivered. Anything we couldn't grow or build indoors or underground.

"Then I found out what people really wanted was the stuff that's sitting out there in Flyover warehouses that no one will deliver here.

"I found someone who had found a stash of stuff in a warehouse that his family owned. But they'd given up getting anything in there back into Cagga. He told me price was no problem, that he'd pay in advance if I could guarantee delivery. So I looked around and found you and this rolling war-wagon you use for deliveries."

Junie interrupted to ask if she and Fido could play catch in the empty storage area. I turned on the stowage lights for them while Dora found his favorite throwing ball under the seat - the one that squeaked. They went off to giggle and pant at each other, back and forth, with squeaks.

"The guy figured your one load of goods could keep him going for years on the black market. Because it was contraband in the PC-controlled ward he lived in. But people couldn't get enough of them, and they hadn't been manufactured for years. Meanwhile, his money wasn't buying him anything he really wanted. And the boxes of stuff you brought was more valuable than any drugs, although the delivery had to be made on the West side and trucked underground to make it over into where he lived by the lake shore.

"That was his guys who came to pick it up from us."

Dora was nodding off by that time, and rose up to peak at Junie, who had curled up next to Fido on some shipping blankets.

Dora stretched out across the two seats with her head on my thigh and the dummy's jacket over her.

And slept until I pulled into the old Air Force base outside of nowhere, Kansas.

I made a few calls, transferred some funds, and the caretaker got a special delivery the next day with papers to sign. He turned over the keys to me and drove out of the base, down the dusty road in front of it. I shut the big gate, then activated the alarms.

Dora, Junie, and me headed over to the old Commissary to use their grill to make some double cheeseburgers and enjoy some real milkshakes. Hand in hand. Family.

"By the way, Dora," I asked. "What was in those boxes?"

She looked up at me and smiled.

"Twinkies."

The Autists

BY J. R. KRUZE

I

I THINK DIFFERENT. Always have. It turned out to be a perfect tool for surviving the Human Purge. Or be the weapon that caused it.

Me and my Carol. And the rest of us Autists.

Not that the world ended, or anything. And if you're an average, run-of-the-mill human, you didn't notice. Most don't. Somewhere around 90-95% don't.

Not that it affected their lives much. They were propped up by the mechanical society they were trained to be part of like cogs in a drive-chain.

I figure at this point that I'm writing for those of you who did see something change, something get better.

You know who you are.

Me, I've always studied history. Kept my bills paid. Told I was a walking Wikipedia on ancient history. (If they could stand to listen to me. I could be a bit raw, sometimes.)

But it's modern history that we're changing. We're evolving. The trick is learning from the past.

The Purge started after World War II. Most of its first stage ended with the Internet. Definitely by 2050. Between those two points was when the centralized control of the media and our schools started unraveling. But all that new technology set evolution in progress.

The second stage started when we autists became more than 1 percent of the world's population.

As trans-human beings started showing up more and more, the old ways of viewing us started failing. Because our numbers were increasing and so we asked for the same rights everyone else had. Instead of being treated like a sub-human with an incurable disease.

Humans were evolving, like it or not. From the "wise" sapiens, we have been changing. Improving. But like all our past, it hasn't been without fighting, scratching, and a fair bit of knuckle-dragging.

Humans were no longer just homo sapiens. Rather it was like the old days of the Neanderthals living down the block from the Sapiens. Dating their sons and daughters. Hanging out, having fun.

From the 50's forward, it's been an increasing scene where a new species has been living among the old, without letting them know it. Because they couldn't see what they refused to understand.

And all we ever wanted was understanding.

So those who refused to understand needed to be protected from harming us, protected from themselves.

The wisest among us quit thinking we were a final version of anything in the homo species. And so the name "homo transire" came into being. Apt that it uses a verb instead of a noun form, if you think about it...

We just called ourselves "autists." A kind of play on words in many ways. But we like to make games out of things. Games are an efficient road to understanding.

Understanding is a set of stepping stones to evolution.

Evolution is forever.

Like love, kinda.

II

I MET REGGIE AT A DANCE.

I'd known him for a long time. The correct phrase is "known of him."

Sorry.

I prefer to hug and touch than talk. So writing is a new skill for me.

And I'm learning so many new skills these days.

Anyway, Reggie was on edge of the dance floor. And I went up and hugged him.

Almost spilled his fruit punch.

He didn't say anything, but smiled and hugged me back.

We stood that way for a while.

A while.

Then he asked me if I wanted to dance.

I said I did if we could hug meanwhile.

So we hugged and shuffled until the music quit.

He's a good dancer.

Then he looked into my eyes and bent down to kiss me on the forehead.

I got hot in my face. [Blushed?]

And then I took his face in my hands and kissed him on his mouth.

A long while.

When I was done, I laughed and ran away toward the girl's room.

I looked back, but he was just standing there smiling.

I felt wet in places I hadn't before. Something felt right about it.

Like when a quintic equation solves with an actual radical instead of an approximation.

Beautiful, elegant, exceeding rare.

And this rare, elegant man found me later on the outside steps while I practiced my mini 4x4 Rubik's cube with my right hand. (Working to get my time down to match my left's.)

He just sat awhile next to me and didn't interrupt. Not that he couldn't, but I was happy just feeling the warmth coming from his thigh. No, we weren't touching. But he was close, so close.

Beautiful, elegant warmth. Rare.

My face got hot again, and finally I put the 4x4 cube into my backpack and just looked out at the starry sky.

He started talking about the possibilities of chaos theory refuting the big bang theory and giving us the stars and their infinite, predictable motions.

I knew he was feeling nervous, so I took the hand he had laying on his thigh, turned it over and held it with my own palm. Both were sweaty. But they felt better together. And our fingers interlocked.

He stopped talking and we both just looked up at the stars.

After awhile, I moved right next to him and pulled that arm over my shoulder, then leaned against him with my head on his shoulder.

We sat for awhile just like this. Quiet. Rare, elegant warmth.

I could feel his pulse through his thigh and arm. It raced at first, then our pulses matched.

Elegant, beautiful happiness.

Feeling right. A kind of purplish blue.

III

CAROL SAYS I TALK TOO much when I'm nervous.

But she's right in so many, many things. I believe her in this one. But I can't feel myself talking too much. Usually when the other person simply wants to do something else, we quit talking.

And so I write when I don't have anyone to talk to. Or when what they call "conversation" doesn't go anywhere at all but around in inane circles about sports or weather or how-screwed-up-something-is-and-we-can't-possibly-do-anything-about-it

So mostly, I quit trying to deal with human conversations. And find something I can do to help them, like clear the table and then go and turn on the TV to drown out their noise.

Nobody watches TV, they just endure it. Helps pass the time.

Like humans don't enjoy time.

Probably because they don't understand it. Or even try to understand it.

Like they have space, time, mass, and energy all defined in terms of each other. So they avoid having an actual workable definition of any of them. And they don't see that they've really defined a system. And systems expand or contract, but never are static.

Like that committee that decided that in order to make their equations work, light had to be a constant speed all the time. (But it doesn't - it pulses. Like breathing.)

The universe is alive. You can hear it on a clear night when you look up at the stars.

The trick is to get your heartbeat to go into sync with it.

Some call this Zen. Others call it true love.

Calves match their mother's heartbeats when they are born, and for a long time afterwards. Human babies and their mom's do, too. Most mother's understand the idea.

Not politicians or media, especially not social media.

Because those ways of thinking don't try to understand. They only try to depress you. To their level. To get you do do what they want you to. Vote someway or buy something.

Carol was different. Our hearts synced soon after we met.

And she was the beginning of how I starting to understand this universe for the first time.

For real.

IV

REGGIE CAN TALK THE ears off a corn stalk. Gawd that guy likes to talk.

When he can't talk, he writes.

Me, I like to hug.

And children. I love children.

And what most people think are "difficult" math problems.

They just don't try to understand what that equation wants. How it smells right when it's accomplished what it wants.

So they use math to solve really dumb things like how a rocket jerks in flight. Instead of looking for things that want to fly, they have to build something truly inefficient that makes a big sound and blows up with a louder one. Because they don't feel when it's right. When the numbers do what they want.

I moved into Reggie's apartment after we danced that one time. His room mate swapped apartments with me, since I lived near a bunch of other girls and he was tired of listening to Reggie. (But I don't think so, it's probably that he'd rather listen to girls giggle while they co-flirted.)

[Is "co-flirted" a word? Too bad if it's not. Bag and Cat are now disjointed from mutual proximity.]

So I'd come back in from work to find Reggie tapping out yet another over-long essay on his computer.

I'd hug him and he'd pause. And his heartbeat would slow to match mine.

Then I'd let him go and move into the kitchenette to make a couple of sandwiches for us. I knew he probably hadn't eaten. Or he would eat a sandwich I made just to make me happy.

And he would finish up whatever he was blogging about. I'd have the sandwiches on a plate and a big mug of sweet tea or something cold (or hot, depending on the season) with two straws. Then I'd come out of the kitchen and bring them all out into the great room. (Why people call it a "living" room is non-sequitur. Living is an action. But they sit and watch do-less TV in it, which is couch-potato logic.)

Our big screen was set to a live feed from one of Cal-Tech's telescopes. (No commercials. No fake news.)

We'd sit and cuddle the night away watching stars without having to be uncomfortable outside.

Sometimes we'd have sex or make love.

Felt good either way.

V

CAROL WAS MY LIVING proof that it wasn't just me.

And while I had been a few years studying all this stuff to make sense out of it, suddenly I had a new box to think outside of, a new envelope to push. Not that I hadn't been going that way.

But she was such a good hugger. It took me out of what I was used to.

Yes, of course that's scary.

For both of us.

Now I had another problem to solve. A big one.

You see, people that think different like us are mostly discriminated against. Like sexism or racism. Autism was just another -ism that should be considered as a bad, impolite word - like "a*tistic".

Just because people think different doesn't mean they are diseased, or need to be "cured."

Practically, there's a much more valid argument that the bulk of humanity needs to be cured of their intolerance. Instead, the most intolerant refuse to understand their own heritage and traditions. They aggregate into cities with other people who think as narrowly as they do. With politicians and corporations who will do anything to get their vote or sell them consumables.

And that is how homo saps are ending their species. Domestic violence, pollution, racking up credit card debt and student loans.

Cities are a failed theorem. Just because people in a mob think differently. And it's not a nice different. Nothing you could or should put in an aerosol bottle or carbonated drink and sell.

The solution to the human problem, the homo sap problem, was to think differently, think better.

Computer design showed us this. Because computers are really dumb. Even the A.I. ones. They only decide based on the garbage you feed them. Good garbage in, good garbage out.

Politics is a dumb computer. It only "solves" things after they go wrong. Bad garbage in, bad garbage out.

That equation means that business will always get their profits before the government can make enough laws to make it unprofitable. And it costs a lot of money into their collective pockets to keep them from regulate against you.

The trick is always to run underneath their radar. To set up your organization so it doesn't make any money on paper and doesn't hurt anyone who would complain about it. (Meanwhile, have a well-paid lobbyist or two on tap.)

And if you can keep an eye on the fads and trends, you can reinvent yourself regularly and disappear from view.

So I started studying modern culture, and started collecting autists.

A non-profit foundation took care of support for them, under the progressive idea of doing something to help all these "disadvantaged" people who didn't fit in. Take the problem off their hands in a "humane" fashion. (Like their old sanitariums.)

We had some people who wrote for grants from the bleeding hearts for funding. Meanwhile, our under-radar businesses were making money hand over fist. Learned that from politician-computers.

We also had some people who studied marketing dispassionately and could write effective pitches. Marketing isn't hard, since it's all laid out in old texts. Humans haven't really changed in 10,000 years - or so they say in their texts. The same emotional "buttons" could be pushed today that would make people buy or donate like they always had.

What was changing wasn't in their books. But we were about to tell them that the change was coming from within. Or maybe we wouldn't tell them at all. Letting sleeping dogs lay, etc.

VI

I REMEMBER OUR FIRST argument.

Reggie was talking loudly on the phone when I got home and was in the middle of another blog post or a paper or something. And he had the big screen 'casting news feeds from somewhere. Only thing missing was some talk show on the radio and maybe a laser light show overhead. It was that noisy. The room stank of bad-colored thought.

Reggie was over-saturating his senses to keep him focused on something.

I came out of the kitchen with our sandwiches just as he threw his phone across the room. Away from me, down the hall toward his bedroom.

Then he cursed.

And sat and did nothing.

His heart was racing, his breaths ragged. His hands were shaking.

So I sat quietly on one end of our couch and waited for him to come over.

He didn't.

He kept typing into his computer.

I turned the big screen over to the Cal-Tech channel to watch the stars.

After awhile, he noticed. And got up, took the remote, and turned off the TV.

Then threw the remote down the hallway toward his bedroom.

And went back to his computer and continued typing.

I sat on my end of the couch and waited.

After awhile, a tear came down my face. And it was hard to breath without sobbing.

So I got up and left. And went to my bedroom. Threw myself down on my bed, grabbed a pillow and cried into it.

I thought I wasn't making enough sound for Reggie to hear.

Then I felt the bed move. He was sitting on one corner of it. Turned back toward the door. Like he could leave if he was interrupting something I was doing that was important.

Not touching me.

But I could feel his warmth. Hear his heartbeat. Smell his thoughts.

When I rolled over, I saw he was looking out the doorway toward the hall.

We stayed that way for awhile.

And I made my heartbeat match his. It took a while.

When it matched, he looked over at me with a sadness on his face.

"Sorry," he said.

"Me, too," I said.

And he laid down next to me, put his arm across my shoulders, across my chest, his head in my hair.

"You smell good," he said.

"Just for you," I answered.

And we laid that way for awhile.

Eventually, I rolled over and pushed up against him, like a pair of spoons.

And our thoughts smelled the same as we went to sleep like that.

VII

IF IT WASN'T FOR CAROL, none of this would have happened.

She was my sea anchor in the storm. Kept me able to focus on what was needed as I plowed ahead over choppy seas and swells.

Because she was so different than me, but more of the same difference.

We were able to spin off our marketing into a for-profit company of its own (because apparently people don't believe old books.)

We found the trick is to have only Autists running things, and find some avid-empaths to act as intermediaries between them and the human freelancers. The people we hired to execute the campaigns we wanted to run. And then pushed these campaigns through social media by buying bot-time and pin-pointed Facebook and AMS ads both as tests and to convert the key buyers in key markets to our line of thinking. Selling what they wanted so they'd buy what they needed.

Discovering avid-empaths was the key. They were also autists, but their skills were from being too empathic. That was almost opposite of most people who were considered "afflicted" with autism. Like most conventional wisdom, 90% or more wrong. It came from considering the arbitrary idea that there was a natural balance to things. If Autists generally had problems communicating socially, then there were people who would be too social and so seem "scatter-brained."

Tracking down these people also found that they had trouble keeping jobs. But they could concentrate on the emotional values of anyone and get into instant rapport. So we hired as many as we could find. Perfect match.

Carol wasn't empathic, according to the "scientific" definitions. But she could feel. And she had a beautiful mind. One that smelled in colors. Perfect for me. And the reason I could keep going.

Our main campus became a think-tank like no other. Because we attracted the most brilliant, and even a few savants. We also took care of a lot of people no one else wanted to deal with. The ones who never talked, or sometimes got violent.

The trick in most cases was to get them out of the upsetting environment into somewhere predictable and safe. Our mix of savants and empaths, plus the necessity to survive as a group of humans in an intolerant world kept us going. Made us whole.

Everyone helped out they way they could best. The entire campus became a sort of massively parallel living computer.

All we wanted was to understand others and be understood.

We succeeded in that, and so almost magnetically attracted more talent from all over the globe.

Eventually, we duplicated the campus exactly in several different places across the U.S. and Canada. And a few countries like Switzerland that had a tradition of protecting individual rights.

In those countries, you'd see economic revivals a few years after one of our campuses was built and operational.

We never took any claim for this. We just said we were problem solvers. We "thought so far out of the box that the box doesn't exist - just the most optimal solution."

And each campus was left alone, once it got profitable enough to pay its own way and repay its set up costs. And those funds would be earmarked to build another, and so on.

Because the model was a working system. Based on the 5-10% of the most workable truths out there. These were derived from a huge cross-study of our oldest human philosophies. Like that old saying, we studied history in order to not have to repeat it.

The other advantage of keeping the design exactly the same was to enable us to have physical meetings and conferences. Because few of us liked random change. If we could come into a space that was just like the one we had left, we could more quickly settle in and get back to work. As it was, sometimes it took people months to get ready for such a change like traveling.

Our autists who lived in rural areas would remodel their houses following the our designs, like a room or wing of one of our campus buildings for the same reason. So someone who was over-stressed could retire to one of their rural homes as a guest to wind down.

The trick was to stay out of cities, but on their outskirts. Close enough to be available for consultation, but not close enough to be infected. Or regulated.

Carol brought up the next phase to me, and it took me a long time to get ready for it.

VIII

"WE'RE EXPECTING," I told Reggie said one night over sandwiches.

"Expecting what?" he asked.

"Our baby," I answered.

He was quiet after that for awhile.

And then he saw my worry look. So he hugged me close, closed his eyes and breathed into my hair.

"You bless me," he finally said.

I looked up at him with teary eyes.

"Are you upset?" he asked.

"No, these are happy thoughts leaking out," I replied.

He just cuddled me close to me and I could feel his thoughts as they smelled of satisfaction. Even if he thought he couldn't leak happy thoughts on his own. At least I could.

IX

OF COURSE, OUR NEW family meant a lot of changes, a lot of things. Mostly, an idea that had been on my back burners for awhile.

We'd long taken in families so they could learn to deal with autist children. And sometimes, the child would stay on as staff, and the family would visit from time to time. We usually bought a large lot of land when we built, to keep the campus isolated and secure. So building small visitor cottage-sets wasn't a big deal. And all this helped with PR as our empaths told us.

So having babies and raising children of our own became a project that gained a lot of interest in our campuses. There was no shortage of volunteers to become nannies and teachers, especially among those who themselves were pregnant.

Carol finished off or turned over most of her math and programming projects so she could help other women in her condition and also learn the skills of raising an autist child.

HER NAME WAS BRIDGET. And she was beautiful. Her toothless grin was lop-sided and heart-melting. And that's the first time I leaked happy thoughts, the first time I saw her smile.

On the other side of this, we worked on long studies into heredity and genomic data sets. Of course, we had to throw most of it out and work with what actually produced results.

And realized we were creating and responsible for moving the human condition forward, evolving it. Homo transire in the making.

While we Autists all agreed on traditional marriage, we also knew that our best survival route was being able to have the widest possible combinations and mixes of genomes. And that fit in socially with the urban-decayed idea of "sleeping around" and "open relationships."

All it meant to us is that we had very large families. And that we needed to keep track of daddies and mommies so their babies could grow up to know their best choices of bed-mates.

X

SO REGGIE AND I HAVE a dozen now.

And they are all individuals and unique and beautiful.

Their thoughts all smell different colors. A rainbow in their classrooms. If you look for it.

Reggie encouraged me to write more, so now I can even do long paragraphs.

But I like the short ones best.

Like the punchline of solving an equation.

BRIGITTE IS NOW EXPECTING her first.

She turned out to be a high-functioning empath. Something Reggie or I never expected from our talents.

Brigitte also runs her own campus, and we come to visit once a year or sooner. Although I'm going to stay with her before she delivers. She always likes my hugs.

XI

I PICKED UP THESE PAPERS just recently to add some last notes.

The grand experiment that Carol and I started a few decades ago has worked wonderfully.

The cities imploded with crime and taxes, as we predicted. Our solution proved itself when they came asking for our help. Not that they listened much. But if they wanted our loans, there were conditions.

We run training programs through what they used to call "community colleges." Those graduates are the executives we then angel-finance to start businesses and provide jobs for their city people.

Our organization also bought out several hospital chains after they bankrupted. And we provide essential clinic services, as well as doing first aid training and drug-withdrawal services.

No, we never say that homo sap humans are stupid. They do take longer to train sometimes. And there are huge gaps in what they should already know from their traditions. Their schooling systems failed long ago. And since we are "religious-based" we don't get a lot of flack from local governments. Especially as we are cleaning up the messes they created.

In addition to all that, we work to get them to turn their empty city lots into mini-farms, so they aren't so dependent on corporations to get their food to them. And help them have off-grid backups when their water and power (frequently) fail.

Corporations already know that we can improve their bottom line if they follow our unorthodox advice. They may not understand how we figure things out, but they know our solutions make more money for them. Otherwise, we go to their nearest competitor and help them out instead.

Most of the big corporations don't exist anymore. Mostly because they wouldn't listen. If they are still around, they had Autists running them all along, even if those execs and board members won't call themselves that.

I figure that Homo Sap still has a few hundred years left before they cease to exist. But they'll live in comfort for the rest of their time. We'll make sure of that.

Because when you work in understanding, then you work with compassion.

Meaning: we just saved their asses in spite of themselves. For as long as they live.

The Caretaker

BY C. C. BROWER

HERMAN GAUSS FOUND a caretaker through an ad he placed.

As a reclusive writer, he didn't much care for what he got, but had some wishes. Since he'd never married again, the idea of having a female moving about the big empty house made him both worried and content. He had been happy to live quietly at the end of a long, dusty road, but found his cleaning habits left too much dust around.

He wanted to write, not clean house. He didn't want his solitude interrupted, but would appreciate having the dust gathered out of the corners and the occasional hot meal he didn't have to prepare himself.

So he placed an ad through an agency. He paid them to find and pre-interview the applicants. They would send over one at a time, only sending the next in line when an earlier one disqualified themselves.

And the reasons for the disqualified applicants seemed inconsistent and even frivolous. But the company was only paid to send applicants, so the money would keep coming to them until Herman ran out of it, or they ran out of applicants. (Word can get around about certain ads...)

Maggie was herself quiet and happy to have such a job. She was a student of writing, but had never published. Her shyness found her many admirers, but never a long relationship. That's not to say she didn't have strong opinions. And perhaps those were what drove her would-be lovers away. She never talked about her personal life, even when asked.

How she got hired was a bit of a mystery. She wasn't outspoken much, but was firm and unmovable when she was. It wasn't that all things should be a certain way, but certain things should be kept in certain ways.

The hiring company took this minor loss of income in stride.

HERMAN GOT USED TO the thick curtains on the west being open in the morning, and those curtains on the east only open when the sun had passed the house peak, where the west curtains would be closed. He didn't mind that if he came in early from his walk, he wasn't allowed back in his own study until the cleaning was finished.

Maggie didn't work to keep the porch as spotless as the rest of the house inside. So when Herman was refused access to his inner chambers, while she was cleaning, he would come out here. He took the rough broom and ash shovel, and pick up the worst-offending dirt clods and dried mud clumps. He'd even pick up his boots to put them outside on the steps so that he could empty the tray they sat on. All to help get rid of som of the dust. At least those in the form of dirt clumps.

In Spring, he would find occasion to take his heavy tan overalls and dark brown coats to put them into a standalone, faded, porch cabinet out of the sun. Heavy gloves would go into porous bags made from pillowcases, putting in sets onto one of its upper shelves.

However, he wasn't permitted to clean the windows or screens of that porch. Maggie would have a fit, in her own quiet way, if he tried this. If they needed painting or repairs, then he could take them down to work on them.

The house soon became Maggie's as much as Herman's, although he had title to it.

While Herman was busy in his study for hours, Maggie would finish up her housework and do some writing of her own on the kitchen table. Herman had noted that she always had a yellow legal pad in her bag and would find her writing at it when he came out into the kitchen for more coffee.

AFTER A YEAR, HERMAN gave her a room of her own to write in.

Her long, filled-up legal pads stacked up neatly in a corner of the room until they were nearly as high as the desk top. That study oak desk and her ladder-back chair with its woven rush seat, plus a small goose-neck lamp, were the only furniture in that room. They were placed at a definite angle to her window, not aligned to any wall. An oval hook-rug, created with brown, tan, and a few green yarns as accent, fit under the desk and chair. This was the only covering for the wood tongue-and-groove plank floor.

Her current pad was placed at an angle where she could write easily and read quickly. The pages were all flattened back into the original position, so each would stack neatly once filled. At the end of her writing, a sharpened pencil was placed as a book mark on top of the last incomplete page, under the filled pages on top. A small pile of fresh pads were placed along the far left corner of the desk, precisely against the edges.

There was a white, chipped porcelain jar of pencils on the desk, within easy reach, but not close enough to get in the way. These pencils were always kept sharp and the points up. Only just enough pencils that they leaned away from her, able to be grasped easily with an almost casual gesture. Another matching jar was to the left of this, with dulled pencils facing down. Maggie would deposit a dull pencil to pick up a new, sharp one in a single, efficient motion.

The single drawer in that simple desk held more supplies of the same.

One small tin trash bin, set next to the front right table leg, carried any trash away daily, after the writing was done.

The walls were plain, paneled over the original lath-and-plaster. While they showed scuff marks and tack holes from the children who had grown up in them, there were no nails or screws sticking out to hang things on. The one exception was a dual set of antique-brown coat hooks screwed into the door back, just above eye height, which held Maggie's shawl or jacket, depending on the weather.

HERMAN'S STUDY WAS not so tidy. Its walls were filled with shelves. Books were crammed into their place with various bookmarks. They were of all sizes and widths. Some covered with ragged dustjackets, others were scarred and scuffed paperbacks. If a book was pristine in condition, it was usually in a pile on the floor. Once Maggie tried to straighten those piles into a neat and tidy alignment, but Herman wouldn't have it. Apparently the corners sticking out told him what book it was and what was in it. He didn't expect to have to read the script on the spine to do so.

A big wide table was used as his writing desk, with an old keyboard and all-in-one monitor on it. Old mugs held a variety of pencils, pens, and markers. Pads and notebooks of graph paper stuck out above or beyond the books in stacks next to the computer, and between the table legs at it's base. A pile of thumb-drives had its own zippered binder, which was kept open by the stacks of them.

The study was big enough for Herman's double bed. A single night stand was at the side nearest Herman's desk. Maggie changed the sheets on this weekly, and rotated the covers with the seasons.

MAGGIE WOULD ONLY DUST and sweep and tidy in that room. No papers changed position. She did empty the trashcan once a week. Herman would sometimes throw a wadded paper into it and then recover it. After a spat and a fit about a certain thrown-out paper, Maggie found a duplicate of his trash can and would rotate the new for the old, keeping the spare still filled with last week's "trash" in a closet near the study door. If Herman knew of the arrangement, he said nothing. Maggie did find that closet door ajar every now and then...

OTHERWISE, THE HOUSE was as it had been for over a hundred years. Herman had spent some of his writer's earnings to have it restored after he inherited it, and before he moved in. Many of the floor joists were replaced, and the house was inspected to ensure there was no rot anywhere. The windows were replaced with modern ones that looked the same. The house was tight and draft-free when he was done.

To the rest of the world, the house looked the same as it had always been. Barn red with gray trim. The farm itself had no barn, as it had tumbled down years before and gradually rotted away. Herman kept cattle and the only sign of it was a corral with a loading chute, as well as the graveled drive to it. The cattle grazed everywhere there were fences to keep them in, and trimmed the trees as well. Of course, they left random placements of manure divots, gradually being reabsorbed into what had formerly been lawns.

When a tree would die, it would be left as is, and cattle would use it for scratching. If it was close enough to the house, Herman would cut it up for firewood. The bigger trunks were left, as Herman didn't see any need to work at cutting and splitting huge slabs just in order to get them small enough to burn. Instead, he would quit cutting at the point where the wood no longer fit his fireplace opening. Meanwhile, new sprouts would grow, if they didn't get trimmed by the cow's grazing habits.

Herman held that the farm was there for solitude and inspiration. It had raised a good number of kids, none of which were much interested in agriculture. There was a small garden where Herman raised various plants that grew themselves from year to year. He only planted what would grow back on its own. Herman would fertilize by collecting the cattle divots in the fall and placing them appropriately in the garden. Blackberry and gooseberry brambles grew around the fences, plants that cows would normally leave alone. Fruit and nut trees were left from the original farm, and Herman would replace these as they died off.

Maggie would visit the farmers' market for any seasonal vegetables. Herman stocked the freezer with beef he had processed. Chickens provided eggs from their standalone shed near the garden.

Herman would often bring fresh fruit in from his travels, which Maggie would make into jelly and jam. Sometimes breads or cakes.

Hard farm work, mostly in quiet, was Herman's crucible for his work. The only sounds were the birds in the trees, the occasional cow calling for its calf, and the patter of his keyboard.

Maggie's own quiet cleaning assisted her inspiration.

THE HOUSE WAS SPARE, minimalist. For the renovations, Herman had given away most of the furniture, and didn't replace it once he moved in. Relatives had taken anything they held valuable, and charity organizations were glad to take the rest.

The kitchen contained the most furniture, and had four ladder-backed chairs around an oak table. It had a formica top, rimmed in stainless trim around its curved corners. Painted plywood cabinets were built in, although held little besides some canned goods and boxed foodstuffs. Stove, refrigerator, microwave, sink completed the spare outfitting.

The living room had a simple, padded oak bench for a couch, an oak coffee table and two brown padded chairs with tall backs, all arranged facing the old fireplace. Herman had installed a fireplace insert to cut down drafts. Another hooked rug covered most of the wood floor. Two floor lamps by the chairs completed the furniture. Paneling covered the plaster walls. Here, too, there was nothing hung on those walls. The mantel of the fireplace was bare. This was a room kept clean for necessary visitors, which were few and far between. The spartan condition of the room wasn't inviting for them to stay long or come back.

ONE WINTER, HERMAN got quite ill. This was when Maggie moved a double bed into her own room upstairs, along with a wardrobe for her clothes. After she nursed him back to health, she never moved out again.

Neither Maggie or Herman talked about this much. Or said much when they did answer someone's question.

People in town might have talked about this, but it didn't matter to either Maggie or Herman. Maggie did the weekly shopping for food and house supplies. Herman visited the local weekly livestock auction regularly. He was there to check the prices for his cattle, and as much to get inspiration for his books. In town, or at the auction, they had conversations, but were known to just smile and nod more than voice any opinion.

Both seemed content with how things went.

They would talk over meals, in quiet and short sentences. Otherwise, the silence of the big farm house was only affected by the season's storms that occasionally thundered, or whistled, or roared.

The porch was most affected by that weather, more than the occupants.

In summer, the screens would let some wind-blown rain in.

By the end of fall, the windows would replace them and be battered by gusts.

In the winter, the windows would frost over. Both Herman's and Maggie's boots would bring in snow, sometimes ice.

The spring would rotate the windows back to storage to let fresh spring air in again.

The house inside would stay temperate and clean. Both writers would be hard at work in their comfortable silence, regardless of temperature or wind outdoors.

MAGGIE RECEIVED A PRESENT one day. Herman had a laptop delivered for her.

This was one of the few times they had a discussion outside of meal times. Maggie seemed to protest, but Herman repeated that he thought that would help speed her writing progress.

He revealed that he had read several of her yellow pads and found them to be quite good. "Sufficient for publishing," was his phrase. Maggie blushed, one of her rare few times.

Herman also had a satellite installed that year to bring them Internet access, but no TV. Before this, Herman would mail a flashdrive of his works to his publisher. What mail he got before that was in letter form or he answered on his phone.

His quiet mentorship of Maggie got her first book published. And they started sitting in the living room in the evening, each in their own tall padded chair. Herman had gotten them both e-reader tablets and they read each other's works.

Maggie wrote Romance, Herman wrote mystery-adventure stories.

They'd make notes in the margins and as bookmarks of sentence improvements and apparent plot holes. Their sharing sped both of their works, and improved them.

Herman started putting love interests into his stories. Maggie started including more mystery and action in hers.

Eventually, they became co-authors on a few longer stories. And readers started finding the other's works. Both Maggie and Herman became well-known under their own names, as well as many pen-names.

When Maggie started bringing childbirth and child-raising scenes into her stories, Herman brought this up at one of their meals. She thought this was an interesting element that she wanted to explore. She started a children's series. Herman produced a series with a family adventure in it.

UNKNOWN TO HERMAN, Maggie had added a freestanding shelf to her room, and had put books on it. When this was filled, she started stacking books on the floor beside it. They were neat, tidy stacks and organized by size with the largest and thickest nearest the floor. A small stool kept the lowest one high enough to be swept under.

One day, Maggie found that one of the kitchen chairs had been moved to her room, and a book had been left on it. A bookmark was in a particular spot. She left it exactly as she found it. Day after day, she saw that the bookmark moved further through the book. And when it was about to reach the end, another book took it's place and the process continued.

Herman soon found a nightstand had been placed on the far side of his bed. A book was on it, with a bookmark. He noticed it, but didn't touch it. It's bookmark moved through the book gradually, and then another book would replace it.

ONE DAY, HERMAN STOPPED Maggie and surprised her with a hug. This became a daily occurrence they both enjoyed.

Maggie started going on walks with Herman around the farm to check on the cattle he raised, to help him repair the fences.

Herman was of no use to her in cleaning the house, but started gathering wild flowers for the kitchen table. He also moved some wild roses next to the house, which he said was to keep the cattle from rubbing on the house-corners. Both knew that was a "stretch" as none of the cows had ever been permitted to scratch themselves in that fashion.

One stormy, windy night, Maggie joined Herman in his bed. Herman visited hers the following evening.

Some months later, Herman brought an antique single bed with new springs and mattress from town. He assembled this in the other upstairs bedroom. Maggie later brought back a wardrobe and chest of drawers, plus a nightstand. Herman then brought a small set of shelves. And put her series of children's books in it, neatly arranged. Maggie had his series of family stories placed on a bottom shelf.

HERMAN AND MAGGIE STILL live and write in that old farmhouse at the end of their long, dusty road. In the evenings, they still sit in their tall padded chairs and make notes on each other's writing. Meanwhile, a child is between them, quietly playing with his toys or reads books on the hooked rug that covers their living room floor. In the afternoons, you can see the three of them walking around the farm, hand-in-hand as they check the cattle and get their inspirations for more writing.

Their child has plenty of ruled pads to draw and write in.

And a sister on the way.

Keyboard In the Sky

BY R. L. SAUNDERS

One

HORACE HACKETT JR. was head down on his desk, the laptop filled with rows of b's and the machine bleeping. Horace's nose pressed neatly on that letter, regardless of the machine's discomfort.

Nearby were several empty bottles of a variety of alcoholic beverages.

"Looks like it was beer, then whiskey with a beer chaser, then straight whiskey as the beer was all gone."

Julie Montcalm was looking over the disheveled mess of the dorm room though the open door.

Behind her stood Micah De Wolf.

Both students were in the same school as Horace. And both were similarly disgusted by the state of Horace and his dorm room.

Laundry was everywhere but the hamper, with scattered pages of print outs. The printer was blinking and obviously out of ink. Several empty cartridges sat nearby, and more on the floor. They had completely missed the trash can. Some of his school texts hadn't.

Shelves for those books were filled with food wrappers and RPG manuals. In and amongst them were grade reports and various bills from equipment dealers and pawn shop receipts.

Micah crossed behind her to the keyboard on it's stand against the wall. Moving some old shirts and unmentionables over to the bed, he clicked the device on and started a riff with the volume dialed low.

Julie meanwhile had crossed to Horace and pushed his head to the side, stopping the insistent beep. She brushed his thick locks away from his face with a soft touch, more as an elder sister than an editor asking after her story. The alcohol on his breath rose to her nose and she stepped back, raising her hand to it as if to shield it from further offense

At that, Horace moaned and slowly squinted his eyes to see who was bothering him. He saw someone standing there, sideways in his vision as it cleared. Slim, in tight jeans lit from the hallway light, it was obviously a her or a she. The curving hips on long legs was definitely not his room mate or any of the many female visitors that infrequently graced the male dormers. These were black jeans, cut for dual purpose of business while displaying her feminine charms. Not that he'd ever bed this one. He recognized the ring on her hand as it left his forehead.

His head jerked upright and collided with the unlit desk lamp. The effort made his vision swirl again. Rubbing the bump was more a habit than needful. His scalp was numb from the result of all those bottles that had emptied themselves into his mouth not far below.

"So it's obvious that there is no story for me tonight." The tight jeans had a commanding voice.

Horace's ears felt assaulted by the volume. He opened his eyes wide at this. "Julie! I'd say this was a pleasant surprise, but apparently you're here on business."

"Do you even know what day this is? Do you know the Atworthy College Quarterly is due to ship for publishing tomorrow? Do you?!?"

Horace held his ears with both hands, knowing her voice could pierce through concrete and so his hand would do little to protect his throbbing head.

"Oh, is it that time already? I was just finishing up when I must have dozed off."

"Dozed off after a six-pack and a quart of cheap whiskey? Or..." At this, she pulled a skimpy piece of lingerie off the top of that lamp, holding it up as evidence before his eyes, "Did you have a little company to help you empty them?"

Horace focused on the sheer article she was dangling in front of him, tried to grab it, and missed as she cast it accurately into the trash can.

"Whoever the owner of that, I doubt she'll miss it."

Horace knew there was no response needed to that comment. No comment he could add other than to change the subject.

Micah was playing a soft tune in a direful key, as if to bury the conversation they were having, or set the theme for what was coming.

"I said I nearly completed your story, just polishing up the next draft of it."

"Since when did you work in drafts? That's why you got the job. You always write clean copy from the start. Engaging action and 'the reader transported into the adventure within seconds.' Wasn't that your last review? Or did you write that one, too?"

"Well, that was a good story. But this one is even better."

She picked up a few print out papers from the floor. "What is this, romance? Or a tawdry sex romp between werewolves and vampires? We can't be showing this to Atworthy College Alumni!"

"No, no, that was for Sheila. I was just showing her how any plot fits into a different genre with a little re-writing. Read closely and you'll see how O. Henry became D. H. Lawrence within the modern forbidden love of popular paranormal..."

"Oh, this was just another effort of yours to bed another undergrad by prostituting your writing gifts."

"Selling stories to potential publishers is either whoring all the way or not at all. Silvie has a blog and wanted some racy material for it. Evidently she left here without her copy."

Micah had changes the music into something more sprightly, with a traveling theme.

Julie glanced to the trash and frowned, "Among other things."

"Well I wasn't aware of her leaving enough to notice..."

"And the promised story? Should I be ready to re-shuffle the contents and drag up some overused 'classic' from the morgue because you missed another deadline?"

Her arms now crossed her chest, which Horace noted created an enticing effect in the soft fabric covering it. Tracing the buttons up to her collar and jawline gave him something to focus his eyes on. At that, one of her arms reached out and grabbed his chin to focus his eyes where they should be.

"Well, Mr. Observant? Can you get your mind on the work you promised to deliver? And off female anatomy?"

"Well, Jules, that's a tough option with you in the room."

She spun on her heel in disgust, arms now akimbo on her hips.

Micah looked over from his energetic keyboard sweeping to see Horace now focused on the accented area in between Julies arms. At that, Micah paused for effect a full measure.

Julie, realizing she had fallen for another or Horace's ploys, sat down on the rumpled bed, and crossed her legs away from Horace. Stooping to pick up an empty bottle from the floor, she raised her head as the pulled the bottle into his Horace's vision. She pointed its neck at him like a stiletto blade.

"Now do I have your attention? Let's get your mind out of the gutter." She flung the beer bottle past him to land expertly on the lingerie in the trash. In one fluid move, she snatched up her Cappuccino with its secure lid and thrust it into his hands.

"Drink up. You've got work to do."

Horace removed the top and carefully sipped the hot, sweet liquid. While it had no immediate effect, they both knew it would eventually.

Micah resumed with a Brahms lullaby as a sarcastic comment about Horace's condition.

"No, really, the story is almost there. It has a great plot. A hunk of a hero rescuing a strong-willed lady who gets imprisoned by a notorious villain, all set in the Caribbean..."

"Wait, Horace, isn't that just like one your Father wrote? One of his 'greatest hits'?"

Horace paused for only a short moment. "'All that's ever been told has never been new.' The point here is that I can write any story I want and make a new page-turner out of it."

Julie was caught up in her original idea. "Wasn't that the one where he took his friend and put him into the story as the villain?"

"Yea, some say his greatest work. But that's not this one. I can do his stuff much better than he ever did. Because he only ever wrote for a single character, himself. All the other characters were standing like cardboard cutouts. Pulp fiction melodrama where the characters only reacted to the plot. But that was the day, and that was what he was good at. People wanted that type of entertainment."

"Look, we just need a decent, long piece to hold the issue together. And it has to be good enough to make sure the Atworthy Alumni are impressed and will shower down donations. If you can't do that, then I've got to find someone else." She uncrossed her denim legs and began to rise.

"No, wait. Settle down. I've just got to wrap up a few details in the dialogue and add a little more color to the ending. You'll have your story."

"And by midnight tonight. No later. I'm going to have to get the line-editor and proofer up early as it is, but they've already been told to expect your stuff and are giving up their Sunday to have it all ready by Monday publishing. And you'll be sending it to my cloud account so I can follow what you're doing."

"Whoa, I don't do oversight editing. My stuff is original and complete when I say it is."

"That might have been for other stories. On this one you've worn out your last favor. I need to know you're working on it, and not shacking up with some bimbo who knows she can flash her chest or skimpy shorts at you. This isn't just some click-bait to get traffic."

"No, this is prime stuff, top notch, real entertainment."

"It better be. I don't have time to mess with anything else. Of course, receiving your final grades depends on it."

"You didn't..."

"Remember, you had to sign for that advance."

"I thought it was just a release."

"Since when have we made you sign a release? Although you did look a bit hungover."

"I was - er - late for a party, er, meeting. What did I sign for?"

"That until that story arrived, the school would be able to hold your grade report. And that means your dear parent's purse strings would be harder to loosen for your next semester."

Horace slumped in his chair, lounging back, almost hitting that desk lamp again.

Micah rolled into a minor key with his melody, matching the darkening scene in the room.

"Well, I'm for it then. Better get to work." At that he brightened. "You should see how this starts out. Swashbuckling is back again, along with the paranormal..."

"Just no vampires or zombies, OK? Remember, it's Atworthy Alumni that you need to impress, not your female writer-groupies."

"No, no, it's a real classic. Caribbean conflicts with English vs. Spanish. Privateers versus the almighty Armada. And mysterious happenings due to the native Amerindian influences working against the Catholic church interests."

"You are going to be sensitive to minorities in this one? If you're just revamping your dad's one-hit wonder, then you've got to do more for Indians than call them lying spies. And then there's that muscular pin-headed dark flunky..."

"Oh, come on, you know me better than that."

"And why I had to ask. Your dad could get away with that in the '30's, but now we have all kinds of sensitivity committees who can't censure your stories, but can raise a ruckus with the sympathetic agenda-pushing press."

"I get it - your job depends on this story."

Julie bristled at this, pointing a manicured finger in his direction, "Don't get thinking you can put me over a barrel. I've already got another story ready to slip in, if or when you screw the pooch on this one."

Horace leaned back. "No, this story is rolling out like clockwork. I'm just revising the second act of it now, right as the hero is getting into massive trouble over his head. It's a great plot, all driving suspense and conflict. Mystery and Romance to boot. You'll see."

Micah brightened the tempo and went back into a major chord, similar to an action soundtrack by Williams.

"And no plagiarism. I've got a copy of your dad's work, so you'd better make this good. Original. No copy/paste/rework."

Horace's mouth opened in shock, eyes wide while his rest of his body relaxed. "You don't mean you are copy-checking my work. I'm shocked."

"Oh, you're about to say you've never pulled his or other people's stuff up to pass them off as your own."

"Copying the masters is a time-honored tradition painters have used..."

"And plagiarism can get you expelled along with anyone who edited or approved it. So don't try my patience."

"It's easier to pull from real life. Like Micah over there would make a great model for the villain. Totally modern day. Aristocratic bloodlines, but a commoner's ancestry with his parents mixing according to current norms."

Micah saw where this was going and stopped the accompaniment. "Wait, I've read your dad's story. This is where you write me into it and all hell breaks loose. My life goes to hell and I have to listen to some damned typewriter in the sky telling me how I'm going to act."

"Oh come on, Mikey, that's just nonsense. Fantasy. Never happened in real life."

"You haven't talked to my Dad about that. He had nightmares for months after your dad wrote him into the story."

"It's just modeling. Take Julie here, she's a much better 'Lady Marion' for that story than the cutout pasteup that my dad used. Auburn-haired, take-charge sort of gal who sees what she wants and goes after it. No-nonsense, but a heart of gold."

Julie brightened at that and tucked her hair behind her ear, smoothing her blouse and leaned on one hip.

Micah continued. "No. You're not using me in this one. What's that smell?" He got up, looked around to see if there was some recent spill he'd sat in or near.

Horace pushed on, "Imagine if Julie were there, the story would have turned out so very different. The men would have been eating out of her hands. And your sensible, hard-working approach to your craft shows in your schoolwork and would make the villain far more intelligent and discerning.

"These days of writing have to take the characters into account in writing the story. You just can't have hackneyed melodrama pulled from some Plot Genie. Readers want real people in their stories, believable. So real they want the next installment in the series. We can do this up into a real page-turner. The college mag will have another collectible on their hands!"

Micah muttered, "Whatever. I've heard this before. But what is that smell? Is your toilet clogged again?" He moved around Julie to the dorm's bathroom and entered.

Julie shook out of her reverie, "Just remember you have a midnight deadline. No funny business. If you can deliver half of even what you're promising... Look, I don't care. I want something that will be a decent piece that doesn't offend anyone but entertains them. It had better be good and better be on time. I don't want to spend all night fixing your goofs and then have to throw it away. Don't waste my time."

With that she stormed from the room and pulled the door tight behind her with a thump.

The bathroom door was closed. Horace had to get to work. Picking the other empty bottles off the desktop, he added them to the wastebasket with a mental note to check across the hall for more trash bags. As he did, he smiled as the contrasting colors between them and the bright feminine article there. Then he nudged the rest of the bottles under the desk out of any accidental kicking range.

This was going to be some serious writing, he thought. Well, he always worked better under pressure.

Picking up the coffee again, he could almost smell Julie's perfume on the cup. But that was probably his imagination working again. What a gal she is. Taking a deep drink from the cooling liquid seemed to clear his head. Minimizing all the other windows on the laptop screen, he began again.

The clattering of the keyboard soon became the only sounds in the room.

Two

MICAH FOUND THE ODOR in the bathroom but wasn't sure what was causing it. The door seemed to shut on his own, as if by reflex. In the darkness, he flicked on the switch. With a pop, the light went out. As his eyes accustomed to the darkness, he saw a series of steps going down toward some misty light source way below. Turning back to grab the door handle, he almost toppled off the step he was on.

There were no walls, no door, nothing but these old and moldering steps he was standing at the top of.

It hit him then. Damn that Horace Hackett! He's writing me into the wrong story. This isn't his dad's "Blood and Loot", this is his dad's other only hit, a disjointed horror story they had to call weird fiction just to classify it at all.

Damn that Horace Hackett.

Well, OK, let's get this over with. I'm supposed to find my hat and 4 hours of my life. But I can fix that. I know how he ended that story.

So Micah DeWolf started down the steps to his doom.

Three

WHEN JULIE CAME TO, she was laying down in sand. She brought an arm across her eyes to shield the sun. When did she put on gloves and what was this white linen she was wearing? It wasn't the simple blouse she'd put on to see Horace...

She sat up. That was no blouse, it was a full gown with what felt like pearls sewn into it around the neck. And there was a wide hat with a silken strap nearby.

As the sound of the booming surf reached her ears, she looked around. A toothy series of rocks were being washed by a restless sea. To her right, a craggy point reached up and posed a brownish silhouette against a crystal blue sky.

Turning her head, she saw a great bay horse munching grass just inland of where the beach ended. As she struggled to her feet with the folds of long dress making her rise less than elegant, she also noted that she was wearing long leather riding boots, the air proved she was wearing nothing else under that long dress. The form-fitting dress holding her top in, but exposing a bit too much flesh for her taste.

How did she... where was she? No. NO. HE DIDN'T!

"Horace Hackett. You ASS!"

The there were no echoes against that booming surf.

This was "Blood and Loot" again. Damn that Horace Hackett. His father's greatest hit. He said he wouldn't.

But one thing consistent about Horace was that he'd kept to his dad's legacy. Say whatever you want, do whatever you want. Just keep people happy telling them whatever they think they want.

Now she was in his story. But that's OK, she new how this one ended.

Wait, what's this? In a side pocket of her dress, neatly sewn and positioned to hide itself, was her smartphone. And it had a full charge. Of course, no bars. But somehow it was getting a Wi-Fi signal. She got into the cloud file sharing and looked up Horace's story.

Of course, he hadn't actually finished it. He was only at the beginning. And she had just been written into it. "Flame-headed woman," he had written. Pulling a lock of hair up to look at it, she was impressed. Her hair had never been that red. And it must have grown a foot longer. Gorgeous, even for being wind-blown and not a speck of sand in it.

Her dress was form-fitting, and tight around the waist. But it looks like she was a few pounds lighter. And maybe a cup-size or two bigger. Horace, you devil.

She scrolled back to find the backstory. Let's see. Irish father, a land owner and spoke mostly rubbish with a very poor accent. Horace never could get dialects right. Big land holdings, and she was his only heir. Could ride and fight with a sword or musket. So far so good. Otherwise, the story just started with her fully grown, single, and "ripe." She'd have a few more words for Horace when she got back. Fiction writers could do whatever they wanted, but when they are dealing with real people...

Wait. She was now fiction. She paused for a moment. There it was. The sound of plastic keys clattering in the sky. Great.

Like father, like son.

She then scrolled back up and saw the words had continued without her. So far, so good.

On a lark, she pulled up the Hackett elder's work. Let's see. This had her entering the scene pretty quickly. The villain was supposed to wash up on the beach and she was supposed to keep her own squad from killing him.

As if on cue, the horse whinnied and came over to her. The reins now were over his neck and on the pommel of that English side-saddle. So much for grazing. She stroked the gelding's nose as he continued forward to nuzzle her and bury his nose in her flaming hair. Probably likes the lavender scent, she thought. Julie pocketed the smartphone.

But how am I supposed to get up on this huge beast? And loop my leg around that saddle to hang on? Usually they had servants to help...

And suddenly, not only was she mounted , but galloping down the beach toward musket fire in the distance. Not only did she know how to ride and control this animal, but could even be a cover girl for Horsewoman Monthly. As if on cue, her dress parted to show her cleavage to the sun and wind. The galloping seemed in slow motion which showed off her new feminine charms. (Mental note: Horace would get words about this, too, when she got back.)

Coming up on her first real scene in the book, she saw the villain, a Spanish don, defending himself on eight sides by her troops. He was holding his own. Dirk, the black-bearded tall one was saying something to Red. The villain just killed one of her men with a point to the throat, then another with one to the heart. Finally, someone knocked his sword out of his hand. And that was her cue.

The horse had moved her right up to the action, and the words came out of her mouth, "Stay! Back, you gutter sweepings! Dirk, hand him his sword, if he'll permit a fatherless varlet to touch it!" (Boy, that was really stupid line-choice there. Like anyone would treat their own staff like that. Even in those ages. Basically calling an employee a bastard to his face. Note to self: Have to clean that up.)

She heard a noise behind her. "And get out of here before my groom starts laying the 'cat on you." Oh, and here's the stereotypic black oaf, seven-foot tall with a cat-o-nine-tails that he's swishing menacingly. (Gawd, you'd think that Horace Jr. would have fixed his dad's plot holes.)

So her squad then leaves her with this guy that has his weapon back. She's on her horse, but even her groom is gone. Nothing but the beach, this villain and the three guy's he's killed.

Then the villain suddenly gets a hat with feather, swoops it off his head as he bows, and then falls to the ground, senseless, landing on one of the men he had killed.

Now, how is she supposed to get him back to her father's place with no one around? (I guess this is why Hackett simply had a scene shift...)

Four

MICAH SAW A DOORWAY about thirty steps down, and moved toward it. A few steps down, there was a peal of thunder and the earth rolled together over his head, putting the whole flight into darkness. (OK, that's weird. He'd started out from a second story bathroom.)

As he felt and groped his way forward, step by step, he felt something banging against his leg in his pocket. Feeling for it, he put his hand in the tweed pants (funny, he had been wearing some chinos back in the dorm room. If this had been "Blood and Loot" they would have been pantaloons, so the small favor of pockets were welcome, itchy tweed or not.)

Punching the side of it illuminated the space. He turned on the flashlight and was able to see the rest of the way down. While some of the steps were three feet tall and others merely inches, he was able to make the distance as evenly as possible under the conditions.

The landing had no door. OK, this was where something else happened. Turning off the flashlight app, he opened up the shared folder and found that he had a copy of that other story in it. Scrolling along, he found where that was supposed to happen and then went further. There is was. The point where an old, demented lady opened the door. Switching to editing mode, he put the cursor there and started typing.

In Micah's version, the feeble light came on and a door knocker with Medusa on it magically appeared. And instead of knocking, he simply turned the unlocked door knob and flooded the stairs with bright Caribbean light coming in from the windows of the room beyond. Micah then entered the room and closed that door behind him.

No old lady, no snarky young boy, no mystery here. "Blood and Loot", just like was supposed to happen.

And then - poof - he found himself naked in a big four-poster bed with a bandage on his head and his side. Great. So much for subtle scene shifts.

Right on clue, a black servant wearing only a white gown came in the room with a tray. He helped Micah sit upright and fluffed the pillows behind his back. Then he put the tray on Micah's lap and left.

Melon, a bottle of wine, some sweet buns, a pot of coffee, and an envelope. (Which meant the tray was huge to hold all that. Another Hackett plot hole.) Micah opens the envelope and smells the lavender, reads the horrible version of English, and gets out of that letter that Lady Marion hopes he's doing better and can join them this afternoon.

Here's where he suddenly remembers the audition, and the tray had somehow moved over to the side of the bed. What Micah really remembered was finding that smartphone. Where did it go this time? He went over to the piles of clothing all cleaned and neatly folded. Rummaging through them, he found it. Full charge, still. So far, so good. Opens up the file-sharing app and scrolls down to that place in the story he was supposed to be in.

Let's see. OK, skip that. Micah started typing. Gym shorts with pockets. Poof. That was a little less drafty. Now, skip the servant helping him get dressed. Poof. Fully dressed and stuffy in all this humid climate. At least the shoes were comfortable.

Next, skip ahead and...

Poof. There he is, looking out the window and just had told the servant to summon the mistress.

And he was hearing the clatter of the keyboard in the distance. He heard the door open, the rustle of silk as the lady bowed. He then turned and bowed himself.

Shock and awe resulted as they both rose.

Micah and Julie saw each other. Micah dressed as a Spanish count, Julie with her long and very red hair (flaming) piled high on her head with a gorgeous form-fitting dress that swept the floor.

Micah was the first to recover and reached inside his pantaloons to the gym shorts where his smartphone was secured. He opened up the editing app and saved it to "draft" mode. That would keep Horace from changing things for a little bit.

Julie saw what he was doing and cocked her head to listen. No clattering keyboard.

She said, "That was a smart move. He can type away, but it won't affect us until we take it off edit mode." She got her own smartphone out and did the same. Her story was already scrolled to that point.

"I wish I had thought of that before. But I didn't suspect we'd both be here."

"Yea, that was a surprise to me. too. But you sure clean up nice. Never thought your hair was that red. And Horace can sure turn a nice phrase on how to dress you. How you got into such a tight dress is beyond me."

"It was one of those 'poof' moments where it just happens. I just have to make sure I keep my hand on my smartphone when there's a scene change. These dresses don't necessarily have pockets, unless I edit them into it. Oh, and I also give myself some more comfortable underwear. Some of these period dresses are real scratchy. Bloomers hadn't even been invented. Airy under all this."

"Hey, I don't mean to be coarse, but I have to get this out of the way. Did he give you a bigger rack?"

Julie blushed and then nodded, "It seems like it. But I haven't had a chance to check, since we haven't gotten to any of the scenes were this character is even remotely disrobed."

"I think we can move around in this story pretty much any way we want."

"The bigger problem is that Horace is making just as big a mess out of this as his dad did. Plot holes that have plot holes. This is going to keep me into an all-nighter just editing this into shape. I've still got to get that issue out tomorrow."

Micah dropped down on the bed and gestured to the tray. "Hey, help yourself to some sweet buns and coffee. Or maybe you'd like melon and wine." He grabbed the wine and poured a glassful.

"I'm starving, thanks." She flounced down on the bed, pulled up a sweet bun and chomped into it.

Micah sipped his glass of wine and passed the bottle over to Julie. "Try this, it's really good. A bit of a jolt, but sweet."

Julie got the cup that came with the coffee and filled it with wine. She then sliced off a piece of melon and chewed it as she looked off into space. "Have you got a plan for this?"

Micah pulled up his smartphone and started scrolling with one hand. "Now the original story has the villain surviving and the hero disappearing under a collapsing front porch. Lady Marion ends up in the villain's arms but there's no trace of her at the end."

"Well, we'll have to fix that. Needs a decent romantic ending. Has to include a happily-ever-after."

Micah stopped and looked at her. "You know that means us. Our characters."

Julie thought that over. "You know, it's probably a good way to get to know you better. But it's just fictional characters."

"Right. Just fictional characters."

Both were scrolling on their smartphones for a bit.

Julie cut the silence next. "Boy I can save us a lot of work on editing later if we do it now. Look, we can go in and out and fix things."

Micah moved over to her side, "And if we go through to note the plot holes and fix them as we go, then the whole thing will roll right through."

Julie pointed out on his screen, "Look, we can do the whole thing from here, edit it in advance and then flip right to the ending."

The sun didn't move for several hours. All the story's characters stayed in place, the wind and waves and birds kept up a sort of looped rhythm while Julie and Micah did their editing. The big bed was comfy, and they bantered back and forth to fix things. Julie took the big picture approach with the overall story arcs, and Micah would fix the little scenes so it all fit together.

Eventually, they had everything the the way they liked it. Both were happy with the story.

During all that editing, they'd gotten out of the most uncomfortable garments. The tray was empty and on the floor, along with an empty wine bottle and dishes. Micah was in just his t-shirt and gym shorts. Julie was in a halter top and bikini briefs. They were lying side by side and smiling.

"You know, Julie, that was fun. Almost as good as sex."

Julie propped herself up on one elbow and looked at him. "Are you serious? Sex is way better than editing."

Micah looked deep into her eyes. "I just meant that I'd never had so much fun with anyone before like that. Not that I would ever ask you just to have a romp so we could compare things."

"No, of course you wouldn't."

"No, of course I wouldn't. Neither would you."

"Neither would I."

And silence continued while they continued their mutual gazing.

Eventually, Julie leaned over and planted a long kiss on Micah.

When the came up for air, Micah asked, "I don't mean to be unappreciative, but can I ask you what that was all about?"

Julie smiled. "Well, if I have to have a reason, it was for how you complimented my dress and how I fit into it."

"Oh that. You do look nice. All the time. I don't know how you do it. But I usually don't have a chance to tell you about it, because it's either Horace of someone else around who would then make fun of me. I'd never hear the end of it."

"Really? How long have you been thinking that?"

"Years. Years and years. Ever since we were kids growing up on the same block. Visiting on holidays and such."

"No. You're kidding."

Micah shook his head slowly.

Julie leaned over and gave him another peck on the lips.

"Now wait a minute, why was that so short?"

"I like to tease."

"Hey did you ever think of something? We've got the world on pause. We can do whatever we want and don't have to tell anyone about it. Just us and our fantasies."

"Yeah, I was wondering when you'd get around to that idea."

"OK, two for me being the slow one." With that, he reached up and pulled her arm out so that she dropped down on her back, then Micah rolled half-way over on top of her, one arm across her chest and holding her other arm down. Almost in a whisper, he said, "Now, teacher, what do you want me to learn?"

Five

HORACE WENT DOWN TO the canteen to get some more coffee. Like a pitcher full.

Kurt von Rachen was at one of the tables waiting for his microwave to beep. He had a pad and mechanical pencil with a large eraser. Kurt was making wild notes and scribbling things down as fast as he could.

"Hey, Kurt, what's going? You're going to run out of pencil lead or get a cramp, I don't know which first."

"I'm just sprinting while my microwave cooks my Raman noodles. Something I picked up in my last community critique."

"Oh, the one where you try to write down all the ideas you can get as fast as you can? It would help if you actually turned the microwave on."

"No wonder it was going so well. I thought I was going to set a record."

"I think the point was to be aware of all your inspirations and to be able to get into the Zone simply, not setting idea-production records."

Kurt paused and sat up, looking at Horace. "You're probably right. It also explains why I'm so hungry. I don't know how long I've been sitting here. But I'm about out of paper with this pad."

"OK, let me help." Horace punched the start button. "It will be about a minute."

"What are you up to today? Busy improving on my old man's stuff."

"Well that could only be 'Blood and Lust.'"

"That's 'Blood and Loot'. Loot. But I'm thinking I might get heavier into the romance story arc. And your title could sell better, particularly if I put a bodice-ripper scene or two in it."

"Well, don't write anything you'd be embarrassed about later."

"Me? Embarrassed? Not likely. Plus, it would put a pink tinge on that uppity editor I have to deal with. She is so straight-laced."

"Julie Montcalm? Oh, well in that case, do what you want. I've sworn off editors. Now I just self-publish everything. My audience will tell me what they want. I don't need some editor telling me to do massive re-writes. One and done, that's my new model."

"How's that working for you?"

"Well it's fine, but did you ever notice that the characters tend to write their own stories? At least editors would tell me that my inciting incident was blasé or I didn't compound my complications enough, or my story twist wasn't dramatic or surprising enough. Hell, since I've just started asking he characters what they were up to, they give me all sorts of stuff I've never thought of before."

"Yea, characters act strange sometimes, like they were actually alive. And then when I start to write the next scene, it flows out like someone had already written it, that I was just there to type it out. Still exciting and everything. But like the whole thing is out of my hands."

They were both silent for awhile.

"Kurt."

"What?"

"Your noodles are getting cold."

"Thanks."

"See ya."

"Later."

Six

BOTH FULLY DRESSED again, Julie wondered out loud to Micah if she should type in a scene where a maidservant does her hair.

"No, it will be fine when the next scene starts. Look." He took the edit off pause, punched 'update all changes', and then hit pause again. Sure enough, her hair was perfect, there was a touch of rouge on her face, and lips, and she smelled of lavender.

"OK, lets scroll through this as a double-check."

"No, let's don't. No second guessing. Just scroll through to the end and skip all the naval battles and such."

"OK, here goes..."

As they entered the scene, the sound of clattering plastic keys met their ears.

With shocked looks, Julie and Micah realized that Horace was editing the ending. Just as they arrived in it.

Seven

IT WAS ALMOST MIDNIGHT when Micah finally swam ashore and then climbed into the heights above Nombre de Dios. By sneaking through the battlefields back to his own cabin, he had discovered all the clues. They added up, finally. Now he solved the mystery of how Bristol had defeated the Spanish fleet. By taking a force in through the unfortified rear flank, he took the fort and turned their guns on the Spanish fleet. Then English then crushed the unsuspecting Spanish in their own trap.

Unlike what the original book, the typing continued up in the sky. Clattering away.

Worse, he must have lost his smartphone in the action. His only hope was to find Julie. Otherwise, between Hackett and his Bristol character, it's probable that all their work would be undone. Worse, they could both meet a tragic end.

His only companion now was the hot, sultry wind in the dark palm trees overhead somewhere. The smoke rising from the sacked city hung thick in the air, adding a greasy feel to even breathing.

The English vessels rode the silent waves in the harbor while their crew were practicing their unlimited debauchery on what was left of the town.

While the original Spanish admiral had met his end before this point, Hackett's dad had continued the story of Mike DeWolf far afterward. And that is what the keyboard was still clicking away at.

His Nibs was still working "improving" his dad's greatest work into his own.

Regardless, this was the end of the book. Micah had to hope that the revisions he and Julie had created were left alone.

Sadly, Horace Junior had some of the same cheap approaches to writing his dad used. Both had used massive word output to simply power through their careers, without the real phrasing or plotting talent that made perennial bestsellers. They both got inspired from deficits in their bank accounts.

But that gave Micah an idea that might just work. If Julie still had her smartphone, it would help.

Meanwhile, in the book Micah's character had been as a "swordsman without peer, a military genius, a clever and even treacherous gentleman." So those would be his hole cards to play.

All his crew was dead, even that pin-headed, over-muscled stereotypic flunky who tailed him during the whole story. They were all dead. All he had left was dragging himself through these tangled woods toward the darkened cabin his character had occupied so long.

Micah saw lights in the windows showing through their shutters. But he wasn't here to just peep through cracks and skulk. Horace had written in his rapier at his side and and a tireless arm. (Probably that unrequited love sub-plot...)

Stepping up to the porch, Micah found a buccaneer sentry sprawled there, bottle just falling from his slack grip onto the porch floor.

Drunk was a mild word for it. Mike pulled a pistol from the sash that circled the sentry's pudgy gut. Holding the gun in his left hand and pulling the sword with his right, the door had to be opened with a swift kick.

The scene was romantic. A beautiful table lit by tall yellow candles that made Mike's crystal and gold gleam in their soft, flickering light.

At the far end, sat Julie as Lady Marion, as gorgeous as ever. She was smiling, even more gorgeous in her simple gold gown. Julie heard the sound and smiling even though she was looking at Micah in the doorway. Or maybe because of it.

Bristol, with his silk shirt and gold sash, started to his feet at the noise. Micah noticed romance written into the scene, with items like "candlelight still in Bristol's eyes."

"Gog's wounds ! Who's this ?"

"Oh come off it, Bristol. I'm Miguel St. Raoul de Lobo, and my friends call me Micah. But my friends don't take over my house and burn the city I've been caring for. Nice silverware and gold cups. Oh, right. Those are mine, too."

"Damme!" said Bristol. "Ye're a ghost!"

"Oh, come on. Just because you've been lead to believe your invincible doesn't mean that someone else can't play that game. It's just the way you were written. But we can fix that quick enough. You're about to be edited out of this story."

Julie was white as she looked from Mike to Bristol, her hand moving under the table.

"But ye're dead!" cried Bristol. "With my own eyes I saw it!"

"And like you've had all this 20-20 vision with a bulletproof insanity to boot," said Micah. "Come on, get the rest of that script out of your mouth."

"But why ... have you come back?" said Bristol.

"To kill you. So pick up that rapier and let's go at it."

All that talk made no great effect upon Bristol. Being written in with a charmed life for so many books in his shallow series made him stereotypically afraid of nothing. Bristol picked up his rapier from the arms of the chair beside a wall and calmly flexed its steel.

Micah almost gave in to the urge to blow his brains out at close range, but realized that it would alarm Julie, and make a mess in editing this story. He knew he was tired, exhausted. There's every chance that Bristol could skewer him before he could even defend himself. Writing or no writing, this was a dangerous mess.

The chattering keyboard above was not reassuring. And prompted words from his mouth that weren't his.

"Maybe you English fight before your women," said Micah. "I don't. There's light on the porch."

And Bristol followed his own script, snorting with derision, "Marion, please pardon me while I kill this gentleman once and for all."

And then strode past Micah, through the broken door and onto the porch.

Julie wasn't watching, her head was looking down. Probably avoiding the conflict. Micah thought for a brief moment that she was completely out of character, both for the character Marion and for her.

Micah avoided the plot hole of trying to shut the broken door. He paused past the doorway and looked at English hero Bristol taking sitting there, taking his boots off.

Micah resisted the urge to simply skewer him and be done with it. Again, to avoid editing problems later.

"You found her very glad to see you I've no doubt," said Micah, following the script to feign jealousy. Like anyone could be as shallow as these Hackett caricatures.

"Aye," said Bristol. "And I've a debt to pay you, you hound, for sullying her fair name."

"Like that bothered you so much you couldn't keep from asking her to marry you," said Micah.

"So I did," said Bristol.

"And she accepted," said Mike, "and then it went blah, blah, blah. All this stuff about a very touching scene, marching in triumph through the streets of London, your name on every lip, blah, blah, blah, and that at last she had found a man brave enough to command her humbleness blah, blah, blah, blah. Rest of her life spent worshiping the ground you walk on, etc. And then she kissed you."

"Of course," said Bristol. "But ... how did you know?"

"Did I mention you are very poorly written in all your stories? The titles alone should give you a hint. So I know a lot."

"I hope you know I do you favor to fight you. I've a town full of my men—"

"All drunk," said Micah, "Just look at what they accomplished. They'll blame it on the Spanish, of course. And at villainous priest will imprison and torture any witnesses. Look, have you got your boots off so you can get a better grip on the planked floor yet?"

Bristol shrugged.

Micah could hear the keyboard chattering in the silence.

Then came another pitifully-written script from Horace. "I fear," said Mike, "that you'll never live to spend the millions in bullion you found here today. For, Tom Bristol, I intend to run you through."

"Garde!" cried Bristol.

Their blades crossed and, with furious attack and defense, they went at each other.

Micah's blade suddenly flew from his hand as Bristol's blade swished. Tom's kick took the pistol away in the next moment.

Bristol now had a point at Micah's heart.

"Did ye think you're so different than I?" Bristol was gloating. "Other than my birth in England and your's in that hell called Spain, we might even have been comrades in arms had we shared the same country of origin. I've followed your trail for years. A worthy opponent, for sure. It's just a shame you took the darker route to your own fame."

"And what would you know of worthy opponents? Your scripts have never had an inkling of compassion for anyone except your over-sized ego. You've never gone beyond beating every bad guy with superior swordplay and witty repartee, not quite as sharp as your miraculous and ever-ready blade."

Bristol was puzzled at this. Nothing in his background had ever prepared him for someone giving him a retort with a blade ready for his heart.

Micah saw the confusion in his eyes. "Can't take the truth? What would you do without that blade or a pistol? And what do you think is going to happen to your life once you've returned to England? Did you ever look up whatever happened to the other privateers in history? No wonder you want to marry some rich girls for their Dad's wealth. But check it out - it doesn't matter. You've been given a complete carte blanc to kill as many enemies as you can catch. But what do you think happens the day after they sign the armistice? Your orders are invalid. Then they can come after you and string you up from your own yardarm or haul you right back to rot in prison based on your alleged "war crimes". Think about it. Just pause and think it over."

The point no longer pricked his chest, and it lowered slightly. But a lung puncture wouldn't help things.

Bristol shrugged, "And how do you claim to speak for history that hasn't happened? Is this some devil's work? Trust a Spaniard to be impious and cursed from all their contact with those insane priests you support. How could you know the future and tell me about it with such impunity? "

Micah no longer heard the keystrokes. "Because I read a lot. All writers read a lot. What I never told Horace is that I practiced writing as much as I practiced my music. And you only get better the more you do - if you're working to improve your actual craft, you aren't there to just make money off your fast fingers and a glib approach to life. You're just manipulating people to get what you think you want."

He pushed the point of Bristol's blade aside. "Look, even if you have millions and billions stashed away, when you get something by deceit and force, then you're riches will be worthless. They only buy you loneliness and fear. Until you can trust no one really. That's called paranoia. Your last days are spent in hiding. That's the lesson all history has shown. Spaniards and English, there's always someone opposing your goals. That's what people want to hear about. That's 'having your name on everyone's lips.' And it's never true. A few years later, it will be someone else's name, and then someone else after that."

At that, Micah turned away from Bristol, who by then had dropped his rapier point to the floor. "You live the story you want to live. Money and fame isn't permanent. Because people worship your legend, and that's not real appreciation. How you got the money and fame comes back to you. Want to live your life in fear and die alone? Go ahead, keep traveling the road you're on. It will get you there. That's what history keeps saying."

Bristol gritted his teeth. His fist clenched the grip of the sword he held. Breathing became faster. This was a hard truth to swallow.

"Turn, you coward. Face your fate like a gentleman, not the scourge you were raised to be."

Micah only turned his head to look directly into Bristol's angry face. He was waiting for the typewriting to have a blade instantly show up in his hand.

Nothing happened. Bristol just fumed, standing there. His moral code prevented him from killing an unarmed man in the back.

Micah knew this. Bristol threw down his rapier and charged.

Micah at first thought that the fury of Bristol's attack was the cause of the floor's shaking. That didn't explain the lantern jiggling unless the foundation was faulty. Not likely. These buildings were brick and stucco. Something was shaking the scene.

Then he remembered the end to the story he was in.

The shaking was soon so violent that it threw both of them down. Bristol, cursing, struggled up and fell again. Micah saw the porch roof start coming down and scurried back like a crab.

Lightning flashed down in the sky, lighting the woods where trees were falling. Micah got up off the porch floor where he and the hero Bristol had fallen from the earthquake. The porch fell and covered Bristol along with his sleeping, drunken bodyguard. All that was left was Bristol's rapier. Micah didn't bother picking it up, but went to see how Julie was doing inside.

She was yelling for help as she couldn't get a beam out of her way to get out of the cabin. The rain had started slashing down, soaking them both. Micah simply reached in and pulled her across the opening above the beam.

"What's happening?" she cried out.

"This is the big ending. We have to run down this path to get away from the building." Micah grabbed her hand and pulled her along with him as they ran.

The earth shook again, and they found themselves down into the water. Julie and Micah swam for each other and out away from the cliffs.

"I didn't think this was going to be so violent," Julie yelled above the roar of the wind, thunder, rain, and waves.

"I don't think this is part of the story," Micah yelled back. "We should have simply had THE END show up in big letters."

"Is this what happens when a story is published?"

Micah found a floating spar, and pulled Julie to him. He felt every inch of her respond as they kissed in the deep water.

As they did the rain quit, the skies cleared, and the waves calmed. The moon lit up the now romantic scene.

Big letters appeared in the sky.

Fade to black.

Eight

WHEN THEY QUIT KISSING, they were in her apartment bedroom. Micah was dressed in his t-shirt and shorts, Julie in a halter top and bikini briefs. Both were soaking wet. Micah had one arm around a pillow and the other holding Julie close to him.

The lights in the room were off and a moon was shining in through the window.

Her laptop came alive with a quiet chime and lit the whole room with a light-blue glow.

They untangled themselves from each other and the bed sheets and covers. Then got up to see if Hackett had come through.

It was 11:59 pm. There was a notice that the file had been updated.

As Julie sat at the desk and accessed the file, Micah looked over her shoulder, one hand on the chair back behind her.

They scanned through it and it was almost exactly the way they had fixed it.

Micah stood up and stretched. "That was certainly something. Wouldn't want to go through that again."

Julie said, "Well, not all of it. It does look like everything is just fine here. That gives me a few hours before my line-editor and proofer will be up. Like a regular night's sleep."

Micah looked down at Julie. "Or time for something."

"Yeah, something."

Nine

THE ATWORTHY ALUMNI magazine was a great success. Horace Hackett's story was printed with a byline of Micah DeWolf as researcher. That story also had a short bio of Hackett saying that when he had begun writing himself, he found that the 30's and 40's style writing his dad was famous for wasn't the only way to write, and felt that he could contribute a new version of it to the world.

That was Julie's idea. She had warned him about plagiarizing his dad's stuff. But congratulated him on breaking into the romance genre. Hackett always wondered about that afterwards. She had such a big smile on her face for weeks.

But she never asked him to write for her again. Said it was too strenuous.

Micah passed his audition, but turned down playing for the Philharmonic.

They both moved to another small college town after graduating, and started writing Romance novels in their spare time.

Her Eyes

BY J. R. KRUZE

I

I LOOKED INTO HER EYES and my soul was gone.

Like I never existed in my own body. Or more like I had a different one, now.

I could feel her arms, her legs, the silky smoothness of where she shaved and where she didn't. Medium height, brown hair, blue eyes - I knew these from looking at her from the outside. But from the inside out, your eyes didn't have color, your hair only showed in a mirror or when you grew it long enough to pull out in front where you could see it. And you hardly felt hair growing where it shouldn't unless you felt it for yourself.

I put my new hands around and over my new body to feel the textures, the curves. Raising one hand and arm in front of my eyes, I saw alabaster white skin, like I'd never been out in the sun. This body was trim, smooth, exercised and fit.

I was wearing her clothes and underclothes, where they bound and where they supported. Even feeling the coolness on my feet where I'd kicked my own shoes off.

Then I moved my hand higher, across my/her chest.

"Hey, watch it!" A voice came in, the hands dropped, arms straightened, fists clenched.

"Buddy, we're in this together, for now, so keep it clean." That voice was obviously in command.

"Who are you? What am I doing here?" I asked.

"I'm Rosa. This is my body and you are a visitor." The voice named Rosa was tough, but as smooth as her hips that I could still feel through our knuckles.

"But what am I doing here?" I repeated.

"You're a volunteer. Simple. You asked to be here." Rosa replied.

"No. You're kidding. This is slavery, this is..." My own voice halted.

Rosa turned to look at my own body. All 6 foot, 4 inches of it. Sandy hair, broad shoulders, tanned dark by the sun. Wearing my own clothes, the denim pants, chambray shirt, scuffed leather boots, and a frayed and faded blue ball cap with a seed company logo on it. And "I" had a blank look on my face until I didn't. Then winked an eye back at me, with a wry smile.

Then that me, all dressed up, walked over to the cheap "solid" door to this two-bit flea dump of a hotel room. Unlocked the chain, turned the dull stainless-steel door knob, opened it. Just before I went out, I picked up a small knapsack. Two steps and I was gone. At least thoughtful enough to shut the door behind.

I was trapped in someone else's body in a room that was also borrowed. Probably paid by the hour. But how long I would be in this body was another question. My ride had just left for parts unknown.

"Relax." Rosa said, trying to comfort me. "we're in this together. Quit worrying so much. It gives you wrinkles around your eyes and your forehead that you can't get out."

Our eyes closed. That was better. Calming after a fact.

"That's right, settle down. It's always a shock at first, but you'll do fine. Let's get to know each other a bit before we have to leave." Rosa's calm approach slowed our heartbeat and our breathing became more regular.

"Now, do you want the 50-cent tour or do you want to just see where this rabbit hole goes?" Rosa felt honestly interested, concerned for my well-being.

"Thanks. The main question I should ask, is 'How?'" I was calm now, curious.

"I don't know the science to this, but you volunteered to try it all out. All I know is that it works. You're here, I'm here, and for the next few hours, we'll have to get along inside my skin and bones. Probably more important is your Why." Rosa felt as curious as I was.

"Why? I don't know why. It's like I just woke up here. Where's my memories? What just happened?" I could feel our back tense and those fists uncurl into straight fingers spread out as far as they could.

"Shh. Be quiet for a bit. Getting excited won't help. There are simple answers. Let's have a drink." Rosa again was calming me on purpose.

Our body walked over to the Formica wood-grained chest of drawers with the large mirror on the wall above it. I could see exactly how petite she seemed, but I knew this body was trained and toned. There was hardly an ounce of fat anywhere. Scanning up, I noticed tailored fit of the blouse and slacks. Shoulders were broad, which again meant athletics. Hair was brown with light, natural tints. So we saw some sun occasionally. The eyes were a piercing blue. With the irises wide in this dim light, I could almost fall into them again...

Our eyelids shut, firmly. "You don't want to go there. That's why we avoid mirrors. Some have been found in front of mirrors and take a long time coming back. If they ever do. The first thing we are told is to only look into real eyes." Rosa was giving me tips to survival.

She continued, calmly. "Now relax again. You got us all excited. It takes some getting used to. If you want, we can lay back down and pleasure yourself to get that out of our system. It's quite exciting to share all that with someone. You can't get closer than this." A smile crossed our face, wistful. Our hands found a long-toothed hair brush on the dresser top, then we turned away from the mirror and opened our eyes again, if only to keep our balance.

Meanwhile, Rosa took our hands and arms to brush our long hair out, starting with the tips and then longer strokes until she could get to the scalp. The sensation of the brush on scalp and hair was unique and soothing. Our body relaxed noticeably.

"Yeah, you guys just crop it short and use a comb. You miss 90% of the fun of having a mane like this."

Gradually, she could smoothly brush from top to bottom with no hitches. The hair was brushed silky smooth again. And it felt great.

We sat down on the bed, sideways to the mirror and laid the brush down on the crumpled sheets and coverlet. We crossed our legs.

"How long is this going to last?" I asked.

"Not long. Could be hours, could be days." Rosa said.

"Days?!?"

"Oh, come on, we've been over this. Just calm down. Your body is being taken care of quite well." Rosa replied.

"What am 'I' doing and where did 'I' just go?" I asked.

"You don't need to know right now. Just know that you are getting paid to do a job that only you can do. I can't get in there. So you're just doing your regular job as far as anyone else knows. So relax." Rosa raised one hand to look at our nails.

"Well, I guess I'll just have to wait it out." I said.

"Yeah, I can tell when you're up to something, so don't even try it. There's no lying in here. Our long-term memories are shut off for now so neither of use can try anything. Also, we don't have any money in here, and both of our ID's are gone." Rosa replied.

We looked around the room, avoiding the mirror, and verified that the room was completely bare. It had no closet, only a faux leather orange stool to hold a missing suitcase, below a chrome plated shelf with hooks below it. The bathroom door was missing as well as any curtain for the shower. The mirrored door on the bathroom cabinet was open, exposing bare shelves.

I started to ask, "I supposed that knapsack..."

"...was our clothes and ID." Rosa finished.

"Nice." I said.

"So, what do you want to talk about?" Rosa asked.

"How are we going to talk about anything if we can't remember anything?" I asked in turn.

"Just being polite. Otherwise, we can just curl up and sleep it off. Your body should be back pretty soon." She said.

"Should we lock the door?" I asked.

"He took care of that on the way out. If we put the chain up, it just complicates things." She answered.

"How do you know what you know, if your own long-term memories are gone?" I asked.

"Not gone, just unavailable. I get to keep enough to calm you down so 'we' don't do something stupid with this body. At least until you get back with whatever you were sent to get." Rosa said.

"Oh, so if things go wrong, we're stuck here. Even if our ID was found in here somewhere, we can't be lie-detectored on stuff we don't know." I said.

"That's right. You're catching on. Worse comes to worse, we become a ward of the state and get a new ID and a new life. Together." She said.

"And meanwhile, I just have to keep calm. Just let the whole deal go down. Roll with it." I said.

"You got it. But that worry you just let fly - you noticed I'm in good shape. There's a lot of training with that if anybody gets funny ideas about how helpless I am. All that memory is stored in muscles, which kicks in if it's needed. Just like you can't hold your breath to die. Autonomic reflexes kick in." Rosa explained. "And all this I'm saying is just about all I know right now."

We laid back on the bed, felt the disheveled coverlet and sheet make wrinkles below us. There was one bulb in the light fixture, behind the cheap orange-yellow diffuser that was held on by a single screw-knob at slight tilt.

I raised one of our legs to ease the tension in our back. The stiff mattress was a little too hard to be comfortable. Probably easier to clean that way. I looked over to find a pillow and pulled it under my head. All easier to explore the seams in the off-white and water-stained ceiling tiles.

"It is always this boring?" I finally asked her.

"Couldn't say much. I seem to know that I've been in worse scenes, but those are vague ideas. I'm pretty sure I don't want to probe too much, as that would be risky." Rosa said.

"You have a point there." I said.

We could feel the central air pumping the air in and out. It had a mild scent of Lysol or some cleaner they used in the filters. A steady temperature in the high 70's probably. So the coverlet would be enough to keep someone warm.

"So neither of us know anything."

"Right."

"We don't remember anything."

"Correct."

"All we got is what we have, which is nothing."

"You got it."

"And other than unlocking that door and run screaming down the hallway for help, which would just get us locked away, we really can only lay here and wait."

"Yup. Sleep is probably the best option. Neither of us can remember any jokes or stories, after all." Rosa was pragmatic. "Here, just relax – let's take some deep breaths and count to a thousand..."

II

I AWOKE TO BEING CRUSHED by a body on top of me, lips against mine, and the feel of a grizzled face giving me whisker burn.

Male arms were holding my own against my sides. Through my thin blouse, I could feel the roughness of his jacket, the hard seams pushing through. I couldn't move.

So I relaxed.

When my body pulled my face away from ours, I opened our eyes to look into mine and got a shock. Rosa was looking back at me through my own eyes.

"Hey there, cutie." That was my voice, but Rosa's words.

"Well, handsome, now what? If you don't know what comes next, and I don't...?" Rosa's voice, my words.

"All I know is that mirror trick again. Look deep into my eyes. Kinda dumb saying, but that's how it works." Both my sets of eyes focused on each other, irises wide.

The world spun. Almost like a merry-g0-round when you unfocus and let the world just spin around you.

Then it stopped.

I was back on top of Rosa, looking back at her, and was pinning her arms down, my weight on top of her so she couldn't move. Home again.

"If you don't mind, you're making it hard to breathe." Rosa was talking from her own body now.

"Oh, sorry." I pushed up off her, to sit on the end of the bed, and then realized that could have been a mistake.

Rosa said, "No, there are some moves I could have done that would have left you with some serious hurt."

"Wait, you can read my mind?" I asked.

"It will pass in a moment. You'll still get some thoughts of me from time to time, but just consider them dreams from a night you don't recall too well, and they'll pass." Rosa rose and shook her long mane back into place.

"A kinky one, to boot." I rubbed the back of my neck. "Wait. I still don't remember anything."

Rosa had gotten the knapsack open and fished out her ID. "You will. Best thing is to wait here for a bit. You won't know where you are, and sometimes people can get a bit sick to their stomach when the memories return. I'm queasy myself right now. But it will pass."

"What if someone comes?" I asked.

"Just tell them you don't remember anything, like you just blacked out." Rosa turned to the mirror and tucked in her blouse, straightened it. Turned away instead of checking her makeup. Those eyes again.

All this I saw from the back, which was still an admirable view. Yes, I was starting to feel like myself again. I glanced at the mirror and then twisted my head away.

She saw that reflection and turned to face me, one hand on her hip.

"You don't have to worry about that now. Only I do." Rosa reassured me.

Rosa then recovered her slip-on flats by the edge of the bed and put them on her sock feet again. Looking around the room, she picked up the brush and any clues she had been there, stuffed it into the backpack, then zipped it up and slung it over a shoulder.

Again she swung her hair away. I remembered that image also from a bar as a hazy recollection.

Rosa came over, leaned down, took my chin in her hand and kissed me lightly on my cheek. "Thanks John. That was a night we won't remember."

"So John's my name?" I asked.

"No, 'John' is everyone's name. I don't have my memories back, either, but I know I've got what I need in this knapsack. Directions and tickets, everything I need. Or at least I hope."

She kissed me once again. "Wish I could stay, but it would only get us both in trouble. Take care of yourself. Stay a while and leave when you feel like it. The room is yours until later this morning."

Then she swept out the door like the wind.

I looked at my watch. It was just before midnight.

That queasy feeling came in, so I laid back and closed my eyes. Nothing else to do right now.

III

THE SUN WAS TURNING the curtains the color of the ceiling light, showing details to the room I'd rather not know.

I sat up on the bed, and rubbed my face with my hands, then pushed them through my hair. Looking over to the mirror, I got up to check out what I looked like. Same 20-something I'd been before I had this dream. Or at least I think I was.

Still couldn't remember anything.

I pulled out my wallet. A few twenties, but no ID's. No pictures of anyone. Great.

Some change in my jeans pocket, a comb. I pulled that out and looked at it. Rosa was right. At least I remembered that part of it. A combed head doesn't feel like a brushed one. But the rest of what we did that night was fading. Now I could remember little of her.

And still had the taste of the mixed drinks in my mouth from the night before.

Hungry.

I got up, picked up my ball cap off the dresser. The rest of the room was empty. Coverlet and sheets mussed. Made sure everything was in my pockets and moved to the door.

Helluva one-night stand. Don't even know her name, now. All a blur.

I walked out and left the door open for the maid. Headed down the concrete walk, with one hand on the smooth metal railing. Brown paint was flaking or worn off in most places. Like the yellow paint on the wall's concrete blocks. Typical two-story strip mall motel. Don't know how I got here, but knew I was hungry. Felt the grit in my eyes like I'd been up most of the night, even though I'd just woken up.

Down to the asphalt parking, sticking to the cracked concrete sidewalk. Pulled my ball cap down against the rising sun. It was too bright in the East, and was starting to reflect off the windows of modernist buildings on the opposite side of the street. Four lane traffic with parking on both sides.

It was warm and getting warmer. I wouldn't need this jacket much longer today.

I kept to the sidewalk and avoided the larger cracks. Up ahead was a McDonald's. That would be safe. Eating-wise. There were all sorts of food places around, but I wanted something familiar.

That was the point. Find some familiar things. Maybe then I could get my memory back. Hell, I didn't even know what city I was in. Figured it must be L.A. from the trees and all the asphalt. Everything fake. Growing palm trees must be easier on the maintenance or something. But they sure are ugly.

I got a couple of dollar-menu items, several in fact. They'd fill me up until I could get a real meal somewhere. And those few twenties would have to last until I got somewhere.

I took the plastic tray with the white-sacked food items over to an empty window seat. The plastic feel of the benches and table top was cool and clean. That was another advantage to McDonald's, or any good name brand. They were always cleaning. I wolfed down the tiny burgers with all the white-bread buns. The cola was too cold to do more than sip at first. Fries topped everything off. Like everything there, all generic. No memory of where it had come from, like me.

Drink finally finished, I rose with the tray, put the cup with all the wrappings in the trash can on my way out. Tray wound up on top, just like the sign asked. I turned and palmed the door open.

Two cops were waiting for me. Blue uniforms, sunglasses reflecting the still-rising sun. Guns on their hips in holsters. Each had one hand near their own, the other out to keep their balance. You could hear the dispatcher coming from somewhere, either their black push-to-talk mic on their shoulders or that cop car that I could only see hood and trunk behind them.

"Josh Wilkins?"

My blank face probably wasn't helping things. "Officers, I couldn't tell you. But could I get my wallet out for you?"

One motioned to go ahead with their free hand, the other hovering near their gun. Cops. Guns. That meal wasn't sitting well already.

So I used a thumb and forefinger to fish out my wallet from my hip pocket. Pointedly kept the others out in the air. The other hand was holding my arm out away from my side, also empty and extended. I might be white, but that doesn't mean things couldn't go south pretty quickly. I just wanted to help these two officers keep as calm as possible.

Obviously, something was up. I only wish I could remember more than eating at McDonald's. This must be L.A. Those palm trees and all the asphalt. I could hear a freeway nearby, and the street outside the parking lot was four-lanes. That was all I really knew. And my name was Josh something.

One of the officers took my wallet from my fingers, and opened it, getting the same blank spots I did - where the ID's should have been.

My hand went wide and pulled that arm out to the other side. I didn't even try to adjust my cap, just lowered my head against the sunny glare.

One nodded to the other. "We've got a report of an incident exactly matching your description. You need to come with us for an interview." He handed my wallet to me, and I took one hand to put it back in my pocket.

The other officer circled behind me as the first one motioned for me to come toward his car. I was right, that car was behind him, a typical black-and-white with lights and rolled down windows with dispatchers talking through it.

Before we could get much closer, a black unmarked four-door sedan screeched and bounced into the parking lot on the other side of the police car. The cops and I stopped in our tracks. Again, their arms moved to hover hands over their gun butts.

The driver's side door of the black sedan opened and a female driver popped up. Dark suit jacket, brown hair tied into a bun on her neck, she was holding up a badge with ID in a wallet. "DHS, fellas. This one is mine."

She rounded the back of their squad car with an easy jaunt, the suit flipping open to expose her white blouse, and matching dark pants. Sunglasses completed the official government look. She gave the officer in front a closer look at her ID badge. While she grabbed my arm and started pulling me toward her car.

"Call it in if you want. This is Homeland Security and you don't want to touch this with a barge pole. You'd be up to your ears in paperwork for a month if you tried." The suit was pulling me around to her car as she talked.

Both the officers just stood there. They looked at her, looked at each other, then walked to their car to call in her badge number and name.

"Hey, I'd love to stay and chat, but this guy is needed downtown. Thanks for finding him. We've been on his trail for months." With that, she opened a back door on the passenger side and pushed me inside, just fast enough that I didn't have time to say or do anything else.

When she got in, she pulled out quickly and eased into traffic on our side of the road. Within minutes, she had pulled down ramp and was on the freeway headed north east. I could tell that by the sun coming in the closed window on my side.

We drove in silence for a while. Passing one exit ramp, she took the next one. Then stopped at the next cross street to turn right and through a maze of short turns that wound up in a neglected residential area right by the freeway. She pulled into an old wooden garage with white vinyl siding to match the house next to it.

"Just wait for a moment." The female suit turned on a police scanner along with another device and was listening. The sound was only high enough for her to hear. After several minutes of chatter, she turned it off again, leaving the other device on.

"OK, Josh. You're safe for now." The female suit pulled off her sunglasses to show a pair of piercing blue eyes. "Unfortunately, I wasn't able to tell you much last night. Because I didn't know. But now I do. And I have to apologize."

She looked honestly sorry. But I was still confused. Her eyes looked familiar, but that doesn't mean squat. I was staying quiet for now. The only thing I knew for certain was that those burgers in my stomach were having a hard time of it.

"You still don't remember anything, do you? You have no reason to trust me, but I'll tell you that they will come back. All your memories. Even what you did tonight.

"For right now, we have to get out of this car and start moving again. Watch the door, it's a tight fit."

She opened her driver-side door and was able to get about a foot of clearance before she hit the garage inside. I got about the same. But my bulk had a harder time than she did. So she was waiting for me at the end of the trunk when I finally got free.

"Here, put these on." She had brought a black garbage bag with her and was busy stuffing her suit jacket into it. From hooks on my side of the garage, she pulled down two jackets and caps, handing one to me. "It's an extra large and should fit."

They were jackets for a cleaning company. Long and white with emblems on the back. Like scientists wear in labs. Hokey, if you ask me. But they covered just about everything. She had her sunglasses back on and the white ball cap covered just about everything else.

"Quick, come this way." We went to the opening. She looked both ways. "See that van over there, our side of the street? Go over and open the side door and get in the back. Walk, don't run. Now." And gave me a little shove.

So I walked quickly toward the white panel van with the same emblem we had on our jackets and cap. I opened the side door and got in, then shut it behind me.

I could see her shut the garage doors and padlock them. Then she rounded the front of the van and got in the driver's side. She threw the garbage bag to me.

"Undress. Put clothes you came with in the bag. Everything, even your underwear. Leave out that coat and cap I just gave you. That garment bag behind you will have everything you need." She checked the mirrors and moved out onto the residential road smoothly, like nothing had happened.

Inside the garment bag had khaki slacks, a button-down blue cotton shirt, and a medium brown tweed jacket with elbow patches. White cotton socks, slip on Hush Puppies in my size, and a pair of skivvies.

I got them on in the dark panel van. There was one bench seat, which was bolted sideways, so I had plenty of room. The van was clean, no equipment in it. Painted a uniform grey.

As I stuffed the rest of my clothes in the black bag, I asked, "OK, what's next?"

She glanced in the mirror, "Now that's a good change for you. More respectable."

"If you say so." I replied.

"Now we're going to blend in. Put your coat and cap back on over the rest and come up here." She was watching the road and driving slowly to blend into traffic. We weren't on any main road that I could tell, but were back on four lanes again. The sun had been ahead of us for a bit, and then we turned back north east for a while. I could see more mountains showing up ahead of us and to our right.

We drove in quiet for some time. Windows up and A/C on. The windows, even in front, seemed to have a slight tint to them. I started to scrape at the passenger side.

"Don't do that." She was terse, almost snapping at me. "That stuff keeps anyone from taking a picture of us."

I put my hand down in my lap with the other and sat looking straight ahead.

"Sorry. We're just on the clock. I'm Rosy. That might help you a bit. We spent some time together last night."

I looked at her, but didn't recognize much with the cap, sunglasses, bunned hair, and white work coat. Cute, though.

"So now you've apologized twice and have me in a van going god-knows-where and have me suited up like a professor. What's the deal?" I said.

"You're right. I owe you some answers. Here's one you can deal with: we made love last night and something happened so you can't remember anything about it. Meanwhile, the cops have you confused for someone else who looks a lot like you. I'm just here to save your butt." She said.

That short answer was clipped and succinct. She was right, I could deal with it. And if we made love, I'm certain we both enjoyed it. Just wish I could remember what we did, how, and how many times. That brought a smile to my face.

"What's making you smile now?" she asked.

"What you said. Probably was nice, for both of us." I replied.

She smiled. "Yes, it was very nice."

Quiet took took over again. The sun shifted as we drove south east. Traffic was smooth and we tended to stay in the right lanes and let the speeders pass. We were going slightly below the speed limit. A few more turns, across a bridge, and then we pulled up onto a two-lane street next to a grassy park. There were oaks here, and maybe those were magnolias.

She stopped the van in one of the free parking spaces, and turned off the engine. Reaching into the glove compartment, she pulled out a tube of skin lotion and a hand mirror.

"Here, put this on your face and neck." Meanwhile, Rosa climbed into the back, taking the keys with her, and removed her jacket and cap. She stuffed them into the garbage bag, then opened another garment bag which gave her a flowered blouse and a rose-colored jacket. She swapped her own shoes out for a comfortable pair of walking shoes. She pulled down her bun and put back into a long ponytail.

I could see this from my mirror as I finished the face cream. It was clear when it went on, but turned the color of my skin into a light brown.

"Here, hand me that." She took the tube and mirror from me and touched up where I had missed. Her thumb and index finger took my chin and pushed it back and forth. Then she dabbed on any areas I'd missed.

Rosa then loosened her blouse down to her bra and turned the collar down. She used the mirror to apply the cream to her as well, looking over everything before she put the cap back on and put both cream and mirror into the plastic bag.

"Girls have the problem of men wanting to look where they shouldn't." She told me as she buttoned back up. "And our new ethnic isn't supposed to have tan lines."

Rosa said, "Hand me your wallet."

I did. She took out the money and put the wallet in the bag as well.

"Now the white work jacket and your cap." I gave her those. And they also went into the bag.

From under the driver's seat, she took a small package and pushed it deep inside the bag. Then she took two opposite sides of the bag and tied them together, the tied the other two sides the same. She took the van keys off the van bench seat and took the key fob off the ring. Then pulled a wide-mouth thermos from under the drivers seat, opened it carefully and then put all the keys into it. She took a plastic tube taped to the top of the lid off and broke the seal, dropping it into the thermos while quickly screwing the lid back on.

"Time to go." She climbed back up to the driver's seat and checked the mirrors one more time. Then she stepped out and closed the door. I followed suit on my side. She came over to me, put her arm in mine and walked us across the park toward some sandstone brick buildings on the other side.

Once we were half way across, we stopped at a water drinking fountain in its center. All the concrete paths met here and sloped down into a storm drain just by the fountain.

Here she took out the key fob and locked the doors with it. The lights blinked once, the horn sounded, and then the van windows blew out as a fire started inside.

"You keep looking at it. That's what we should be doing, just like anyone else who might have seen it." She dropped the key fob to the concrete and stepped on it, then pushed the broken parts into the drain with her toe.

"OK, that's enough. We're normal Los Angelinos and it's not our van, so we're going to keep walking." Rosa took my arm again. We moved along, deeper into shade. We then started curving our approach so that we eventually were going at right angles to the direction we started.

"Here's the deal. You're an absent-minded professor, and I'm your loyal assistant. If anyone asks, you simply don't know. Now, here's your money. Put it in that wallet inside your chest pocket. That gives you ID to match up with your story." Rosa continued us walking.

I put the wallet back inside the jacket and covered her hand with my other one.

"What was the explosion for?" I asked.

"We needed a controlled burn to get rid of the DNA. But that van had nothing to do with us. Our car is just on the other side of this park and we have just come from the art museum across the street from that park." Rosa rattled this off like she'd been doing it for years. Maybe she had.

The van on fire was getting hard to remember even now. For all I knew, we really were in that museum. "Well, if you say so. That's fine with me."

Rosa looked up at me, her flat shoes making her even smaller. She looked a bit concerned. But she still looked cute. I smiled at her. "Whatever you say goes."

Turning back to looking down the path, she patted my hand with her other one. "You'll be alright. I promise."

Shortly, we were at a car. White, gray upholstery. A sporty late-model Buick. Thin white-walls. It looked like half a dozen other cars in this neighborhood. Probably the point. She had me go to the passenger side while she felt under the front left fender. She pulled out a little magnetic container and a key. Unlocking her side, she opened the driver's door and unlocked mine from there. We both got in.

I scooted the seat back as far as it would go and reclined it so I wouldn't hit the interior on any bump. Plus, I was a bit tired already from all the excitement. Putting on the seat belt cinched the deal.

She glanced over, then back through her mirrors, pulling out slowly although there was no traffic. Soon we were back on a four-lane city street going north east again. The sun was up by now. Tinted windows helped the glare.

"We're going to be driving for a while. If you want to nap, you should. Here." Rosa handed me a straw hat to cover my eyes. It had a flowery hat band that matched her top.

"Thanks. For everything." I said.

She smiled sweetly and patted my hand again.

At least I could still remember her name.

IV

THE DREAMS WERE WILD. Some job where I was working at making movies. Lots of people on the set, few actors. Scene changes, lighting setups for every new scene, changing with every set. Some director everyone was treating like he was a god or something.

Another job where I was caring for an orchard and turning off valves every few hours after I'd turned on others. All in the desert somewhere. Grapefruit. All you could eat. If you wanted them.

L. A. The Rodney King riots. Watching the fires start up across the city. Here, there, over there. They marched in almost straight lines. Standing outside in a line around the property to show people they aren't welcome to loot and riot here. I guess it worked. We were bored standing there and finally the word came that we could go back to our jobs inside.

Then I stopped at a bar for a drink and saw this girl further down the bar. Wearing a short, black, low-cut one-piece. She had eyes so blue they almost shone in the dark...

"Hey" she said. I smiled.

"No, HEY." It was Rosa. We were driving. I'd been asleep. Dreaming.

"We're going to stop and get some gas. I'll go in and get some sandwiches and drinks. You stay here and keep that hat on, OK?" Rosa smiled again.

That was a killer combination she had. Blue eyes and a smile that melted you inside.

I nodded and put my head back. I could see under the brim that we were on the furthest outside row of pumps. More gray concrete and yellow curbs. No buildings nearby. Rosa had pulled another jacket out of the back and walked off wearing a cowboy hat which was a few sizes too big. Made her look a lot younger.

I woke up again when she came back and the car dinged as her door opened. She had changed into a black one-piece again. She handed me a bag with sandwiches and drinks. Then put another bag into the back seat. She threw the cowboy hat on top of it, but kept the jacket on.

We pulled out of the station and back onto the highway. Just dual lanes in each direction now. We were heading east, and the sun was behind us. The ride was smooth.

I set the seat up and took off the straw hat. Opening up the bag, I saw the sandwiches were both ham and cheese on rye buns, with pickles and some special sauce of some sort. The sandwiches were cut in halves. Two canned ice teas. I opened one of the sandwiches at one end and handed it to her. Then I opened a tea and put it into her half of the center console. My sandwich and tea came next. I was surprised how hungry I was.

When I got done with my sandwich, she handed me the other half of hers.

"That's all I needed." She said.

I nodded and finished off hers as well, then the rest of my tea. That hit the spot.

We traveled in quiet for a while.

"Rosa?"

"Yea?"

"How's this memory thing work? I can remember your name and that there's something between us, but little more than that. Those dreams were pretty real, but were they actual events? I just don't know." I bit my lip at that.

"It's gradual. But you're right, there's something between us. And as long as you don't have your memories, I'm tied to you. It's like I'm living both of our lives at once. I'm getting your memories as well as my own. That's why I came back to keep you safe." Rosa said.

"So it's not permanent. I'll get it back, eventually." I said.

"Sure. It's different for different people." Rosa said.

"Is this one faster or slower than other people had?" I asked.

"Well, the faster ones tend to still take a while to get it all back. But you're far from the slowest I've seen or worked with." Rosa replied.

"So you've been with other guys before me?" I asked.

"And gals. But ladies don't tell." She smiled at this.

"Why didn't you just leave me?" I asked.

"Because we are tied together until you do get your memories back. That's what makes an operation like this so tricky." She said.

"What operation?" I asked.

"All you need to concentrate on is getting your own memories back. Anything else I tell you won't make sense and you won't remember it, anyway. Like this - what color was that van we rode in?" Rosa asked.

"Van? I don't remember any van. Just this car." I said.

"Exactly. We could have been in several vans or none." Rosa said.

Another few minutes of quiet passed.

"What did you mean that you're living both our lives at once?" I asked.

"There's the problem of this transformation. We kinda swapped bodies, but not quite. I got the heavy load of both sets of memories, with all the emotional content. You just got to forget. But right now, when you see something, I get the memories that get triggered and you don't. Even something simple like driving a car gets tricky if we don't both stay calm. If you get excited, my adrenals act up so I can respond." Rosa frowned at this.

She relaxed her brow and continued. "It does have its benefits. You love almost anything on rye. But I told them to keep the hot mustard sauce off it as it gives you indigestion. And I don't want to be burping gas because you didn't eat right. Meanwhile, you get a sandwich you like. And tea, not soda. Better than those fast food burgers you ate. Side of fries and a coke. Good thing I got you when I did. Eating that crap food doesn't agree with you. I know. I feel it."

"So you and I are tied together physically without touching?" I asked.

"For now. But it's not too bad. Like I said, this isn't my first rodeo, so I'm a bit used to it. A bit. Not entirely." Rosa said.

"What about dreams?" I asked.

"I get these too, as long as we're connected. Even the ones you don't remember." She said.

"Must make driving hard." I said.

"Only gets bad when you're having a nightmare. Or a daymare. I'll pull over to the side of the road if it's going to be bad and wake you up." She said.

"Wow. That's a big load on you." I said.

"Well, the pay's worth it. I guess." She said.

"Why would a pretty girl like you need to do anything like this?" I asked

She smiled. "I've got other talents, like you do. Ever wonder why you and not some other barfly?"

"Did cross my mind. But you probably know that." I said.

"I can't read your thoughts, but I can feel your memories. Your empathic to a higher level than others. You care about people more than they care about you. The only trick is that high empaths like you often become recluses or develop extremely thick skins to keep people out. You just hadn't been in L. A. long enough, and you're young enough to not recluse yourself completely." She said.

"Oh. There must be a lot of science behind this." I said.

"A bit. More like where the heavy spiritual meets the extreme science that the government secret projects deal with." She said.

"Is that where this is from?" I asked.

She didn't have time to respond. A big semi veered a little close, forcing us to put two tires off the pavement and slow down.

It corrected and roared up in front of us and then slowed again. Meanwhile, a big black SUV had come up on our left and was matching our speed as we came back onto the road.

"Crap." Rosa said. "This isn't good."

The semi in front continued to slow while the SUV matched our own slowing speed. Rosa was peering in the mirror behind as much as she was looking forward.

I leaned forward to look out the mirror on my side. A blue, tall, one-ton pickup with dual rear wheels was coming up from behind. We were being sandwiched.

"OK, hang on. This is going to get tricky." Rosa warned me. She had two hands on the wheel, with white knuckles. I grabbed the handles and upholstery that would give me a grip, then pushed down on the passenger firewall with my feet as best I could.

Rosa braked suddenly, forcing the white pickup behind us to do the same.

Then she swerved in behind the SUV on her left in that tiny space it made.

She accelerated to push the nose of our Buick right against its bumper. As it slowed, we started pushing it.

The white pickup behind us then swerved and accelerated to the road side, scattering pebbles and dust as they drove.

Soon, they were right up next to us. The space tightened so that the pickup's double-cab passenger side started rubbing on our driver's side. We were being forced back into our first lane.

Rosa braked, jerked the wheel to the right and put us over onto the other roadside opposite. Slowing quickly, she was able to let the semi, SUV and pickup get slightly ahead. Then she twisted to the left again and was immediately behind the pickup over on the roadside.

Brake lights everywhere. The pickup's rear bumper was approaching our windshield fast.

Rosa saw an overpass railing coming up and braked hard. She drove back to the other side, screamed up behind the semi and then off the other side as soon as the overpass railing finished.

The white pickup wasn't as lucky. It clipped the railing with its front bumper and fishtailed, then tumbled sideways across the highway.

Sparks and parts flying away from it.

Rosa was navigating through the steep embankment grass on the side of the highway, keeping our own car from flipping. I could see the semi continuing to slow.

Then the tumbling pickup hit its trailer and forced it into a sideways slide.

She got our Buick slowed enough to turn and go at right angles to the access road. Twisting sharply, she was able to turn the Buick around and onto that access road.

We then followed the access road to the underpass and moved under it, stopping.

V

A LOT OF RED LIGHTS on the dash, but the engine was running, and we had all four wheels.

"Take a deep breath. You have to calm down." Rosa was looking at me hard, her blue eyes piercing through her chalk-white face.

"I can do this, but you have to bring your own heart rate down. Now."

Then she grabbed my thigh and nearly punctured my slacks with her fingernails.

I complied. Breathing deep and slow, Deep and slow. Feeling the heartbeat lessen. Forced my hands to unclench. Deep and slow.

Rosa's face got some color back. She was doing the same as I was. Her trick was twice as hard as mine. Her grip on my thigh relaxed. And she patted it. "Good boy. Nice job."

Looking out our mirrors, "I didn't see where the SUV went to. We can go north or south. South doesn't have anyone there for miles. Further from where we need to go. But less likely they'll be looking for us with a single car." At that she, turned the car around in a U-turn and waited for a local car to come by. Then she pulled out behind them and matched their speed, a safe distance behind.

"We're going to have to do this old school. Pull out the map in the glove compartment." Rosa said. She pulled off onto the next country road, into an old driveway where some farm house used to stand. The oak trees sheltered us from above, and we couldn't be seen from the road.

I handed her the map.

"Our advantage and disadvantage is that we are off the grid. This car had the electronics modified so we couldn't be traced. And we don't have cell phones. But we can't call anyone, either. They'll only know we're in trouble when we don't show up."

She took the map and looked it over.

"Here." She pointed. "Now, we can't use the interstates any more. State roads are probably OK, but not in this car." She traced some lines south of us. "That dot. That's where we should find something. Can't be a rental. We're looking for a salvage job. Something that would blend in. Let's go."

We got back on the gravel road and followed it east and then south. I kept an eye out for planes or helicopters, although I suspected that satellites could find us as easily, if it came to that.

We finally rolled into that dot of a town. It didn't even have a stoplight. But it did have a salvage yard. Peeling white paint and an old concrete island where a gas pump used to stand. Dirty windows everywhere they still existed. And rows of old trucks that pushed back into the hardwood trees behind it. One 60's model Ford truck out front that was only in primer gray and missing its tailgate. It was sitting under a big maple tree that was probably as old as the building. All had seen better days.

We pulled in front of its garage door and stopped. Rosa rolled down her window and honked the horn.

No response. Honked again. Still nothing.

Finally, she reached under the seat and pulled out some high heels. Shrugged out of her jacket and took the straw hat that matched her blouse off my head. She popped the hood and the trunk. Then got out. She grabbed a package out of the trunk and dropped it in the driver's seat.

She stuck her head through the window. "Take that cowboy hat out of the back and recline your seat way back. Don't answer any questions. Just act like you're so carsick you don't want to move again. But don't over act. OK?"

I nodded.

She had a tire iron in her hand and did something to the engine to make a huge cloud of steam rise up. She jumped back with her hand holding her hat and nearly fell off her high heels - if the young guy with grease covered bib overalls hadn't caught her.

I couldn't hear the conversation very well, but Rosa suddenly caught a Southern accent and became completely helpless. She leaned against him and allowed him to put an arm around her while he tried to keep from looking down her front, unsuccessfully.

By the end of it, he was nodding, and she hugged him like a long-lost relative. Then she came back to the car.

"Get my big purse out from under your seat and open up that package into it." Rosa whispered to me. "While you're at it, clean out everything in that glove compartment."

The purse was a big black shoulder bag, with plenty of room in it. The package contained stacks of hundred-dollar bills, all used and none fresh. She took the shoulder bag and slung it over one shoulder, then carefully wobbled on the gravel toward the dingy-windowed space that was apparently the office.

The young guy met her at the door and she pulled out several stacks of bills for him. He fingered them, but didn't count them. Then he pulled the keys to that truck out of his pocket, along with the rabbit's foot on its ring. She added one more stack to his open hand and then reached up to kiss him on his cheek. He turned red and put the money behind his back.

Rosa then got in the truck and started it up with a roar. She made a surprised face for the benefit of the guy and then pulled around back of the car.

The truck had a set of white, hinge-topped storage bins in the back, which were mostly empty. She took everything important out of the car trunk and put them into those bins. Then came around my side and helped me into the passenger side of the truck.

Meanwhile the young guy got the car into neutral and pulled a long winch line out from inside to tow it in.

Once it was inside, she waited patiently for the garage door to close, standing in the shade of the big tree out front. He came to the door, and she smiled, waved, and blew him a kiss. Then she teetered off to the truck and got in carefully, closing the door.

Slipping off her high heels, she put her pumps back on. Pushing in the clutch and shifting into low, she tested the transmission by letting it out slow as she pushed on more gas.

"He said it was just a bit touchy, and he's right. You can't beat one of these high school shop class projects when you can find one." Rosa smiled, happy at the bargain she'd found.

Once she was out of site, she opened it up more. it had a light rear end, like all pickups. They were going down gravel roads now. The gray of the truck matched the clouds of dust they threw up behind. Straightways were fine, but the curves took some careful cornering. Still, Rosa was happy with this truck. To me, it seemed to match her brash side. Just as the Buick had matched her elegant side. Still, we seemed to be making good time.

As darkness fell, we got back onto a state highway to find somewhere to rest for the night. We passed several roadway motels of various repute, but finally pulled into one of the bigger towns and found a bed-and-breakfast.

A great old house, surrounded by oaks, walnuts, and hickories. Plenty of room to hide the truck in the back. We could also come and go through the back door without being seen.

The gray-haired, doughty matron was more than happy to accept cash. I don't have a clue what name we signed up under. Rosa didn't tell me.

There was a gas station that had pizza up the street, so the matron sent one of her young cousins to get a couple for us. He was back quickly and so Rosa gave him a big tip. Fortunately, some of those stacks had 10's and 20's in them, as we didn't want to be remembered for our cash. We also took two adjoining rooms. Not to appear chaste, but also because Rosa was concerned as I hadn't recovered faster by now. She told me she wanted me to get all the rest I could.

After some pizza and some iced tea the matron provided, I did get right into bed. I was exhausted. Rosa must have been at her wits end as well.

In the middle of the night, my dreams woke me. Strange ones. But somehow, they didn't seem real to me. Like they weren't mine. Something strange was going on. So I laid there, awake. Listening to the night air and the various animals outside. Dogs barking at unseen and unheard coyotes. The occasional cat-fight. Owls hooting back and forth.

Then I saw an odd bluish-green glow pulsing from under the door to Rosa's room. I heard some rustling there and thumping like the bed was being wrestled on. There was also some low voice, like a man talking.

The glow continued while the thumping got more faint and stopped.

I got up and carefully made my way to the door. Through the crack, I could see someone sitting on her bed, although I couldn't see Rosa. He was mumbling something, but the crack wouldn't let me see what was happening. That glow was over to the right. Where Rosa should be sleeping.

Now if I just butted in, there might be someone else in the room to surprise me. Then we'd both be in trouble. So I quietly went out through my room's door to the hall.

Then I knocked on Rosa's door loudly and called out, "Are you alright in there? Hey, I've got some more pizza if you want it!"

Then I ran in my sock feet back to my room, quietly shutting my door.

Next, I rushed to the double door and flung them open.

The man who was sitting on the bed looked up at me, with the blue-green beam coming out of them. I blocked my eyes and jumped across the foot of the bed to knock him on the floor, with me on top.

Another younger guy in a suit turned from closing the door to the room and came toward me. I rotated the older man's face to him and hit him with that blue-green look I'd avoided.

The younger guy froze and then sank to his knees. I kept the old guy's face directly on him until the younger dropped to the floor, eyes wide open.

Pointing the older man's face to the floor, I got up to look at Rosa. She'd been tied down and was now just staring off into space. I was concerned that we had already been making too much sound. Seeing a mirror above the dresser, I had an idea.

Picking up the older man from the back, I propped him up against the dresser, using his own arms to hold him there. Squeezing his hands into top dresser drawers, I twisted his elbows around to lock against his ribs.

His face was against the mirror. I adjusted it to make him look only into his own eyes. Then his body completely stiffened into that position.

At that point, I went back to look at Rosa. She was still out of it, eyes looking across the room at the other corner near the ceiling. No waving in front of her eyes did anything. I untied her arms and leg, then used those ropes to truss up the young man on the floor. Just in case he came to. And for good measure, stuffed a doily in his mouth as a gag.

Then I scooped up Rosa in my arms and carried her to my bed. Closing the double doors between the two rooms, I locked them on my side. Rosa was still out, eyes wide open. I felt her forehead, no fever. At her neck I got a pulse, it was slow and steady. Her breathing was regular. It looked more like a trance. Where I got all this, I didn't know. I wasn't even certain my name was Josh. But I could identify trees and animals, so this seemed like some sort of selective identity scene.

More to the point, Rosa was my only way out of this. There was one chance I needed to take. She said she still had both of our memories in there. What went in must be able to come out.

I took the pillows on my bed and fluffed them under her head until her head was more or less looking down toward her feet.

Then I climbed above her and situated myself so that I'd be able to look into her eyes and yet not cause her difficulty breathing by my weight. Just in case we both went zombie catatonic if this didn't work.

Finally, I looked deep into her eyes. They were still blue. And deep in there, I seemed to see a bluish-green spark...

The room shifted, disappeared. It became something like a hall of mirrors.

I saw Rosa, I saw my own face. I saw me looking at Rosa, looking at me, looking at Rosa. Then two Rosa's. Four. Sixteen. Over a hundred...

And then just one. The girl in the bar. When she looked at me that night, it seemed like the whole world had stopped. Just for a moment, I got a glimpse of eternity. Then the barkeep came up. "The lady bought you a drink." He said.

I saluted her with the new drink, finished my old one, and joined her at that bar end.

Later, she and I were in that seedy hotel room, standing just inside the closed door, embraced in each other's arms. She turned me around facing the bed and pulled me down on top of her.

"Hey do you want to see something really wild?" She asked, in between long kisses.

"I've seen a lot of things already." I replied, when I could get a break for my mouth.

She put her finger on my lips and said, "This you haven't. How would you like to see the world from my view? Look at everything we are about to do through my eyes?"

"You mean like watching me make out with you? Kinky." I said. But the idea was interesting, novel. "Sure."

"Look deep into mine. Do you see a little blue-green spark in there? Look deep..."

And then I saw her just go blank, staring up into space.

Through her eyes, I saw myself get off her and stand up, straighten my own clothes. Then I picked up her purse, after checking for ID in it, and putting it into a knapsack. I pulled on my jacket and cap, slung the knapsack over my shoulder, took the chain off the door and left. I checked outside to make sure I had the hotel key and then used it to lock the door.

Once down stairs, I went over to a black Chevelle. Feeling under the driver side fender gave me the key to get in. Soon I was on the road back to my workplace...

A cough woke me up. Rosa had shut her eyes, and we were both in the bed-and-breakfast. Smells of bleached doilies and wet grass replaced the grit and grime of city.

Rosa raised her hand to her face and rubbed her eyes. Then looked at me.

"You big lunk. What do you think you're doing?" Then she remembered what had happened after the pizza and our good nights.

She looked at my room and then looked at the light coming under the double doors from hers. The blue-green glow was still there.

"Time to go. Get off me." She said.

I complied, rolling over to the other side of the bed and then rising to my feet.

"How did you get me over here?" She asked.

"I carried you." I replied.

She looked at her simple night gown. "Well, I can't leave like this. How did you leave them in there?"

"The guy with the eyes is staring into the mirror, and the other one collapsed on the floor. I tied him up with the ropes I got off your arms and legs. Oh, and stuffed his mouth with a doily." I said.

"OK, should be fine then. I'm going to get my things and come back here to get dressed. Then we'll go out the back." She turned to the door, stopped, and turned back.

"Oh. You might need some shoes. And pants."

VI

WE WERE BACK ON THE road pretty quickly after that, pushing down back roads again, but having to go slower due to the potholes and narrow bridges. While a truck traveling down back roads at 3 am would be highly visible, you had to be up at that time to see anything.

Still, there were people out looking for us. Luckily, the truck's owner had installed a cute little floating compass on the front window, one that was fluorescent. So we could tell in a general form whether what direction we were going, even we didn't know what road we were on.

Just keep going north-east.

"How much did you learn while you were looking inside me?" Rosa said, after some miles had passed behind us.

"I wasn't looking very long, and you woke up in the middle of it." I said.

"Don't lie to me. I can tell, you know." Rosa replied.

"Everything I used to know. Plus what I did that night." I said.

"Anything else?" She asked. The truck slowed down.

"Ok, everything." I said.

At that she brought it to a stop. "Everything?"

"Back to the dress you wore at your prom and your first kiss." I answered.

She turned off the engine and shut out the lights. The darkness swallowed us until we could see by starlight.

"So you know what I do and why." She said, finally.

"And I know why you came back for me. But I also found something else out." I said.

"What's that?" she asked.

"You're wrong about what you told me. Sure, these memories fade, but you stay connected to anyone you want to stay connected with. The more..."

"The more you get emotionally involved with them the more the connection stays in place." She finished.

"And so, Houston, we may have a problem." I quipped.

"More than you know. It's that old saw that's misquoted. 'Knowledge is power' is only half the equation. Responsible action is the other half."

Rosa went quiet at that.

She finally spoke. "They've got more powerful empaths than me. You saw a sample of that tonight."

"But those weren't our guys." I said.

Rosa smiled and touched my hand in the dim light. "It isn't 'our guys' any more. You're going to have to have some time to digest all you learned. You got a lifetime of mine, plus some glimpses into others. And now, like your own memories, they won't exactly be under your control. You'll have dreams of things. You'll get sudden inspirations. And you'll find talents you had no clue about."

"I can deal with that." I said.

"Yes, I know. You could do my job better than me. Eventually. Right now, we have another problem." Rosa said.

I just waited for her to figure out what she wanted to say.

Rosa finally spoke. "Those guys hate one thing, and that's one thing that could wreck all their plans."

"And what's that, Rosa?" I asked.

"Love." She replied. "An empath in love with a normal human is bad enough. Generally, that takes them out of the game. They've been recruiting orphans and raising them in nearly isolated conditions for years. But they also know that they can only keep them effective for just a handful of years. Once they have interacted with enough people, they learn how to love and why it's important to living."

I took my time answering this. "And this was your last mission, I was your last client."

"And we were both going to be retired after this. You would have wound up in a ditch somewhere, and I would be kept as a lab rat for the end of my days." Rosa put her face in her hands.

Putting my hand on her shoulder, "I saw that, too. But it doesn't have to be that way."

"You know how powerful they are, what connections they have..."

I could hear the warble in her voice. Rosa was almost crying.

"But you and they overlooked one thing. Think back to your training, the point about qualitative and quantitative magnification." I said.

Rosa raised her face out of her hands and reached into her black shoulder bag for a tissue.

"Your point?"

"'Two empaths in complete sync are more powerful on exponential scales.' That's what they taught you. But because they kept all their empaths separate, they could never explore that observation. Because empaths in love couldn't be controlled." I said.

"And so they usually just 'liquidated' those assets." She replied.

"However, they also forgot that this talent works outside of time and space. The more intentional effort they put into controlling this ability, the worse control they had. Their efforts would spiral into failure." I said.

"And so they said there was a limit to the capacity of any force." She replied.

"So they quit trying to get more than something like 80% effective." I said.

Rosa turned toward me. "If you and I could make this work, we could recruit and train an organic movement that would de-power these government agencies, regardless of what politicians and their military types wanted."

"Exactly." I said.

We were both quiet for a time.

"So, you're thinking what I'm thinking?" Rosa finally said.

"You know it. One mind, two bodies." I said.

"OK, I'll drive, you shield. We've got all the time we need for this." Rosa started the truck, turned on the lights, and then turned around at the next gravel road intersection.

We were taking the fight to them. Only we weren't going to fight by their rules.

VII

LATER THAT WEEK, SEVERAL simultaneous 'accidents' happened at various secret government research facilities. People disappeared from jobs. And jobs disappeared.

Budgets were re-written, discovering they had been printed years ago. Staff now reported to different areas and had desks waiting for them.

Pardons were discovered as issued by presidents who had been out of office for decades.

Administrative projects were left without staff or budget or administrators to oversee them. Soon, there was no more research on empaths or on 'extrasensory perception' experiments of any type. At least any files that anyone remembered.

In some forgotten and decommissioned missile silos, people began arriving for work. Actually, for training. Deep underground, their lessons started in earnest. The deeper underground the better the solitude, and so, the better the inspired ideas and places to practice at developing their abilities.

This had been financed by one-time grants from governments. Those grants were then converted to various funds and investments that grew over time. All this had happened years prior and recently reached maturity.

Within months, small communities developed around those underground silo's, similar to the growth of boom towns around mining and oil drilling.

But satellites never showed these on any photo map. You couldn't find them on Google. And most electronics didn't work within several miles of those locations. Spy Planes sent over these areas would either malfunction temporarily, or become re-routed. Several reconnaissance drones were "lost" only to be found later, way off course.

Governments left them strictly alone. Because they could read minds at a distance. Politicians learned to never mention them in their speeches, or face "curious leaks" about the other secrets they were hiding. There was no such thing as "government secrets" with any of these empaths around. Military wouldn't send anyone near those locations. Oddly, as they found out, there was no limit to empathic skills. Once someone mentioned any locations or subjects, anything they knew would become public record. No secrets, means no government. "Live and let live" became a workable model.

Oh, and lots of peace broke out that the media wouldn't report. Funny how those things work out.

It's not worth covering here how mega-corporations started having trouble with collecting data on private citizens, much the same as the NSA. Mystery leaks of damaging data to online media by untraceable anonymous sources. Massive databases discovered, accessible to anyone.

The world became a bit more honest and respectful. Just a bit.

Rosa and Josh lived and worked at one of these training facilities. They raised some fine children and trained them. And all their children married and had fine children. All of them have their own talents. They all live quiet, prosperous lives. Loving families. No secrecy, plenty of respectful privacy.

Rosa and Josh are there yet.

While reporters are always nosy for a story, if anyone did interview them, they'd only get a broad smile. And probably invited for some fresh, hot pizza and a tall glass of iced tea. Meanwhile, they'd lose interest in whatever they had come there for.

They'd come back with a story, but it was never what their editor sent them for. And all the notes about it would disappear from their computers, written notes would be displaced...

You're welcome to visit them. Just look into their eyes. You can see they are telling the truth.

Did You Find the Strange Secret in This Story?

ALL OUR STORIES CONTAIN a strange secret.

Hidden right in the middle of the story. In plain sight.

Whether or not you recognize that secret - it changes you as a reader.

And our stories won't read the same the second time - or the third, or ever again.

Because you, the reader, have changed.

Let me give you a small book that tells you exactly how this works.

You may have heard about it:

"The Strangest Secret" by Earl Nightingale.

Contains "The Strangest Secret" transcript by Earl Nightingale, and selections from other books he referenced in that Gold recording.

Limited Time Offer

You can download your own copy of this book –

as long as its still available.
Visit: https://livesensical.com/go/ssc-join-now/

Related Books You May Like

All our Latest Releases[1]

BOTH FICTION AND NON-fiction – each with links to major online book outlets as well as author discounts.

Speculative F[2]iction [3]Modern Parables[4]

OUR SHORT STORIES AND anthologies – all in order of most recent release.

The Strangest Secret Library[5]

ALL THE FULL REFERENCES mentioned in Earl Nightingale's Strangest Secret Library available for instant download – through your online book outlet of choice or with our publisher's discount.

---

1. https://livesensical.com/books/?utm_campaign=related-book-ad&utm_source=ebook
2. https://livesensical.com/book-series/fiction/?utm_campaign=related-book-ad&utm_source=ebook
3. https://livesensical.com/book-series/fiction/?utm_campaign=related-book-ad&utm_source=ebook
4. https://livesensical.com/book-series/fiction/?utm_campaign=related-book-ad&utm_source=ebook
5. https://livesensical.com/book-series/strangest-secret-library/?utm_campaign=related-book-ad&utm_source=ebook

Books on Writing & [6]Publishing[7]

OUR COLLECTION OF MODERN and classic references on how to improve your writing in our modern self-publishing age.

Did You Like This Book?

HOW ABOUT LEAVING A review with the vendor?

Otherwise (or in addition) you can leave your recommendations on:

- **Bookbub**[1]

The whole point is to enable others to find books that you liked reading.

Which then helps you find more great books to read.

And...

Feel free to share this book!

---

1. https://www.bookbub.com/recommendations

Did you love *Fantasy Romance Anthology*? Then you should read *A Romance Reader: Short Stories From New Voices*[2] by J. R. Kruze et al.!

Being able to escape into the wonderful world of romance is always a pleasure.

This set of short stories are an amusing way to find yourself into new worlds, with new lovers working out their difficulties and eventually end up with their happily-ever-after result.

Some are ghosts, some introspective writers, some CIA-government types, a couple of futurists, some socially disadvantaged, and a young couple with hidden abilities.

All in contemporary settings (for the most part) and perhaps something you can relate to (well, we can always *want* the superpowers, anyway.)

Lose yourself in these worlds and become young at heart again with these short reads to fit into any schedule...

Short Story Anthology Containing:

- The Ghost Who Loved by S. H. Marpel- Ham & Chaz by C. C. Brower & J. R. Kruse- The Caretaker by C. C. Brower- Mind Timing by R. L. Saunders & C. C. Brower- The Autists by J. R. Kruze- Her Eyes by J. R. Kruze

Excerpt:

IT WAS FATHER'S DAY. They were all still dead, and I was again dry-eyed over their grave.

I came this way every year, for the past few, as it was also my birthday. Such as it was.

Growing older just meant more sadness for me.

Father, Mother, and younger sister all passed that night. Horrific car accident. All decapitated or crushed instantly, head-on collision with another car, that seemed to come out of nowhere.

I was the only one remaining.

And I couldn't even cry anymore.

Of course my heart ached. But it was almost the dull, screeching creak of some massive pump whose bearings were failing and overheated from lack of grease. The grease of kindness, of human love.

Why was I still here? What reason did I have for existing? I didn't know. All I knew was that I kept going from day to day, month in, month out, and then showed up back here again - once a year.

Graveyards are funny things. Why they exist is such a morbid concept. Small and huge monuments erected to incite the memory of the fallen. Like it was the old Japanese ancestor worship. But just because they weren't remembered after a few centuries, didn't mean the ache went away. Only the persons who had the ache. To their own plot of earth and monument - or not.

People visited. And opened up that ache fresh to the sting of memory once again, like a wound opened to the air. Painful, abrupt. The ache continuing long after the bandage was re-applied.

Like that guy over there, a few rows over. Downcast young face. Blue jeans, black sweater jacket, high-top basketball sneakers. And that cute brown hair, those nice cheekbones. Why did he come here? Did it ever help him move on - or was he like me, a magnet for more punishment?

Scroll Up and Get Your Copy Now.

Also by J. R. Kruze

Parody & Satire
R. L. Saunders Satire Collection 02

Short Fiction Clean Romance Cozy Mystery Fantasy
Voices
To Laugh At Death

Short Fiction Young Adult Science Fiction Fantasy
A Goddess Visits
Story Hunted
The Case of the Walkaway Blues
The Lori Saga: Escape
One Thought, Then Gone
On Love's Edge
Synco
The Case of the Naughty Nightmare
A Goddess Returns
A Nervous Butt
Max Says No
A Dog Named Kat

Short Story Fiction Anthology
New Voices Vol 001 Jan-Feb 2018
New Voices Vol 003
J. R. Kruze Short Story Collection 01
A Writer's Reader: Short Stories From New Voices

New Voices 004 July-August 2018
A Humor Reader: Short Stories From New Voices
A Mind's Eye Reader: Stort Stories From New Voices
A Mystery Reader 001: Short Stories From New Voices
A Goddess Visits 2
J. R. Kruze Short Story Collection 02
Voices Anthology

Speculative Fiction Modern Parables
Her Eyes
Death By Advertising
The Lazurai
When the Dreamer Dreamed
The Autists
Toward a New Dawn
Ham & Chaz
The Lazurai Returns
The Case of the Forever Cure
The Girl Who Built Tomorrow
A World Gone Reverse
The Girl Who Saved Tomorrow
The Girl Who Became Tomorrow
The Autists: Brigitte
The Arrivals
Root

Speculative Fiction Parable Anthology
Tales of the Lazurai
A Romance Reader: Short Stories From New Voices
New Voices Vol. 005

New Voices Vol. 008
Fantasy Romance Anthology
J. R. Kruze Short Story Collection 03
A Short Story Reader's Bookshelf

Speculative Fiction Parable Collection
New Voices Vol 002 Mar-Apr 2018
An SF/Fantasy Reader: Short Stories From New Voices
C. C. Brower Short Story Collection 02
New Voices Volume 6
The Girl Who Built Tomorrow Collection
New Voices: Vol. 007

The Hooman Saga
The Hooman Saga: Book One
The Hooman Saga Library 01

Watch for more at https://livesensical.com/book-author/
j-r-kruze/.

Also by C. C. Brower

Ghost Hunters Mystery-Detective
The Spirit Mountain Mystery

Parody & Satire
Becoming Michelle
Our Second Civil War
R. L. Saunders Satire Collection 02

Short Fiction Young Adult Science Fiction Fantasy
Snow Gift
Vacation Amok
A Long Wait for Santa
Mind Timing
The Hooman Probe, Part II: Salvation
Peace: The Forever War
Return to Earth
Snow Cave
The Emperor's Scribe

Watch for more at https://livesensical.com/book-author/
c-c-brower/.

Also by R. L. Saunders

Ghost Hunters Mystery Parables
Smart Home Revenge

Parody & Satire
Keyboard in the Sky
Cats Typing Romance: Two Short Stories
Rise & Fall of President Frump
A Sweet Fortune
Becoming Michelle
R. L. Saunders Satire Collection 01
Our Second Civil War
R. L. Saunders Satire Collection 02
Beltway Gremlin
The Lonely Witness
The Chardonnay Conspiracy
The Writer's Journey of John Earl Stark 01

Short Fiction Young Adult Science Fiction Fantasy
Mind Timing
The Tunnel People

Synco
The Integrity Implosions
The Maestro

Short Story Fiction Anthology
New Voices Vol 001 Jan-Feb 2018
New Voices Vol 003
A Writer's Reader: Short Stories From New Voices
New Voices 004 July-August 2018
A Humor Reader: Short Stories From New Voices
A Mind's Eye Reader: Stort Stories From New Voices
A Mystery Reader 001: Short Stories From New Voices
J. R. Kruze Short Story Collection 02
Voices Anthology

Speculative Fiction Modern Parables
For the Love of 'Cagga

Speculative Fiction Parable Anthology
Tales of the Lazurai
A Romance Reader: Short Stories From New Voices
New Voices Vol. 005
Fantasy Romance Anthology
A Short Story Reader's Bookshelf

Speculative Fiction Parable Collection

An SF/Fantasy Reader: Short Stories From New Voices
C. C. Brower Short Story Collection 02
New Voices Volume 6

The Hooman Saga
The Hooman Saga: Book One
The Hooman Saga Library 01

Standalone
The Writer's Journey of John Earl Stark 02

Watch for more at https://livesensical.com/book-author/
r-l-saunders/.

Also by S. H. Marpel

Harpy Redux
The Case of the Sunken Spirit
The Harpy Saga: Sister Mine
The Training: Mysti
The Training: Star
The Training: Sylvie
The Training: Tess
The Faith of Jude

Ghost Hunters Mystery-Detective Anthology
Ghost Hunters Anthology 3
Freed

Ghost Hunters Mystery Parables
Ghost Hunters
Why Vampires Suck At Haunting
Ghost Exterminators Inc.
The Haunted Ghost
Faith
Harpy
The Ghost Who Loved
Two Ghost's Salvation, Book One
Falling
The 95% Solution
The Case of a Cruising Phantom
Clocktower Mystery
Smart Home Revenge
Finding Grace
The Mystery of Meri
Time Bent

The Lori Saga: Faery Blood
A Very Thin Line
Dark Lazurai
Lilly Lee
Hermione
When Cats Ruled
A Case of Lost Time
Enemies & Bookends
Hermione Anthology
The Tao of Mysti
When Death Died

Ghost Hunters - Salvation
Two Ghost's Salvation - Section 01
Two Ghost's Salvation - Section 02
Two Ghost's Salvation - Section 03
Two Ghost's Salvation - Section 04
Two Ghosts Salvation - Section 05
Two Ghosts Salvation - Section 06

Mystery-Detective Fantasy
Witch Mystery: Beth
Wish Me Luck, Witch Me Love
Last Witch Dance
Witch Mystery: Dixie
Witch Mystery: Raven
Witch Mystery: Ruby

Parody & Satire
R. L. Saunders Satire Collection 02

Short Fiction Young Adult Science Fiction Fantasy
The Case of the Walkaway Blues
The Lori Saga: Escape

Short Story Fiction Anthology
New Voices Vol 003
New Voices 004 July-August 2018
A Humor Reader: Short Stories From New Voices
A Mind's Eye Reader: Stort Stories From New Voices
A Mystery Reader 001: Short Stories From New Voices
Witch Coven Harvest
J. R. Kruze Short Story Collection 02

Speculative Fiction Modern Parables
The Lazurai Emergence
A World Gone Reverse

Speculative Fiction Parable Anthology
Tales of the Lazurai
A Romance Reader: Short Stories From New Voices
New Voices Vol. 005

New Voices Vol. 008
Fantasy Romance Anthology
J. R. Kruze Short Story Collection 03
A Short Story Reader's Bookshelf

Speculative Fiction Parable Collection
New Voices Vol 002 Mar-Apr 2018
An SF/Fantasy Reader: Short Stories From New Voices
C. C. Brower Short Story Collection 02
New Voices Volume 6
New Voices: Vol. 007

The Hooman Saga
The Hooman Saga: Book One
Moon Bride
Blood Moon
Moon Queen
Moon Shadow
The Moon Cleaner
Alice in the Moon
Moon Rebels
The Hooman Saga: Book II, Part 2
The Hooman Saga Library 01

Watch for more at https://livesensical.com/book-author/
s-h-marpel/.

About the Publisher

"We Become What We Think About."

A veteran publishing imprint and a practical philosophy for life, Living Sensical Press has been active publishing new and established authors since 2006.

We take advantage of the new Print on Demand and ebook technologies to enable wider discovery for authors.

We publish in most of the major genres of fiction and non-fiction.

Our current emphasis is in speculative fiction modern parables.

For More Information, Visit:

https://livingsensical.com/books/

CPSIA information can be obtained
at www.ICGtesting.com
Printed in the USA
LVHW090103121219
640185LV00001B/4/P